What peopl

"*The Sapphire Flute is a steady burst of imagination and adventure. What a great start to the series!*"—James Dashner, author of *The Maze Runner*

"*This book has everything I read fantasy for: excitement, adventure, engaging characters, and a storyline that is completely unpredictable. Not to put too fine a point on it, but Karen Hoover is one heck of a writer! Now I just want to know when I can get my hands on her next book.*"—J. Scott Savage, author of the *Farworld* Series and *The Lost Wonderland Diaries*

"*A delightful tale filled with action, magic, and enchanting characters you're sure to love!*"—Julie Wright, author of *The Hazzardous Universe*

"*This is one of those books I can picture myself reading when I was much younger—I think it would be among my most-loved books of my pre-teen and teen years, along with A Wrinkle in Time by Madeleine L'Engle, The Oval Amulet by Lucy Cullyford Babbitt, and Lloyd Alexander's Prydain Chronicles. Perhaps it may be presumptuous of me to rate The Sapphire Flute so highly. I do so because this story resonated with me the same way those did. I can see myself re-reading this book many times down the road, as I have the titles I mentioned above.*"—Melissa Owens, of *Melissa's Bookshelf*, book reviews

THE ARMOR OF LIGHT

BOOK 2 OF THE WOLFCHILD SAGA

KAREN E. HOOVER

TIN BIRD PUBLICATIONS

The Armor of Light

by

Karen E. Hoover

Book 2 of The Wolfchild Saga

ISBN: 9781463663100

The Armor of Light / Karen E. Hoover

Tin Bird Publications

Dedicated to my
sweetheart,

Gary Hoover,

My very own knight
in shining armor with
the golden voice.

PROLOGUE

The girl called Shadow crept into the glade, the magelights of Javak shining their unnatural blue glow over the city. Unlike a true fire, the magelights never flickered. They were unwavering, neither hot nor cold—and yet the glow seared into her eyes, leaving floating balls of blinding light impressed on her retina long after she turned away to hide in the shadows of the forest. The girl blended herself to the darkened lengths of shade cast by the tall pines in the moon's glow. She faded into nothing, an extension of the natural balance of light and dark, unnoticed, unseen.

The teacher came next, the one called Dragon. Careless, the teacher was fully in the meadow before slipping on the dragonhead mask, features fully exposed to view. C'Tan would be furious if she knew. Shadow was stunned at Dragon's true identity. Had she not seen the face, she would not have believed.

At the mage school, Dragon was the kind teacher, always willing to take time to help a student. But here in this glade, she heard only the harsh and bitter, fury and hate for the academy and for Ezeker in particular. Dragon at last pulled down the mask, covering the face, the dark contours of the black drake leaving all but the eyes hidden, then leaned against a tree to wait.

The guards came together, Magnet and Seer, male and female, their faces already covered by the plain helm that hid them—but Shadow knew them. She had known since the first meeting. There was no mistaking Seer's terse alto tones and Magnet's rich baritone. His voice was as familiar to Shadow as her own—a voice she both loved and despised.

The voice of her father.

The three masked figures watched each other warily, never trusting. Stillness descended over the glade with their presence, as if the very insects could feel their malice.

They stood in silence until the deep beat of wings coming from the east pulled all eyes up to watch the descent of the Mistress, current owner of their souls, by rule of their true master, S'Kotos.

C'Tan flew in on her dragon. Behind her sat a young boy, his arms wrapped around her torso. The black beast back-winged, stirring the pine needles and dust into a frenzy about the group, their hair whipping in the wind.

No one moved. They stood as if frozen until C'Tan dismounted the dragon and leaped to the ground, leaving the boy to dismount the black beast on his own. He moved as if he were born on a dragon and came at her side, his stance too mature for his years.

"Who is the child?" Seer asked.

C'Tan did not answer, but instead threw her words to the darkness where Shadow hid.

"Show yourself, Shadow."

"Yes, Mother," the girl answered, fading from darkness to a semi-transparent gray that still left her face and figure a mystery.

C'Tan grimaced. "I have asked you not to call me that, girl. Do you wish to give away our plans with a slip of your tongue?"

"And who is there to hear, Mother? They already know that—" Shadow stopped with a grunt of pain. Her shadow cover wavered as she collapsed to her knees and looked at C'Tan in astonishment. The blonde woman's arm was outstretched, her hand hooked, claw-like. Shadow's insides felt as if they were about to burst. She fell to her side, the pain was so great, but she refused to give her mother any further satisfaction. The pain stopped immediately when C'Tan dropped her hand. Shadow sucked in a deep, sobbing breath and scrambled to her feet.

"Do not question me, child." C'Tan spoke in a deadly whisper. "There is too much at stake. Do as you are told."

"Yes, Moth . . . Mistress." Shadow faded back into darkness.

There was silence for a long moment as C'Tan glanced at each person, then to the boy at her side. The child couldn't have been over eight or nine. He grinned up at C'Tan with cold eyes. Shadow felt a pang of envy for the boy who stood so close to her mother, but she squelched it quickly. There was no use in longing for that which would never be.

C'Tan finally spoke. "The Chosen One has come." She didn't need to say anything more. Everyone stood a little sharper, the intensity in the glade increasing. "Laerdish has failed us. His true nature has been discovered and he has fled with barely his life. But he has managed to get us some useful information. They have accepted the Chosen One to the academy."

Now their voices leaped over one another, asking questions. C'Tan quieted them with a single motion.

"Her name is Ember Shandae and she will arrive with the next intake, but . . ." she paused, her eyes gleaming. "I have a plan. I believe you all know Ian Covainis?" She gestured to the boy and was greeted by stunned silence as the boy stepped forward and bowed.

"You must be joking," Shadow's father, Magnet, growled.

"Have you ever known me to joke?" C'Tan quirked an eyebrow in his direction.

Magnet scratched his nose beneath the helm. "Actually, no, I have not."

"Nor do I joke now. Ian, tell them," she demanded of the boy.

Shadow had to admit there were certain similarities between this child and the man she knew. The protruding ears, the shape of the nose, the smile that held no warmth—yes, it could be, though it seemed impossible.

"I found the girl, Ember, outside of Karsholm. I captured her and planned to bring her to the Mistress, but she shapeshifted into a wolf and escaped with a pack. I didn't find her again until I got to Javak and discovered that she had shapeshifted into a boy. I alerted Laerdish, and he tried to make her look like a fraud, but it backfired on him. She can read all the colors of magic, people. Every one." The silence around him spoke for itself. "The Mistress thought it might be good if we could plant an agent into her class—someone who can get close to her while she's vulnerable. And since I've had the most experience with her, C'Tan age-regressed me so I could hide in plain sight." Ian's young voice was at odds with his tone and words. "Much as I might wish it, I cannot do this alone. The girl is smart and trusts very few. We'll need to work together if we hope to succeed, and I can't do that with your anonymity. It has served its place, but now is the time to let yourselves be known."

Ian waited in silence. Nobody moved or spoke. He shook his head and ran a hand through his wavy hair. "All right then, if you won't trust me with your identities, we need to have an alternate way to contact one another. Any ideas?"

Seer snorted. "And why should we help you?"

"Because I said so," C'Tan answered for Ian. Seer glared from beneath her helmet, but said nothing more.

"Let's use the sending stones and establish a password in case we need to meet in person," Magnet said in his deep voice.

Shadow shivered.

"A password? Such as?" Ian asked.

"Wolfchild," Dragon growled. "Make the code wolfchild."

Ian smiled. "Wolfchild it is. Now, first we must gain the girl's trust, bring her into our circle, and turn others against her as often as possible so she has nowhere else to go."

"And what is that supposed to accomplish?" The woman sneered again.

"Why, it should be obvious," the man-turned-boy leered, which looked strange on his nine-year-old face. "We get the Chosen One to trust us, chain her with her weakness, and lead her away from the light of

Mahal to the darkness of S'Kotos. If we can't defeat her, then she must join us—or die."

Shadow shivered, but she did not leave. If good or evil were carried through the blood, she had no choice. *With parents like these, who needs enemies*, she thought as they pulled her into the circle and planned Ember's demise.

CHAPTER ONE

There was still ash in the sky when it began to rain. Ember watched the fat droplets pound against her window, turning Javak a murky gray as the moon rose over the city of magic. He was still out there somewhere. She could feel him watching her from the darkness, could feel his ever-present spirit as aware of her as she was of him, now that she knew who he was—now that she knew her father was still alive.

With a sigh, Ember Shandae turned from the window and threw herself back on the bed. Three nights—three sleepless nights she'd spent in this room since the mage council had accepted her into the academy. Three nights of tossing and turning since Laerdish had made his betrayal known—and three nights since Ember had discovered that the white hawk who'd been watching her for so long was actually her father.

Ember sat up and surged off the bed once more to pace the small confines of the room, her thoughts and feelings a whirlwind of which she could make no sense. She had to get some rest. She'd never survive in the academy if she couldn't sleep. "This is ridiculous," she said to no one in particular.

Suddenly feeling claustrophobic and desperate to do anything to relax, Ember grabbed a towel, her weather charm, and a change of clothes and headed out the door. She walked quickly down the hall, her soft boots shuffling across the marble floor of the council house.

She'd been surprised at first when she'd been told to stay in the room Uncle Shad had arranged for her, but it made sense in a way. The people closest to her were nearby to protect her if necessary—Uncle Shad and DeMunth, Ezeker, Aldarin, and now her mother and Paeder. They'd all taken rooms near hers, though they didn't seem to suffer the same trouble with sleeplessness that Ember did.

Ember left the council house and crossed the water bridge. She walked quickly through town. Only the pitter-patter of raindrops that didn't touch her and the thundering waterfalls escorted her through what had been a bustling market the day before.

Everyone was gone now, with only crumpled paper and mounds of rotting food on the ground, and occasional feathers floating across the wet grass to show anyone had even been there.

Ember shook her head. *Why can't people pick up after themselves?*

She arrived at the women's bathing quarters and quickly checked herself in. The bath girl was asleep on a pad just inside the door. The girl who had nearly given Ember trouble at her trial didn't stir as Ember tiptoed past to write her name in the book and leave a thumbprint.

Within five minutes, she had undressed and slid into the water. The edges were lukewarm and shallow, nowhere near what Ember needed to loosen the kinks that had settled in her shoulders. She waded slowly to the deep waters and swam toward the waterfall cascading from the cliff high above. Her toes found the sandy bottom once more as she neared the falls. Ember stepped directly into the stream and let the liquid begin its heated massage.

The tension immediately faded. The water was almost too hot—pleasurable to the point of pain.

It was perfect.

Ember closed her eyes and sat on a boulder sunk just beneath the waves. With her muscles relaxing, she could at last address the issues that had kept her sleepless these many nights.

First, her father was not only alive, but had become a messenger of the Guardian Mahal. She didn't know how to feel. She was happy he was alive, disappointed he thought so little of her that he'd never told her he was there, angry that he'd been gone all these years, and elated that he had healed Paeder. She had to admit, she was also a little intimidated, knowing he worked for one of the creators of Rasann. She wanted to get to know him, wanted desperately for him to never have died, wanted to give him the tongue-lashing of his life and throw herself into his arms and never let go.

She felt like her insides were one giant pot of soup with opposing flavors—pineapple with hot peppers and potatoes and a handful of dirt for good measure. Her heart ached with the lack of a solution. More than anything, she wanted to sit down with her father and just talk and resolve the conflict stirring within her.

That thought led Ember to the second, and probably more challenging, of her troubles.

She was the first white mage in three thousand years. She didn't know how to use her magic, and there was no one around to train her. The weight of responsibility was overwhelming. A white mage was supposed to help heal their world, to mend the net of magic that surrounded Rasann. Ember did not know where to begin, and neither did anyone else. What was she supposed to do? Teach herself? How could she mend a net she couldn't even see?

Although they hadn't yet left for the school, Ezeker had quizzed her endlessly since her acceptance into the academy, guiding her sight in what ways he could. He seemed to be a wonderful teacher, but Ember just didn't see things the same way he did. She understood the concept clearly—she just couldn't put it into practice.

"So there you are," a relieved voice echoed across the waters. Ember jumped, her eyes snapping open as she scanned the room for the figure she knew she'd find on the other end of the voice. She wasn't disappointed.

Feeling a little guilty for not telling anyone she was leaving, Ember sank her shoulders beneath the surface and swam slowly toward her mother, enjoying the slow transition from hot water, to warm, and almost chilled.

Marda held up a large towel and stepped forward as Ember stood and climbed from the water. Her mother wrapped the towel around her without a word.

It was a sign of their changed relationship that her mother didn't chastise her now, but put her arms around her daughter, as if Marda could feel the struggle within her—and also a change between them that Ember let her do it. When Marda let her go, they walked, mother's arm around her daughter as they went back to the dressing rooms.

Marda glanced down at the sleeping bath girl, her eyes flashing when she recognized her. She glanced at Ember, a wicked twinkle in her eye, then took the ink from the sign-in table and, using a corner of Ember's towel, dabbed dark streaks across the girl's cheeks and down the bridge of her nose.

Ember gasped. "What are you doing?" Marda put her finger to her lips and continued marking the girl. Ember clamped a hand over her own mouth and stifled an appalled giggle. She couldn't believe her mother would do such a thing. It was a harmless prank, really. The ink would wash off—or so she hoped—and Ember enjoyed knowing her mother could let down her walls enough to let her daughter see her this way.

Putting a finger to her lips to remind Ember not to laugh, Marda put her thumb in the middle of the girl's forehead, one last black oval, then set the ink pad on the floor next to the girl and stood. "Let's get you dressed," she whispered to her daughter before they moved on.

It was strange, being comfortable with her mother now, since their past relationship had been so challenging. Once the truth was out, Marda had become a different person. She was softer somehow, more full of purpose and compassion. And though she was still strict and kept close tabs on Ember, she'd finally given her daughter some of the freedom she'd craved for so long—being able to visit the baths so far from her rooms being an example of what she'd gained.

Mother and daughter went to the dressing room, Marda standing guard while Ember dried off and scrambled into her clean clothes, slipping the weather charm back around her neck last of all. Ember would not step foot outside without it until the skies stopped spitting rain and mud.

The next morning, it was still raining and Ember had been forced to leave the weather charm behind, much to her consternation. No charms or talismans were allowed during practice, and today her new class had moved outside to the fields of Javak—the city that wasn't looking so magical at the moment. She wiped dripping bangs from her face as she straightened and watched her soon-to-be classmates use their magic to clean the garbage left from the mage trials, and to make matters worse most of them were half her age. One couple had paired up, with the boy levitating the garbage off the ground and the girl incinerating it with a thought. Another girl made the wind blow everything in one direction, where a young boy circled it around him and then shot it outward to the garbage bin. Yet another girl made it disappear entirely.

And then there was Ember. She stabbed downward with a sharpened stick and picked up the trash the old-fashioned way. Things were supposed to have been different once they accepted her to the mage school. She was supposed to be able to use her magic just like anyone else. But for some strange reason, her magic wasn't working. Her attempts at conjuring a fireball had summoned nothing but a plume of smoke. She couldn't teleport the garbage, she couldn't make the wind blow it away—she couldn't even change it into something else. All she could do was bend over and pick it up or poke it with a stick.

"Worthless," she muttered aloud. "What good is magic if I can't make it work for me?" She stabbed hard at a sodden mass of paper. The stick penetrated something hard, the length vibrating like the handle of an axe when chopping hard wood. She pulled on the wood, but it wouldn't budge. She got down on her knees and looked closer. The stick wasn't wedged in a crack, as she'd thought. It was completely embedded in the rock. "How'd I do that?" she wondered aloud, standing and twisting the stick until a sharp snap freed it from the stone . . . minus the bottom three inches.

Frustrated, she threw the stick and yelled, the piece of wood tumbling end over end across the clearing. All the kids in the class stopped to stare for a moment before they went back to picking up their garbage, using their powers.

"Feel any better?" her stepbrother said from beside her. Ember jumped and turned in a single motion.

"Don't do that," she growled. She took a deep, shaky breath and let it out in one explosive blast before answering his question. "No. No, I don't. Why can they use their powers and I can't? What's wrong with me?"

"Nothing," Aldarin answered, putting an arm around her. "The whole point of this exercise is to learn how to use and control your powers in a safe environment. Sometimes it takes a little longer."

"At least they had lessons," Ember said, glaring at the group spread across the grass. "All I got was Ezeker telling me to do what feels best. I need a tutor! How am I supposed to learn without someone to teach me?" She snorted. "Do what seems right. Right now, doing what 'feels best' means poking somebody with a stick."

Aldarin laughed. "I don't think that's what he meant."

Ember turned her glare on him. "I know that, but it sure would get my frustration out. I don't understand. I can't even change the things I touch anymore. What am I doing wrong?"

Aldarin shook his head. "I'm not the person to ask, Sis. Only you would pick the one magic nobody knows anything about. You'd think that being a white mage, you could use all the colors of magic."

Ember snorted. "Yeah, that's what I thought too. Evidently not. There's got to be a textbook or some mage's journal from the past. Surely they would have kept some kind of record. I'll never get this without some help."

"Wait until we get to the mage academy. The library is endless, and you never know what you might find in there. We can hope."

"Right now that's all I've got," Ember said. She picked up another stick, pulled out her belt knife, and began whittling once more.

They had unwillingly dragged Ember before the mage council, her abilities and very identity thrown into question. She'd finally proven herself by reading the colors of magic for all seventy some-odd members of the Mage Council, and she could still see magic now. She could discern every shade and color of magic in all the people she saw . . . but she couldn't tap into her own power.

Ember was grateful Aldarin stayed quiet while she whittled the stick to a point. The frustration inside of her bubbled and boiled like one of Ezeker's potions, and there was no way to release it except to stab at the garbage. When she dreamed of being a mage, she'd never imagined how hard it could be.

Her new stick sharp, Ember went in search of more trash. They had mostly cleared it already after four hours of work in the large field, so Ember left Aldarin watching the class and went another direction, eager to get away from her classmates and try some of her own magic in private, where she wouldn't continue to embarrass herself with an audience.

She headed toward the permanent buildings on the west side of town, angling down the alleyways for trash that might have been blown about in the storm. Everything was wet. Muddy ash had collected against the buildings and window ledges.

The mage shields suddenly surged to life in a blue wave. Why it had taken so long to get the mage shields working again, she did not know. Ezeker had his up in a matter of hours. Maybe he was just better at magic than the Magi in Karsholm. that made Ember jump, then Ember sighed with relief when the rain stopped pinging off her head. The field and paths would dry out soon and at long last the mud would be gone.

Ember came upon a U-shaped meeting of three buildings that had trash heaped against the walls. She sighed. People were such slobs. She took her stick and canvas bag and moved to the corner, still thinking over her problem.

How could she learn about white magic when there were no books, no teachers, and the only person who knew anything was one of the Guardians who had created the world? What was she supposed to do? Pray for a teacher? It actually tempted her to do just that. She stabbed downward, collecting a soggy mass of paper on the end of her stick, then paused. If her father would talk to her, maybe he could get a message back to Mahal to see if he really *could* help her find a teacher.

Ember heard shuffling footsteps behind her, but paid them no mind. It was most likely another student searching for more garbage, just like she had done. It wasn't until sizzling heat and the crackle of flames were almost upon her that she instinctively dove for the mud, a fireball slamming into the stone wall just past where she'd stood. She rolled over and looked up, scrambling to find some place to hide, but she was cornered. Trapped on three sides, the only open space was filled with flittering shadows in the shape of people.

Her heart racing, Ember took her stick in her hands, wishing it were a sword, a polearm, a spear—anything but the wimpy wood she held. A flash of heat sparked across her palms and the weight in her hands suddenly increased, the wood shifting from warm and alive to cold, hard metal in an instant. She didn't even question it, but took the gift for what it was and rushed forward, hoping to take the enemy by surprise. She raced into their midst, swinging the iron rod like a club and aiming for the empty space between them.

An arrow flew at her from out of nowhere, Ember never having seen the shooter. The shaft flicked through her hair, just inches from her neck. In an instant, Ember dropped the rod, and with a surge of overwhelming power, instantly became wolf without any of the slow changes she usually experienced. Her body flared with pain, but with the adrenaline pumping through her, she barely registered it. Suddenly, her sight and sense of smell heightened. The shadows still flickered, but they seemed to slow as her perception changed. And when she could not see them, she could certainly smell.

They moved in to surround her. Ember gathered herself and leaped directly at the man in front of her. He hesitated just long enough for her to bare her teeth and take him by the throat. Warm blood gushed into her mouth as she bit down, but her usual gag reflex was buried in her wolf survival instincts. The group of shadows rushed toward her. Ember let go of the man and he sank to the earth, clutching his throat and gurgling.

In an instant, she jumped over him and raced toward the field and the protection of Aldarin. She ran full tilt, running faster than she ever had, when she hit what felt like a brick wall. She yelped as her nose rammed into solid air and her body flipped up. She saw stars for a long moment, then shook her head and growled. They stalked toward her, more slowly now as they realized the danger she could be to them. The man whose throat she'd nearly torn out still lay on the ground, jerking spasmodically. The flickering shadows seemed to race from place to place, a zipping blur that put them here one moment, there the next, and Ember couldn't focus on them long enough to defend against them.

Her mind raced. She couldn't do this alone, but it appeared they had created a shield to hold her in, and she had no idea how to break through. She didn't know how to fight. She didn't know how to use her magic. She was alone, defenseless, but for her teeth and whatever magic would sporadically work for her. Terror built, and she backed slowly against the shield wall, wishing with all her heart that it would let her through. The shadowy people picked up their pace and raced toward her, though still in a zig-zagging blur.

She backed farther away, the pressure building behind her and seeming to crawl up her body as she stepped rearward, her tail between her legs, her lips pulled back in a snarl, blood from her victim and drool mixing to drop in rivulets to the ground. The closest person raced toward her and she jumped away, the growl rumbling in her throat.

Suddenly she was not alone. A figure in glowing yellow armor landed at her side, his shining sword cutting toward her attacker, slicing him neatly in half, top and bottom hitting the ground separately. The shadows stopped and held still for a moment. DeMunth didn't give them a chance to attack again. He raced toward the figures as they turned to flee, his feet moving so fast, he seemed to have wings. Ember sat stunned for a brief moment, then raced after him. She couldn't let him fight alone.

But her efforts were in vain, for by the time she reached DeMunth's side, her attackers had reached the U-shaped building, leaped to the rooftop, then jumped skyward and disappeared.

CHAPTER TWO

Kayla trailed her fingers through the water wall and stared into the depths of the sea. The thin membrane that held the sea at bay glowed with an eerie blue light that drew the creatures that lived in the depths to investigate. In addition to the near-constant school of fish that seemed to follow Kayla wherever she went, tonight there was a family of sea turtles and a manta ray. The latter fascinated Kayla, and she unconsciously dug in her bag for her flute. Not The Sapphire Flute, not for this, but the flute Brant's father had given her when she was eleven years old.

She pulled the instrument to her lips and let her fingers run up and down the keys, a quick stuttering of scales that made the school of fish dart away, then slowly collect just outside the wall again, their bodies tilted to the side much like a young child's cocked head, listening to her tune.

Instead of falling back on her standards like *Darthmoor's Honor*, Kayla tried something new—something she'd tried only with The Sapphire Flute before. She played from her soul a random sampling of notes that blended, became measures, and eventual songs written for the sea, written for the visitors who swept back and forth across her field of vision. She played for the fish and for the sea turtles, for the manta ray and for the sea itself. She played for the sand tunnel and the waterways that traveled across the floors of the oceans the worldwide and felt a surge of majestic gratitude flow back toward her. It almost stopped her playing, so surprised was she, but instead she redirected her efforts high, up beyond the sea to the heavens, where the Guardians lived and had breathed life to the world. She played a question for them. *Where should I go? Where should I go?*

And finally the answer came, a whisper of thought that seemed to echo from the heavens and through the water. With relief she heard the words she'd wished for these last three nights. *Go home, Kayla. Go to Brant.* That stopped her playing abruptly, her heart suddenly pounding in her chest, a mixture of fear and joy. Go home to Brant? It was all she'd wanted these three nights full of nightmares. She'd seen him fall, released by the dragon high in the sky. She'd seen him plummeting to his death and had played to save him, but every night she awoke with his cry of pain as his body pounded the earth. Had he survived? She'd held him up as long as she could, but had he truly been safe? Was he injured?

The questions had kept her sleepless and indecisive. She knew she needed to go to the mountains behind Javak and find the birthplace of the flute. She knew she needed to find The Wolfchild, the chosen one, and find the true player of The Sapphire Flute, much as it pained her. But how could she do all that, knowing her fiancée could be injured, or worse—dead?

Kayla stared past the wall once more, her fingers reaching through the water membrane to touch the rubbery edges of the manta ray. It nudged closer, nearly caressing her hand before it jerked to the side and streamed away in a burst of speed. The school of fish and sea turtles followed immediately after, and it was only then Kayla saw the two bubbles of light swimming toward her. It wasn't until they were nearly upon her that she realized it was two of Sarali's people, the MerCats, coming by for a visit. Kayla stepped back, her palms suddenly clammy and nervous as they leaped through the water wall as if it were nothing more than air, tails swishing as they stared at her.

18

They crouched, looking part beaver and part jaguar, before they melted and pulled upward into human form. When the transformation was complete, they gave her a slight nod and strolled down the sandy walkway toward where Kayla had left Sarali and T'Kato sleeping. Unable to help herself, she followed the two beings, not sure whether it was to protect her friends, or listen in on whatever was important enough to bring the MerCats here.

Before the two reached Kayla's friends, T'Kato rolled to his feet, knives in hands, and Sarali sat up and brought her knees to her chest.

"What do ye want, Niefusu?" Sarali asked, looking up at the taller one, who was a hair taller than Kayla.

"Father wishes ye to join him for an audience," the shorter one said.

"I was not speaking to ye, Jihong," Sarali nearly snarled. Kayla was surprised. Though she'd known Sarali only a short time, she had always been mild-mannered and polite.

The shorter one called Jihong bowed low, almost mockingly. "It matters not who answers, little sister. His reply would be the same."

"But I want to hear it from his lips," Sarali barked again, surging to her feet. T'Kato closed in, standing by her side and looking as if he'd jump in front of her, should the need arrive.

The tall one, Niefusu, finally deigned to answer. "Father wishes to see ye. Would ye please grace us with yer presence, princess?" He bowed, not full of anger or scorn like Kayla would have thought, but a more deep, deep sadness that sang through his voice.

Kayla startled. "Princess?" she asked, but Sarali ignored her. Kayla moved closer and stopped only when the short brother blocked her way. "Why didn't you say anything?" she asked, stepping to the side so she could see the girl she thought was her maid.

Sarali exhaled sharply. "Because it wasn't important. Now hush," she said, looking at her brothers. She seemed undecided for a moment, but a glance at T'Kato hardened her. "Me marriage be sealed. He cannot be breaking it now, and I be on an errand that cannot be delayed. Tell Father I most graciously decline his offer, though—" she paused for just a moment and glanced at her husband, then mumbled—"I would stay if me could."

19

Niefusu bowed. Jihong snorted and turned his back on her, only to see Kayla watching. She still fumed at Sarali's betrayal and dismissal. The girl outranked her, even though they came from differing kingdoms. She wasn't sure how she felt about that. Jihong's snarl turned into one of guarded pleasure as he saw her. "It was ye we heard playing?" he asked.

Kayla nodded.

"Ye are masterfully good. It is an honor to hear one such as ye. Thank ye for gracing me ears with yer music." He nodded once more, then stormed past Kayla and dove into the wall of water.

Niefusu also bowed to Kayla. "It truly is an honor, me lady." He nodded to his sister and T'Kato. "I am sorry, but Father insists." At that, several more MerCats stepped through the water wall, armed and in fully human form. Before T'Kato could draw his sword, he had been disarmed and thrown to the sandy earth. Sarali leaped toward her tall brother, a snarl on her face, and Kayla could see her animal nature shining through the polished exterior. Before she could reach Niefusu, one guard had taken her about the waist and thrown her through the water wall.

Niefusu leaned over T'Kato and, in his musical voice, asked the thrashing tattooed Ketahean, "Do ye wish to remain here, pinned to the sand, or would ye rather accompany yer wife into her father's presence?"

T'Kato immediately stilled. He swallowed and answered, "I will accompany you, if you will return my weapons."

Niefusu nodded to the guards, who immediately handed the knives back to the Ketahean. He came to his feet and swung at the guard, who remained just out of reach. The other two took a step toward T'Kato, but Niefusu raised a warning hand to hold them back. "Our argument is not with ye, discipled one. We wish only to converse with our sister in our father's presence, and then ye may be free to go on yer way."

T'Kato stopped and narrowed his eyes, confusion clear on his face, then nodded sharply before stepping past Niefusu into the water wall. The tall MerCat turned to Kayla. "And what of ye, me lady? Shall we accompany ye to the surface?"

Kayla nodded her head, packed her flute back in its rosewood case, and stuffed it in her satchel. Then, on a whim, she pulled The Sapphire Flute from her bag and raised it to her lips. "Do you know what this is?" she asked, her voice vibrating the instrument to life, a small echo sounding down the waterways. Niefusu's eyes grew round as he nodded. Kayla played a single note and the surrounding air chilled until their teeth chattered. Then she pulled the instrument from her lips and put it away. "I am its guardian, and they are mine," She said, nodding toward the wall where both T'Kato and Sarali had gone. "Where they go, I go."

Niefusu met her eyes, then gave a sharp nod, much like the one T'Kato had given just moments before. He took Kayla by the hand and led her to the wall. Her heart raced as she stepped near the membrane that held the water into place, unsure what this man intended. He stepped through first, his hands still on her hips. Holding her in place on the sand, he swung around to meet her lips with his own, only the skin of the water separating them. Kayla was so surprised she forgot to breathe for a moment. Then Niefusu exhaled and the skin holding back the water wall grew around her head to form a huge void that let her inhale.

Her mouth tingled as he backed away, took her by the hand, and led her to a chariot pulled by what looked to be dolphins. This chariot was horizontal, with a sled-like surface, a handlebar for them to grip, and a ledge for her feet. He settled her on the sled, wrapped a cord around her waist, and showed her where to place her hands, then he stepped up beside her and hummed a note that set the dolphins to moving at a breakneck pace.

Kayla always felt a little claustrophobic with the bubble around her head, and her natural inclination was to pant, but she didn't want to drown on her way to meet the king of the MerCats, so she inhaled slowly. Kayla felt odd knowing that her serving girl was actually a princess. How had that happened? How had Brant not known? And why would Sarali settle for the life of a servant, when she had had so much more? She'd had the notoriety, the position that Kayla had sought for most of her life, and she had left it willingly to marry T'Kato?

Kayla didn't understand and wasn't sure she wanted to. Losing everything she'd gained after working so hard for so long was still a bitter taste to her. She knew in her head that it had no meaning, really—but the reality of everything was so far beyond the life she ever envisioned for herself that she still took comfort in her dreams of normalcy. She wanted to be the duchess of Driane. She wanted Brant to be her husband. She wanted lots of little children running about her feet and a nursemaid to care for them.

She was seeing that the life she'd imagined was really just a fantastic dream.

The carriage surged through the ocean at a breakneck pace, and Kayla noticed the surrounding beauty. From somewhere, purple magelights throbbed, setting the world around her to dancing in a strange wave of light. The seaweed, if that's what it was, grew tall, like giant blades of grass undulating in the current. Schools of fish and sea serpents peeked from behind the fronds of fern-like growth. A manta ray, maybe even the one she'd played for earlier, surfed at their side, his movement strangely bird-like as he kept the dolphins company. She let go of the bar long enough to reach out a hand and touch his rubbery flesh once more and he let her, a slight tremor easing through his length before he looked at her with flattened eyes and nearly smiled.

When Kayla turned back to the sight in front of them, she looked beyond the surging backs of the dolphins to see a city, a sparkling gem of a palace, glittering before her. Two other sled-like chariots entered the massive front gates, and Kayla assumed they carried Sarali and T'Kato. She glanced behind her to see several more chariots with the guards who had attacked T'Kato following. She truly was a captive, whether she'd gone with them willingly or not. It scared her more than anything, aside from losing The Sapphire Flute. She set her eyes on the MerCat palace and steeled her nerves. Whatever lay ahead, she'd handle it with the best she had within her, be it with the power of The Sapphire Flute or the charm she'd gained in ten years at court.

CHAPTER THREE

Ember's jaw dropped in wolfish surprise as the shadow figures seemed to evaporate in thin air. DeMunth snarled in frustration, his muscles bulging beneath his armor. Ember startled and looked again at his biceps. The golden armor that had once been a breastplate had grown to cover his arms, but they fit like a second skin, not like traditional armor. She could see the shape of the shoulder armor and greaves overlaying his arms, but she could see the skin beneath it, as if she were looking through yellow-tinted glass.

His brow beaded with sweat, though he had not really exerted himself all that much, and it was cool enough outside that Ember would have shivered, if she had been in human form. It was a puzzle she didn't have the answer for at the moment.

"*Where'd they go?*" he asked in his melodious mind speech.

Ember shrugged wolfen shoulders, then afraid he would not understand her body language, she answered, "*I have no idea, but I'm not going to complain. I thought I was dead for a moment there. How did you break through their shield?*"

He glanced at her over his shoulder, one eyebrow raised expressively. *"I didn't. You backed through it. Once you were through, they evidently took it down. It was there one moment and gone the next. Maybe you broke the magic when you passed through it. I am unsure."*

She'd backed through the shield? Ember had a hard time believing that. She'd not been able to get any of her magic to work, and dispersing a shield you didn't create was hard and powerful magic. How could she just back through it and not even know it? Having no answers, she let it go for the moment and moved closer to DeMunth, wanting to touch him, but not daring. She liked him too much for either of their good. *"Thank you for your help. How did you know I needed you?"*

DeMunth quirked his head and looked at her, puzzled. *"I am unsure. Something inside me spoke and told me you were in need."* He shook himself and reddened. *"It sounds as if I am losing my mind, I am sure, but perhaps it was the voice of Klii'kunn speaking to my soul. You* are *the wolfchild, after all."*

Ember wasn't sure how to feel about that and didn't have time to pursue the thought any longer as Aldarin and the rest of her class came running around the building at that moment. Her step-brother's sword was drawn and the look on his face was one of panic and fury. When he stopped and found them standing there with no enemy in sight, he spun in confusion, looking for her attackers.

"Where'd they go?" he asked, echoing DeMunth.

The mute shrugged and pointed skyward. Aldarin glanced in the direction of his finger, then looked at Ember. She shrugged her wolf shoulders and tried to speak, but her words came out as a random series of yips, snarls, and growls. The children in her class backed away, one of them pulling a fireball from thin air he seemed prepared to throw. Ember immediately surged to her feet and growled at the boy, who yelped, dropping the fireball to the ground. The grass caught fire, and for the next few minutes, the whole group stomped at the sputtering, sodden grass.

Ember spent that time changing back to her human form, not sure how she did it this time when she could not before. One of the youngest of the group stopped his fire stomping to watch her, his eyes huge as her body stretched and changed into its normal appearance, like clay molded by an unseen hand.

When she was back to herself and her clothing in place, having suddenly appeared to replace her fur, the boy whispered a single word, the awe in his voice near adulation. *"Wolfchild,"* he mouthed. Just that whisper of sound was enough for the rest of the class to spin and look at her. Varying degrees of confusion, awe, and fear crossed all their faces.

She ignored them and turned to Aldarin. "They're gone. They disappeared. Poof. Like dandelion puffs on the wind."

"That's impossible," one kid sneered at her.

Ember quirked an eyebrow. "Then where are they?" She spun around, her hands stretched out pointing. "Because they're obviously not here."

"Maybe he would know," DeMunth mindspoke to her, pointing to the gasping man whom Ember had attacked.

He was still alive. Her stomach sank now, remembering what she had done, the feel of his blood spurting into her mouth, the coppery warmth coating her tongue. The memory made her gag, but she fought it down and ran past the ogling students.

Before she could think about it, she reached for his throat and covered his hand with her own. It was a pointless act, she knew. His skin was gray, and blood flecked his lips and spurted from between their joined fingers as he gasped for air. Despite his attack, she wished with all her heart she'd been able to think before tearing into his throat. Granted, she'd been defending herself, but she couldn't stand the thought of this man's life on her conscience. She'd killed no one before, not even in defense. If she could take it back, she would.

At that thought, a warm, yellow light spread through her hand and into the man's throat. His eyes got big as could be, and he gasped, trying to scramble away from her, but the power of the yellow held him down. Then in streaks came green intermixed with the yellow. Ember could do nothing but watch in awe as the magic of light and the earth burrowed into his throat. How she was doing it, she didn't know. She'd been working hard for days to get her magic to manifest in doing simple things, and nothing had worked. Now she held her enemy to the ground as if it were nothing. If she could heal this man so that he wouldn't die, maybe she could find out who had attacked her and why. Maybe she could finally get some answers.

Her class had followed her from the sputtering fire and now surrounded her. Aldarin and DeMunth stood amidst the children, but the small class had grown as other members of the community were drawn by her magic like moths to a flame—Ezeker, Shiona, several council members, and even more city dwellers. They had all gathered around to watch as she poured magic into her attacker hoping to save his life.

It pulled at her, like fibers from cotton, spinning something of herself in the healing. She focused, trying to feel exactly what it was she was doing, putting more and more of her essence into the magic until something snapped. Suddenly she floated outside of her body, a white cord stretching upward and out, connected to something she could not see. Glancing down, she followed the line of two more cords connecting her to two separate people in the crowd—people who had yet to notice her problem.

One of those cords went to Ezeker, and the other, stronger, cord connected her to DeMunth. Her body still knelt, frozen over the attacker, who gasped now, his breathing fine—but Ember knew something was wrong. She wasn't in her body. It wasn't moving. Ezeker glanced up and shook his head, then reached over and tweaked the cord that ran through her spirit self to her body. Immediately she found herself back where she belonged, gasping like she'd just run a marathon. She fell back from her attacker and lay on the grass, not caring if she got wet or not.

That's when the muttering began. *"Did you see?" "She's the Wolfchild. I saw her change!" "Impossible. No one can heal that kind of injury!" ". . . might want to separate her from the other candidates."*

Ember tried to slow her breathing so she could get a handle on the situation. There was no way they were going to keep her from the school or the other students. She wasn't dangerous, just untrained. She sat up and looked at her attacker. Where his throat had been torn out, the skin was now smooth, but it was tattooed with an intricate layer of yellows and greens that kept him silent at the moment, almost like the manacles placed on Ember when she'd been imprisoned by the mage council. The man scrambled to his feet and amid all the people jumped skyward—or at least, attempted to. His feet never left the ground. He tried again. And again. Nobody said a word or did a thing. They just watched as he stopped, realization crossing his face. Whatever magic had sent his compatriots skyward would not work for him. Ember had literally bound him to the earth.

Ezeker stepped forward and took the defeated man by the arm. "Come on. We've got some talking to do. Aldarin. DeMunth. Bring Ember."

Ember tried not to be shocked. They treated her as if she were a prisoner. She had done nothing wrong, and yet her step-brother and her friend each took one of her arms and marched off the field with her, leaving the rest of her class to clean the grounds alone.

"Ezeker, you can't just ignore this!" Shiona said, pacing back and forth from one side of Ezeker's borrowed office to the other. "Ember is the first white mage in three thousand years. She needs twenty-four-hour supervision. We can't let her be taken or destroyed before she has a chance to learn what she can to heal Rasann. The world is more important than one person's freedom or will."

Marda answered, but not the way Ember would have expected. She had thought her mother would be livid over a comment like that, or agree wholeheartedly that Ember must be protected at all costs. "Shiona, remember what we stand for. If you take away Ember's freedom, you remove from her the very gift the Guardians gave us in the beginning, and we become no better than Laerdish or C'Tan."

"I know! Don't you think I understand that? But Ember is a priceless gift, the first chance we've had to undo some of the damage the last three millennia have caused. Isn't it better to sacrifice the one than lose the many?"

"And what if you were that one?" Marda asked, picking up a statuette from the desk and fiddling with it before turning to Counselor Shiona.

"What if it were you being asked to sacrifice all? Would you be so willing to give it up then?"

Shiona didn't answer. Her jaw set stubbornly, but her eyes were reflective.

Ember was about to breathe a sigh of relief when her mother continued.

"I do not agree with taking Ember away from the other apprentices. She needs to learn, and they could learn from her. I do not agree that she should be put in a locked and guarded room and not be allowed to leave. But . . . I do agree that she needs protection, and DeMunth has proven himself perfectly capable on more than one occasion. I would ask that he be permanently assigned as her guard through the duration of her training, and perhaps into her life as a white mage. The Armor of Light is a keystone of great power, and it is growing already. I think we shall not find a more capable guardian."

"What?" Ember rose to her feet. "You're giving me a babysitter? How is it my fault that I got attacked? Why do I have to be punished?"

"You dislike my presence?" DeMunth asked her in mindspeech, the hurt more than obvious in his tones.

"No, that's not what I meant," she said, turning and answering him aloud. "Of course I enjoy being with you. I just want my freedom, too."

Ezeker finally spoke. "I believe Counselor Marda is correct in this. You need a guardian, Ember, whether or not you like it. C'Tan is not the only one after you. This attack today . . ." he stopped to scratch his beard, his eyes worried. "This is something new. We are not sure who they are or what magic they use, but they are unfamiliar to us. I think it would be in the best interest of all of us to travel through the caves tonight and get you settled at the academy. We can protect you there. DeMunth will come. Aldarin and White Shadow, too. We shall make you as comfortable as possible, but it is time to leave."

"I'll be going as well. Paeder can care for the farm himself now, and I can use the portals to visit him whenever necessary," Marda said, giving Ezeker the look that always said arguing with her would be useless.

Shiona clasped her hands together and tapped at her chin. "I . . ." she started, drawing it out. "I know it is expected that I return with you and go back to my duties as an instructor, but I would prefer to do some field work, if that would fall under your approval, Master Ezeker?"

His brow quirked skyward and his head tilted to one side. "Oh, what did you have in mind?"

"I've heard rumors of other attacks, one most recently in Peldane at a manor called Dragonmeer. Supposedly another keystone appeared there, The Sapphire Flute, and C'Tan left Dragonmeer in ruins while pursuing it. The holder somehow escaped her clutches and fled, nevertheless, I would consider it an honor to investigate."

Ezeker's eyes lit up at the mention of The Sapphire Flute. He pretended to think about it, but Ember knew what his answer would be even before he gave it. "I would agree. Go, then, and go soon. Use the portals, or the journey will take you a month. The portals will have you there in a day or two."

Shiona nodded her head and turned to go, then turned back to ask another question. "But what of the prisoner? What is he saying about the attack?"

Ezeker's mouth set into a grim line. "Right now he says nothing. We've got him in the academy prison, guarded, spelled, and chained. He's not going anywhere. We'll get the answers one way or another."

Ember didn't like the way he said that, and it surprised her. She'd never thought of Ezeker as being a violent man.

Shiona left the room then and DeMunth stood. *"When do we leave, sir?"* he asked Ezeker in his mindspeech.

The mage stroked his mustache before he answered. "Pack everything you need now. We'll leave within the hour."

CHAPTER FOUR

The huge gates leading into the jeweled city of the MerCats were magnificent. Kayla had never imagined that lava rock, magelights, and underwater plant life could combine in such a manner as to be more beautiful than King Rojan's throne room. Nature in its most resplendent parade had completely outdone all the gold and satins adorning King Rojan's halls.

She tried not to ogle as the chariot passed beneath the majestic arches of the underwater city whose name she did not know. The palace itself was faced with coral and sea anemones, a constant shift of color and movement that would have taken her breath if it weren't already absent with awe and the bubble of air that was mere inches from her nose. Kayla reached over and tapped Niefusu on the shoulder, and when she was sure she'd gotten his attention, she pointed at the bubble surrounding her head. He gave her a toothy smile, then let go of the sled with one hand, scooted closer, and kissed Kayla again, breathing out the air that expanded her bubble and allowed her access to oxygen once more, though his kiss had her head spinning. Why he felt he needed to kiss her to increase the bubble, when Sarali so obviously hadn't, was beyond her. Though, she hated to admit it, especially with her thoughts so recently on Brant, the man certainly knew how to kiss. He left her dizzy with delight and all those other cliché terms that had made no sense to her until this very moment, though Brant's kisses had come close.

Those thoughts brought her full circle back to Brant. She felt guilty for enjoying the kiss and scooted away from Niefusu, which he obviously found humorous, since he grinned at her action.

Niefusu steered the sled toward a huge coral archway, tall enough for six men to stand head to toe with room to spare. They passed beneath the immense doorway and into what could only be a stable, though it was like no stable Kayla had ever seen. The stalls for the animals didn't just run along the sides of the structure like in a normal barn or stable. They also ran from floor to ceiling, four levels high. Kayla was seeing how living a life underwater could be very convenient, in the design of storage space in particular.

The sled came to a stop in the center of the building where T'Kato and Sarali hovered in place near the animals' caretaker. He unhooked the dolphin that had pulled their sled without even a glance in their direction while Niefusu and Kayla released the bar and swam toward the other two. They immediately turned and headed toward a human-sized doorway nearby. Instead of swimming through it, Sarali stopped and took the doorway in her hands, pushing her feet toward the sand so that she nearly stood vertical, then stepped through the doorway and dropped a few inches to stand in the air-filled room.

Kayla didn't know why she was surprised after spending so much time in the waterways, but she was. Evidently the castle was underwater, but had no water in it. Kayla followed T'Kato, grabbing the doorway as Sarali had done and stepping through the doorway, rather than swimming. It was a strange sensation. Her breathing bubble popped as soon as her face was through the skim of water, and she dropped to the sand without stumbling. She was grateful for that, at least. She didn't want to look a fool in front of the royal family of this water kingdom.

That thought stopped her for a second. She distinctly remembered Sarali telling her that she'd lost her father, just like Kayla. She glanced at the MerCat woman and the question popped out of her mouth before she could stop it. "I thought you said your father abandoned you as a babe." Sarali glanced at her, then at her brother who was just stepping through the doorway, and leaned in close. "I lied," she said, her voice low. "Ye needed the moment to know ye weren't alone, so I lied. I'm sorry." Kayla wasn't sure what to feel at that. She'd believed her, wholeheartedly.

Jihong walked toward them, and Sarali's face darkened. She pulled her head up and growled at her brother, but he paid her no mind. He turned when he saw he had their attention and without a word led them through the hallways of the castle. Sarali was fuming. She held herself rigid. If she'd been in her cat form, Kayla imagined her hair would stand on end with a puffy tail standing straight in the air. Kayla had never seen Sarali like this, every bit the annoyed and inconvenienced royal Kayla had faced daily throughout her life. She couldn't believe she was the same girl whose darling lilt and ever-helpful attitude had made Kayla admire her so few days before.

Niefusu passed them and went to Jihong's side, angling toward a doorway. They stopped, Jihong opening the door with a low, sweeping bow and letting Sarali in before him. It seemed to annoy her even more, as she seemed to step purposely on his foot as she stormed past, though he acted as if nothing happened. Niefusu glared at the shorter brother as he passed by, but Jihong grinned his hard smile and came in behind them. T'Kato gestured with a hand for Kayla to fall in before him, and he brought up the rear.

The halls were lined with mother-of-pearl. Several MerCats stood along the hallway, at the end of which was an obsidian double door, taller than the trees Kayla had raced through three days before. Two dark guards hovered before the doors, which they pushed open as Sarali approached.

The room they entered was more grand than anything Kayla could have ever imagined. The pillars were sand, hard as stone, the walls more of the mother-of-pearl, and the décor was natural seaweed. Even the pictures seemed to move, and in the middle of the back wall sat a man and woman, with crowns of starfish and pearl upon their heads. They both stood at the group's entrance and nearly raced with open arms to Sarali.

The girl stopped them with an upraised hand.

"That's close enough, ye two. What in the world would ye be thinking, dragging us all the way down here when ye knows we've got work to do up top?"

The queen answered. "We wouldn't have brought ye here if it wasn't for dire need, me daughter. The airways be collapsing all across the kingdom. The passageways. In cities. In homes. Even in our castle here, half the rooms be filled with water that won't leave. We need help and didn't know who else to ask. None of the magi can clear the places once they fill with water and, we don't know why."

Sarali seemed concerned, though still upset. "It's because the net of magic around Rasann be collapsing, Mum. I cannot do a thing about it."

The king spoke up. "How goes the search for the Amethyst keystone? We thought that perhaps if ye'd found the stone, ye might be able to help clear the water once again. And it's more than the water. The hot pots are roasting people in their homes."

At that, Sarali seemed truly upset. Her eyes got big, and she stilled completely. "What do ye mean?"

"Just what I said," the king answered. "The pots have gone super hot, for no understandable reason. They be fine one day, and the next we find everyone in the home boiled alive. Many a time, the pots go back to normal after they super heat, but not always. Sometimes there be survivors, and other times not, but the world is falling apart, daughter, and we'd hoped with ye being the heir, ye might help us find a solution."

Sarali shook her head. "I'd heard rumors, but hadn't believed them." She tapped her lips for a second, then glanced at Kayla. Her eyes lit up, and she turned back to her parents. "I cannot fix everything, Mum, Da," she said, nodding to them. "But the keystones are manifesting, showing up here and there, and once they come together, the chosen one should fix the unraveling. I may not have The Amethyst Eye as of yet, but T'Kato found the bearer of The Sapphire Flute. Maybe she can fill some of the waterways here with air once again."

Kayla tensed as Sarali told the king and queen about her and the flute. Would they hurt her? Would they try to take the flute for themselves? Why would Sarali tell them, when she and T'Kato had warned Kayla about this exact thing? She couldn't help the wave of fear that washed over her and had her stomach in knots. T'Kato had pounded the idea of not playing the flute into her head. But she had successfully used the flute to save Joyson and Brant, to defeat C'Tan. So long as she held the flute, nothing could harm her. If C'Tan could not take the flute from her, then neither could a simple MerCat.

The king and queen seemed full of hope and Kayla couldn't dash that. Niefusu already knew she had the flute, though she worried about Jihong and his antagonism toward Sarali. That was a story she was going to have to get from the princess. Kayla glanced his way and caught him eyeballing her, and it was not with admiration. Chills raced up her spine. Evidently he'd already figured out who had the flute, but even if he hadn't, Sarali's introduction and her playing of her other flute earlier would have given it away.

"Mum and Da, this is Kayla Kalandra Felandian, Duchess of Driane of the kingdom of Peldane. She is the bearer and current guardian of The Sapphire Flute." The king and queen nodded their heads toward Kayla with what seemed to be respect, then raised their eyes to hers. The queen spoke for them both.

"If ye wouldn't mind, Duchess Kayla, would ye help us fill the rooms in our home once again? I know ye don't have time to fix the kingdom," she rushed on, "But if ye could just fix a few of the spots that are most important, we'd be most grateful."

Kayla glanced at Sarali, trying to keep the anger out of her eyes, then glanced back at Sarali's parents. "I'd be honored to help, Your Majesties. I'd fix them all if I could, but time is pressing."

"Then why don't ye just leave the flute here and let us do it for ye?" Jihong said, stepping forward. "Surely it will work for any player. We can fix our kingdom and ye can be on yer way, and when we're done, ye can return and retrieve yer flute."

Kayla's stomach burned at that, though she shouldn't have been surprised. Jihong was turning out to be exactly the kind of man she'd expected. Still, there was no point in antagonizing him further. "I'm afraid I can't do that," she answered. "I've been sent on a mission with this flute, and I can't be delayed any longer than I have already." She scooted closer to the door.

Jihong strode toward her, meeting her near the door. "I'm afraid I must insist," he said, reaching for the flute. Kayla scampered away from him, at which point he spat out a few choice words and turned into his MerCat self. T'Kato raced toward him, but the beast sent a bolt of purple light toward the tattooed man that sent him flying across the room.

The king shouted. "Jihong! That'd be enough!" The guards charged toward him, but he drew a shield in the air that shoved them back against the wall, then he put his focus on Kayla.

She hadn't expected him to try to take it by force, but she would not let him have the flute, any more than she'd let C'Tan take it. If this boy wanted a battle, he'd get one.

Kayla put the flute to her lips and sent out a freezing sweep of sound that instantly created a shield of ice before her. Jihong sent out his purple spear of light. It reflected off the ice and hit the wall of the throne room, leaving faint streaks of black with amethyst undertones. He sent another spear, and she turned to deflect it. This time it hit one clam on the wall and shattered it into a million pieces.

That scared Kayla. If the light was that strong, she was in trouble. Taking the shield of ice in front of her, she played the flute again and bent the ice up and around her so that she stood in a bubble. That angered Jihong and he sent wave after wave of light at her, all of which glanced off the ice or stuck in it like a spear. By this time, everyone had either left the room or were hiding behind the furniture and pillars. Sarali looked ready to chew stone, she was so angry, and the king and queen were not far behind her. The king continued to yell at his son, but the boy didn't appear to be listening.

Tired of his game, Kayla took the offensive. She sent out a crystal of ice to encase Jihong's hand. The pulse of electricity in his fist grew as he struggled to blast open the ice, but nothing would happen. His angry face turned to his left hand and a ball of lightning grew there too, so Kayla encased that hand in a ball of ice as well. The furious Jihong raced toward her then and pounded on her ice shields with his icy hands, but nothing happened, not to her shields, and not to the rapidly growing icy fists.

Afraid he would hurt himself, Kayla surrounded Jihong with ice, leaving his head and neck free so he could still breathe. She only hoped this duel would end before it damaged the boy with frostbite.

As if the king could hear her thoughts, he stepped out from behind his throne and stormed over to his son. "Are ye insane, boy? Ye'd be so desperate to make a name for yerself that ye'd go against one of the chosen?" The king smacked Jihong on the back of the head, the boy's chin ricocheting off the ice on his chest. The boy glared at him in sullen defeat. "I'll ask the girl to thaw ye if ye promise to behave, but I'll not have ye seeing her again while she be here, understand? Yer to be sent to yer rooms." At that, he turned to Kayla. "I apologize, Duchess. Me son has no patience nor tact. Ye'll be safe now." He gestured the guards forward, then nodded to Kayla.

Still guarded and in her bubble of ice, Kayla thawed Jihong all at once so he fell to the sand, shivering. The guards picked him up by the arms and carried him from the room, apparently to be locked away for the rest of the evening.

Once the adrenaline subsided and Kayla felt safe, she melted her ice bubble and walked over to enter the conversation with Sarali and a now-awake T'Kato. He looked none the worse for wear, though anger rolled off him in waves. It was a good thing Jihong was gone or Kayla was afraid T'Kato would have killed him—though at the moment, it wasn't as repulsive an idea as she would have thought. She was angry at the boy as well.

"Could ye at least stay for dinner and a night, me girl?" the queen asked, her lilt very much like Sarali's.

The princess who had been Kayla's servant tipped her head and grinned. "I think that can be arranged, Mum. Thanks for the invite. And could ye arrange a small gift of thanks for Kayla's work in clearing the water from the castle?" Her mother, the queen, nodded. "But of course. It be only expected for her kindness." Sarali winked at Kayla, then turned and walked for the obsidian door. Kayla followed after, hoping she wouldn't have to spend much time in water-filled rooms while helping to clear things. She wasn't about to be kissed by Niefusu again.

CHAPTER FIVE

C'Tan pulled the bronze mirror out of thin air, opened her satin robe, and let it drop to pool about her feet, then let the illusion of beauty fall from her features. It was her daily routine, begun after her servants had dragged her from the fire after she and Jarin battled and he had died. It reminded her of what she lost, of what she'd given up in her decision to serve S'Kotos. Hair the color of golden apples and her beautiful features faded away, and she stared at the fiery scar snaking its way across her bald head and down her face. The usual anger burned inside her, rising up in a volcano of hate. Usually the hate was for Jarin, her half-brother and the man who had scarred her this way. It was Jarin's lasso of fire that had sparked the flame in her clothing and hair, though S'Kotos had used it to mark her as his—her master's way of claiming and torturing her both.

Things were different now. The volcano of anger, disgust, and hate rose, but it was not for Jarin this time. It was for herself. Her weakness had led to Kayla's success. She should have known better than to trust Ian to find Ember Shandae. She should have done it herself. The disgust rose to such a heat that C'Tan lashed out at the bronze mirror.

It shattered into a million tiny pieces.

The cloud of slivered glass hovered before her, splitting her image and reflecting the same horror, the same weak and imperfect woman she had become. For one brief second, she remembered what she'd been once, long ago when she was young and carefree, before she'd been burned with the hate of S'Kotos toward her murderous bastard of a father and Kardon turned her to the Guardian of Fire.

Fractured. That's what she was. A fractured soul, bits and scraps of what could have been and what was, illusion and reality, all mixed into one jumbled mess, just like the fragments of glass that hung in the air before her. The first crack had come when she'd murdered her father as he lay in his own vomit in the street, bellowing his drink-sodden song. The truth about him had broken her, and she had taken his life with anger so huge it had stolen her innocence and turned her into the scarred wreck she had become. The memory sickened her and she sent it back into the halls of history from which it had emerged. The man deserved what he got, no matter the price she'd paid.

With a shove, she pushed the glass pieces back into their brass frame and fired them to the melting point. The metal glowed with the heat she pumped into it, the molded images along the edges melting, but she didn't care. She put the glass back into one piece that again reflected her naked and scarred body, and looking at it then, she felt only one thing.

Empty. Like a wine sack that had been dumped in the dirt, she was deflated, overused, and full of holes. Completely and thoroughly empty.

"Mistress?" a deep voice echoed through her head. Grateful for the distraction, C'Tan banished the mirror, replaced her robe, and tied the sash.

"Yes, Drake?" she answered her dragon. He never disturbed her unless the news was urgent. C'Tan had learned early on she could trust her dragon mount more than any other being. He had always been true to her.

"I have heard from our spies at Javak. The girl you want, the one named Shandae, was attacked this morning and nearly killed." Drake was silent after that, knowing her well.

C'Tan went from empty to livid in an instant. *"Do you know who was responsible? Was it Kardon?"*

"I know not, Mistress. It was a group I've not heard of before. They move like shadows, flickering in and out of the light, much like your daughter, but different. Here one moment, there the next. If it is Kardon, I do not know where he made his connections, though I have heard it whispered he plans to overthrow you and become the master once again." Drake was quiet for a moment before continuing. *"I would much prefer that you remain the mistress. Kardon is . . . painful."*

C'Tan understood what he meant. Kardon's treatment of the dragons was the final thing that had made her rise up against her master, but when it came time to kill him, she just couldn't find the strength to do it, despite S'Kotos' urging. She'd killed her father with hardly a thought. He was vermin. But Kardon? She couldn't, and she worried that another battle now would destroy her. She was too fragmented, too distracted by so many things. The search for the keystones, the search for Ember, the search for Kayla, and now this attack on Ember as well? She couldn't juggle it all and keep things quiet at home too.

Well, forewarned is forearmed, or so they say. If Kardon *was* responsible for the attack on Ember, C'Tan would take care of the problem once and for all.

She stormed to the door and threw it open, surprising the guard who stood just outside. "Summon Kardon. I wish to speak with him immediately." She didn't wait for an answer, just slammed the door shut, then turned to her wardrobe and decided what to wear for the day. She thought her red riding leathers would do nicely. Yes, after she took care of Kardon, she believed a ride would calm her nerves.

The old master-turned-servant came quickly at her summons. She made him wait outside her door while she finished dressing and selected several knives to accentuate her outfit. One at the hip. One for her boot. One for each thigh. And one hung behind her, just at shoulder height.

With the last knife tucked away, she opened the door and let her servant in. She didn't give him time to think, just took the knife from her right hip and thrust it into his stomach. It wouldn't kill him. The man could heal himself faster than she could do much damage, but it would hurt. Oh yes, it would hurt.

He doubled over in pain and surprise, but C'Tan did not let go of the knife. She shoved it deeper and twisted. "We seem to have a problem, Kardon, and I remember telling you once that the next time you betrayed me, I would have your heart."

Kardon looked up at her, hate and confusion battling in his eyes. His mouth grimaced with the pain. "I've done nothing to betray you, Mistress."

C'Tan twisted the knife again, and he cried out. "Please, Mistress, I do not know what you mean! Tell me what I have done to deserve this punishment."

Unsure now, C'Tan withdrew the knife. Kardon gasped, the blood splattering her obsidian floor. "The girl. Ember Shandae. She was attacked this morning at Javak by a group of shadow people. They meant to kill her. Have you gone against my wishes, Kardon? Are you trying to kill Ember and seek the reward our master will give you?"

Kardon placed his right hand over the hole in his stomach, power and heat flowing through his hand to heal the damage. He stood up straight with a grunt. "I have heard of the attack, yes, but I give you my word I had nothing to do with it. I've already got agents searching out the attackers. It's a group we've neither seen nor heard of before. Something entirely new. How is it you came by this knowledge before me?"

C'Tan waved away his question and wiped her knife on the hem of his shirt. "That, my dear, is for me to know and you never to find out. I have my agents too."

Kardon grimaced. "Of that I am sure, Mistress. What would you like me to do about the matter? I know what the master wants, and the soulstone still plays a heavy part in that act." He glanced across C'Tan's room to the altar that sat beneath her window. C'Tan kept it there to remind her of her goal and why she continued to follow S'Kotos when her love for him was long dead.

"Ember must join us or be bound to the stone, Kardon. There are no other options in S'Kotos' eyes, do you understand?" C'Tan said, walking over to the soulstone but never touching it.

"I understand completely, Mistress. And for what it's worth, I'm in full agreement. There are no other choices," Kardon said as he bowed from the room, his hand still covering the bloody hole in his tunic.

You've got that right, C'Tan thought. *There are no other options when S'Kotos is in charge.*

CHAPTER SIX

The cold, foggy mist conjured by the magi to cover their exit from Javak set Ember to shivering, despite the warm-spelled cloak Aldarin had retrieved for her. It wasn't so much the clammy cold as that she couldn't see anything coming at her from the darkness. She'd learned not to trust anything that eluded her eye as of late, and in this fog she could barely glimpse DeMunth marching in front of her, let alone Ezeker or Marda before them. She could feel the warmth of Aldarin behind her and could hear the muffled steps of her co-inductees into the Academy of Magi, but beyond that, the city was silent.

Ember's thoughts went back to her experience in healing her attacker and what had happened at the end. Had she really stepped outside her body? What was that white cord that had sailed off into the distance? And why was she connected to DeMunth, of all people? Ezeker, she understood, but DeMunth? Her mind boggled at the thought, and she wished she'd talked to Ezeker about it while she could. There'd been no time since the afternoon meeting. They'd been busy packing and gathering everyone together. Then the magi had called up the fog and told the students to march toward some indeterminate spot that no one could see. She hoped Ezeker knew where they were going, because, in her eyes, they marched toward a solid wall of rock.

After what seemed an hour of walking, but was probably half that, the group came to a silent halt and Ezeker called her forward. He stood next to a strange outcropping of rock and had his hand on a nubby protuberance. Ember looked at him expectantly, but he still said nothing, just handed her an ordinary-looking stone and pointed at the knobby rock, then pointed at her. Ember took the hint and pressed the rock against the knob.

For a long moment, nothing happened and Ember felt silly, but then a dim light scanned her hand and the rock she held against the stone. She was astonished when the wall of the rock melted into itself, like a river bank after a storm. It collapsed and opened a pathway into the mountain.

Ember had to stop herself from exclaiming with awe. Obviously, the mage academy wanted to keep this a secret, but what a secret it was. Each of the candidates was brought forward, handed a rock, and asked to touch the knobby stone, and one by one the cave seemed to accept them, the entrance growing larger and larger with each child who approached until the last of the mage recruits had been introduced to the stone and Ezeker led the way inside.

It was a whole new world in the cave. Ember felt like she should have been afraid—claustrophobic—but she didn't. The cave spoke to her in ways little else ever had, like it knew her somehow. The walls lit up around her and reacted to the presence of magic. It was eerily fascinating—but strange. In the distance, she could see the tunnel still opening up, as if she were walking through the inside of a giant balloon one of the village entertainers blew up to charm the children. Ember couldn't take it all in. There was so much to see.

In some places, the walls were black obsidian, shiny, like glass. In others, they were clear as quartz, and she could see figures in the depth that never really materialized. Those figures made her shiver and gave her an ill feeling that crept up and down her spine.

The light cast from the walls was an odd color. Just like the stone itself, in some places it cast light of bright sunlight yellow, and in others it was a mossy green or sapphire blue. It was the strangest thing, and yet Ember felt at home here, despite the figures in the stone.

The sound of the group's footsteps echoed off the walls, sounding louder than they really were. Every scuff and stomp was accentuated and cast back on the group. Ember jumped when Ezeker started talking.

"Lessons begin now, my dears. This mountain, as I'm sure you can tell, is not your average stone and dirt. It is alive and is the origin of all the keystones the Guardians used to bind magic to our world. It is a special place, and one that has gained a sentience of its own. It welcomes the members of the Academy of Magi as it would its own children, and protects them just as strongly. We actually housed the Academy within the depths of this mountain, all the rooms created for us by the manipulation of the mountain's stone." Ezeker's words echoed back to the group just like the footsteps, but different from the shuffle of feet, his words came back clear and undistorted.

"Many people have tried to break into the mage school through some means or another. None have succeeded. The mountain envelops them—eats them, I guess you could say. The stone you used to gain access to the mountain is your keystone—not to be confused with the keystones created by the Guardians." He waited for the chuckles to stop before he continued. "These innocent-looking black rocks are your passport into the mage academy. Do not lose them or you may end up like those the mountain has found trespassing against her."

Just as he said that, a section of quartz to the left of the group lit up. Several of the children screamed. All of them backed quickly away from the wall, but it wasn't until they were behind her that Ember saw what had frightened them.

Encased in the quartz was a man. He stood frozen in the glass like stone, as if in solid ice, preserved perfectly. One hand stretched out toward them, the other had a sword raised as if to strike, his mouth open in a scream, but only his eyes told that it was in terror and not fury that he struck. He was dressed in armor that could have come from any of the kingdoms across the continent during the last two hundred years. Things had changed little. Ember took a step closer to better see the man, feeling neither fear nor revulsion.

A snarl sounded from behind her and a figure rushed forward, pushing her aside and to the ground as he struck at the crystal wall with his glowing sword again and again. Ember looked up in shock as DeMunth, now covered from head to knee in glowing yellow armor, a sword seeming an extension of his right hand, swung at the man embedded in stone as if he were one of Ember's attackers from that morning. His sword struck deep gouges in the crystal, sparks flying from the wall as he hacked at the face of the stone.

The mountain shook around them. The children screamed in terror and clung to each other. One of them cried. Ezeker finally found his voice, and what a voice it was. It shook the earth around them and nearly burst Ember's eardrums.

"DeMunth DiCartier, what in the name of all that's holy do you think you're doing? I demand you halt this instant!" Ember glanced up at her old friend to find him nearly glowing with power. He might not be strong in magic, but he had his own kind of power.

DeMunth jabbed at the frozen man one more time before turning to the master of the academy. He tried to answer with his mouth, but all that came out was a collective series of yowls and snarls. Ember knew something was seriously wrong.

She scrambled to her feet, raced the few steps to DeMunth, and spun him around. Rivulets of sweat ran down his face to collect on his collar, and the armor of light was flickering on and off. Worst of all were his eyes. They were blank, unusually bright, and kept wandering back to the man caught in the crystal, DeMunth's lip curling upward in a snarl.

Ember reached up, turned his turned his head until his eyes met hers, and spoke to him in mindspeech. *"DeMunth. What's wrong? You're going to hurt yourself or somebody else. You need to stop attacking the man in the crystal. He is no threat to you."* When his eyes still wandered to the frozen man, Ember added, *"He's no threat to me."* At that, his eyes snapped on Ember's, locked on as if they were the only place of safety in the chaos of his mind.

Finally, he croaked in his normally melodic mindspeech. *"Help me, Ember. I . . . I'm . . . I'm not sure what's real anymore."*

Ember turned to Ezeker. "Did you hear him?"

Ezeker shook his head, nibbling at his mustache while gripping his hands together so tightly, his knuckles turned white.

"He says he's not sure what's real anymore. I think something's going on with the armor. Every time he fights for me, the Armor of Light covers more of his body, and he seems to get feverish. It's affecting him somehow. He needs help, or restraints—something until whatever this is passes."

Ezeker nodded slowly. "I would wholeheartedly agree. Marda, help me with him, would you?" Ember's mother stepped forward and tucked herself under DeMunth's arm while Ezeker took the other side. He turned a head over his shoulder and spoke to the initiates.

"Children, we must hurry. DeMunth is ill, as you can see, and we need to get him to the healers as quickly as possible. If you don't mind, I'll give you the rest of the lecture later. We'll go as quickly as we can toward the first portal, and from there, we'll hop through a few more before reaching the academy. Students, are you ready? We'll be moving fast—keep up."

A few teary sounds of agreement came from behind Ember. Ezeker and Marda moved forward quickly. Some of the younger kids had to run to keep up, which started the tears flowing again. "I want me mum," the youngest boy said, sniffing.

Ember fell back to put an arm around him and squeezed. "It's going to be fine. I'll help you. This first part's going to be a little harder because we have to go so fast, but once we get to the school, it will all be okay. You'll see."

The boy still cried, though he nodded at Ember and clung tightly to her.

"What's your name?" she asked, trying to distract him.

"Markis." He ran his hand across his snotty nose, then wiped it on his tunic. Ember tried not to cringe.

"Markis, huh? Where are you from? Tell me about home." All the while, Ember pulled the boy along, almost picking him up and carrying him over one patch of rough ground where it looked like there'd been a cave in. Perhaps it was from the light earthquake that had shaken them when DeMunth attacked the crystal.

"I'm from Peldane. Do you know where that is?" the boy asked, looking up at her with brimming eyes.

Ember did, but she shook her head no.

"It's three weeks to travel there overland. My mum and da both serve at Duke Domanta's home. It's called Dragonmeer, though I don't know why, since I haven't ever seen any dragons there. My mum serves in the kitchens and my da is a horseman. Even my big brother Joyson serves as one of Master Brant's fetchers." The boy seemed to find his voice as he described home, as Ember hoped he would.

"I've never heard of a fetcher," she said. "What's that?"

"Oh, he runs errands for the Domantas, but mostly for Master Brant. He fetches things. You know, a fetcher." The boy seemed exasperated that she didn't know what he was talking about.

"Oh, a fetcher! Around here, they call them gofers. You know—go fer this, go fer that . . ."

The boy giggled, the last of his tears gone. "Hey, you're pretty nice," he said. "Thanks for helping me."

It surprised ember he would thank her. Most kids weren't that considerate. "Well, you're welcome, Markis. So, what color of magic are you?" She could have looked, but she felt like he still needed some distraction, especially as they came up on the first portal.

"Yellow, orange, and red. They said three is pretty rare." He puffed out his chest and grinned.

"Wow—three colors is really amazing. You're going to do great at the school. I can feel it," Ember said, her focus elsewhere. Ezeker and Marda had reached the portal with DeMunth and he was fighting them, pulling back and thrashing about as if determined to keep from passing through. "Hey, Markis, are you going to be okay now? I'd really like to go and help my sick friend."

Markis looked up at her, his eyes worried for a second, but when he looked at DeMunth, he pulled his shoulders up. "Yes, miss, you can go help him. Thanks again for helping me."

"Any time, Markis. You ever need anything, you just ask for Ember, okay?"

Markis grinned and nodded emphatically. "Oh, yeah. Ember. I heard about you! You're the one who can turn into a wolf and can do white magic." Ember groaned inwardly. The rumors were spreading already. The boy continued, oblivious to her thoughts. "You bet, Miss Ember! I'll see you around!"

There was no time to think of rumors right now. She had to see what she could do for DeMunth. She couldn't just leave others to care for him. There was a bond between them, and though she didn't understand it, she had to honor it. She'd gotten through to him before—maybe she could do it again.

She gave Markis a squeeze, patted him on the head, then sprinted up to where DeMunth so adamantly refused to cross into the portal. Ezeker looked at her gratefully as she took the mute by the hand and looked into his eyes. She mindspoke again.

"DeMunth! You've got to go through the portals if you want to get better. They won't hurt you. They're just like doors. Come on. I'll walk through it with you. It's going to be okay," she said and pulled gently on his hands. He seemed beyond hearing, but his eyes locked on hers once again, and something connected between them. In the back of her mind, Ember wondered if it had anything to do with the white cord she'd seen stretching between them earlier.

One step at a time, she pulled him toward the portal, turning around and taking both his hands. She walked backward through the portal and pulled him through. The portal zipped them at a frightening speed from one spot to another, and in the single moment, they passed through.

The stone was unique here, muddy browns and grays with dingy light leading them to the next portal. Some of the children had obviously never been through a portal before, and had varying responses. Some were giddy, talking excitedly, and couldn't wait to travel through the next one. Others were crying, and terrified to go through again.

Ember, on the other hand, was slightly nauseated. DeMunth still followed her, though he seemed weaker than he had before, as if his strength were being sapped somehow. The sweating had stopped, but now he shivered as they stepped into the next portal. It was much longer than the first, and Ember thought she was going to pass out. As she tumbled out of the portal, she gasped for breath. DeMunth stepped forward woodenly, as if he were a reanimated corpse. His eyes still looked as if they burned from within, but the Armor of Light had completely faded.

Ember broke eye contact with DeMunth long enough to seek out Ezeker, who quickly stepped to her side. "How many more portals?" she asked, gritting her teeth at the pressure DeMunth was putting on her fingers and the panic she fought with each step.

"Only one. Can you make it that far? How can I help?" He asked, sounding concerned.

"He seems to get worse with each portal, but I don't know what you could do to help."

Ezeker nodded and stood on DeMunth's other side as they passed through the portal. It was a good thing he did, for when they exited the final portal, DeMunth completely collapsed and landed right on top of Ember. At least she'd broken his fall enough that he hadn't lost his teeth along with his tongue.

Shad ran to her as DeMunth fell. Evidently, he'd come to the academy ahead of the rest of the group. He helped roll DeMunth off of her. She was extremely grateful, as the weight of him was making it very hard to breathe. Then a couple of guards reached down and lifted DeMunth. The guards, a man and a woman, threw DeMunth's arms over their shoulders. His head lolled from side to side and his skin was cold and clammy when she touched it.

They turned to take DeMunth away, when the male guard gestured toward a stone desk where the children were gathered. "Why don't you just step over there to the registrar and get your uniform and room assignment? We'll take care of your friend, no problem."

It wasn't until they eased DeMunth onto a litter and carried him off, Ezeker and Shad at his side, that Ember could follow the guard's instructions. Torn between running off after them and doing as she was told, she decided she'd better follow protocol and get a room assignment. She stood in line behind all the little initiates, feeling awkward as the oldest one in the group. They were each handed a stack full of robes. Markis got a red robe with one yellow sleeve and the other orange. Other kids had solid colors, some had one color on the bodice and another on the sleeves. One girl had five colors with the tunic separated vertically into three colors, and the sleeves were two other colors. It was almost dizzying.

Ember's turn came. The lady behind the counter looked up. "And you must be Ember Shandae," she said, welcoming Ember like she was her granddaughter. Or like Ember imagined a grandmother would act, considering she'd never actually had one.

Ember nodded to the woman, who went to the back of the closet and came out almost reverently with an armful of white tunics. "I've been waiting a long time to hand these to someone. Welcome, Ember. I hope to see many more of your kind in the coming years."

Ember was a little embarrassed and not sure what to say. She took the robes and stammered a thank you, then turned away, not sure where to go next. All the kids in her group looked at her with something akin to awe and whispered amongst themselves, pointing at Ember and moving out of her way as she tried to get past them. A teenage girl, not from Ember's class, stepped forward and took her by the elbow. The rest of the littles from Ember's class parted to let her by, and even though Ember didn't know the girl, she knew immediately they would be great friends.

Or so she thought until the girl opened her mouth. Once they got around the corner and away from the crowd, the girl stopped and turned to face Ember. "Look, I know you don't know me from the queen, but we're roommates, so you're stuck with me. I'm Lily. I'm a third-year student, and if I can pass my finals, I'll make master in another year. Why didn't you come here when you were younger? You're going to be so far behind, you'll be forty before you graduate. Come on, our room is this way. I've got the north side, you take the south. I'll help you find your classes tomorrow, but then you're on your own. Got it?"

Ember was too stunned to do more than nod.

"Good. Follow me, then." Lily took off with a long, gangly stride that left Ember scrambling to keep up and wondering what in the world she was doing here.

As Ember hung up her white tunics on her side of the closet, she noticed that Lily was one of the girls with many colors. She had six.

Shad had told Ember a few days before that to have six colors was almost unheard of. Three or four was amazing, but six? It was almost as rare as the white. From the look of the robes, Lily's primary colors were orange and red, but when Ember concentrated on the girl and looked, Lily's brightest colors were purple first and red second, with swirls of every other color.

Everything but white.

Suddenly Ember understood why Lily was unhappy having her as a roommate. Until Ember showed up, Lily had been the best of the academy. What made it worse—Lily actually knew how to use her magic. Ember's shoulders sagged. If Lily knew how useless Ember really was, she wouldn't have been worried. What good was magic if you couldn't use it?

Everything Ember did was an accident. And she was back to the questions that had plagued her that morning. How was she supposed to learn white magic when there was no one around to teach her?

As she climbed into bed in her new room at the mage academy, the place she had always dreamed of being, she was still no closer to enlightment and hoped some solutions would come with the start of a new day. If only her father would show up again, she might be able to get some answers, but what were the chances of finding a white hawk while buried in a cave?

Longing for something she couldn't quite name, Ember turned to the wall and tried not to cry herself to sleep.

CHAPTER SEVEN

Kayla exited the throne room and waited in the hallway for T'Kato and Sarali. Instead, she once again got Niefusu. "Thank ye for agreeing to fix the flooded rooms," he said. "Mum and Da have asked me to escort ye about the palace and help ye clear out the most important spots. Would that be all right with ye?" He thrust out his elbow for her to take his arm. She hesitated for a moment. Every time they were alone, this prince did all in his power to kiss her. Did she really want to take that chance? But then there was the question of offending the king and queen. When she thought of it that way, there really wasn't much of a choice.

She refused his arm and instead gestured down the hall. "Lead the way, Prince Niefusu." He seemed mildly disappointed in her gentle refusal, but he did as she asked and led her down to the far end of the hall, then spiraled up a ramp way—evidently what the MerCats used instead of stairs—and down another hall on the second floor. All the rooms had round windows in the doors, and she could see the water that had filled each one of them.

It was overwhelming, she had to admit. "You want me to clear all of them?" she asked, disbelief in her tone, she was sure.

He looked at her over his shoulder. "No, not all. The king and queen's suite first, and then perhaps the library, if ye wouldn't mind?"

Sighing with relief, she followed the handsome prince down the hall and to the double doors at the end.

He threw open the doors to a suite that was more magnificent than any Kayla had ever seen—but it was completely under water, and strangest of all, the water stood like a wall where it had butted against the doors. Kayla reached her arm into the water, just like she had in the waterways. It was eerie.

"Why doesn't it fall?" she asked, pulling her arm out and shaking it off.

Niefusu shrugged. "We don't know. All the flooded rooms be that way. As if the air in the hall be enough to keep the water standin', but the pressure in the castle be not great enough for it." He trailed his fingers across the surface. "One of the great mysteries of these last days."

"Last days?" Kayla asked. "What are you talking about?" She dug in her satchel for the Sapphire Flute and pulled it out.

"The world is unraveling, lass. With no white magi to fix Rasann, she be falling apart. Haven't ye noticed the volcanoes, the storms, heard the tales of the merpeople thrown onto beaches to drown on dry land? The earthshakes? No?" he asked as Kayla shook her head. "The end of the world, I be telling ye."

Kayla wanted to laugh, but he seemed so serious. Could he actually be right?

She shook her head. No. It was impossible. She refused to believe it, but rather than offend the prince, she got to work.

Putting the flute to her lips, she blew a single note. Ripples spread across the surface of the water. It was quite beautiful to see. She moved to another note, the acoustics in the hall hanging on to the first so she harmonized with herself. The water shook like jelly, and then it collapsed, flooding the hallway. Kayla didn't know what she'd done wrong, but in a panic, she froze the water, creating a wall of ice to block the flood. Unfortunately, she forgot that she and Niefusu were standing in it, and froze their feet to the floor, ankle-deep.

Kayla reddened as Niefusu looked down, then at her, and laughed. She focused the flute to thaw the water just around them, then stepped back and tried to think what to do. She couldn't just release the water, which is what she'd been thinking when the flood started. She had to push it back out into the sea, but she wasn't sure how to do that.

She stepped closer to the wall and searched the room through the ice. The room had two windows looking out into the water. If she could get the water to leave through those, she could clear the room.

"Let's try this again," she said, more to herself than to the prince. He nodded and stifled his chuckles.

With the flute at her mouth, she concentrated on what she wanted the water to do. She pictured it very clearly in her mind—the ice melting, the water pushing inward toward the wall and flowing out the windows. She took a breath and blew her first note, high and powerful, putting her intent into the sound.

Everything went just as she imagined it, with one small exception.

She forgot the windows were closed.

The ice in front of her melted, the water pushed toward the back wall, uncovering dripping cabinets and a sopping bed. It seemed to condense somehow against the back wall, and then the windows exploded, shattering outward into the sea. The water cleared quickly after that, and Kayla sealed the gaping holes with ice. It would have to do for now. Next time she'd have to remember to open the windows first, but at least now she knew what she was doing.

As an extra thank you for the king and queen's kindness, she continued to play, sucking the water out of their clothes, their mattress, their blankets, and furniture—everything had all the water pulled from it until it was as dry as if it had hung on a clothesline.

Satisfied with her work, she turned to Niefusu. His jaw hung open and his eyebrows almost reached his hair. "How did you—but—you just, " He couldn't seem to finish a sentence. Now it was Kayla's turn to laugh.

She patted him on the cheek as she walked out the door. "Magic, my dear boy. It's simply magic."

He seemed to take that statement seriously, and it was all she could do not to bend over in laughter. Instead, she asked, "And where would I find the library?"

He led her down another hallway she hadn't noticed before, one that went perpendicular to his parents' bedroom, and at the end he opened the doors to a vast library and looked inside, his face morose. "It be killing me to see all me books waterlogged. Think ye can do the same here as ye did before? I'd appreciate it ever much."

Kayla nodded, though she wasn't sure. This was going to be a much bigger job. Remembering her previous mistake, she asked, "Are there any windows in the room?"

He nodded.

"Do they open?"

He nodded again.

"Would you mind swimming in there and opening every window you can find?" she asked, hoping he would say yes.

He stepped close and took her hand. "Are ye sure ye wouldn't like to join me? I can make an air bubble for ye," he said, a twinkle in his eye.

She pulled her hand from his. She would not let him kiss her again, but she couldn't be rude.

"No, thank you. I've had enough water for the day," she said instead.

Niefusu chuckled and stepped into the water. No theatrics or showing off. He just stepped forward, then swam up to the top, toward the ceiling, where round windows lined the entire room. It took him a good ten minutes to get them all open, but eventually he swam back to the bottom and stepped through the doorway, then shook himself.

Kayla got soaked whether or not she wanted to. Niefusu's smile was so infectious that instead of being angry, Kayla laughed, and had a hard time stopping in order to play the flute.

With only an occasional hiccup and snicker, she played the flute and pushed the water out the windows like she had before. It was a large room, so it took longer, but to save time, she pulled the water from the books as each section cleared, adding it to the mass that surged outside. Finally, the room was done, the books barely damp, and Kayla exhausted and starving. She let the flute fall to her side, her arms suddenly rubbery. It was all she could do to keep standing.

In an instant, Niefusu was at her side, his arm around her, supporting her. "Whoa, lass. That was a bit too much for ye, wasn't it? What can I do to help?" He seemed genuine.

She did not want to like this guy—she was engaged, after all—but he made it so very hard.

"The case for the flute." He reached around her and pulled it out of her bag, then held it open while she placed the flute within its safety. Then he practically carried her to a chair in the center of the room she'd just cleared and made her sit. He pulled up an ottoman and held her hands, watching her face with a concerned look.

It became embarrassing after a while. She pulled her hands away and tried to stand. "I'm fine, now. Thank you." That's what she meant, but her body didn't agree, and flopped back down in the chair before she could get her legs under her.

"Ye most certainly are not fine." Niefusu's voice was stern. "Ye need some warm food in ye and a good rest. Here." He wrapped his arm around her waist and pulled her onto her wobbly legs, then bent over and scooped her up as if she weighed nothing. "I'll get ye to the kitchens. We'll take care of ye."

Kayla objected, but Niefusu wouldn't listen, and she gave up as she caught the scent of something delicious wafting down the halls. "How do you cook down here?"

He chuckled. "Building a fire isn't impossible, though we don't do it much. Mostly we use the hotpots." He wound down the spiral ramp and walked through the hallway they'd first entered.

"Hotpots. Aren't those what your parents said were overheating and boiling people alive in their homes?" she asked, alarmed.

Niefusu was solemn when she expected laughter. "Yes, they be."

"And you still use them?" She was astonished.

"What choice do we have?"

He was right. Under the water, what choice did they have, really? It was either use what they had, or eat cold and raw food all the time. Even so, they were taking a chance.

When they got to the kitchens, Kayla put her hand on the flute in her bag for comfort and looked at the hotpot. It looked like a cauldron of stone grown from the seabed. It had an orange glow about it and was filled with bubbling water.

She wished she could see below it, down into the heated part to see if it was in danger of exploding, and as quickly as she thought it, she felt the power of the flute surge through her hand. Her mind dove to a vein of magma that ran under the ocean floor. She could see where the heat had surfaced through cracks in the ground like miniature volcanoes. There was a fissure just below this hotpot too, and though it was not in danger of erupting today, it would soon if something wasn't done.

Kayla wanted to help, but she did not know what to do, so she did the only thing she could.

She asked the flute.

The answer came in a tumble of information pouring into her mind like a downpour. It was a flood that came so fast it was hard to interpret. She tried, but it was useless. Finally, she told the flute to use her and just fix the thing.

Surprisingly, the flute did exactly that. The boiling slowed to a simmer, and Kayla's mind returned to her surroundings. She collapsed on the spot, sitting hard on the sandy floor in the middle of the kitchen.

Of course everyone was at her side in a moment, wondering what had happened, but no one knew how close they had come to perishing when the hotpot erupted. No one but her.

Niefusu picked her up again, looking at her strangely, and carried her to a table in the corner. He dished up a bowl of soup for her, then gave her some strange crackers to go with it, rather than the bread she usually had. She dumped the entire plate into her soup and ate so fast that before he could dish up a bowl for himself, the soup was gone. He refilled her bowl and brought sea fruit, things she'd never seen nor tasted before, but they were delicious, and slowly her energy returned.

About that time, Sarali and T'Kato came into the kitchens and found her there. She filled them in on what she had done and told them about the hotpot and how close they had come to being injured or killed. Sarali paled at the story, but promised to tell her parents.

60

Everyone thanked her, of course, and pushed more and more food on her until she could eat no more.

T'Kato and Sarali walked Kayla and Niefusu back upstairs, said good night, then dove into one room and left Kayla alone with the prince.

"Thank ye again," he said, opening the door to another water-filled room for her.

"I can't sleep in there," she said. "How am I supposed to breathe? I don't have the energy to clear another room tonight."

He didn't say a word, but turned so they faced each other and stepped backward into the water, pulling her to him so their lips met at the junction between water and air. He blew out, the bubble once again forming around her head like gravy skimmings. His lips were soft and gentle, and seemed to move against her mouth in exactly the manner she liked, mimicking her every move. Every time he kissed her, the world narrowed down to just the two of them and it was so easy to get lost. She couldn't quite manage to pull away, despite her commitment to Brant. Ugh! She'd sworn she wouldn't let him kiss her anymore, but it was so hard to say no. He was so good at it!

This time, he did something different. When he blew out, he pulled her head into the water and bit her neck. She cringed and exhaled a scream that came half out of her neck and half out of her mouth. As he pulled away, he lunged again and bit the other side of her neck, just below her ear. Kayla screamed again, but this time all the air came out of her neck, and none from her mouth. For a moment, it scared her and she jerked away from him, back into the air, but he kept hold of her hands and grinned at her.

When she calmed enough to be rational, he pulled the hair back from his face and pointed at the gills fluttering below his ear, then pointed at her, caressing her neck gently. Kayla could feel she had her own set of gills now, and realized there was no bubble of air around her. She was breathing under the water.

Somehow Niefusu's bite had given her gills. Was this the gift the king and queen had talked about?

That thought was enough to give her the strength to push Niefusu away. He came toward her again and leaned forward for one final kiss,

61

but she put up her hands and wouldn't let him come closer. She was engaged. She couldn't do this.

He smiled at her, then backed out of the room and let her swim inside, pulling the door shut behind him.

Not knowing whether she could trust Niefusu, Kayla pulled the Sapphire Flute from her bag and froze her door shut, sealing the seams with ice, before she made her way to the hammock and lay down to sleep.

It was a long time before dreams came to claim her, and even then they were filled with kisses.

CHAPTER EIGHT

Ember awoke to a ball of cloth hitting her in the face, interrupting her dreams of endless tunnels and suffocation. She sat up in bed and looked around at the unfamiliar space. Cave walls. Beds on either side. A closet at the end and a nightstand to her right. That's right, she was at the mage academy. Her roommate stood in the doorway, her hands on her hips as she stared coldly at Ember. Ember looked down to find her new white robe sitting on her lap. Evidently Lily had thrown it at her.

"Time to get up. Breakfast in ten and classes in forty. You slept through bath time, so you'll have to go as is. Better requisition an alarm stone or learn how to make your own," she said with hardly any emotion. At that, she stepped through the curtain, giving Ember some privacy.

Groaning, Ember slipped out from under the covers, fully expecting the floor to be cold when she set her feet on it, but was pleasantly surprised by the warmth. She stood and scrambled into some clean underclothes and pulled the white robe on over her head, letting it cascade down her body to her ankles. She had no idea how the clothing clerk had done it, but she had made Ember's just the right length, and it didn't itch. It was soft as silk, but not shiny. The material puzzled her, but she had no time to think further about it. She glanced in the mirror on the wall by the doorway and saw her messy hair, ran her fingers through it, then pulled the stringy mass back and wrapped a leather cord around it. It would have to do until she had time to bathe again.

Ember wondered about DeMunth as she stepped through the curtain to find her roommate leaning against the wall, waiting for her. Was he going to be all right? She wished she knew. As soon as Ember appeared, Lily shoved off the wall and walked down the hall to the right, the smells of something yummy assailing Ember's nose the closer they got to the kitchens. A left turn, and then another right, and they entered the dining hall. Small, circular tables sat around the room and people stood behind a long stone counter that ran the length of the far side of the room. The whispers started as soon as she walked in the room, but she was too hungry to care. The closer they got to that counter, the stronger the smell of food became. Ember's mouth was watering by the time she picked up a plate and started down the line after Lily.

Ember stopped and took sliced apples and peaches from the first station, biscuits and gravy from the next, moving down the line and pulling food from each tray. She loaded her plate like she hadn't for a very long time. Mum would have never let her eat like this at home, but Ember didn't care. She was nearly starving after the stress of the last week. She took the sliced fruit, biscuits and gravy, eggs, bacon, and a glass of milk and juice. She was juggling her food and looking for a place to sit when she saw the twins sitting at a table near the door. Ember couldn't help the smile that spread across her face. It'd been too long since she'd seen her step-brothers Tiva and Ren. She took the lead, Lily following behind as she made her way toward the boys.

"Mind if I sit with you guys?" she asked, actually feeling a little shy, but giddy with excitement to see them.

"Em!" Tiva leaped to his feet, took her food and set it on the table, then gave her a big squeeze, his hair minus the stinky oil he usually rubbed in it. Ren was right behind him with a more gentle hug, his dark eyes smiling. "Of course you can sit with us! Mum will be down soon. Isn't it wonderful that she's teaching at the school now? I never even knew she could do magic, did you? They're letting me and Ren out two days a week to help Da with the horses too, thank heavens. Da needs the help and this gives us a break from our studies. Gives us the best of both worlds." Tiva rambled like he hadn't seen Ember for weeks.

When she could get a word in, Ember sat down and pulled out a chair for her roommate. "Have you guys met Lily? She offered to room with me so I wasn't stuck with the littles. Wasn't that nice of her?" She took a bite of her biscuits and gravy and almost choked, it was so delicious.

"Sure. We've met." Tiva said, looking a little leery of the girl, but she seemed oblivious. "We were in the same group. You know, came to the academy at the same time, but so far as I know, you've never taken a roommate, Lily. Why now?"

Lily shrugged. "I had a change of heart. I know how it feels to not fit in, so I took pity on her." Ren nodded and grinned at Lily, his shy smile taking on extra warmth. Lily looked at him out of the corner of her eye and turned a little red. Ember was surprised. Ren? Ren and Lily? The girl was so outspoken, she didn't seem like Ren's type. Ember shrugged. Who could ever tell with these things? She tucked the thought away in her head for another time.

Marda walked in the door and headed toward the food line. She was about to pick up her tray when it flew out of her hand and across the room toward the doorway. Marda stepped back in surprise, then ducked as a bowl of hot cereal and a plate of biscuits sailed over her head, a splatter of the gravy nearly hitting her.

Ember started to her feet, but Tiva reached out and held her wrists from across the table. "Let go, Mum needs help." She tried to shrug him off, but he ignored her and just grinned his usual grin.

"Mum's fine, Em. Just watch. I love when Tyese does this." He muttered the last, glancing toward the doorway. Finally Ember saw who he was talking about. A young girl, her red hair half covering her face, leaned over a notebook and scribbled frantically. She glanced up once at the line, her brow beaded with concentration as the food items sailed one by one to her tray, then down the hallway to her right. What in the world was she doing?

Ember watched as another tray detached itself from the pile and filled quickly with food before sailing toward her, barely missing one of the students. A booming voice shouted from behind the counter. "Tyese! What have I told you about magic in the dining room? Stand in line or get out, but no flying food!"

Tiva burst out laughing. The girl glanced Ember's way and gave a mischievous grin before she scampered down the hallway after her flying food. Ember turned to her still-laughing brother as the chatter once again resumed in the room. "What in the world was that all about?"

"Tyese," Lily answered for him, as he seemed to be choking with laughter. Typical Tiva. "She's been here for a couple years now. Keeps mostly to herself. She's only got one color, but it's strong, and manifests differently than most." Ember waited for her to continue, but instead of explaining further, Lily resumed eating.

"And?" Ember drew out the word and loaded it with expectation. Lily glanced at her, then put her spoon down with a sigh. "She has yellow magic, meaning that everything for her is about sight. Most yellow magi can visualize things and they happen, or manipulate light, but Tyese uses written words or pictures to make her magic happen. She's been helping the Master Librarian for two years now to get his books in some semblance of order."

Ember's mind reeled. The girl looked too young to have been here two years already. "How old is she?"

"Eight," Lily answered, then resumed eating as Marda joined them, looking puzzled and slightly disgruntled. Ember decided not to mention the splatter of gravy in her hair that evidently hadn't missed her after all.

"So she came to the academy when she was six?" Ember asked. Lily nodded. "And why won't she just come in and get her food? She doesn't seem like a troublemaker, unlike Tiva here." She kicked her step-brother under the table. He winked at her.

"No, she's not a troublemaker. Actually, quite the opposite." Ren took up the telling now. "She's an orphan. Nobody's ever been able to get a straight story out of her as to what happened, but Ezeker found her and brought her in. She's afraid of crowds. She's fine in small groups, but she can't attend regular classes because she's terrified by the sound of so many people. I'd guess it throws her back into whatever it was that killed her parents. Anyway, she gets meals for herself and the Master Librarian. It's part of her duties here. She usually comes at odd hours so there aren't so many people, but every once in a while, we get to see a performance like today's. It's kind of funny to watch, but I got clipped by one of her juice glasses once and it's not so fun to be in the midst of it. About like being in the barn when Tiva levitates the cows. You just have to run for cover and get out of the way."

Tiva objected. "Hey!" But aside from elbowing Ren, he said nothing more. He actually seemed a little proud of his escapades.

The table was quiet for a few minutes while everyone ate. Ren was much slower than usual, as he kept glancing out of the corner of his eye to watch Lily. She acted as if he didn't exist, though her face still burned red. Ember wanted to laugh out loud, but didn't dare. Lily already was inclined not to like her because she'd just bumped her from her position as the best in the highest ranking student in the Academy. If Ember wanted to get along with Lily, she'd do well to try to set her up with Ren rather than laugh at the way they tried, unsuccessfully, to ignore each other.

The table suddenly got very crowded when Ezeker and Aldarin joined the group, food in hand. It was like a Karsholm village reunion, with the exception of Lily, who didn't seem to mind. These were almost all people Lily knew, after all. Marda was a new addition, but Lily didn't seem to have a problem with her. She was probably used to being the teacher's pet, with as many colors of magic as she had.

Ezeker started speaking almost as soon as he sat down, mouth full of food. "So, have you gotten your class schedule yet, Ember?"

She shook her head. "Lily said she'd show me my classes after breakfast."

"She did, did she?" he said, glancing across the table at the girl. She met him stare for stare and went one notch up in Ember's estimation. The girl was not intimidated by anyone, it would seem. "Well, you're in good hands with Lily. We decided to put you in Green and Orange classes." He put his hands out to stop her objection before she could voice it. "Those are the colors where your magic is manifesting. You healed your attacker, amazingly so, but you still don't seem able to control your magic under normal circumstances. After lunch, you've got a few hours of one-on-one training with Shad. For now, your evenings are your own to practice or peruse the library in search of information on white magic."

Ember was a little surprised with how full her day would be, but knew she shouldn't be. Her time in Javak had been filled with testing and small bits of training, so it should be no surprise that her schedule would become even more hectic once she arrived at the mage academy. She was here to learn, after all, though she wasn't sure how much good the classes would do, since she didn't seem able to tap into magic the same way every other mage did. But if that's where Ezeker thought she should be, then that's where she'd go. She nodded, then asked the question that had been on her mind.

"Where is DeMunth? Is he going to be okay?" She suddenly felt ill with all the food she'd eaten, remembering her tongueless friend shaking and sweating as he pounded against the crystal wall with his sword.

No one answered. Ezeker avoided her eyes for a long moment. Her stomach dropped. "Is he dead?" she whispered.

Ezeker placed a hand over hers. "Oh, heavens no, child. We're just not sure what's wrong with him. He fell into a coma when he passed through the portal last night."

"Can I see him?" she asked, suddenly desperate.

It was Marda who answered this time. "Perhaps this evening, he will feel better and up to company. For right now, involve yourself in your school work. We've assigned others to guard you until DeMunth is awake and back on active duty." She glanced at Ember's face, meeting her eyes. "He's going to be okay, sweetie. Don't you worry."

Ember *was* worried. She couldn't help herself, but as her family left the table one by one and went to their separate classes, she realized that there was nothing she could do about it. Her mother was right—she needed to throw herself into her classes. She had to learn how to manage her power, one way or another.

As Ember followed Lily to the green room, the whispers and pointing continued. She looked down at her robes to be sure she hadn't spilled anything on them, and finally realized that the problem wasn't that anything was on her robes, it *was* her robes—or the color of them, anyway. She was the first white mage in three thousand years. Nobody had seen anyone wear the whites for three millennia. Of course they were whispering and staring at her. She was thrilled to be at the mage academy, living this dream she'd had for a lifetime, but the attention was hard to take. She'd never been one to stand out in a crowd, and now here she was at the center of one.

The moment she stepped through the doorway into the green room, she was overwhelmed by the smell of life. Wet earth and living green were all around her. Ember reached out to touch a plant, but Lily grabbed her hand.

"Don't touch anyone else's work. You'll contaminate it." She tossed her long brown hair over her shoulder and made her way toward the front of the room. Ember wanted to be offended, but she could understand Lily's point. She just wished she'd been nicer in saying it.

Lily approached a tall man with reddish-gray hair and a goatee. He wore spectacles and had bright green eyes. His smile was kind and welcoming as he spoke with Lily, then glanced up at Ember. His eyes traveled the length of her white robe. He looked excited and apprehensive at the same time as he stepped past Lily and approached Ember, his hand outstretched.

"So you're the one we've been hearing so much about. Ember, is it?" he asked. "I'm Master Stravin. Come in, come in. Sit, sit, sit. Find a spot, and we'll begin shortly." He gestured around the room with his thick hand. "A white mage. Who would have thought I'd live to see this in my lifetime? My, oh, my." He was nearly breathless, and it made Ember uncomfortable. She felt like a new toy for the magi, rather than a person.

The kids came into class in groups and as individuals, but either way, they stopped and stared at her every time. It made her wish she could change her shape and be in disguise again, like she had been in Javak.

The door shut when a chime sounded, and Ember counted the members of the class. There were seventeen people ranging from a seven or eight-year-old to someone who looked to be near thirty. Class began with Master Stravin asking a couple of the older students, including Lily, to come and help him. The students took up a crate of seedlings and set one in front of each student. After what Lily had said, Ember was afraid to touch hers, so she waited for Master Stravin to begin his instructions, her hands folded in her lap. She wasn't even willing to touch her desk until he said she could.

"Okay, class. Today we are going to work on our growing techniques. We want to send healthy energy into our plants and strengthen the roots and stems, and make the plant look like this." He held up a full-grown bush with berries growing from it. Ember looked at her seedling, then back at the bush, and felt the impossibility of the task. How in the world was she supposed to do that when she couldn't even do any of the magic she'd been able to do before?

Lily took the desk next to hers and pulled over close, seeming almost friendly as she went into teaching mode. "Do you know how to tap into the green magic?" she asked.

Ember shook her head.

"Well, we'll work on that. Ezeker asked me to help you because I can access the most colors of magic. Hopefully something will make sense and you can learn to use your white magic too. Now, to begin, reach your hand out very gently. Don't touch the plant—just hover your hand over it and see if you can sense the green magic."

Ember took her hand out of her lap and reluctantly reached out. She closed her eyes, and immediately the green magic of the seedling sprang behind her eyelids. She could see it—could see how the small roots buried themselves deep in the soil and sucked at the nutrients and water. She could see how the leaves reached for the special magelights that were supposed to duplicate sunlight—but there was still a wall she could not reach through. "Okay, I see it," she said. "What do I do now?"

"Really?" Lily sounded surprised. Ember wasn't sure why. Seeing the magic had never been her problem. "Well, then, the next step is to touch that energy and add to it. Almost talk to it and tell the plant to speed up and grow. Do you think you can do that?"

Ember was afraid to answer, so she shrugged. When Lily scowled at her, she spoke. "I can try."

Her hand hovering over the plant, Ember attempted to push through the barrier that kept her from touching the green magic, but nothing happened. She brought her other hand up from her lap and cupped both hands around the plant, but the wall seemed impenetrable. She built up the energy within her, frustrated, then touched the plant like she had her face when she'd wanted it to mold and change, and with her touch, the wall fell, and all the pent-up energy blew into the plant in one swell.

The seedling thrust upward, thickening to the size of her wrist in an instant, breaking out of its small clay pot and scattering the soil about the room. It had grown to a six-foot bush on Ember's desk in a matter of seconds, and Ember and Lily both opened their mouths in astonishment. Master Stravin rushed forward and carried the bush from her desk to a large, trough-like pot at the end of the room. He quickly dug a new home for the huge bush, then returned to Ember, who was now red with embarrassment as everyone stared at her.

"Well, well, that was a much faster grow than we'd planned on, but it will do. It will do." He beamed at his new student, and Ember wanted to shrink under her desk. It was hard to be happy that her magic was working when it created such a mess and she had so little control over the results. She sat for the rest of the class saying nothing and pretending Lily wasn't there, whose defenses seemed to have dropped just a bit with Ember's blunder. She seemed more genuine, though she didn't speak to her until the chime rang for class to be dismissed.

"Orange class is next. This way, Ember," Lily said in an almost kind voice. She took Ember by the elbow and steered her down the hall, away from the dining room and their living quarters. It was quite a distance from where they'd been, but they made it to class just in time. The chime rang twice, and the door shut behind them as they stepped into the room.

This classroom was completely different from the green room. It had stone tables with stools set before them, and the tables were multi-leveled. Lily led Ember to the middle of the room to the only remaining stools, got her seated, then brought over two large, squared pieces of soapstone one at a time. She then hiked herself up onto the stool and used her teaching voice again.

"Okay, now, I've been told that orange magic was your father's strong suit."

71

Ember interrupted her. "Really? I didn't know that. What does an orange mage do?"

The rest of the class had all gone to work without the teacher saying a word. Ember could finally focus in on what Lily was saying. "He was a master stonesmith. He could mold and shape any stone or wood with the heat of his hands alone, and did much of the decoration around the halls. You didn't know that?"

Ember fought the tears that welled up in her eyes and looked around the room. The upper half was decorated with knotwork that looked like vines running the entire circumference of the room. Unable to speak, she pointed at the knots and Lily nodded, a slight smile on her face. Unable to help herself, Ember stood and approached the carving, tracing the lines all around the room. In the middle of the door was a large, knotted symbol. Ember brushed it with her fingers, then turned to go back to her seat. Her da had made that beauty with his own hands. She felt a pang for him and wondered where the white hawk was now that she was buried in the caves. Would the mountain let him in? Would she see him again?

Everyone in the class watched her with a mixture of awe and fear as she returned to her seat. Ember realized that was just going to be part of life for now. There was nothing she could do about it, really, but for today, she was in a room where her father had sat, had worked, had created a masterpiece—and she had the chance to do the same. It provided a comfort nothing else could give her.

She turned to Lily, who had remained silent this whole time. "So, teach me," Ember said, touching her own stone.

Lily started to speak, but Ember made the mistake of putting her hands on her stone after all the emotion had built up from seeing her father's creation. Her hand melted into the stone, embedded in it like a piece of clay, and she couldn't get it out.

Lily looked appalled. "What did you touch it for? Didn't I tell you not to touch things until you were told?"

Ember felt like a three-year-old, but those were the only words she heard Lily say. The rest were a string of nonsense to her ears. She imagined going through life with a club hand. Anyone ever needed a hammer, all they'd have to do is yell for Ember. Soapstone, being soft, would eventually wear away, but she wanted the stone off *now*. She put her energy into it, wrapped up the fear, and smashed the stone down on the table. Instead of it cracking or letting her hand free, it exploded . . . and the table along with it. Pieces of granite and soapstone blew outward, screams and cries coming from the dust.

The mistress of the orange room spoke up. "Everybody outside! Let's see who's injured and assess the damage. Come on out with you. Let's go." Ashamed, Ember moved to the door and filed out with the rest of the kids. The last person to leave was a small woman with braided hair and glasses with darkened lenses. She moved from child to child as if she could see them, but Ember realized quickly that the woman was blind.

Several guards had come running at the explosion, and the Mistress sent the injured children with them to the healers' hall. Only four would require stitches, but everyone had inhaled the stone dust, including Ember.

After dismissing the class, the woman turned to Ember and extended her hand. "I'm Mistress Vanine. Are you the one who made this mess?"

Ember slowly nodded, then realizing the woman couldn't see her, she answered. "Yes, I'm sorry. It was an accident."

Mistress Vanine stopped her there. "I realize that. I should have paid more careful attention. I'm sorry for my lapse, girl. You're new to class, yes? Have you a name?"

Ember nodded again, not thinking. "Yes, ma'am. I'm Ember. Ember Shandae."

The teacher's face lit up. "Ah! The new white mage! It is a pleasure to meet you, even under these circumstances. I hadn't realized you would be in my class today or I would have given you my personal attention. Stone sculpting is no easy task, though your father was beautiful at it."

"You knew my father?"

Mistress Vanine nodded. "Yes, I did. He was in my entry group. Poor little guy, only six and so gifted and having to be with all the olders. You've got a bit of the opposite problem here, I see." The woman smiled, making it obvious the pun was intended.

"Yes, I'm a bit old to come to the academy, but my mother held me back until now."

"That sounds like her." Mistress Vanine chuckled. "Your mother was another of our group members. She used to be my best friend. I'll have to see if I can weasel the story out of her."

"I'd love to hear her version of it," Ember said, which made the teacher laugh.

"Oh, I'll bet you would. Well, enough excitement for today, eh? Why don't you run on to your next class? Lily can help you find where you need to go. Again, a pleasure to meet you, Ember."

"Thank you, Mistress. It was nice meeting you too, though I wish the circumstances were different," Ember said, looking around the destroyed orange room. It would take a while to repair the damage, she was sure, and she wondered what Mistress Vanine would do in the meantime. All because Ember couldn't wait to learn to mold stone like her father.

It looked like orange magic wasn't one of her gifts after all.

CHAPTER NINE

Kayla awoke from dreams of kisses to banging on her door, powerful enough to jar her from sleep. She sat up from the hammock and without a thought, hummed a tune that thawed the ice from around the door she'd put there the night before to keep out unwanted visitors.

It wasn't until T'Kato stormed in the room that Kayla realized she'd done magic without the help of the flute. She wasn't sure how that was possible, but obviously it was, since she'd just done it. Perhaps becoming guardian to the flute had enabled her to use its powers. She didn't know, and T'Kato wasn't giving her any time to think about it.

He swam toward her, held the back of her head, and brushed back her hair as best he could underwater, so that he could clearly see the gills Niefusu had given her the night before. For some reason, he didn't seem thrilled about them, though why they should bother him, Kayla wasn't sure. She was grateful for them. Now she could breathe independently instead of relying on Sarali's bubbles or Niefusu's kisses. She only hoped that once she was on land, the gills would not be visible. She had enough trouble with her Evahn ears—the last thing she needed were gills added to the mix.

T'Kato growled when he let go of her head. She would have thought he'd be happy, as having the gills should speed up their journey, but he seemed almost livid at the sight. He picked up her bag, then gestured for her to follow him. She swam as quickly as she could, but she did not have his advantage of webbed hands and feet, and he quickly outdistanced her.

Still, she did her best, and eventually they reached the royal stables. Kayla stopped in the doorway and stared at the array of animals like she hadn't the day before. There were the dolphins that had pulled the sleds, but there were also sea turtles, sea lions, giant sea horses, a squid, and more animals that she could not name. None of these were hitched to the two fine chariots that awaited them, though. Kayla wanted to rub her eyes. The animals that would pull the chariots were shaped like horses, but were almost invisible, as transparent as the water they were made from. Only their constant fidgeting and movement made them visible at all.

She wanted nothing more than to approach one of the beasts and pet it to see if it felt anything like an actual horse, but she didn't dare. Instead, she turned her attention to Sarali, who was arguing with her father. A giant bubble enveloped the king, his daughter, and eldest son. Niefusu glanced at her, fire still in his eyes, and Kayla blushed, turning away from his gaze. Jihong was nowhere in sight.

Kayla discovered something interesting about the way sound travels underwater when Sarali leaned forward, her face red as she shook her finger in her father's face. As the princess yelled at the king, Kayla found she could hear every word they said. She had to strain a little to interpret it, but she understood the gist of the conversation.

The king insisted that Sarali stay behind to help with the challenges their kingdom faced. "Ye cannot be a leader if ye aren't willin' to do the things a leader does. Sometimes that be inconvenient," he said, rational and calm. Sarali was fuming.

"And what am I supposed to be doing about the promises I already made? What of Kayla? What about the promises I made to her? How can

I be protecting her when I'm down here?" she said, throwing her arms out so her fingers skimmed the surface of the water surrounding them.

"T'Kato can handle it," the king said, glancing at the tattooed man. "And I'll send Niefusu and Jihong to take your place."

Sarali objected, but the king raised a hand. She stopped talking immediately, though she looked as if she were about to explode. "I have spoken," he said with a ring of formality. "We cannot do this without ye, Princess. Ye have the most power of us all. If any can fix this problem and save our people, it be ye. None other."

Sarali slumped in defeat, and even from this distance, Kayla could see tears brimming in her eyes. "I don't know how, Da! I don't have the power Kayla and her flute have. What am I supposed to do?"

The king took Sarali in his arms now that her anger was gone. She collapsed against him, but still did not release the tears. She clung to her father as if he was comfort personified.

And now Jihong entered, carrying a satchel and swimming toward the back chariot. He cast a neutral glance Kayla's way, then ignored her as he packed.

Kayla wanted to help. It devastated her that Sarali wouldn't be joining them. The thought of spending days alone with three men was terrifying to her. Jihong had tried to kill her, Niefusu seemed to have his heart bent on having her for his own, and T'Kato—well, T'Kato was just scary. Period. But she saw no other choice. If only she could help speed up the process for Sarali, maybe the princess could join them.

That got her thinking. Was there something the flute could do to help Sarali? She nibbled at her lip and took a deep breath through her gills. It was still odd, feeling the air coming through her neck rather than her nose or mouth. She shunted aside the distracting thought and focused on what the flute might do. She obviously couldn't just give it to Sarali. But could she create something that would breathe air into the rooms? Maybe even cool the overheated hotpots?

An idea formed in her mind. Kayla scanned the sandy bottom of the sea for a stone of some kind. It took her several minutes, but she finally settled on a large seashell—a conch, she believed—that sat in the corner. She swam to it and picked it up, then nearly dropped it. It hadn't been washed into the corner by the currents, but had walked there on the back of the crab that lived inside. Something clicked in her mind, and she smiled. The crab made it even better.

Kayla set the conch shell back on the floor. Raising the flute to her lips, she hummed, creating a small bubble around her head that she expanded once the water had cleared and she could blow across the flute. She made the bubble grow larger and larger until it reached the sand and encompassed the conch shell at her feet. The crab within must have been frightened, for the shell rocked and bobbed and moved away from her. She froze it with a small trill, feeling only slightly bad for the crab. She was about to make it something so much more.

Twisting the sound, and with a firm purpose in mind, she sent the music and the thought of air and cold to the conch. It didn't freeze as Jihong had when they were battling. Instead, it glowed a pulsing blue and rose into the air. Kayla tried to give the shell and the crab instructions with music alone. No words were spoken, and yet she spoke to the shell and asked it to become a token of power for Sarali. She keyed it, tuned it to Sarali's energy and being so that she connected it to her as if it were a part of her. Hopefully, it would work like the flute, and Sarali could use it to clear the flooded rooms of water, but with it being keyed to her, no one else could use it. It was hers alone. She asked the newly created air elemental crab to cool the super-heated hotpots and save the people. She asked it to use the power of the flute to save the sea people, MerCat and other, and she felt an intelligent nod in her direction.

The crab lived and had become an elemental of air. Kayla opened her eyes and saw the crab swimming out and around the shell, increasing the bubble of air, trying to drain the room dry here. She sent out a burst of sound along with a thought to make it stop, then lowered the flute, walked over, and picked up the shell. She turned to face Sarali to find that everyone was staring at her. Evidently, they'd never seen someone create an elemental before. Jihong, Niefusu, and the king looked a little scared and in awe. T'Kato seemed proud, and Sarali had a mischievous gleam in her eye. Kayla swam through the bubble, letting it pop at her exit, and entered the bubble the king had created for his conversation with his daughter.

"Here," Kayla said, handing the conch to Sarali. There was a spark of blue light as the girl's hand connected with the shell, and Kayla felt it make the last connection to Sarali. She wouldn't have to worry about the crab elemental going rogue now. "I'm sorry I can't stay behind to help, but this will clear a room for you and cool your hot pots. It's not much, but it's the least I can do after all your service and friendship."

Sarali didn't say a word, but those brimming tears were back. The princess stared at Kayla for a moment, then hugged her. The conch shell dug into Kayla's back, but she didn't care. "Thank you," Sarali whispered before giving her a tight squeeze and letting go. Kayla grinned as the girl released her. She wasn't used to being hugged, except by Brant, but Sarali was like the sister she'd never had, and she felt bonded to her like she had no woman in her life and she was going to miss her. She couldn't bring herself to express all of that, so instead, she answered Sarali, trying to get her emotions under control.

"You're most welcome, Princess," she said.

Something connected between them, and Sarali said, very seriously, "You watch out for me rascally brothers. Niefusu seems to have taken a liking to ye, and the boy is as stubborn as the wind. Watch yerself with him. Trust T'Kato, and take care of him, would ye?" she nearly begged.

Kayla was pretty sure T'Kato was much better at taking care of her than she would ever be at taking care of him, but she couldn't stand the look of worry in Sarali's eye, so she nodded and hugged the girl again. "Come back to us soon. It won't be the same without you."

"Oh, I imagine ye'll manage somehow," Sarali said, moving to stand beside her father.

Kayla took that as the sign to go. She swam to the front chariot, trying to get far away from Jihong, only to discover that Niefusu had already ensconced himself there. She glanced at T'Kato. He beckoned to her, and she swam toward him. He created a small bubble around their heads. "Watch out for Niefusu. He is not all that he seems. I will protect you from Jihong." That was all he said, but it was enough to put Kayla at ease for the moment. She swam back up to the chariot and took hold of the bar, settling as far from Niefusu as she could. He chuckled, flicked the reins, and the chariots surged into motion, climbing toward the surface at a steep ascent that had Kayla's ears popping every few minutes.

The water lightened as they neared the surface, the sunshine brightening even the ocean's depths, and at last they burst through the barrier between water and sky. The chariot skimmed across the top of the water, the horses racing like the wind toward land. Kayla watched them with fascination. They were the same texture and tone as the sea, but in the shape of magnificent stallions, bringing whole new meaning to the term "Sea horse." Such beauty. She had seen so many things in the last few days that she had never known existed, and she felt as if her mind had grown from the experience.

The wind was exhilarating. It whipped through Kayla's hair, sending it flying every which way, but the most fascinating aspect of the ride was that the horses went fast enough to keep the chariot on top of the water, much like a boat skimming across the waves. The wind was a roar in her ears, making conversation impossible, but it dried her clothes quickly, even if it crusted them with salt from the sea water. Kayla tried to gather her hair into some semblance of order and tie it back into a bun, not caring who could see her ears.

She leaned into the wind and closed her eyes. The chariots were still quite a distance from land, and even with horses like this, it was going to take a while to get there. The shore was a dark smudge on the horizon and she had no idea where she was—whether the coast was anywhere near Dragonmeer, or the other side of the continent. She only knew she was in the above the sea, and the need to see Brant pressed at her like a weight on her chest.

Niefusu slid to the floor of the chariot and motioned for Kayla to join him. She shrugged, turned, and sat, her head just below the lip of the chariot. It quieted things significantly.

Niefusu handed Kayla a small bag with breakfast in it, then leaned toward her ear. "How do you like your gills?"

Kayla reached up to touch the gills in her neck, then without answering, dug into the food packet and ate. She relished the leftovers from the night before, dinner for breakfast or not. "They're nice," she answered. "Definitely helpful with swimming underwater, though I wish you'd warned me ahead of time. You about scared me to death when you bit me."

Sarali's brother chuckled. "I apologize, me girl. I hadn't meant to scare ye. I only wished to give ye a special gift." He took a bite of his own breakfast.

"Why was T'Kato so upset to see them this morning?" she asked.

Niefusu was quiet for a long moment. "Well, like I said, they be a very special gift. Not given to many." He cleared his throat. "To any but a chosen few."

"A chosen few?" she asked, getting a nagging suspicion that set her heart to racing and put lead in her stomach. She set her food down in her lap. "And why was I chosen?"

The prince actually reddened. "I was hoping to make ye me mate," he said without the embarrassment that seemed to glare through his skin. Kayla was so taken aback, she wasn't sure what to say, though it was no more than she'd been expecting to hear.

"I'm already taken." Kayla tried to brush her hair behind her ears as the air threw it into her eyes. "I'm engaged to be married. I just assumed the gills were the gift your parents said you had for me."

He looked a little chagrined, but he laughed. "Oh, it's a gift, all right, but not the one Mum and Da had in mind. This gift is given only to the husband or wife of one of the MerCats. Always. It looks like I should have waited until I knew yer status. I'd apologize, but I'm afraid I wouldn't mean it."

Kayla felt herself redden and glanced back at the men's chariot. Jihong stood at the head with T'Kato, staring at her with a resentment she'd rarely seen, as if he had heard every word they'd said. Niefusu made a rude gesture toward him, which just made his brother's glare deepen all the more.

The gills on Kayla's neck felt odd—like little fine hairs tickled by the wind, even in her hidden position. She reached up a hand and fingered them. They sat just below and behind her ears and felt like small feathery slits in her skin. She wondered what they looked like and if she'd have to get used to wearing her hair lower on her neck to hide them. Something told her it probably wouldn't matter. What part she'd played in society was over, and she suspected that the adventures ahead would change her in more ways that would make it hard for her to reclaim her status. It was regrettable, but she didn't see any way around it.

Niefusu leaned over and yelled in her ear once more. "Ye might as well get a bit of rest while ye can. It's a trek of many hours before we be reaching land, and who knows how much farther beyond that until we reach Dragonmeer. The time will pass faster if ye sleep." He pulled open a pocket on the side of the chariot and removed a couple of small pillows and a blanket made of woven water reeds. Not the softest things to rest upon, but they blocked the wind and kept her head from bouncing up and down on the floor of the chariot.

Not caring about propriety, they stretched out, their heads nearest the horses, their feet facing the open back end, and curled up together to sleep.

Kayla awoke when the wheels started turning. She sat up with a start and realized they had reached land and were rolling up the side of a cliff to get to the top. It surprised her to see they were now climbing the same cliffs where she had been dropped by C'Tan's dragon just four days before. That meant Dragonmeer was nearby—she'd be able to see Brant shortly. Excitement and nerves built in her, her stomach flip-flopping with excitement. She scrambled to her feet and hung tightly to the edge of the chariot in anticipation, her knuckles white as she gripped the sides.

Things looked more familiar the closer they got to Brant's family home. The sound of hammers hitting stone, wagons rolling across the field, and the hollering of men made it sound like there were many people out working, and Kayla was sure she knew why. When she'd raced back to save Joyson, she'd seen from afar some of the destruction C'Tan's other dragons had caused.

The chariots burst out of the tree line, and Niefusu pulled the water horses to a sharp halt. A young man walked down the middle of the road with a noticeable limp, his arm bound in a sling. He led a horse and it, too, seemed to limp. Kayla glanced around and gasped to see how much damage had truly been done. In the distance, she could see the old cottage that marked the end of the tunnel where she had escaped. It was completely burned to the ground. Bits of the ramparts had been knocked loose from the castle, the field littered with stone. Scorch marks streaked across the walls, and the drawbridge had been thrown off its hinge and was half burned. At the moment, there were boards bridging the gap from road to keep.

Kayla's heart sank at the sight. All this was her fault. If she had not breathed on the flute, C'Tan would not have found her, and none of this would have happened. She held back the tears, but guilt and sorrow ate at her stomach and heart like a ravenous wolf. She felt every scar, every burn, and every displaced stone as if it were one of her bones.

They continued forward at a snail's pace, the man in front of them seemingly oblivious to the chariots behind him. His limp made it obvious he was injured, which probably accounted for his pace, but he stood tall despite it. Finally, Niefusu called out. "Excuse me, chap. Would you mind stepping over so we can pass ye by?"

The man in front of them startled, then turned to look over his shoulder. He caught Kayla's gaze and froze, his eyes as round as little saucers. "Kayla?" he asked, his voice a near croak.

No. It couldn't be. But it was. Crying out, Kayla leaped over the side of the chariot, femininity be damned, and ran to him. As she threw herself against him, his arms were open and a giant smile had split his face. "It *is* you!" He put his arms around her and caressed her hair. "Oh, Kayla, I've looked everywhere for you. Where have you been?"

She pulled back to stare into his eyes, her smile nearly as big as his. "Oh, Brant, I have so much to tell you!"

CHAPTER TEN

C'Tan threw open her door to find Kardon, with head bowed and breakfast on a tray. His way of making amends, she'd found.

She growled at him, "What do you want?" She took the tray from him and set it on the bed.

"The flute, Mistress—" he started, but she cut him off.

"The flute is gone for now, Kardon. I no longer wish to hear of it. Have any of the other keystones manifested?"

"None but The Armor of Light," he said, still examining the floor as if it held something of great interest.

"Also not available at the moment. I am not fighting that Sha'iim priest to get it. Not again." C'Tan took the silver lid off her breakfast platter and threw it against the wall, where it rebounded and skidded across the floor. "If we can't get the keystones, we have to find someone to get them for us."

"Wouldn't it be better to focus on the chosen one for now, Mistress? The keystones will come to her, as I've said before. Why don't we wait for them to gather around her, and strike then?" he asked.

C'Tan kicked the silver dome lid toward him. "Because that is when they will be strongest, you idiot! We can't even take them when they are apart. We need to come up with a better plan. In the meantime, contact our agents at the mage academy and update me on their progress."

Kardon bowed from the room, and she added, "And don't talk to me about the keystones again unless you have a better plan, understand? I can't waste time on this fruitless search, repeating the same mistakes over and again. Fix this, Kardon, do you understand? Fix this!"

"Yes, Mistress," he said, exiting.

She slammed the door in his face.

CHAPTER ELEVEN

Lily was quiet as she escorted Ember down the hall without touching her, avoiding even the barest brush of their sleeves. At first Ember thought she was angry, but as they continued to walk, it seemed more as if she were afraid to touch her, though why that would be, Ember couldn't say.

Instead of leading Ember to her training session with Shad, the brown-haired girl had led Ember to the baths. They both quickly checked in and stripped, then dove into the water and washed their hair free of the dust and rock chips. When they got out of the water, there were warm towels waiting for them, and new mage robes and underthings. Ember didn't know where they came from and would not worry about it. She was clean, her hair washed and combed, and she was going to see Uncle Shad. The bath made it easy to forget the debacle of her classes.

Once dressed and with matching slippers on their feet, Lily led the way deep into the caverns—so deep, in fact, that they had to take a portal to reach the study rooms. Shad stood outside a circular room waiting for her. She ran into his arms and squeezed him tight for a second before letting go. "I know you're my teacher and all now, but I've missed you. I had to do that."

Shad grinned his usual mischievous smile and gave her another hug. "Ah, I'm always open to that kind of thing from my favorite niece." He gestured with his chin toward Lily. "Who's your friend?"

Ember wanted to say, "She's not my friend," but she restrained herself. Walking to Lily, she pulled her over by the elbow, just like Lily had done for her earlier. "This is Lily. She saved me last night after check-in and is my new roommate. She helped me through a lot of messes today and even taught me a thing or two."

"Really?" Shad asked, looking the tall girl over from head to toe. Lily actually blushed under his gaze and glanced at Ember questioningly. Ember could feel the girl's walls coming down bit by bit, which surprised her. Lily's walls should be sky high with all the misadventures of the morning, but it seemed the more Ember messed up, and the more she tried to reach out to the girl, the more Lily responded. It was as if she didn't want to like Ember, but couldn't help herself.

"Well, I've got my own training to do, so I'll come back for you after class, or Master White Shadow can show you to the dining hall and the library," Lily said, backing toward the portal.

Shad nodded. "I'll get her where she needs to be, don't you worry. Enjoy your classes, Lily. It was nice to meet you. Thanks for taking care of our girl."

Lily bobbed her head and waved as she ducked through the portal. And then it was just Ember and Uncle Shad. He gestured for her to enter the practice room, then came in right behind her. The door closed so tightly, she couldn't see where it had been. It was like it sealed them in a cave. Ember's first instinct was to panic, being closed in like that. She put her back to the wall and tried to slow her breathing.

Ember took a moment to look around. The domed ceiling had sparkles of different-colored gemstones embedded in its height, so it almost looked like stars shone down on her. Other than that, the room was plain black-and-white granite, with occasional veins of quartz. She turned back to Uncle Shad, who leaned against the wall, his arms crossed.

"So, I hear you're making quite an impact already." He shoved off from the wall and walked toward her.

Ember wanted to cry, but didn't give herself the release. She just nodded and continued to look around, turning her back on him to further examine the walls, though there was nothing really to see. Shad came up behind her, took her shoulders in his big hands, and turned her around to meet his eyes. "How do you feel about that?"

Ember shrugged, not wanting to talk about it. She knew if she talked, she'd cry, and once she started, she wasn't sure she could stop.

Somehow Shad knew and held her for a moment, then pushed her to arms' length and searched her eyes. He nodded once, then backed away. "Okay, then. Let's get to work. Shapeshifting today. I've heard it's been a bit of a struggle for you lately. What's wrong, do you think?"

Ember's frustration with her inabilities rose and she tugged at her hair. "I don't know. I try to turn into a wolf and get nothing. Then, when I'm threatened or scared, it happens suddenly, without my thinking about it. I don't know if I'm trying too hard or if it's something else."

Shad nodded slowly and sat down cross-legged in the middle of the floor. "Let's try the quiet and easy way first. Sit with me." Ember knelt, then sat and stretched her legs out in front of her. Shad rolled his eyes. "Not like that. Imitate me." Ember examined his posture and adjusted, crossing her legs beneath her, and sat up straight. She put her hands on her knees, palms up. When she had settled herself properly, he spoke. "Now, breathe deeply. In through the nose, then release it slowly through your mouth. In through the nose. Out through the mouth."

Ember did as she was told, but did not know how breathing was going to help her manage her magic, even the shapeshifting kind—though she enjoyed the relaxation. Her mind drifted and she felt the tug of the heart rope again.

Unafraid, she followed it and found herself outside of her body, looking down once more. She continued to breathe in and out like Uncle Shad told her, but her consciousness was gone. It was out there, with her spirit self or energy self, or whatever she was supposed to call it. She floated around the two of them, enjoying the vibrancy of light and energy, seeing the shields guarding outsiders from harmful magic inside, and realized what this room was for. It was like the game Aldarin played when he was young that required him to wear padding to keep from being hurt. This was a magical padding for those inside and out.

Ember looked at the heart rope from her body to Uncle Shad, which was still white, but with a tinge of green, then saw the yellow-white heart rope that led out the wall and, she was sure, down the hallway to DeMunth, wherever he was. There was something connecting them, something more than just a mutual interest in each other. It was something magical.

That thought snapped Ember back into herself, but Shad never seemed to realize she'd been gone. She was going to have to ask someone about this strange ability to step outside of her body—but this was not that day. Today, she had to focus on breathing, and seeing if she could get her shifting abilities back under control.

"Now, Ember, I want you to change your robes, just like you did your dress back home. I want you to change it from white to yellow. Can you do that?" Shad asked in a slow, melodious voice.

"I think so," she answered, still floating a bit in her head. She laid her hand on her knee and wished for the robe to change.

Nothing happened.

She tried again, and again, and again, until the frustration built to the breaking point and she grabbed it tightly and shouted at the material, "Change, you cursed thing!" Something pulled out of her and Ember sagged, her eyes closing automatically, but when she opened them again and looked, the robe had changed to a vibrant lemon yellow.

"Hmmm," Shad said. "That was interesting. Why don't you try shifting into a wolf?"

Shad did it from his sitting position, a slow transition that was fascinating to watch. Ember enjoyed seeing the shift from one form to another, and once Shad the wolf sprawled on the floor, tongue lolling, she tried it as well. She focused on her face.

Nothing happened.

She tried to make the fur grow.

Nothing happened.

It wasn't until the frustration built and she yelled at herself that the shift happened, all at once, just like it had at the field when she was attacked—and oh, did it hurt. Ember lay on the floor, panting and whining with the pain for a long moment before she could gather her paws beneath her and shake herself.

Shad mindspoke. *"When you shift back to human, make your tunic white again. Change now."*

Ember was stunned. Shad had never made her shift back and forth so quickly before. She gathered her energy and shifted, her white tunic appearing out of her fur. Shad changed at the same time and sat back down, waiting for her to finish. When Ember was fully clothed, he asked her questions.

"What do you feel when you shift?" he asked

"Pain," she said, wiping the sweat from her brow and trying to readjust herself so the spot where her tail had been a moment before didn't hurt any longer.

"I know that," he said. "Emotionally. What do you feel when you shift?"

Ember had to stop to think about it. When she'd been attacked, she'd been afraid. Training with Shad, she felt frustrated. In the caves when Ian had kidnapped her, it had been desperate fear. She expressed all this, and Shad nodded his head sagely.

"Emotion is your trigger," he said, as if that made all the sense in the world.

"Huh?" was Ember's literate response.

"You change when you feel potent emotion. How about today, when you turned the seedling into a bush? What did you feel?"

Ember described the frustration of not being able to breach the wall of magic around the plant, and how that feeling had grown until she touched the leaf.

"Ahhhh," he said. "Emotion is the trigger, touch is the catalyst. Do you understand what I'm saying, Ember?"

She shook her head.

"When you feel powerful emotion, it activates your magic, lets you access it somehow. When you touch things, it releases the magic you've built. Emotion and touch. You'd think you were a water mage and physical mage, with the catalysts you've got. Water magi use emotion to access their magic. Physical magi use touch, just like your da did. You are going to have to work on controlling your emotions and using touch before the emotion gets too strong. That's why things happen so fast. It's like you've built up this dam of water and then you take the wall down all at once. You need to be more like a faucet. Can you do that?"

"I don't know, Uncle," Ember said, surprised at his evaluation and realizing he was right. She felt the truth of it deep in her soul. "I can try."

"Good," he said, patting her on the shoulder, then pulling both of them to their feet at once. "Lessons are over for now. How would you like to go see DeMunth? It's lunchtime. I'll bet they'd let you feed him. We can feed you too. You've used a lot of energy and you need to eat."

Ember had heard nothing better all day.

The healing hall was farther away than Ember thought. She'd imagined it being more in the building's heart, where the action was, but they had to travel through two portals to get there, different from the ones they'd come through originally. They evidently scattered the portals throughout the caves.

The healing halls were quiet. Whispered voices only existed there, and the smell of soupy lunch wafted from the area. Shad led Ember into a room that held many people, but to the left lay one that drew her like a magnet—a body still unmoving and barely breathing. Ember felt the draw, nearly shaking at being so near to DeMunth and the fear of losing him. The bonds between them were strong. She didn't know why, but she would not question it. Her uncle stepped to the side to visit with a nurse, who glanced at Ember with a smile.

Ember turned and headed toward DeMunth when Shad stopped her and handed her a bowl of soup. "Eat now," he demanded. Ember's belly growled. She didn't even use a spoon—she drank the soup straight from the bowl, her stomach barely calming when she was done, but it was enough to take the edge off her hunger. Shad then handed her another bowl with a silver spoon and nodded toward DeMunth. "Now's your chance to take care of him, pup. I'm going to leave you for a bit. Call my name in your head when you're ready to go, all right?"

Ember nodded and didn't even wait for him to go. She took the bowl and spoon and walked across the room to DeMunth's side. She barely registered when Shad left. Still shaking and trying not to spill the soup, she sat on the chair at the side of DeMunth's bed. Unsure what to do, she fed him. She spilled a little of the broth on his chest and sopped it up quickly with the blanket. She had to get her mind off of his condition and decided talking to him as if he were awake was her only option.

"Hi, DeMunth. It's me, Ember. You're supposed to be my guard, you know, and believe me, I could have used some guarding today. You should have seen what I did." She told him everything that had happened, all the while dribbling soup into his partially open mouth. When he seemed to respond, she put the spoon in his mouth.

He bit down and Ember felt a moment of panic when he wouldn't let go. She was afraid he would break his teeth. She pulled and prodded gently and finally he released it, but when Ember pulled the spoon from his mouth, the bowl end was missing. It seemed impossible, but DeMunth had just bitten through metal, and not just any metal, but precious silver. She was terrified that he would choke to death on it. But how in the world were his teeth that strong? She was afraid to stick her fingers in his mouth—if he could bite the end from a spoon, he could bite her finger off—but she didn't want him choking, either. She pulled his jaw down with a rolled piece of blanket and called one of the magelights to shine in his open mouth—but what she found was not at all what she expected.

The silver of the spoon had melted and pooled in his mouth like mercury, but instead of blocking his airway or falling to the back of his throat, it was attaching itself in threads to the base of his tongue. It built up silver nerves, blood vessels, and muscle fibers—even a few silver taste buds popped up on the top of his tongue. Ember froze, staring into his mouth for a long moment, her heart racing with the shock and strangeness of it. She was horrified and fascinated at the same time. How could this happen? What was causing it? Then excitement took over and, feeling only slightly guilty, she put the end of the handle into his mouth to see what would happen.

As the silver handle touched DeMunth's tongue, it melted like chocolate, continuing to pool around the silver bud, then adding more to the mass his tongue should be. She gasped as the light of his armor flared up, then something connected in her head. The problem with DeMunth's armor had something to do with his tongue—or lack of one. It sounded ridiculous, but somehow she knew it to be true. Maybe she could help him after all.

Ember set the soup aside and went to the healer's station to grab more spoons, taking them right off the lunch trays, not even caring that the healers would have to find more. She found a couple of forks tucked in a drawer, and with her hands full of silverware, she went back to DeMunth's side and put the utensils in his mouth one piece at a time, watching as his tongue grew, now formed from silver.

She watched in fascination as the Armor, that had begun as a breastplate and grown to cover his shoulders and thighs, burst to life with a bright yellow light and pooled over his body like honey. His tongue was not the only thing growing. Ember's heart raced. She had been right. The armor rolled downward until it covered his feet, then upward until it encased his head in crystalline armor.

Then it changed, firming up, creating angles on his chest and down his arms. His headpiece gained a visor and a sharp angle from the forehead to the back of his neck. He gained gloves and greaves, knee guards and boots. It was lovely armor, made more lovely because it encased DeMunth's body.

And then it faded into his skin, just like Ember's bracelets had when Ezeker gave them to her. When the color faded completely away, he breathed deeply and his eyelids fluttered. Ember tried to give him another spoon, but he pursed his lips and turned his head, rejecting it. Evidently, he had what he needed. Ember set the spoons on the side table and clasped her hands, trying to calm the shaking now that the deed was done. She picked up the cold bowl of broth and dribbled just a little into his mouth. He smacked his lips, then raised his head for more.

Ember's heart thrilled. He stretched, yawning, his mouth open wide and his silver tongue bright and shiny for all to see. It moved just like a real tongue, fascinating Ember. A silver tongue that moved like a human one. This had to be the work of the Guardians. What other reason could there be?

DeMunth sighed, then settled into the deep, healing kind of sleep, and he was going to be oblivious for a while still. Full of relief and excitement, she stood, the stool scraping the floor behind her, then she impulsively leaned over and kissed him in the middle of his forehead and stroked his hair back. She just couldn't seem to help herself. The connection between them was something she'd never known before.

Suddenly, she wondered how old he was. She'd never asked him. He didn't look old—older than her, yes, but only by five or six years, ten at the most. Very young to be sitting on the council, but there was a wisdom about him that was rare, even in people much older than he. She was determined to find out when he awoke. She was positive that he would awaken. There was no doubt.

Knowing there was nothing more she could do at the moment, Ember addressed another of her problems. She turned as the healer came through the door near DeMunth's bed. "Excuse me, could you tell me where to find the library?"

The woman barely glanced at her as she went to tend to another patient. "Certainly. It's at the center of the school. Go toward the dining hall, but instead of turning left, turn right, follow the hall to the end, and enter the double doors. Talk to Master Earl. He'll help you find whatever you need."

"Thank you," Ember said, but the woman seemed to have already forgotten her as she cared for her patients. Instead of feeling bothered by it, Ember turned on her heel and exited the healing hall, and following the directions, found the library in a matter of minutes. The double doors were solid wood, and though heavy, they swung easily as she entered. Uncle Shad had helped her understand herself a bit, but if she could find a training manual or a journal from an ancient white mage, she might figure out how to do this magic thing.

Hopeful and anxious, she walked across the gigantic room to a large stone desk where a spectacle-wearing man sat, a magelight hovering over his shoulder as he read an ancient scroll.

Ember cleared her throat. "Excuse me."

95

The man looked up. One eyebrow quirked in an unspoken question. "Are you Master Earl?" she asked.

He nodded.

"And you are the head librarian?" she asked again. It was hard not to fidget under his gaze.

He nodded once again.

Ember was starting to wonder if his tongue was missing, like DeMunth's. "I was told you were the person to talk to—I'm looking for some information on white magi."

Now both eyebrows went up. The man leaned back in his chair and really looked at her. "You are the new white mage." he said in a much deeper voice that she would have thought could come from his compact frame.

"Yes, sir. Is anything here that belonged to a white mage? A journal, perhaps?" This man scared her a bit. How could someone so slight give off such a feeling of power as to make her squirm?

"Don't you think we would have something like that ready for you, if we knew of it? It's possible there is something within these hallowed shelves, but this library is so old and unorganized. If it's there, I have no knowledge of it." He leaned forward and peered into her eyes. "You could search through these halls a thousand years and not find what you're looking for."

"If they are so hallowed, why are they unorganized?" she asked before she could think.

He stiffened. "Not all the Head Librarians have treated these shelves as respectfully as they should. I, on the other hand, find value in the words of our ancestors."

She'd obviously angered him, though she hadn't meant to. Taking on a humble posture and tone, she asked, "Well, would you mind if I try?"

The man pursed his lips and cocked his head, looking her up and down, assessing her in his own way. "Why don't you talk to Tyese and see if she can help you? If anyone can, she'd be the one." He gestured with his head to the girl sitting behind him. She was hunched over a desk, scribbling in her little book. At that moment, a scroll flew over Ember's head and directly into Master Earl's hand. He grunted, then unrolled it and went back to his studies, completely ignoring Ember. She could see why they stuck him in the library. He seemed more content with his books and scrolls than with people.

She walked past him, her footsteps echoing off the stone walls, though Tyese didn't seem to notice her. Ember stood and watched the girl's handiwork for a moment, now that she could see down the long lengths of shelves to what was happening. Books and scrolls flew from one shelf to another, several soaring over the bookcases at one time. How the girl juggled so many at once, Ember didn't know, though she wanted to. She felt a kinship with this silent, redheaded child.

Ember spoke softly, so as not to startle the girl, though she still jumped the sound. "How do you do that?"

Tyese stilled, but she didn't answer.

Ember remembered what Ren and Lily had said about her that morning. Instead of getting frustrated, she took a chair from the wall and pulled it up to Tyese's desk. She watched her go back to her drawings and list writing for a long moment before she spoke again, this time waiting for the girl to pause before she interrupted her.

"You know, it's kind of hard being the new one here and having a gift that nobody understands," Ember said in a near whisper, looking down. "I've got this gift, see. I'm the first white mage in three thousand years, which is amazing. I mean, it's wonderful that I can help heal the world, but I've got a problem. It's been so long since there was a white mage. Nobody knows how to teach me. I'm not sure what to do." Ember stopped talking and hoped Tyese would respond to her plea.

It worked.

"What do you need from me?" Tyese said in a sweet, but still guarded, voice.

"I wondered if you could find a journal or something that belonged to a white mage. Anything that might give me some understanding or control of my powers. Do you think you can help?"

Tyese looked up from beneath her curtain of red hair and met Ember's eye. "I can try." She was quiet for a moment, then said, "I know how that feels, you know. Not fitting in. Being different. It's hard." She sighed.

"Yes, it is." Ember joined her with a sigh of her own.

97

"I've learned that most of the time, you just have to figure it out as you go. I know it's frustrating, but trial and error is the best way to see what you can do. At least, that's the way it was for me, though I think being a white mage and messing up would cause a lot more damage than a few dropped books." A smile appeared on her lips as she looked at Ember again. She had a charming smile. She should let it out more.

Ember remembered her adventures in class that morning and knew Tyese was right. She needed to practice, but she was going to have to be sure it was in the shielded rooms, so nobody got hurt again. She couldn't stand it if her power ended up hurting anyone else. Or worse—killing them.

"I'll help you. I can't promise anything, but I'll see what I can find," Tyese said, looking shyly down at her book. Ember glanced at her hand, smeared with graphite and ink on the nails and the side of her palm. Such a big job for such a little girl, but Ember was thankful.

"Thank you, Tyese," Ember said. "Is there anything I can do for you in return?"

Tyese bit the inside of her cheek and glanced hesitantly up at Ember. "Do you think you could come visit me again?"

Ember smiled at her and took a chance. She reached out and gave the girl a gentle, one-armed hug. "I'd be happy to."

Tyese gave her a full smile at that, and it dazzled Ember. If only this girl could see herself the way others saw her. Ember decided to help her. She needed to know what a gift she was, not only to the school, but to the people within it.

With nothing more to be done or said, Ember gave Tyese one more hug and said her goodbyes, then left without a word to Master Earl.

She stopped at the dining hall on her way to her room. She had spent more time with DeMunth and Tyese than she'd realized. Dinner had come and gone, but there was still food to be had. She took a plate and packed it with as much as she could. When she got to the end of the line, she asked one of the kitchen workers if she could take the plate back to her room.

"So long as you bring the dishes back in the morning, that should be fine," the woman said with a wink, handing her a silver fork. Ember looked at the fork as she walked down the hall, remembering the metal pooling in DeMunth's mouth to create a new tongue. Oh, was he going to be surprised when he woke up. And with that thought, she walked through the curtains to her room and sat down to eat her dinner before going to bed. She'd never been so exhausted in her life.

CHAPTER TWELVE

Kayla stared into Brant's eyes, so happy to see him. After all the times she'd imagined returning home to his funeral, seeing him in the flesh was almost more than she could take, and she teared up.

"Hey, now, none of that," he said, taking her in his arms.

Niefusu cleared his throat. "Duchess, me think it best if we moved the chariots off the road a wee bit, wouldn't ye think? The travelers will be wanting a way past us in but a moment."

She glanced up at him, then followed the turn of his head to the coach coming their direction. She let go of Brant with reluctance. "He's right. Let's move off the road. Here, Brant—why don't you ride with Niefusu and I'll take your horse until we get you fixed up."

The two men competing for Kayla's hand looked at each other warily, but she would have none of it. She pushed at Brant from behind, though she tried to be gentle with his injuries. She wasn't sure if things were broken or sprained or something else, but he had both a leg and an arm that seemed to be bothering him, the latter in a sling. Niefusu reached out a hand to pull Brant into the carriage.

"Me name be Niefusu. Sarali's brother," he said, still holding Brant's hand.

"Brant Domanta, son of Duke Brantalew Domanta of Dragonmeer, fiancé to Kayla Kalandra Felandian," Brant said in his most formal tones, bowing his head in Kayla's direction.

She wanted to roll her eyes, but resisted the urge. Instead, she clambered into the saddle of Brant's huge white stallion, his half of a matching pair given as an engagement present from the duke.

"I've heard of ye," Niefusu said. "Kayla has spoken much of her engagement to the duke's son." The way he said it made it sound almost an insult, and Brant stiffened. Niefusu continued. "She's quite a catch, yer Lady Kayla. I would have claimed her for me own, but for yer prior claim."

Kayla turned in the saddle to object and froze as Brant's face turned red with anger. "If I were not so incapacitated, I would demand justice for that, sir."

"From the son of a *king?*" Niefusu asked, a smirk plastered on his face. "Wouldn't that be a bit presumptuous of ye?"

Brant pulled away from Niefusu. "What?"

"Me father be king of the sea people. The girl who played the part of yer maid for so long is the heir to that kingdom. Ye would demand justice from me?" His voice went from playful to offended. Brant sealed his lips, still red, though seemingly more embarrassed than angry now, and tried to climb down from the chariot, but Niefusu held him back.

"Now don't be daft, me boy. Ye be injured. What does it matter if I be the son of a king and ye the son of a duke? We both be men, and servants of a king—and we both be wanting to impress a pretty lady, wouldn't we?" He winked in Kayla's direction. She ignored him and stared at Brant, imploring him with her eyes to stay put.

His lips were still tight, but he relaxed in Niefusu's grip and nodded once to Kayla. For now he could ride easy, and just in time too. The carriage was nearly upon them.

Jihong pulled his chariot to the side of the road, and Kayla guided the stallion a few steps to the right until they were all on the grass as the carriage passed, the driver barely looking at them. Once the dust cleared, they pulled back out and headed to the crossroads.

There was a clearing there, purposely created for those who needed a resting place before going one direction or the other, wood already set in the firepit, ready to be lit.

T'Kato got out of the chariot before it even came to a stop and pulled Kayla aside. "What was that all about?" he asked.

Kayla shook her head. "A bit of not-so-friendly competition between the boys. I don't know what to do, except let them battle it out for themselves."

T'Kato nodded, as was his way, then added something more. "You are wise in this. When it comes to affairs of the heart, a man is not to be toyed with. Make your choice clear to them both by your actions alone. Don't say anything to them about it. It will be easier for the loser." T'Kato turned his back on her then and went to start and tend the fire. Niefusu and Jihong hobbled the horses near the sweet grass to feed and took care of the chariots. Kayla at last had a moment to tend to Brant's injuries.

She marched over to her fiancé, who stood watching T'Kato feed the fire, took him by the elbow, and pulled him toward a copse of trees nearby. Brant yelped when she first took his arm, but then followed her willingly.

When they got to the trees, she turned around to talk to him, but he was already leaning forward and she moved right into his kiss. With a sigh, she wrapped her arms around his neck and tried to show him just how happy she was to see him.

When Brant's breathing became ragged and she knew hers would soon be as well, she pulled away from him with a laugh, her fingers still twined in his hair. "Oh, how I've missed you!" she whispered with all the passion she dared.

"And I you," he said. "I've been looking for you for days. I was so afraid you were dead after the hounds found your blood at the top of the cliff by the sea." He choked up.

Tears fell freely then. He had been as worried about her as she was about him. In her eyes, there was no greater sign of his love.

But she hadn't come here to kiss him. She'd brought him to these trees to heal him. She pulled the Sapphire Flute from the bag slung at her hip and put the glowing instrument to her lips.

Brant's eyes got huge, and she knew what he was thinking. She did her best to reassure him. "Don't worry, love. C'Tan had her chance and lost it. I've fought her and won—for now. I can play the flute without fear."

Brant's eyes were still wide as she played, but shortly he began to relax as the pain she could feel flowing through him faded. Her mind went with the music of the flute, deep into his shoulder where the ball had come free of the socket. Into the bone below his bicep, where it had fractured in a spiral. Into the muscle of knee, shoulder, and arm, bruised and aching with rips and tears.

She started with the fractured arm and played, begging the flute to heal the bone, to fill the spiral with new bone. As the flute listened, she moved on to the dislocated shoulder and heard an audible gasp from Brant as it slid into place, then a sigh of relief as the constant pressure released. The flow of blood restored itself to normal, and she sent out a final swell of healing into the muscle of his shoulder, arm, and then down to his knee, much like a final pass over a frosted cake, and he was healed.

Kayla lowered the flute and sighed. If Brant's eyes were big before, now they were huge as he took off his makeshift bandage and spun his arm in a circle, then flexed his bicep, and squatted down and back up. He looked at her with something akin to awe before he said, "Thank you, love. That was—indescribable."

Kayla laughed, put the flute away, then walked to him. She was almost into his arms when T'Kato burst into the clearing, his sword out for war.

"You foolish child! Did you not see what your previous playing has done to Dragonmeer? Would you bring C'Tan down upon them once more?" He glared hard at her.

Kayla's anger was immediate and fierce. "Of course I saw, and I feel terrible about it! I know it is my fault Dragonmeer is in ruins. I know it is my fault so many are dead." She took three steps toward the tattooed man and stopped, shaking with fury. "But know this, disciple of Klii'kunn—I was given guardianship of this flute, not you, and I know when it is safe to use it. Your calling is no longer to guard the flute. It is in the hands of its master, and I will use it as the need occurs! You will trust me or you will leave. Do you understand?" Kayla's breath came as though pumped through a bellow and a blue glow surrounded her like a sapphire flame.

T'Kato glared at her for another long moment, then he straightened and thrust his sword into its sheath. He brought his palms together in front of his heart and bowed to Kayla in the Evahn gesture of respect and gratitude.

It was the last thing Kayla expected.

"At last you have found your voice and have become the true guardian of the Sapphire Flute. I will challenge you no longer," he said, then turned and walked back toward the flame that now cooked their lunch.

Stunned by his change in tone and acceptance of her guardianship, Kayla didn't know how to respond, so she just let him walk away. Inside, there was a part of her that knew she'd won a significant victory in gaining T'Kato's approval, but she tried not to listen to it too much. She couldn't afford to with meeting the wolfchild in the future. Who knew where that would lead where the flute was concerned?

Kayla could smell lunch on the breeze, and her stomach growled.

Brant must have heard, for he laughed and took her hand. "Thank you, Lady Kayla," he said, and kissed her knuckles where their fingers met. "I must say, that was the most wonderful healing I have ever received."

Together, they walked back to the crossroads, hoping there was food enough to share.

The sun dropped behind the horizon with the afternoon's activity. Kayla took the time to heal Brant's stallion, and the boys vied for her attention every moment they had. Most of the time, the competition seemed friendly, but a few times she was afraid harm would come to one or the other.

One of those moments was at dinner. Rather than traveling on to Dragonmeer, where Kayla was sure she would get a mixed welcome, they camped in the crossroads clearing for the night. T'Kato brought more wood for the fire, and the smell of applewood tickled her nose every bit as much as the rabbit and root vegetables Niefusu and Jihong had found in the brush. Brant added dessert to the mix with cored apples stuffed with sugar and cinnamon he pulled from his saddlebags, and baked in clay from the riverbank.

Kayla had wanted to scream when she saw Brant slathering the fruit in thick mud, but his wink had calmed her a bit, though it wasn't until the first taste that she finally understood. The clay formed a perfect bowl to hold the juices of the apple and melted sugar, sweet and sour together.

It was the perfect ending to the perfect meal—for everyone but Niefusu. He glared at Brant across the fire and refused the apple baked for him. Instead, he gnawed on the bones of the rabbits he'd snared and watched Brant and Kayla together. His eyes never seemed to leave their clasped hands or the small distance between them.

Brant broke open the apple Niefusu had declined and offered it up to Kayla with a flourish. "My lady?" he said, wafting it under her nose. He knew her too well. The smell of the cinnamon apple was irresistible.

Kayla leaned forward. "Why, Brant, are you trying to tempt me?" she asked, laughter lacing her voice.

"But of course," he said. "Is that not the duty of one's love?" He said it flippantly, but his eyes showed just how much he meant it.

Niefusu made a gagging sound. Kayla was offended—he had seemed so much more refined than that. She refused to look at him and instead gently took the wrapped apple from Brant and answered him with a kiss. When she finished, she said, "Yes, it certainly is."

She could see the confusion in his eyes for a moment. There had been a long pause between his question and her answer, and she had addled him with a kiss. She liked knowing she could do that to him. She took a small bite of the apple and gave him another kiss, this time a quick peck on the cheek. "Thank you, love," she said so low none could hear. Then she looked straight at Niefusu and took a big bite. She sighed and licked her lips. "This is so good." She proved it by eating every bite and drinking the syrup from the bowl.

He stared at her with annoyance that quickly turned to longing as he watched her and Brant, and shortly after, he left the warmth of the fire. She was actually grateful. She hoped he would stay gone for a while—not that she didn't appreciate his hospitality and all that he and his family had done to bring her home, but he was making things so very difficult. Despite her love for Brant, there was no denying what she had felt during Niefusu's kisses. And he was a prince. The son of a king. And the world he came from was so very fascinating. She couldn't help but be drawn to him.

But here was Brant, her best friend since childhood, and now her love. His kisses brought every bit as much pleasure, and there was much to be said for loyalty. She was promised to Brant, and Kayla was not one to break promises easily.

Before she knew it, the apple was gone, the clay broken to pieces and ground into the earth. It wasn't until T'Kato approached them with blankets that Kayla realized both Niefusu and Jihong were gone. "Where are the princes?" she asked. She was afraid he would be angry after her harsh words that afternoon, but he was as amiable as ever, though for him, that was something to be measured in teaspoons. He was loyal, but not friendly.

"They decided to sleep in the river," he said before turning from them and setting up a place for himself on the other side of the fire.

"Sleep *in* the river?" Brant unrolled blankets for them side by side. Kayla was unsure where the blankets came from, but for the moment, she did not care. She wanted only to sleep.

"Well, they are members of the sea court. They live in water by nature," she answered, plumping pillows for them both before sitting on the blanket closest to the fire.

"But how do they breathe?" He threw himself down on the other blanket and tucked his hand under his head.

"They have gills."

"Like fish?" He seemed genuinely interested.

"A bit like that, yes. The gills allow them to breathe underwater. T'Kato has some. So do I, for that matter." She didn't even think as she said it, but suddenly Brant had her face in his hands and was turning her head back and forth. He was going to break her neck if he didn't stop.

"Wait, wait! I'll show you, if you wish." Brant removed his hands from her face and looked at her, worried and perhaps angry. At least, that's what she read from his face and actions.

She pulled her hair back from her neck and tipped her head to the side. "See? Just below and behind my ear? Those are my gills."

Brant approached her more carefully now and touched the feathery slits, then shivered.

"Did it hurt?" he asked.

Kayla's heart melted. He didn't ask why or how she'd received them, but only if it had caused her pain. She took his hands in her own and looked down at their fingers locked together. "A little," she admitted, "But only for a moment. It was worth the pain to be able to breathe under the water."

He sat back, letting go of her hands and leaning against the huge log they'd been sitting on most of the day. "I can't even imagine. What a strange world it must have been. I wish you would take me there someday."

She grinned and leaned forward on her hands and knees. "Then we'll go! What adventures we'll have. Oh, Brant, the kingdom under the sea is like nothing you've ever imagined. They built their walls with coral and pearl, the clams stuck to the walls with their mouths wide open. I have been nowhere more beautiful," she said, knowing the awe she felt would be heard in her voice.

Brant was silent for a long moment, fidgeting with something in his hands before he blurted out of nowhere, "Do you love him?"

He didn't need to tell her who he meant. She knew.

Kayla sat back on her heels and looked at her fiancé. "Brant," she said quietly. "How could I love him? I barely know him."

"But he kissed you, didn't he? I can tell by the way he looks at you." Brant's voice was slightly bitter.

She turned, reached a hand up and caressed his hair. "I will admit, he kissed me under the pretense of giving me air, and he gave me the gills.

He was trying to tooth his mark upon me, because he didn't know I was already taken, and though I have told him time and time again, still he tries to claim me for his own." Kayla sighed, and now both hands held Brant's face, forcing his eyes to meet her own. "But Brant, never doubt that I love you. You are my one true love. There will never be another."

That seemed to be what Brant needed to hear. He smiled, then lowered his face to press his lips to her forehead. "Thank you," was all he said.

In short order they had settled down on their blankets, he with his back to her for propriety's sake, and she, flat on her back, staring at the stars. One would think she would be lost in thought over her conversation with Brant, or the challenge Niefusu had become, but no, the thoughts that plagued her were the words she'd spoken to T'Kato in the clearing that afternoon. She had told him that she was the guardian of the flute, that she was the master and he was no longer needed. Was it true? She'd been told that she was just the temporary guardian, the holder for the player, whom she assumed would be the wolfchild. But if that was the case, why had she told T'Kato she was the master of the flute?

Even in her sleep, the questions continued to haunt her.

CHAPTER THIRTEEN

Ember's dreams were back. The blonde woman she assumed was C'Tan fought with Ember and DeMunth in his radiant armor. Facing C'Tan was also her step-brother Aldarin, who was covered with glowing orange symbols, and the girl with the flute was there. Uncle Shad snapped at her in his wolf form, and strangely enough, Lily was there as well. Six of them against C'Tan. It was odd. The people kept changing, but the dreams were becoming more clear, and once again, the blonde woman stumbled back into a stone altar, collapsing in a heap, and the battle was won.

And then a dark shadow grew from C'Tan's body and the fight was on again. The darkness fought like the Shadow Weavers and devoured magic like it was nothing more than candy. Ember was in full panic mode, helpless in the grasp of this dark being, when a hand on her shoulder shook her awake. She sat up with a start, hitting her head against Lily's as she surfaced from her dreams. Nothing like a little pain to wake a person up.

"What did you do that for?" Lily held her brow.

"I didn't mean to. Why are you waking me? Is it morning already?" Ember rubbed at her forehead, hoping their collision wouldn't leave a mark. She had enough scratches and bruises from stonesculpting class the day before.

Ember watched Lily rub her brow in the glow of the purple magelight. She wiped away a tear, walked to Ember's closet, pulled out another robe, and tossed it on her bed. "No, it's not morning yet," she grumbled. "Councilwoman Marda is here and asked me to wake you. She needs you for something."

Ember immediately thought of Paeder, so recently recovered from illness and brought back from death, and scrambled into her robe. As she dressed, Lily looked at her with a peculiar expression.

"What?" Ember asked, distracted as she pulled on her slippers.

Why did you get them?" Her voice was strange. It was the first time Ember had seen any genuine emotion besides annoyance or anger cross Lily's face, but she couldn't quite put her finger on what that emotion was.

"I didn't *get* them. They were a gift. A present from my dead father for my sixteenth birthday. When I put on the jewelry he gave me, it absorbed into my skin and became tattoos, and I can't get them off, though I wouldn't if I could. I mean, they *were* my father's." Ember wasn't sure why she was telling Lily all this, maybe because it was the middle of the night and she was exhausted and not thinking straight. But it was nice to have Lily at least be decent to her, and she didn't want it to change.

Once she had her slippers on, she left Lily behind and pushed through the curtain that hid their room. Marda leaned against the wall, waiting for her daughter. She smiled as soon as she saw her, pushed away from the wall, and started walking down the hall toward the dining room, but took a left long before they got there.

Silence gathered around them for several minutes before curiosity got the best of Ember. "Where are we going?" she asked.

Marda glanced at her, then back ahead and answered, "To see Ezeker. He has some questions for you."

Ember's heart immediately plummeted. He'd heard about the day before and was going to kick her out of school already. She hoped it wasn't so, but her heart was certain of it, despite their relationship. He had to look after the good of the school, and she was a threat to it. She'd destroyed part of the academy and was obviously a danger to herself and the other students. She just didn't know if he would send her home whole or if he was going to seal off her powers before banning away.

Part of her knew the thought was ridiculous and was probably sleep deprivation and exhaustion talking, but another part of her wondered. Could he really let her stay after all the damage she had done? What if someone had been hurt, or worse, killed?

She dragged her feet, dreading the confrontation with the man she'd always called "Uncle Ezzie," though she'd recently discovered they shared no blood. She'd never been afraid of him before, but then, she'd never known his position within the magic world until they had unjustly tried her before the mage council.

"Hurry up, Ember," Marda said, picking up her pace. She stood at the side of the glowing arch, waiting for her daughter, whose stomach had sunk to her feet. Ember tried to hurry, but she was broken-hearted at the thought of leaving school. Finally, she reached the portal, and they entered together. For several long seconds, they held their breath and raced across the distance before exiting the other side. They turned left and entered another, this one longer, then again stumbled out of an arch. Ember bent over, her hands on her knees, trying to catch her breath. Marda didn't seem affected at all and stood impatiently, waiting for her daughter to recover, before they walked straight ahead and entered the final portal. This time, when they came out on the other side, they stood behind a huge tapestry. Marda stepped forward and pulled the cloth aside. They were in a stone tower with nothing in it but the large cloth and a spiral of stone stairs leading downward.

Ember caught her breath, then, forgetting herself for a moment, asked, "Where are you staying? I haven't seen you at the school except for meals." They started down the stairs, Marda first. She looked over her shoulder and grinned at her daughter, her eyes a-twinkle. "At home," she answered, with no further explanation.

Home? How was that possible? "But . . . isn't that a long journey?" Ember asked.

Marda laughed, her voice ringing out like a chorus of bells. "Look around, Ember. Don't you know where you are?"

Ember looked, but it wasn't until they rounded the last curve in the staircase and she saw the massive stone table with mismatched chairs everything clicked into place. "Ezeker's? We're at Ezeker's tower?"

Marda nodded, her smile spreading clear across her face now.

"Wow," Ember said. "I hadn't realized the mage academy was so large. That also explains how the twins can get home to help Paeder. Why doesn't Paeder just have a portal directly to the school from here? Why go through so many if he doesn't have to?"

"They don't work that way. They go where they go. They have been there far longer than Ezeker's tower." Marda shrugged, and they took the last step into the room and three men came to their feet to greet them. Sweet, bearded Uncle Ezzie took Ember by the shoulders and gave her a quick peck on her forehead. "Come in, come in!" he said, gesturing toward the stone table. Aldarin and Shad scooted over so Marda and Ember could take the outside chairs. Aldarin grinned at her, but Shad was unusually serious. Ember couldn't shake the feeling that she was going to be dismissed from the school.

Ezeker still stood as they seated themselves around the table. "Have you eaten breakfast?" When Ember shook her head, he beckoned to a servant from the dark corner. People came into the room bearing plates of food. Ember hadn't realized how hungry she was until she smelled the delicious aromas.

Nobody said anything as they passed plates around and they all helped themselves. Ember tried not to look at her mother as she loaded her plate to overflowing. She knew Marda would disapprove—she always had. Ember knew it was a miracle she wasn't huge, for the portion sizes she ate. She hovered over her plate, as if she expected her mother to snatch it from her at any moment. It was Shad's chuckle that made her look up. He was glancing back and forth between Ember and Marda, who were so obviously *not* looking at each other. Ember wanted to be offended, but she could see the humor in the situation.

"I've spoken to your mother, reminding her how much energy magic uses. You don't need to worry about your portions anymore," he said, then went back to his own plate as if nothing had happened. Without looking up, Marda said, "I'd forgotten until I started burning my own energy and was suddenly hungry all the time. I'm sorry I've been so hard on you all these years, Ember. I wasn't trying to be mean. I only wanted to raise you properly and help you to be more girlish. I didn't want you to end up like me."

Ember's heart melted at those words. "There's nothing wrong with being like you," she said, then set to her meal. Food was one of the last things they had standing between them, and with those words she found it much easier to enjoy her meal in her mother's presence.

As soon as they were done and the dishes had removed by the silent servants, Ezeker cleared his throat. "I've heard about the, uh, challenges you faced yesterday." Ember's stomach lurched, and she suddenly wished she hadn't eaten so much. "The Academy Council and I have been discussing your particular situation and have reached a decision."

Ember interrupted. "Please don't kick me out, Uncle Ezzie! I didn't mean to do it. I'll do better, I promise. I'll work harder and stay away from the other students. I'm even willing to be locked in a room with a guard at the door, if I have to. Just please give me a chance to learn." Her white knuckles clutched at the table as if it were an anchor holding her to the academy.

Ezeker had the decency not to laugh when he answered. He was very sweet and calming. "Child, we will not send you away. Do you remember the contract you signed at the mage trials?" When Ember nodded, he continued. "Well, that contract doesn't just hold you. It holds us as well. We have a responsibility to teach you, whether or not we know how. You're not going anywhere, my dear. But . . ." he paused and held up his index finger for emphasis. "It is obvious your situation requires some special teaching and added protection. We'll teach you, one way or another. I understand White Shadow had some success yesterday in finding your trigger and catalyst, and that you've also responded rather well to Lily's influence."

Ember nodded, relief settling over her like sunlight on a spring day.

"Until we have a greater understanding of how you learn and you have gained better control, we will hold all your classes in the shielded rooms, and your teachers will be White Shadow and Lily. Are you comfortable with that?"

Ember let out an explosive breath she hadn't realized she'd been holding. "Oh, yes! That would be wonderful!"

"Good." Ezeker smiled. "Until DeMunth is healed, I am assigning two of our best guards to protect you until we find out more about these Shadow Weavers. Rahdnee and Brendae will see to your needs and keep you safe, all right?" At that, a man and woman stepped through the doorway from the basement. They were both dressed in blue and gold armor, swords sheathed at their hip. The man Ember recognized. He was there the first night she'd come to the school, the one who had taken DeMunth to the healer hall. The woman was new to Ember, and though she seemed like a great guard, there was something in her eyes that gave Ember the chills. She was about to object and ask for Uncle Shad to double as her teacher and guardian and then had second thoughts. Ezeker wouldn't have assigned these two if he didn't completely trust them. She'd give them a chance. She didn't have to like them—they didn't need to be friends. Their job was to protect her, and they certainly seemed capable of doing that.

"But what about the orange room?" Ember asked. "Do I need to help fix it? Isn't there some kind of consequence for destroying it? And what are the orange students going to do in the meantime?" Her stomach was back in knots, but she wanted to right any of her wrongs.

Ezeker shook his head. "It's already done, child. It's fixed and ready for classes this morning."

Ember was astounded. "How is that possible? It was totally wrecked."

Ezeker chuckled. "We live in a mountain. We're surrounded by stone, and there are plenty of students who need to practice their stone-crafting abilities. It was only a matter of hours to put it back in better shape than before. We even saved most of your father's work, though I'm afraid the door had to be completely replaced."

She felt a mixture of relief and agonizing loss. She was grateful for what they had saved, but knowing she had destroyed even an inch of her father's work, let alone the entire door, made her want to smash her head into a wall. Ember knew it had been an accident and could not change the past, but it still hurt. It was one more lesson learned. Think before you act. Never panic when dealing with magic. She squelched down her tears and said, "Would you tell them thank you for me? And tell the teacher I'm sorry?"

The old mage nodded. "Absolutely. I'm sure she will appreciate it, though she wasn't angered. She knew it was accidental. She told me she'd love to speak with you again."

Ember was pleasantly surprised at that and promised herself she would do so. She still wanted to hear the stories about her mother and father and how they met.

"One more thing," Ezeker said. "I understand you stopped by the library yesterday?" Ember nodded and smiled. Ezeker suddenly became serious. "I know we've encouraged you to go to the library in the hopes you could find something to help with your white magic, but considering yesterday's events, we feel that it's best you avoid the library for now."

When Ember objected, he put up his hand, and she quieted. "I know how badly you want to find some information, but think about it, Ember. Some of those documents are thousands of years old. They are irreplaceable. If something happened in the library like happened in the orange room yesterday, we would lose information that could never be rewritten or replaced. Until you gain some control over your power, we would kindly ask you to avoid the library. If you need something, ask one of us, and we will see if we can find it for you. Okay?"

Ember nodded reluctantly. She understood what he was saying, but the library had been her one hope of finding someone else like her. And then she remembered Tyese and smiled to herself. She may not be able to go to the library, but she had someone working for her from the inside, someone who had a better chance at finding what Ember needed than anyone else.

The men stood once she nodded and began to talk amongst themselves. Aldarin hadn't said a word the whole meeting. She glanced at her new guards and couldn't help but wish Aldarin was her guardian. At least she knew she could trust him.

She was about to ask Uncle Ezzie about it when Lily stepped down the stairs and approached her, glancing once at the guards and trying to mask her obvious distaste. She stood next to Ember and addressed Ezeker. "Should I take her to lessons now, sir?"

Ezeker glanced at Lily and nodded. "Yes, she is ready. Thank you for your help, Lily. It is a great boon to us all, especially Ember. And remember that teaching always makes you a better student. If you can teach, then you know you have truly mastered the subject." Lily didn't respond, though she seemed to straighten a little at his words, though whether with pride or resentment, Ember couldn't tell.

Lily gently tugged her elbow, letting go as soon as Ember moved. The guards separated, the woman stepping behind Ember, and the man taking the lead. No one spoke as they made their way back up the stairs, through several portals, and at last to the shielded practice rooms.

At the door, the man, Rahdnee, stopped and addressed them. "We shall wait out here for you to finish, then will escort you wherever it is you need to go, Ember. I wish you well in your studies." His eyes met hers and Ember once again felt that magnetic pull he seemed to have, but she resisted. It was like the pull she felt with DeMunth, but there was something dark about it that made her wary of the guard. She gave one brief nod, then turned her back on him and the strange woman who made her so nervous, and stepped into the practice room. The door sealed behind them, blending into the rock wall and separating the girls from the guards.

Ember sighed with relief when the door completely closed—much different from her first experience in the training rooms. "I don't know what it is about those two, but they feel . . . weird. I don't know how else to say it." She shivered as she turned to Lily and caught a strange expression crossing her face. "What?" she asked as she sat on the ground and wished for a pillow.

Lily's mouth quirked as she glanced at the sealed doorway, then back at Ember. She sat with a sigh. "Rahdnee is my father," she said, looking down at the stone.

Ember gulped, then her mouth gaped open in shock. "No! You don't look a thing like him. I'm sorry, Lily, I shouldn't have—" Lily stopped her with an open hand as she tried not to smile.

"You're fine, Ember. I actually agree. My father and I have never gotten along well, and Brendae is just . . . well, you said it. She's odd. She makes me tremble inside, like I would in the presence of a predator."

Ember nodded before she even finished. "I know what you mean. Having her behind me made me incredibly nervous—like she was going to eat me."

Lily laughed outright at that. Ember decided she liked her laugh. It made her more human and likable. "What about your mother? Does she teach here? Or is she a guard too?" The girl quickly sobered and nibbled at the corner of her lip before glancing up at Ember.

"My relationship with my mother is . . . complicated. She does not work at the school. Actually, she lives far away and sent me to live with Rahdnee when I was just a babe. I barely even know her." Lily seemed uncomfortable even saying that much, so Ember didn't push it.

"That must be hard," was all she said, though she was curious to know more. What kind of mother would send her child away?

Lily let out a sigh. "It is. My parents are most definitely odd. I sometimes wish . . ." she trailed off, not finishing her thought, but Ember could follow it easily. She wanted the same thing Ember did—a normal family.

For the first time since they met, Ember felt a connection with Lily, one Lily seemed to feel too, as the girl looked up almost shyly and smiled a genuine smile. It was small, but it was a start.

Practicing with Lily was hard. The girl pushed. They started with deep breathing, and when Ember was in a calm and meditative state, Lily shoved a wave of magic that sent Ember tumbling backwards, heels over head until she lay sprawled on the rock. She got up, dusting herself off, and glared at the girl. "What did you do that for?"

"To teach you not to take anything for granted. You were attacked in Javak. Were you expecting it?" Lily asked, still sitting cross-legged on the floor.

"No," Ember answered, sulking as she sat back down in front of Lily.

"You never know when or from where an attack will come. Be ready for anything. Now, prepare yourself. Don't think—do." Lily closed her eyes and waited for Ember to settle herself.

As soon as Ember breathed deeply, Lily pushed again. Once more, Ember tumbled backwards, and this time came up hard against the wall.

"Again," Lily said, her voice never changing.

Ember wanted to cry in frustration, but she wouldn't let herself do so in front of this girl. Without a word, she sat back down, and before she had even begun her deep breathing, the wave of magic hit. This time Ember's hand flipped up, almost of its own volition, and somehow *shoved*, sending Lily rocking back, though she didn't tumble as Ember had. The girl opened her eyes and grinned. "Good! Now tell me, what did you do?"

"I—" Ember started, then stopped. What had she done? She went back over it in her head and spoke her thoughts aloud. "I'm not sure. No, wait, I—" she paused again and took a deep breath. "I took the anger and sent it out. No, that's not right either. I don't know, Lily. I just did it. Do I have to explain it?"

Lily laughed. "No. I don't need to know how, so long as you can do it again." At the word "Again," Lily pushed once more. Ember rocked back as Lily had, but then leaned forward, pushing that wave of power back at Lily. Then with a surge, she sent the girl tumbling. Lily came up against the wall and stared at Ember with surprise before scrambling to her feet. "Excellent!" she said. "Now, let's move on to something else."

The girl pushed her to try her talent in as many ways as possible, and though Ember was exhausted and sore by the time their lessons were over, she had to admit, Lily was a good teacher. More than good—she was a natural and seemed to know exactly what to do and say to get Ember to react. As they opened the door to leave, Ember almost jumped when the guards stepped to her again, crowding in on her space in a way that made her uncomfortable. She waved to Lily and headed quickly toward the healer hall, the guards practically jogging to keep up.

"What's the hurry?" Rahdnee asked as she leaped into yet another portal, not even pausing to catch her breath.

When she exited, she threw her words over her shoulder. "I haven't seen DeMunth all day and I'm excited to see him."

"You must really like him to be going this fast," Brendae said. Ember didn't answer, and within a few seconds more, she was at the healer hall. She stopped, took a deep breath, straightened her robes, and stepped through the doorway. The guards stayed outside, thankfully. After talking with Lily and spending even a short amount of time with the two of them, Ember had already decided to ask Ezeker to assign someone else to her. They made her feel like she was walking through a haunted forest. It wasn't anything they did or said, specifically. It was more just a sense of their intention, or their energy that made her so uncomfortable. She didn't like it, did not want to spend her days dealing with it non-stop. At least they had the decency to give her some privacy. She took full advantage of it as she pulled up a stool and sat down next to DeMunth's bed.

It was obvious he was no longer in a coma, but sleeping the deepest of sleeps. She tried not to let it bother her as she took his hand in her own and told him about her day, from the early awakening to being assigned new guardians, to the change in Lily and her new lessons. "I wish you would wake up, DeMunth. I need you. These guards they assigned me are just creepy, and I don't trust them. Not the way I trust you."

She paused for a moment and fought tears as she stared at his handsome face. His hand gently squeezed hers. She jumped, her heart racing. Was he waking up? He licked his lips and without opening his eyes, he said, "I'm coming, Ember. Wait for me. I'm coming." His voice was just a whisper of sound with a slight metallic tone to it, probably because of the vibration of sound bouncing off his silver tongue, but her heart fluttered to hear him speak. His breathing immediately deepened, and he was back asleep, but despite the frustration of losing him to dreams once again, she was thrilled to see him healing. It wouldn't be long now and he could replace Rahdnee and Brendae. She'd have her true guardian back, and she couldn't be happier.

She stood and kissed his forehead, then sat back on the stool and watched him for several minutes. When it became obvious he would not awaken again anytime soon, she sighed and stood. Her stomach was rumbling, and though she did not know what time it was, her body was telling her it was time to eat. She gathered her courage and stepped into the hallway, ready to face her strange escorts. She was thrilled to discover that they were gone, replaced by her step-brother, Aldarin. He grinned and put an arm around her shoulders. "I thought you could use some good company for dinner. You up for it?"

"Most definitely," she said as he escorted her down the hall and toward the delicious smells wafting from the dining hall.

CHAPTER FOURTEEN

The moment Kayla found herself in the domed cave, water lapping against the stony shore, she knew she was dreaming again. She'd been here once before, just before her battle with C'Tan, and had longed to return and see her father again. These dreams, it appeared, were truth dreams, as real as if she were awake. Last time, her Evahn father had met her here, but this time she found herself completely alone.

The water surrounded her, but rather than creating a chill, it was like a blanket welcoming her back to the sea. She scrambled up the slope and sat on a stone to wait. She knew he would come eventually, or he wouldn't have called her here. Her heart fluttered in excitement. It had only been a few days since she'd seen him last and she hadn't expected another visit for quite some time. And yet, here she was.

"Hello, Kayla." His melodic voice came from the darkness near the top of the slope.

She quickly stood and faced him, her hands fiddling with the ends of her sash. "Hello, Father." And now she saw him as he came down the hill in long strides, sure-footed on the slick stone. In a moment, he was there and wrapped her in his arms, giving her the welcome she had longed for the first time she'd dreamed of him. She held back the tears his familiar smell brought and relished the moment. He had always smelled of the woods and fresh earth after a rain. And of course, something male and musky.

He pushed her to arm'slength, a relaxed smile stretching his face. "How have you been?" he asked, sitting on the slope and pulling a knee to his chest, hands clasped around his shin.

"Moderately well," she answered, puzzled by his casual nature. "Is there something wrong? Do you have a message for me?"

"Not really," he said. "I just thought we could get to know each other a bit. It *has* been ten years." He fidgeted, seeming a touch insecure. "Is that all right with you?" His smile seemed forced, as if he was unsure how to behave around her.

Kayla smiled. "I am perfectly fine with that. What would you like to talk about?"

He stared at her, his face blank, and then he laughed. "I have absolutely no idea."

She liked his laugh, full-throated and sincere. She wished she could laugh more often as he did. "How is grandfather?" she asked, the first question to come to mind.

Felandian quickly sobered. "He is still unwell. I worry for him. I wish you could know him as I do. He is truly a great man." He rubbed his eyes. Kayla was unsure if it was from tiredness or tears. "But enough of that. I want to know of you. What happened when you battled C'Tan? I was unable to see. Obviously, you were successful, but I want to know the details."

And so Kayla told him, from the moment he had first alerted her to C'Tan's presence, to her battle with the disciple of S'Kotos. She told him of the wall of ice she built across the waterway that would not melt even with balls of flame, and she told him of C'Tan's insanity and the horrific scarring that lay beneath her illusory beauty.

Felandian nodded, grinning widely as she finished. "My daughter. Bearer of the Sapphire Flute and defeater of C'Tan!" He laughed out loud once more. "It sounds as if you are truly master of the flute."

"Am I?" she asked. "It's strange that you would say that. I was thinking about it just before I slept. Isn't the Wolfchild the master of the flute? I think I'm just a temporary guardian, but if so, why does the flute treat me like its master? I'm so confused," she said, twisting the sash around her hand.

He unwrapped the sash and took her hands in his own. "Daughter, I know not. Only the wolfchild can give you that answer, but for now, you are the guardian. Treat yourself as such."

Kayla's heart calmed at the truth of his words, though part of her was still frustrated with not knowing. She really needed to find the Wolfchild and talk to her about the future of the Sapphire Flute.

Felandian chuckled. Kayla looked at him, but he gazed over her shoulder. "It looks as if you have more of your mother in you than I'd realized. Two suitors? Is one not enough for you?" She rolled her eyes. "Well, it's not as if I chose it. I was perfectly content with Brant, and then Niefusu came along. I will admit, he is very alluring. It is hard to say no to the son of a king. Not because of his power," she was quick to reassure, "But because he has everything I never had. And, well, I like him," she admitted, reddening at the words.

Her father put his hands on her shoulders and met her eyes. "Follow your heart, no matter where it may lead. Only your heart will speak the truth, and many times, it is not the easiest choice." His gaze drifted far away. "I see a difficult path for your heart, Kayla. One more challenging than even I have faced, but in the end, you will have peace and love. Never give up on love," he said, then pulled away.

"I think you might want to return to camp soon. Trouble is brewing between your men, and I'd hate for them to kill each other while you slept." He stood and met her gaze. "I love you, daughter. Never forget that. I shall see you again. Now wake up!" he demanded, and as he said the words, immediately she was back in her body, angry voices bringing her to consciousness much faster than she would have desired, especially with the brightness of the sun blazing into her eyes. She turned over and groaned, then inhaled the most beautiful scent she had ever smelled. For a moment she forgot all about the arguing men and buried her face in the aroma. Floral, but not a flower she could identify. As she lay on her side, the sun was no longer directly in her face, and she cracked her eyes open to discover what created such an intoxicating smell.

When she could focus, she gasped. Somehow, during the night, someone had woven flowers into her hair. Roses and petunias, pansies and snapdragons, dandelions and small white flowers she didn't recognize. There were tiny purple flowers and even sprigs of green berries. She thought those might have been her favorite. She wrapped her hands in her hair and lifted it to her face. The smell was breathtaking. She wished she could distill it and put it in a bottle, it was so divine. She tried to sit up, but the weight in her hair made it difficult, and it wasn't until she was fully sitting, her thick braid in her lap, that she realized what the arguing was all about.

She was sure the flower culprit was Niefusu. It was the kind of thing he would do. He had often taken liberties with her body and personal space. He had given her air under the sea by kissing her without warning, then given her gills by kissing and then biting her neck. If he would be so forward as to do those things, weaving flowers into her hair as she slept next to her fiancé would be nothing to him.

But to Brant, it would be an affront upon his claim to her, and a personal insult. He would not look at it the way she did, with joy and to take pleasure in the beautiful flowers. She loved Brant, but he didn't understand the simple things that made a woman happy. He understood other things, like his gift of the charm bracelet and what it meant to her, but something as simple as weaving flowers into her hair would never occur to him.

The sound of four swords being drawn from their sheaths got Kayla up faster than she thought possible. She lurched to her feet and ran barefoot across the clearing to the men. T'Kato and Brant paired off against Niefusu and Jihong, but only Brant and Niefusu seemed serious about it. "She is *mine!*" Brant spat. "You have no claim upon her and no right to touch her without permission—permission which you shall never receive, so long as she is with me."

126

Niefusu's eyes narrowed. "I marked me claim upon her when I toothed her," he said. "I have as much right to her as ye do, so don't be telling me I need yer permission. That would not be for ye to decide, but for Kayla to choose."

Brant actually growled and lunged at Sarali's brother, but T'Kato held him back. Kayla arrived just in time. She thrust herself between them and faced Brant first. "You and I will talk later," she said, glaring at him, then spun upon Niefusu and tried to calm her pounding heart. "And you, sir, *do* need permission to touch my form, especially in my sleep."

His eyes narrowed further, and he seemed about to respond when she put up a finger to silence him.

"It's not that I don't appreciate the gift," she said, fingering the flowers. "It was a beautiful way to wake up, and the smell is delightful. You should open a perfumery." Brant started to object, but T'Kato somehow silenced him, so she continued. "Sincerely, Niefusu, I appreciate your gift and your kindness." She could see him begin to relax as his eyes opened more fully and his hunched, tense shoulders pulled back. When she saw it was safe, she took a chance and stepped to him, taking him by the hand. "Niefusu, thank you, but please remember, I am not yours, nor will I ever be," she said, then gripped his hand when she saw he was about to pull away in anger once more. "My heart is with Brant. My commitment is with Brant. I am promised to Brant. Can you not understand the importance of keeping a promise, of following through with commitments? You are a prince of the sea kingdom. Can you truly not understand the importance of sometimes giving up that which you want because it is the right thing to do?" By the time she was finished, she had both his hands in her own and she looked up into his reddened face. He met her eyes, and she could see the shame there and knew that at last he understood.

"I would have ye for me own," he said softly, "But I hear ye, Duchess Kayla. I hear ye." With those words, he sheathed his sword. She was beyond relieved. Not only did it mean he would not fight Brant, but holding his hand while it gripped a sword was a heavy and uncomfortable weight.

Once he had sheathed his sword, everyone else followed suit. There wasn't exactly peace between them, but there seemed to be at least a truce. Before Brant turned to go back to their bedrolls, Niefusu reached out and placed a hand on his shoulder. Brant stiffened and turned, obviously ready to defend himself, but instead, he found Niefusu's outstretched hand.

"I owe ye an apology, Duke Brant. I should have acted more like the prince I be. Would ye forgive me?" he asked. It impressed Kayla. She knew how difficult it was to back down and then apologize.

She was doubly impressed when Brant's face split with a cautious smile and he took Niefusu's hand firmly and shook it, placing his other hand on the prince's shoulder. "But of course," he answered. "And I hope you will forgive me for my harsh words and for pulling my sword on you."

"Tis already forgotten." Niefusu slapped Brant on the shoulder and put an arm around him as they walked away together. "After all, ye *are* only human." They both laughed at the intended insult.

Kayla shook her head. She would never understand men.

As she stood in the grass wet from the morning dew, still enthralled by the flowers braided through her hair, a boxcar came up the road and turned the corner. When it reached the clearing, it stopped, and a tall, slender man jumped down from the driver's seat and walked toward them. His dark hair was just graying at the temples, and he walked like a man with confidence and purpose. With no kind of fear, he approached T'Kato and gave him a funny little bow, then began whispering to him. Kayla couldn't hear what they said, but instead watched another man, this one prematurely gray but very handsome, also step down from the boxcar, leaving only a sulky teenage boy behind.

The older man then went to one of the horses, which was obviously pained and struggling. He ran his hand down the horse's neck and back, muttering something under his breath, then felt the shaking legs. The tall, thin man walked over to him, and Kayla heard him say, "It's all right. We can unhitch here and have no problems with them. They'll be on their way shortly." The older man nodded without saying a word, and together they took the faltering horse and led it to the sweet grass and small stream that ran on the other side of the clearing.

Curious, Kayla walked toward T'Kato to find out what was going on. She heard a squeal behind her and then a thump, and the clearing turned to chaos. Kayla turned around and watched in surprise as the older man leaned over the horse that now lay on its side, struggling to get up as it shook and shuddered. Jihong, surprisingly, was at his side, and the two of them held the animal down.

T'Kato took in the scene, then came to her side. "Do you think you can do anything with the flute?"

Kayla nodded, then ran to her bedroll and the bag she'd left there, pulling the flute out and, still barefoot, raced over to the shuddering horse.

Without even thinking, she handed the flute to the nearest person, which just happened to be Jihong while she knelt down next to the animal and laid her hand upon its shoulder. "Miss," the older man said, "Be careful. She's been mighty sick for a while now. I'd hate for her to hurt you in her madness."

T'Kato approached. "She knows what she is doing," he said in his deep voice. "Trust her. She will heal the animal."

Beneath her hand, she felt the horse still. Its chest no longer rose and fell. Its heart stopped beating. The energy that gave it life faded, and all that was left behind was a husk of what it . . . Kayla changed her thoughts . . . *she* had once been. She shook her head, unable to help the tears that coursed down her cheeks. She glanced at T'Kato, then at the older man, who seemed to love this mare so much. "Sir," she started, then stopped with a choke. She tried again. "That flute is a gift from the Guardians. With it, I can heal the sick and mend broken bones. But sir, I can't fix dead."

The older man crumbled into himself, his tears falling freely. Behind her, Jihong snickered. "Can't fix dead," she heard him mutter.

Niefusu elbowed his brother. "Be quiet, fool. Now wouldn't be the time."

Angered by Jihong's laughter, she stood and took the flute from him rather sharply. "What? I can't fix dead. Can you?"

His laughter grew worse. What in the world was so funny about being unable to bring the dead back to life?

129

T'Kato pulled the brothers aside and sent them off to forage in the surrounding woods. She knew he did it mostly so she could calm down and the older man could grieve. Then Kayla had an idea.

"Sir, I cannot bring your horse back to life, but I can give her a fitting burial. Is there something in particular you would like?" she asked, kneeling down once more to lay a hand on the shoulder of the quickly cooling beast.

The man looked up at her, his eyes red from crying. He sniffed, then seemed to pull himself together. "My name is Hadril, and that would be a wonderful kindness, miss," he said.

"Kayla," she offered, not bothering with her title. It wasn't doing her much good at the moment.

"Among my people, the dead are usually burned, their ashes scattered after they move from this life to the next. We don't have enough space to bury her, and to tell the truth, I don't have the time. Would that be possible? To turn ol' Maude into dust and spread her ashes around the meadow? She would like that, I think." He smoothed the mare's coat as if she were still living.

"I can do that and more, Sir Hadril," she said, standing and taking up the flute.

He too stood and backed away. "Just Hadril, if you don't mind."

"Hadril it is, then." She placed the flute to her lips and began to play. This time, the music guided itself, up and down, without the trills and complexity of so many of her other pieces. This song was played in a simple minor key, but somehow full of heart and life. The horse's body dissipated like sand in a storm, then swirled around and spread itself in the grass clear across the field. It was only a matter of minutes before the mare had gone from horse, to flesh, to bone, and then to nothing, but as the dust spread across the field, flowers grew until the entire area was covered with a multitude of color and scent that rivaled only that which was wound in her braid.

She turned to Hadril. His tears were back, but his eyes were as wide as any she'd ever seen. "You did this for my Maude?" he asked, awe lacing his voice like sunlight through a wine glass.

Kayla nodded. "I've always had a fondness for horses, and I can tell how much you loved her. It seemed only fitting." She put the flute back in her satchel so she'd have a moment to look away. She couldn't take the quivering of his chin.

"You are special indeed, Miss Kayla. What can I do to thank you?" Hadril asked. The tall man took that moment to come to his side. He also seemed moved by Kayla's act of kindness and began to sing quietly. His song was in a language she did not understand, but the melody was haunting, a farewell of sorts, and she could tell he had a voice like few others. A voice that seemed to be a gift from the Guardians, just as her flute. She didn't know what he said, but she felt his song, just as she felt the flute. When he was done, all was silent for a long moment.

It was T'Kato who broke the silence. "Which direction are you headed?"

The elder, Hadril, answered. "Toward Javak, though we'll turn our route northward just two villages shy of the city of magic."

T'Kato seemed pleased by this, for reasons Kayla could understand. "You asked how you could return the favor. I have an idea that I think will benefit us all. Would you be willing to listen?"

Hadril and the singer looked one another, then back at T'Kato, and nodded.

"Good," he said. "You are short a horse, and I don't see you getting far with just those other three pulling that big wagon of yours. Would you agree?"

Again Hadril nodded.

"Brant? Come up here." Brant, who had been packing up their things all this time, came at T'Kato's call. He took Kayla by the hand and listened as T'Kato asked, "Am I correct in assuming you will travel with us to the mage academy?"

"Absolutely," Brant answered, squeezing Kayla's hand. "I'm not letting this girl out of my sight, especially with the competition around."

T'Kato chuckled. "That's what I thought. How would you feel about joining up with this group, in disguise, and letting your horse take the place of the one they lost for now?"

Brant then turned to T'Kato. "Hidden and disguised? Why?"

131

"To protect Kayla, in particular. We do not know when or if C'Tan will attack again, but also, we are traveling with some rather esteemed company, in case you hadn't noticed, and I think it best if we hide in plain sight."

Brant seemed surprised. He addressed the two men. "Tell me, what do you do?"

Hadril looked at the tall man and answered first. "I am a healer and an apothecary. I travel from village to village and offer services where they are rarely offered. Hadril, by the way." He offered his hand to Brant, who shook it, and turned to the other man, the singer.

"Graylin," he said, speaking his name in a voice as melodic as his singing. "I have two purposes. One is to fix items that are usually irreparable. A bit of magic in me allows it. I also provide entertainment. Sometimes a story, other times a song, but always where it is most needed." Kayla felt an instant kinship with this man.

Brant pursed his lips again, like he always did when he was thinking. He ran his hands through his hair and asked, "What would we do?"

T'Kato smiled, and with all those tattoos on his face, his smile looked ferocious indeed. "I had thought Lady Kayla could join Graylin in providing entertainment. You and I could be bodyguards for the group, and the princes—" T'Kato cringed at his slip of the tongue when he said that, and Graylin and Hadril seemed to notice—" Well, they could provide more entertainment in their non-human form while paired with their water horses. They're natural performers anyway, don't you think?"

Brant laughed. "I agree. If it is all right with Masters Graylin and Hadril, I think it is a fine plan."

The two men looked at each other, grinned, then came forward and shook hands as they began planning how to put things into effect.

CHAPTER FIFTEEN

C'Tan scrubbed at Drake's scales, getting off the muck he'd collected on their last excursion. She could have had the servants do it, but for some reason, taking care of Drake's needs was comforting. She felt almost at peace while scrubbing his neck or buffing his nails. She didn't understand it, but didn't bother to question it, either. Peace was something she had so little of in her life—she wasn't going to turn away what bits of it she could find.

The dragon lifted his left front paw so she could scrub between his toes. "What did you do this time? Roll around in the mud?" she asked the black beast.

His head swung toward her, and he answered in his deep bass rumble. "Not mud. Wet ash. The weather in Javak is horrid. Devil's Mount erupted, just as you'd hoped, but instead of covering the countryside with lava, it's spitting cloud after cloud of ash. And then it rained." The dragon shivered, coughing a small lick of flame he cautiously aimed away from C'Tan.

The woman actually laughed. She knew how much Drake hated being dirty, but especially how much he detested the water. It was just one of the unfortunate side effects of being a creature of fire. "So what did you discover on this little jaunt? Did you find Shandae or the people who attacked her?"

Drake swung his head back toward her and lowered it to her level. "Shandae has left for the mage academy. The group that attacked her is nowhere to be found, though I heard it rumored they have captured one being and he is being held in the cells at the academy itself, though I cannot confirm it as fact."

C'Tan snorted. "Well, I can." She set the dragon's foot down and turned on the hose to wash him down one last time. She primed the pump, then let the water flow in a tremendous burst. If the dragon had been a cat, his hair would have been on end. As it was, he stood on his tippy toes and his tail went straight out. C'Tan was sure to wash under his belly and all the way up his neck. He closed his eyes as she washed the ash off his head, and shivered when she hit his ear hole. When she had washed him down from head to tail, she pushed down the hand pump to shut off the water—a delightful combination of technology and magic—and Drake shook himself like a wet dog.

C'Tan evaporated the droplets before they ever reached her, and even did Drake the courtesy of running heat along his scales. He relaxed into the flame, and when he was dry, turned a smile on her. "Thank you, Mistress. I feel much better now. Is there anything further I can tell you?"

She shook her head. "No, I think you've done what you could. I appreciate your efforts, Drake. Rest now. I'll need you for a ride later."

The dragon nodded his head, and C'Tan turned to leave, all business. She opened the door to her black castle and made her way from the dragon aerie to her workroom. She picked up a particular sending stone, dropped it into a bowl of silver water, and waited.

After what seemed hours, but was probably minutes, the face of her daughter, Shadow, danced in the depths of the bowl, and she said only one word. "Yes?"

C'Tan spoke. "I have heard a rumor that one of Ember's attackers is being held at the mage academy."

Shadow nodded. She always had been a child of few words. C'Tan wondered if she had any part of her mother within her at all. Part of her hoped not.

"Is he in the academy cells, then?"

Again, the girl nodded.

C'Tan caressed the edge of the bowl. "I need you to get something from him—anything that is personally his—and send it to me. If I am to discover who attacked the girl, I need to know more, and he is the only accessible one. Will you do it?"

"But of course, Mother. I always do as you command," Shadow answered, a sneer on her face.

"Everything but to stop calling me 'Mother,'" C'Tan reminded her.

Shadow smiled. It was not a pretty smile. What an aggravating child.

"I shall do as you command, Mistress," she said, and the picture in the bowl faded away.

C'Tan was forced to wait then. She didn't pay attention to the time, just continued her search in her scrying bowl, hoping to find some evidence of the attack against Ember. She had never heard of this shadow power in anyone but her daughter, and she knew Shadow would not dare to rebel against her. Not yet, anyhow. Where could they have come from, then?

After what felt like hours, a single object appeared in C'Tan's sending bowl. She picked it up with a stick, not wanting to contaminate the item with her own flesh. Who knew who else had handled the thing, but the less touched, the better the reading.

She dropped it into her scrying bowl with the silvery water and watched it sink to the bottom. She examined it for a moment before digging at its memories. A black talon with a silver head and hoop was attached to the leather cord . It was beautifully done, but she couldn't place the bird it had come from. It wasn't dragon—that she knew for sure, as it was much too small and yellow instead of black.

Phoenix, perhaps? Well, scrying would give her the answer.

C'Tan waved her hand over the top of the water, heating it and letting the power build just above the surface, turning the silvery liquid into a mirror of the past.

When the energy built enough, she released it, then looked into the bowl. The water bubbled and boiled for a moment, then stilled into a reflective surface that showed her the bird the talon came from was indeed a phoenix, the shapeshifting token animal for the priests of Sha'iim, the guardians of the light magic. Yellow magic. C'Tan growled under her breath. She hated yellow users.

She moved beyond that memory, and up came the memory of the cow from whom the leather had been taken. That was of no consequence. Nor was the silver mined from the hills high above Niedemar. What *was* important were the people who lived above those hills. C'Tan finally got glimpses of the shadow weavers, as she called them, as they looked much like streaks of shadow weaving throughout the village. Most of the villagers seemed innocent, but there was a small group that C'Tan followed with her scrying bowl that were different from the others. They met in secret. She followed the necklace as it bounced against the chest of its wearer, winding down into the mining tunnels where small groups met and talked about destroying white magic altogether. It was a cult, she realized, after watching them train together and listen reverently to a small, wiry man who seemed completely benign. He must be their prophet, she realized. And the things he taught were full of half-truths.

C'Tan was S'Kotos' ear. She knew the truth behind the eruptions and the water rising up to drown entire cities. She knew his plan of destruction and it had absolutely nothing to do with white magic, except to try to deny it a chance to heal the world.

This cult wanted to weed out all magi from existence forever.

It was a dangerous, dangerous thought.

C'Tan sat and pondered until long after the sun had set and then came to realize that because of S'Kotos' plan for the wolfchild, C'Tan could not allow this cult of Shadow Weavers to get to her first. In order to steal Ember's soul, she was going to have to protect her.

C'Tan shook her head, a malicious grin split her face that would have done her master proud. Her servants were going to *love* this change of plan. She gathered the call stones she needed, fished the remnants of the shadow weaver's necklace from the water, and dropped the stones in. She needed to have a meeting with her spies at the mage academy, and sooner rather than later.

CHAPTER SIXTEEN

It thrilled Ember to have her step-brother Aldarin arrive to pick escort her to the eating hall. She had avoided her new guards for a while at least, but she was curious about them, and here was someone who knew more than Rahdnee's estranged daughter did. She turned to Aldarin. "So, tell me about Rahdnee and Brendae. They seem a bit . . . odd," she said, for lack of a better word.

Aldarin chuckled and squeezed her shoulders. "Yes, it's true that they aren't like most people, but they've been here longer than any others. I'd bet a year's pay that they've had a hand in training every guard who has come through these doors in the past twenty years or more. They are well respected, if not well liked. Did you know your tutor, Lily, is Rahdnee's daughter?" Aldarin twisted his neck to look at her.

Ember nodded. "I did, actually. She just told me a little while ago. It's hard to believe. They look nothing alike and don't get along at all. He scares me." She glanced around the stone halls, wondering what time it was. It was so hard to keep track of time underground. Ember ate and slept when her body told her to, with no knowledge of whether it was day or night.

The smells wafting down the hall hit Ember's stomach like a brick, and suddenly she was starving. She almost didn't hear Aldarin's response, she was so busy salivating. "Really? That surprises me. He has such a magnetic personality, I thought everybody liked him. Brendae is another matter, but Rahdnee is a decent guy."

Ember shivered as they took the final turn toward the hall. "Not to me. There's something about him. I can't put my finger on it, but there's something that isn't right. Maybe it's just me." She tried to shake off the feeling. "I mean, I can't help but be upset that DeMunth is in the healer hall, and every time I see the two of them, I think it should be DeMunth there, and not them. So maybe I resent their presence because they aren't him, and I'm worried about him. Or maybe Lily's dislike of her father has worn off on me."

Ember and Aldarin stepped into the dining hall and headed toward the line without even looking around. Ember was starving, with all the magic she'd used up in practice today, imperfect though she still was at using it. If she could swing it, she wanted to go back to the shielded room to practice on her own tonight and see what she could do without someone watching her. Now that she knew how to trigger her magic, she needed to practice control, and that was always hard to do with eyes peering over her shoulder.

Once Ember's tray was full, she turned and followed Aldarin, her mind still on what she could try while practicing, so it was no wonder she didn't realize where Aldarin was headed or who was there until she arrived. Several of the long rectangular tables were joined end to end. It was a veritable sea of familiar faces. Her mother, Tiva, Ren, Ezeker—these she expected—but not Lily, Uncle Shad, and even her step-father, Paeder. The only thing that would have made it complete would have been to have DeMunth and her father, Jarin, there.

Paeder stood at her arrival. Aldarin set his tray down and took hers just before her step-father took her in his arms and held her tight. Ember hadn't seen him for nearly a week and was astounded at the strength that had returned in such a short time. He was still skinny, but his color was back, and those powerful arms that had pinned horses and boys in training were returning to their normal form.

"I never truly thanked you," he whispered in her ear.

"For what?" Ember answered. "I didn't really do anything."

"You did more than you'll ever know, my daughter. Thank you for the part you played in restoring not only my health, but my life." He gave her a spine-popping squeeze and pushed her to arm's length, looking into her face. "My word, it's good to see you!" He hugged her again, then pulled out a chair for her to sit.

About that moment, Ember felt a tug on her sleeve. She glanced down to her left to see little Markis, the boy she had helped through the portals that first night. His eyes were full of tears as he glanced at her and her family. "Could I sit with you, Miss Ember? I don't have anyone to sit with, and I miss my family so. Do you think your family would mind?"

Before Ember could answer, Lily snapped, "There are plenty of empty tables, *child*. Go find one and leave the girl in peace."

The boy glared at her, much more venom in his eye than Ember had ever imagined seeing in a youngling. If they had rebuked her like that, she would have been in tears, but not Markis. He fought back with his eyes, if not his mouth. Ember caught only a brief glance at his face before he wiped it clean and turned back to Ember, the tears still present. "Miss Ember, I miss my da and brother so much. Can I sit with your family just this once?"

"Of course you can," she said before Lily could interrupt again. She stared hard at the girl, who glared right back at her. She turned back to the young boy. "You come sit right here next to me and I'll introduce you to everyone." Lily glanced from Ember to the boy, and watching her face, Ember could have sworn she saw a trace of fear.

Markis stared at Lily, and Ember heard his mindspeech as easily as if he'd spoken aloud, but his mind voice sounded more mature, richer, and chilled her to the bone. He directed his thoughts to Lily, and no one else at the table appeared to hear him, but for Ember, it was as clear as daylight. "*I know who you are.*" Lily paled and looked at him with apparent horror. Ember wasn't sure what to think. Lily glanced at her, and it was obvious by the look on her face that she *knew*. Somehow she knew Ember had heard as well, and she went even more pale.

Lily scooted her chair back quickly and excused herself, saying she wasn't feeling well. Everybody let her go with hardly a word. Markis watched her leave with a look in his eye that shook Ember. Just like Rahdnee, something about Markis was off. He was more than he appeared.

Ember left the dining hall quickly, despite wanting to stay and visit with her family. Markis gave her the creeps, and she felt an urgent need to get away and do the practicing her magic required. Thankfully, she was able to elude Rahdnee and Brendae, as well as Lily, and got to the practice room undetected. She needed some alone time. Ember wasn't used to being with people twenty-four hours a day. She needed some space and practicing was a good excuse. Nobody could fault her for wanting to practice, especially after the mess she had made of the orange room.

Ember stepped through the entryway and turned around, unsure how to seal the door, but evidently it was sensitive to people and sealed itself without her having to do a thing. She only hoped it would let her out as easily.

The first thing Ember did was lie down in the middle of the room and spread her arms and legs out like she was making a snow angel. She wasn't, though a part of her mind wondered if she could actually make a stone angel if she wanted. It tempted her to try it, but instead, she shut her eyes and let the quiet of the room and the hum of magic ease her aches, both emotionally and physically.

After several moments, she sat up and decided she'd better get to work. If anyone asked her where she had been, she wanted to give them honest details, and lying in the middle of the floor wasn't one she wanted to share.

Ember sat cross-legged and started her breathing exercises like Uncle Shad had taught her, trying to calm her heart and mind, just letting herself float for a moment as she gained her focus. When she felt ready, she opened her eyes and wondered what she should try first. She did not know what her capabilities were, so she wasn't sure where to start. Then an idea popped into her head.

She knew a little of what she could do from the disaster she had caused. Her heart raced when she contemplated reproducing those results in a controlled environment. There was nothing green in the room with her—but there was a lot of stone.

Trying not to think about what she was doing, Ember laid her palms flat on the floor, took a deep breath, and *pushed*. Her hands sank into the stone as if it were mud squishing between her fingers. She pulled them out, startled by the texture and slightly disgusted. She'd never been one to play in the mud. It surprised her to see she was shaking. She held her hands out before her and made the shaking stop. She just willed it so, and it happened. Startled, she inspected her fingers for any trace of the rock in which they'd just been immersed, but there was nothing but a light sparkly dust coating them.

Gaining courage from the experiment, she did it again, pressing her palms into the stone until she was embedded wrist deep, then flexed and wiggled her fingers to see if the stone was still moldable. It was, and she pulled out a second time, wondering why the soapstone in class had exploded. It hadn't felt like mud—it felt like she'd encased her hand in concrete. Did it have something to do with the type of stone?

Curious, she stood and went to the wall, where a large vein of red gemstone ran in a strip from floor to ceiling. She touched the ruby-colored surface and tried to calm the shaking that plagued her once more. She was terrified of getting stuck and being unable to break free, and someone finding her in a week hanging dead from the wall. Ember shoved her overactive imagination aside. She could always call Uncle Shad with her mind if she found herself in a dangerous situation. She breathed deep, just like she had while sitting on the floor, then before she could think about it, she shoved her hands elbow-deep into the crystal and held her breath. Carefully, she wiggled her fingers. A pop sounded from the crystal, but it too flowed around her hands like mud, though this muddy feeling was more like slick clay than regular common mud. Not as gritty.

Ember pulled her hands out, relieved that the type of stone didn't matter. If she could work with granite and crystal both, she imagined she could work through anything. She went back to the center of the room. Maybe the ability had more to do with her focus? Ember chewed at her lip, wondering how she could change her focus and replicate the experience she'd had in the orange room. Finally, she sank her hands into the floor and willed it to explode as she made a fist. The stone burst from the ground, little pebbles pinging off her face and body and the walls as she pulled her hands free from the holes she'd left in the floor. Her cheek stung, and she had grit in her eyes, but inside, she was dancing. She'd done it! It really *was* a matter of will.

Looking at the holes, suddenly her stomach clenched. So, she'd managed to destroy part of the room and blow up the floor, but could she put it back? Could she fix the damage she had done? Could she really sculpt stone like her father?

Ember scooped the bits of stone she could find and put them back in the holes, then put her hand over the rubble and concentrated. Nothing happened. She put both hands over the holes and pushed harder, imagining the stone being whole. And once more, nothing happened. The frustration built, but this time, rather than letting it go like she had in the past, she harnessed it, imagined it flowing through a nozzle, and gently reached down and touched the two mounds. The rubble lit with an orange glow, much like that of coals burning in the night, but there was no heat—none that she could feel, anyway, though when she looked at her sleeves, they were definitely smoking. Ember jerked her hands back, afraid her clothing would catch fire. The orange glow dimmed, and Ember was stunned to see the holes almost completely filled with stone. If she hadn't known her fists had just been there, she wouldn't notice the slight depression where the edges had melted into smoothness.

A wave of exhaustion washed over her, and she lay back down on the floor in the spread-eagle position she'd been in before, her heart beating so fast it seemed she'd just run a race. Ember closed her eyes and tried to slow her breathing when suddenly, she was out of her body, like she had been twice before. She looked at the cords that stretched out from her and decided to find out where they went. She touched one and felt Aldarin's voice come through. He was concerned and looking for her. She definitely didn't want to go there. The golden cord had a very distinctive DeMunth feel, and he was still sleeping. The other white cords went to Tiva, Ren, her mother, and Ezeker, all of which she didn't feel the urge to follow at the moment. That left only one. It was faint, a pale red, almost pink, that tore through the wall to her left like an arrow.

When she touched it, there was a feeling of sadness and pain and a fury induced madness like none she'd ever known. It was so overpowering that she couldn't help herself. She grabbed hold of that line and whipped through the wall and through several others before finding out who was on the other end.

Ember found herself in a room somewhere far away from the busyness of the school. It was a small room, still in the caverns, with only red stone walls and a large stone bowl filled with water in the center of the room. Rahdnee knelt before the bowl while the voice and image of a woman berated him. It was a voice that sent terror through Ember, for it was a voice she knew very well.

A voice that had haunted her dreams for as long as she could remember.

C'Tan.

"I am sick of your excuses, Rahdnee. Are you working for me? Or have you switched sides and begun working for Ezeker again?" the woman snarled. Rahdnee cringed, though whether in pain or fear, Ember wasn't sure. She was so stunned to see him there, she couldn't move, could hardly breathe, for fear C'Tan would see her, even in her ghostly form. Ezeker had, so she wasn't sure who else might.

"I serve you, Mistress. Always you." His voice was not scared, like Ember had assumed, but was full of adoration and a hint of sadness. Evidently C'Tan had a powerful hold on him.

"Then why do you consistently fail me? I've told you to turn the girl to our side or bring her to me to be sealed in the altar. Why is she not yet in my care?" C'Tan's voice was nearly a snarl.

Rahdnee again curled forward, this time in obvious pain. Somehow C'Tan was hurting him, even from far away. "I'm working on it, Mistress. They've assigned me as her guardian until her true guardian heals. I'm doing the best I can."

Again, a wave of cold chills settled over Ember. They were talking about her. C'Tan was still after her, just as her mother had always feared.

Rahdnee continued. "I've raised your child, haven't I? What more can I do to prove my loyalty?"

Ember stopped cold and replayed in her head what he had just said. He'd raised her child? The wheels turned and Ember suddenly realized what that meant.

Lily was not just Rahdnee's daughter. She was C'Tan's. Her roommate was the child of her greatest enemy.

At that revelation, Ember fled back to her body. The instant she was back in her form, she ran to the door, which opened at her touch, then raced down the halls, through the portals, and without thinking, found herself in the healer hall at DeMunth's side. She felt safe with him, even if he was in no condition to protect her. She knew she should go straight to Ezeker and tell him what she had learned, but she didn't dare leave at the moment. What if Rahdnee was out there? Or Lily? Or Brendae? If the other two were in collusion with C'Tan, it would make sense that Brendae would be as well. No wonder Markis hated Lily so much. Somehow, he knew. Ember's heart softened toward him, though fear still held her captive.

Instead of doing what she knew she should, she pulled up a chair and held DeMunth's hand, her heart still racing with all the discoveries and the new threat to her. Instead of telling Ezeker, she leaned forward and told DeMunth all about it. When she was finished, the Armor of Light flashed bright and he squeezed her hand, as if he had heard every single word. He struggled to open his eyes, and for just a moment, they focused and locked on hers. "I'm here, Ember," he whispered. "Stay with me." He dropped back into his deep sleep, but Ember felt comforted by just that bit of interaction with him. She leaned forward, wrapped her arms around his stomach, and laid her head on his shoulder, wanting to feel as close to him as possible.

She was still in that position when she fell asleep.

CHAPTER SEVENTEEN

In Kayla's mind, it should have taken but a few minutes to hitch Brant's horse to the boxcar and be on their way, but it was several hours before they were ready to go. T'Kato insisted that they each play their role to perfection, which of course comprised instructions from him, as well as dressing the part and adding face paint where necessary. The princes were not happy about the last, but since they were part of the entertainment, it was essential.

What was *not* required was for T'Kato to use semi-permanent ink to paint tattoos all over their bodies. Evidently, he had some hard feelings where his wife's brothers were concerned as well. It was all Kayla could do not to laugh when they washed their hands and realized they were stuck with the skin decorations for a few weeks, at the very least.

Brant had to dress like a tough bodyguard, which basically meant an entire change of clothes and a tight-fitting leather cap, all of which Hadril and Graylin had in their boxcar. Kayla's fiancé was also told to let his facial hair grow, much to his displeasure.

Kayla's costume required the least work of all. She wore what she had on and left the flowers in her hair. The only addition was several bracelets and anklets that sounded like seashells clacking together as she moved. The brothers, Hadril and Graylin, wanted her to go barefoot, but T'Kato insisted she wear the boots he and Sarali had sized for her. She was grateful for that. Her feet were too soft to walk barefoot. She was already paying the price for running around that morning with no shoes, trying to stop the boys from killing each other.

Finally, it was time to go. Jihong and Niefusu each climbed into a chariot led by a water horse. T'Kato rode up front with the sulky boy who drove the horses. Kayla had yet to learn his name. She and Brant had the pleasure of sitting on the tailgate of the wagon and watching the road fall away behind them as they moved. Niefusu eyed them for a while until Brant took her hand, his fingers interlocked with hers, and stared at the prince until he moved ahead off the road and passed the wagon to ride in the front.

Brant still didn't release her hand. Not for many hours, and by the time they pulled into the next village, her fingers were numb and she was irritated by his possessiveness. Didn't he know she was committed to him?

Evidently not.

Just as she was about to hop off the back of the wagon, Hadril flung the boy who had been driving the horses out the back of the boxcar.

"You're worthless, Jayden! I've been teaching you this stuff for months now. How many times do I have to tell you not to combine the sheepsmith with the steelwort? It's poison! If you weren't my sister's kit, I'd send you packing right now." Kayla turned to look up at Hadril. His fury was obvious in his stance and the trembling he seemed too angry to hide. The boy, Jayden, picked himself up from the dirt and glared at his uncle. His lip had split open in the fall and a trail of blood ran down his chin and dripped onto his shirt. He didn't seem to notice.

Hadril growled and threw his hands in the air. "I can't get any kind of good help around here," he grumbled under his breath. "Doesn't anybody know anything about herbs anymore? And here I've got this huge order for the Dellian and I've got little to show for it. I'll be up all night at this rate. Stupid kit," he grumbled, slamming things around the counter.

Jihong stopped his chariot and got out. He walked to the boy and put his hand on his shoulder. "Are you okay?" he asked in a low voice. The boy didn't answer, still frozen in anger. Jihong pushed a rag into his hand. "You might need this for your lip." That got Jayden's attention, and he wiped the blood away. He glanced at Jihong, but he didn't move.

Handing the reins of the chariot to Brant, Jihong hopped up into the boxcar and approached Hadril. Kayla knew Brant well enough to know he had no idea what to do with directing a team of horses. He was a one horse man, But at least taking the reins made him let go of Kayla's hand. She stood and hopped down from the wagon, but still she heard Jihong speak to the apothecary. "I know a bit about herbs, sir," he said.

Hadril was quiet for a moment, and Kayla turned to watch them, curious, though she still neither liked nor trusted the prince. "Really? Show me," Hadril said.

"What would ye like me to make?" Jihong said. The tinkling of glass followed his words.

"A love potion."

Jihong laughed. "There's no such thing."

Hadril cocked his head and smiled. "Good. You do know a bit. How about making a healing potion for the lung sickness?"

Jihong was quiet for a moment. "There is no cure, but there is a syrup that can ease the symptoms. Is that what ye wish?" he asked.

The apothecary had a full smile now. "Oh, aye. Make me a bit of that and I'll make you my apprentice. I'll even pay you a bit."

Jihong shook his head. "Money is of no concern, sir. But I'd be happy to help ye. What be the point in knowing about a thing if ye can't use it?"

The boxcar was mostly dark, only a small lamp lighting the space, but Jihong seemed busy combining ingredients into a cauldron and boiling it over a mage-heated stone.

"Kayla," T'Kato said from behind her. Kayla squeaked and turned around to face him.

"Don't do that! You scared me!" she said, her heart still racing.

T'Kato chuckled. "Good. You need to be more aware of your surroundings."

Kayla wanted to hit him, but she knew it would do no good. "What do you need?" she asked instead.

"Your sheath, if you don't mind. The one your father gave you," he said with no apology.

Tears sprang instantly to her eyes, but she didn't let them fall. "Why?"

"You'll get it back," he said, putting a heavy hand on her shoulder. "You have my word."

She didn't want to give it to him. It was not only precious, but it was one of the few things she had of her father's. And yet she dug in her bag and handing it to the large man. Before she let go, she asked, "I have your word? I'll get it back?"

He nodded, then put his right hand to his shoulder and bowed. "On my honor, Lady Kayla. It shall be returned."

Somehow the gesture made her feel much better, though letting go of the gem-encrusted leather was like letting go of her heart.

Jayden stared at the sheath with hungry eyes. He'd probably seen nothing so magnificent. Kayla didn't blame him and let all thought of him leave her head as she turned back to the boxcar at Hadril's chuckle. "Well done, my boy! Well done! We may get that order finished after all!" He put his hands on Jihong's shoulders and squeezed. Jihong didn't even flinch. "Thank you, prince. I know you don't have to do this, but I appreciate it beyond words."

Jihong seemed a little embarrassed. "Just Jihong, sir. I be no prince here, and happy to be helping."

Hadril laughed again. "Well then, let's get to work!" He turned his attention to the boy. "Jayden! You are now the official driver of the boxcar. I've got a new apprentice."

Jayden glared at Jihong, hatred filling his eyes like a black cloud. It worried Kayla. He was too young to hate so much, but the boy nodded, went around to the front, and evidently clambered up to the driver's seat, for the boxcar moved once again until it circled and stopped in a field just outside of the village.

Graylin jumped down from the side of the driver's seat and approached Kayla with a tin cup in hand. The boy, Jayden, jumped down and ran into the village almost before the wagon came to a stop. He still looked angry from his earlier reprimand, and she doubted she'd be seeing much of him during this stop.

When Graylin reached her, he spoke. "And now the fun begins," he said. "Are you ready?" He took a swallow from the cup, what looked like plain water, then set it down on a stump and pulled out a multitude of instruments from compartments beneath the wagon. A guitar, a lap harp, a pennywhistle, and many more. "You never know what you're going to need," he explained when he saw her eyeballing the instruments. "It's all about feeling the crowd's energy and knowing what their soul desires. I'm sure you know what I mean."

Kayla's heart pounded, but not with fear. Actually, she found herself rather excited about performing again. She hadn't realized how much she missed it until that moment. She nodded her head in answer to his question, and he grinned at her.

As Graylin pulled out the instruments, Hadril and Jihong were busy pushing the side of the wagon out and locking it into place with sticks so that it formed a canopy. The countertop that was their workspace under normal circumstances became a sales counter for the apothecary. It was a rather ingenious arrangement, actually. Everything seemed to have a dual purpose.

Once he had everything he seemed to need, Graylin handed Kayla a couple of instruments and moved away from the boxcar. He used a tree stump to prop up his larger instruments and laid the smaller ones upon its surface, then turned to Kayla. "Now, this is the way it's going to go. We're going to set up magelights to draw the people once it gets on toward dark. They already know we're here, I'm sure, and will come soon to make their purchases from Hadril. They will also bring things for repair, which means I've got to leave my instruments and do some business. Can I trust you to watch them until I return?" he asked.

153

Kayla was almost indignant in her response. "But of course you can. What kind of person do you think I am? I know the value of an instrument, and I am not speaking only of monetary value."

Graylin put his hand on her shoulder and met her eye. "I know you are not, and your answer was as I had hoped and believed. I shall make business as quick as possible. In the meantime, feel free to play the instruments, if you so desire. Or warm up on your own. Anything we can do to draw people to us or announce our presence will mean more earnings for all of us." He patted her shoulder once more, then took off for the boxcar at a jog. It looked like two sets of steps had been set up before the counter, one on each end of the boxcar. Kayla assumed one was for the apothecary and one for the tinker.

Kayla's belly grumbled, as per usual. It seemed she was always hungry, despite how thin she stayed. She had often wondered if her father's Evahn metabolism made her burn her food as quickly as she ate it. She could think of no other explanation. But as she always did, she ignored the grumbling stomach and distracted herself. She picked up the smallest flute. It was transverse, like her own, but was about a third of the size. She put it to her lips and blew. A deafening squawk came from it. She pulled back, startled, then, determined to master the thing if it killed her, she tightened the positioning of her lips and tried again. This time, a very high-pitched sound came out, something akin to her flute, but high enough and loud enough to make the dogs of the village howl.

Grinning, and feeling like she was getting the hang of it, she played the opening notes to Darthmoor's Honor, then transitioned into something of her own, her fingers moving faster and faster across the keys, and within just a few minutes, she was almost as comfortable with the miniature flute as she was her own. People gathered. One or two children at first, dashing across the field as fast as their short legs would carry them, and then they stood and gawked as if she were some strange animal on display. It tickled her, and so she danced among them, weaving in and out of the people as the crowd increased, and they began to laugh and relax with her vibrant tunes. Breathless, she finished her playing with the highest note she could hit, then twittered down to the lowest, then pulled the small flute from her lips with a flourish. The people laughed and clapped so hard, she was afraid they would hurt themselves.

"Thank you. Thank you," she said over and again. They just wouldn't stop clapping. She made a motion with her hands, hoping it would make them stop. It had the effect she wished for, but then they stood there staring at her as if expecting her to play again. Surprised and tired, she put the small flute back where Graylin had left it and pulled out her own silver flute. She played something slow this time, giving herself a chance to catch her breath, and it amazed her when just seconds into her song, a voice joined in, giving words to the emotion she tried to play. Without looking, she knew Graylin joined her.

The song he sang was not the song she played, but it melded and fused with her tones so perfectly, it was as if the writers of the two unique pieces had meant for them to be played together. It was amazing, and Kayla herself was lost in his voice, though she continued to play. How she wished she could sing like that. She could sing—all Evahn could—but not like Graylin. His voice was angelic—as if the Guardians had come and put the gift of sound into his voice box. Together they ran through several more verses, he coming to join her, then walking amongst the people as he sang, his hands as full of expression as his voice. He was such a fascinating man. Why did he travel with an apothecary? Was Hadril his only family? And then he stopped singing and nodded to her. The song was done. She finished up the melody she had started, her last note fading away into nothing. The crowd was silent and still after this performance, as if applause would degrade the music they had just made. Instead, they bowed their heads to the performers and whispered something Kayla could not understand, but evidently Graylin did, for he bowed and whispered to them in return. Kayla curtseyed, not knowing what to say. Graylin nodded his approval, then walked slowly to her. "Why don't you let me take it from here for a while? I'd like to use you again, if you don't mind, but I'd especially like for you to play the blue flute as a final number. Are you willing?"

She almost said no, but strangely nodded at his request. As she walked back toward the boxcar and Graylin began singing again, accompanying himself with one of the guitars, she wondered what in the world she was thinking. The Sapphire Flute was nothing to be toyed with. It was not created for entertainment. It was created with a purpose in mind. It had power—dangerous power. But something inside told her it was okay—the village needed to hear its voice, even if it wasn't to battle evil or heal anyone individually. They, as a group, needed the light of the flute—and so she said yes.

When she got to the boxcar, she went around and sat on the tailgate, still thinking on the Sapphire Flute, but the voices of Hadril and Jihong quickly distracted her. They were like the barkers in Darthmoor's shopping district, selling their wares. Who would have thought a prince of the royal sea court could be such a convincing salesman? She shook her head.

Brant chose that moment to sit down beside her and take her hand. It irritated her for a moment. Hadn't he held her hand long enough on the trip here? But then she chastised herself. He was her fiancé, her love, and best friend. If he wanted to hold her hand, he had a right.

"The show is about to begin. I heard you playing out there. You were magnificent," he said, all in a rush.

Kayla pulled back and looked at him, her head cocked. "Brant Domanta, are you nervous?" she asked, feeling the sweat of his palms. He wasn't holding her hand out of love, but for comfort. She saw him redden under her gaze and he stammered a denial. She grinned. "You are! You're nervous!"

He reddened even further, then hung his head, looking up at her through his lashes. "You always knew me too well. Yes, I'm nervous. T'Kato is big and strong and he's been trained with weapons since he could stand. I will be like a fly under a hammer to him. I'm not just afraid of getting hurt—I'm afraid he's going to bash my head in!"

She was kind enough not to laugh in his face, but instead took both his hands and looked at him square on. "Love, T'Kato is one of the most gentle men I've ever known. Yes, he knows how to handle himself, and yes, he's big and scary and strong, but he would never hurt you. He knows that if he did, I would have to kill him." She was only half joking, but it had the effect she wanted, and Brant grinned. "Now, go out there and put on a great show. You're going to be fine. I promise," she said, praying to whatever gods or Guardians were up there that she was telling the truth.

She needn't have worried. T'Kato was practiced enough to make it look as if Brant were a challenging opponent, though she knew he truly was not. It was all for play. They sparred back and forth, first with swords, then with axes and daggers, and then with long poles. T'Kato even let Brant snake in a hit or two that she knew would never have bothered the man, but it was kind of him to let Brant seem the better in their battle. It also did a lot to hide T'Kato's true strength and power if they were attacked. A very smart move on his part.

After the battle show, there was a lull in the entertainment while the people went back to purchasing things from the apothecary or bringing their broken items to the tinker. Kayla walked around the group playing softly, a little nudge in her playing to send people scampering home for those items they'd forgotten needed repair. It was a small thing she figured would help both the tinker and the villagers.

After about half an hour, Niefusu and Jihong came out to the center of the clearing, riding on the backs of their water horses. As soon as the people saw them, they murmured, and Kayla heard more than one gasp of appreciation. The two just sat there, their backs straight, as if they were living statues for a minute or so. It seemed like forever, and then, as if they had timed everything perfectly, they moved at the same time. They rode past each other in a straight line, then turned quickly so they both rode in a clockwise circle, the water horses picking up speed as they rode equally opposite one another. When the transparent animals had reached a speed that seemed impossible, they turned and raced toward one another. The princes leaped to the bare backs of the animals, balancing with one foot on the mount's shoulder and another on its rump. It looked as if the horses were about to collide. The tension in the air was nearly palpable, and then at the last second, the brothers jumped from the backs of their animals, met in midair and took hold of each other's shoulders, then shoved away, landing on each other's mounts, backwards, still standing as they had been before.

The tricks increased as the night wore on, and last of all the brothers raced toward one another and leaped, transforming into their MerCat forms at the last second and landing on the ground. They spun and stalked toward each other like mountain lions, stopping mere inches apart. A woman screamed, and just before they reached one another, they transformed into their human shapes again and embraced, laughing, then turned and bowed to the crowd.

The villagers, awed by the show, applauded and laughed as the tension diffused, and the princes walked away from the circle, their water horses following them with no bridle.

And then it was time to finish up with music once again. Graylin met Kayla in the middle, the magelights having gone into the air long before, casting a blue glow over the scene.

"Ladies and gentlemen," he said, his voice somehow carrying to the far reaches of the crowd, "We would like to give you three final numbers before we bid you good night. Mistress Kalandra has agreed to accompany me on the first two numbers, and will finish with a special number for all of you," he said, calling her by the name they had agreed upon. It wouldn't do to call her Kayla when they were in disguise, though what she was about to do with The Sapphire Flute may just give her away after all they had done.

"Can you sing?" he asked beneath his breath while leaning close to her.

Surprised, she wasn't sure how to answer. "Well, yes, but not like you," she said.

"It doesn't matter. Do you know *Still She Be*?"

Kayla had first heard that song at Brant's home, sitting upon the landing when they should have long been in bed, and she had loved it ever since. She nodded. Graylin moved to the center of the circle, his head hanging. Stillness gathered around him as he sang the first note, a wordless note that grew in a minor key. He sang the first verse then, telling of a woman he loved, a woman he longed for while he was off to war.

Kayla's palms sweat as she waited for the second verse, her cue to take over. She had no problem playing the flute in public, but this was her first public vocal performance and she wasn't sure how it would be. But then it was time to begin, and she no longer had time to think. Instead, to overcome the nervousness, she put herself in the shoes of that woman waiting for her man to come home, not knowing if he would return dead or alive. She put the longing and heartache she would feel into the song, just as she would have with her flute, and then the third verse came and she and Graylin blended together in harmony so sweet, she could barely stand it. It nearly overpowered her with emotion, performing with this man. He was too good for her, and she finally understood how Brant felt when she asked him to play his flute with her. She felt so completely inadequate, and yet so thrilled to share in Graylin's gift. And before she knew it, the song was done.

The people responded as they had before. Not with applause, but with tears, bowed heads, and murmurs. It seemed a sign of the utmost respect, and Kayla found she preferred it to raucous applause.

With hardly a pause, Graylin picked up the lap harp and strummed a note that immediately let Kayla know what he wished to play. There was only one song that began with that chord. It was another quiet number, one usually sung to children before bedtime. One Kayla's own mother had sung to her. Emboldened by her moment of singing with Graylin, she kept her flute in her bag and sang again, this time carrying the melody while he hummed a harmony and played counterpoint on his harp. It was beautiful. Haunting. Everything music could and should be, and long before she wanted it to end, it was done and Graylin gave her the floor, gathering his instruments around him so he could sit on the stump.

Kayla pulled the case for the Sapphire Flute from her bag and set everything but the instrument itself on the ground. The villagers gasped at the glowing instrument. For a panicked second, she wasn't sure what to play, but then she realized that so often, it was that way. She didn't know what would come from the instrument until she placed it to her lips and created sound. All she knew was this village needed something, and all she could really do was give breath to the instrument and let it lead her into what it needed to play.

With that thought deep in her heart, she closed her eyes, brought the instrument to her lips, and blew. It was soft, just as her performance for the people of Darthmoor and King Rojan had been. Merely a breath of sound that grew to something more and pulsed with a life of its own. She put her thoughts on the villagers and her heart into the flute, and the instrument took over. She didn't know how she played it, but the song was simple and incredibly complex at the same time. She didn't know if she'd ever be able to play it again, but the images that came to her mind as she played were those of earth and water, love made, and heartache healed. It was of corn grown tall and strong, and strength in the villagers—strength of heart, strength of body, and strength of mind.

It seemed the villagers had lost hope with the drought and the loss of their crops. Kayla was leaving a blessing from the Guardians with this village. She could feel it flowing through her, and if anything had made her know the Guardians were real, it was at that moment, as they poured their love and healing through her and the flute. Kayla suspected she glowed with the power of the instrument once again. She could feel her hair flowing around her, though not a breeze stirred. She wished she could see it, because if she looked anything like how she felt, it had to be beautiful.

Eventually the song was done, and it faded as it had begun, with barely a breath of sound. It reminded her so much of that moment in Darthmoor, but this time, there was no sound when she finished. No collective sigh or breath. Nothing but the occasional sob of a villager. When she opened her eyes, they were all on their knees, and not a single dry eye could be found. Even Graylin had tears streaming down his cheeks.

It was he who finally moved. He stood, propping his guitars on the stump once again, and came to her. He wrapped his arms around her and squeezed, then took her shoulders in his hands and kissed her gently on each cheek, whispering a single phrase as he neared her ear. "Thank you."

His action began a cascade of reactions from the villagers, who came to her and did the same. They embraced her, kissed each cheek, and gave her their thanks, sometimes still sobbing. Kayla hadn't realized how many people were in the village. She lost count quickly and was overwhelmed by their response. She wasn't used to being touched or appreciated or thanked.

Near the end, a large man approached her, tears still flowing down his cheeks as he repeated the same gesture, but his thanks were different from the others. "Thank you," he said, and then added, "Please, Mistress Kalandra, may I provide you a place to stay and food to eat at my inn? It is a small service to repay what you have given us."

Kayla's stomach growled again at the mention of food. It had been a long night, and she'd forgotten how hungry she was. Without even consulting the others, she accepted. "Thank you, sir. I have little to offer but some entertainment, but I would welcome a bed and some food."

He grinned like he'd just won the village lottery. "Thank you, Mistress Kalandra! Thank you! You need to do nothing more unless you wish. The entire group is welcome. Please. Come soon," he said, grabbing her hands and squeezing tight, then he turned and ran toward the village, presumably to prepare for her arrival.

With a few final hugs, kisses, and thanks from the villagers, Kayla was able to go and tell the rest of the group of the blessing of a bed and hot food for the night. She was pretty sure they wouldn't mind.

CHAPTER EIGHTEEN

Ember sat up with a start, her lower back wracking with spasms that had her whimpering as she arched against it. Evidently she had fallen asleep while leaning on DeMunth's chest and her body was paying for it now. She shut her eyes and used her knuckles to rub at the kinks, but it wasn't working. She stood, about to bend and stretch as best she could, when a large hand reached out, turned her around, and told her with his mind voice, *"Straddle the chair and sit."*

Ember looked over her shoulder to find DeMunth sitting up in bed and looking as refreshed and whole as ever. The knot in her stomach and ache in her heart immediately eased, knowing he was okay. He swung his legs off the side of the bed and nudged Ember down on the chair so the back was facing her. Then his hands went to work.

Those thick, callused hands that had seemed so strong on a cudgel now gentled as they kneaded her lower back like bread dough. He wrapped his fingers around her waist and used his thumbs in a circular motion that made her want to melt. She relaxed against the chair, not even caring that wooden slat dug into her cheek. Whatever he was doing felt *good*.

Ember sighed as he moved upward from her lower back to kneading between and beneath her shoulder blades, then moving into her neck. It had felt nearly tight as stone as of late. She'd most definitely had a lot going on in her life to cause stress, and it had settled right into her shoulders, though she hadn't realized how much so until DeMunth found the knots and roots roping through her muscles. She groaned, not sure if it was in pain or pleasure.

DeMunth chuckled, his voice taking on a metallic tone it hadn't held before. She wondered if he even knew he had a new tongue. Had he discovered it yet? And what was it like? Was it hard and cold like metal? Or warm and soft like a flesh tongue? That thought left her a little breathless, especially as DeMunth chose that moment to dig his strong fingers into her hair and scalp. It felt so very good. She didn't want him to ever stop.

"You have *got* to show me how to do this," she said aloud the moment she could force her thoughts into coherent order.

DeMunth chuckled again, that same metallic tone ringing bell-like through his voice, though he didn't answer her vocally. *"Massage is one of the techniques the priests of Sha'iim taught me. It is very valuable in creating a meditative state."*

"You can say that again," Ember said, leaning her head back into his hands. She felt completely malleable, and yet unable to move. She'd never felt anything so wondrous and was disappointed when he gave her hair one last tug and stopped. Ember groaned and turned around quickly, wanting to grab those hands and put them back in her hair.

Instead, he captured her hands and, one at a time, picked them up and used his thumbs to press away the tension. Ember leaned back in the chair and closed her eyes, still unable to form thoughts. He pressed on the fleshy part of her thumb and stroked it as if he were molding clay, then stretched her palms and twisted and pulled on each finger individually, then moved up to her wrist and elbow. Then he repeated the process on the other hand.

When he was done, Ember's hands sat relaxed in her lap, and she could barely move. She could see how it could induce a meditative state. Or sleep. She definitely felt like she could fall right back to sleep at the moment, could especially fall back into DeMunth's arms.

She pulled away from that thought. He was DeMunth. Council member and her elder by far too many years for her to consider any possibilities with him. And yet . . . she couldn't deny the pull she felt toward this man. It felt almost as if they were two halves of the same whole, but she had just come to trust her family—how could she so fully trust this stranger she barely knew?

She didn't understand it, and yet somehow she did exactly that.

Unwilling to face the thoughts any longer, she turned to meet his eyes. "Do you remember anything from the last few days?"

DeMunth cocked his head in his quirky way. *"I remember defending you from the shadow people. I remember coming to the caves and entering. I vaguely remember attacking somebody I thought was a threat to you and falling through a portal, but beyond that, it's a blank. It's been days, you say?"* His surprise tickled her mind.

Ember filled him in on the rest: How his armor had failed him and he'd fallen into a coma. How she talked to him after her disastrous classes and fed him soup. How the spoon had melted in his mouth and she'd fed him multiple spoons before the armor came back. DeMunth watched her dumbfounded, but she could see his tongue moving in his mouth. He looked like he wasn't sure whether to be happy or appalled.

"So you can talk now. You said my name when you woke at first, then you fell asleep again." Ember blushed. "I think maybe the armor knew your body was incomplete, and that's why it reacted the way it did. It couldn't completely fit itself to you unless you were whole, because as soon as your tongue formed, it flared up bright as could be, covering every inch of you."

"I can talk now?" he asked, his mental voice hesitant.

Ember nodded. "Try it."

He leaned in close, his hand coming up to caress her jaw line. Chills ran through her. That was not a massage type of touch. It was very, very personal. Ember's stomach fluttered about. DeMunth leaned in close, his breath so close she could feel it brush her face, and she caught the scent of his soup and the metallic tang of his tongue. "Ember," he said, his face registering surprise and joy as his mouth actually worked. "After all these years." He sighed. "It feels marvelous to speak. Ember," he said again, a huge grin spreading across his face. His eyes softened as he met hers and spoke her name once more. "Ember," he said in both mind and voice, then leaned forward and met her lips with his own.

Ember had never been kissed like that before. She'd had mum kisses, brotherly kisses, and even a quick peck from one of her schoolmates when she was a child, but she'd never had a kiss that made her melt. She'd always thought the idea of a kiss stopping your heart or your breath was childish or silly, but now she felt it herself and understood.

Her breath stopped, her heart fluttered, and she couldn't get enough of the taste of him. His lips were soft, his jaw unshaven and prickly, but she didn't care. His silver tongue darted between her lips and she finally tasted him and realized that his tongue was every bit as warm and supple as a human one would have been. She reached her arms around him and threaded her fingers through his hair, inhaling every bit of him she could.

The kiss affected her to her very soul, and for a second it thrust her back out of her body, watching as the heart rope between them changed from a thin thread to a chain thick as a sailor's rope. It was beautiful, but a chain nonetheless, and in that moment it pushed her back into her body and she pulled quickly away from him. It left DeMunth panting, his eyes hungry. Ember knew she looked the same. Her body wanted nothing more than to be reunified with him and to melt until they were completely one being enmeshed in the other, but she couldn't. She didn't dare. That chain had her scared. Chains meant she was captive, reminded her of the experience in the cave with her kidnapper, Ian Covainis. She knew it was ridiculous to be afraid of DeMunth, but the reminder of her terror, feeling so helpless, threw up the walls between them once more.

She scooted back, the chair scraping along the stone floor as she stood. DeMunth looked at her, confusion obvious in his eyes.

"What's wrong?" he asked with his newfound tongue. She would have thought his voice would be scratchy with disuse, but then he sang nearly every day. That probably accounted for the clarity. Ember shook herself. Right now, she couldn't think about it. She had to go. She had to get some space before she fell under his spell. She needed to think.

"Class. I've got to get to class. And breakfast. I've got to go. I've got to go now," she said, backing toward the door, knowing she made little sense.

"Wait, I'll go with you," he said.

Just then, Lily, Rahdnee, and Brendae stepped into the healing hall, looked around, and spotted Ember. She froze in place, unable to say anything to anyone about what she'd discovered, that C'Tan was Rahdnee's master and Lily's mother. If she told DeMunth, he wouldn't be able to defend her—not against three of C'Tan's most chosen disciples. She debated on whether to tell him the problem using the mindspeech that had grown so normal between them, but no. If he knew she was in danger at all, he would do anything he could to guard her. To protect him, she had to leave, but she couldn't leave without them. They approached her and acted as if nothing was wrong.

"There you are!" Rahdnee said. "You've been eluding us, you little rascal." He rubbed Ember's head as if she were three instead of sixteen. "It's class time. We're to escort you to the training room. And look, we even brought breakfast." He grinned in a way that made Ember uncomfortable.

"Excuse me, who are you?" DeMunth asked from behind her, his metallic tongue resonating in his voice.

"I'm sorry, I'm Rahdnee. We've met, but you don't remember, I'm sure. I carried you here when you passed out." Rahdnee reached across Ember and shook DeMunth's hand. She wanted to bristle, to shove him away, but that would only make matters worse. She couldn't let him know she knew his secret, or DeMunth would die and she probably would as well.

DeMunth shook Rahdnee's hand, his eyes brightening as a smile lit up his face. "Ah! Well, thank you, then. I appreciate it. And I assume you're taking care of my girl while I'm laid up?" He said the last almost as if he owned Ember. It made her feel a little prickly.

167

"Yes, sir. We're taking your place until you are well again," Rahdnee said, turning and rejoining Brendae and Lily.

"Good. Take good care of her. I intend to relieve you of your duties soon."

Rahdnee chuckled as if he had no problem with that, but Ember knew his orders. That had to be one of the last things he wanted. Now she feared even more for DeMunth's safety. What if the guards tried to poison him or kill him in his sleep? She had to tell someone, and soon. She glanced at Lily. Just as she was starting to like and trust the girl, she turned out to be on the enemy's side.

Or was she?

Ember watched Lily glance from DeMunth to Rahdnee, then to Ember. Her eyes were full of concern and fear. If Lily was afraid, maybe there was more to her than what her parents designed her to be.

Ember stuck it in the back of her mind. She turned to leave when DeMunth took her arm. "Will I see you later?" he asked, sounding almost desperate.

Ember hesitated, then nodded, glancing at the temporary guards. He dropped his hand from her arm and she left with her three enemies, hoping against all hope that they wouldn't try something today. Not until DeMunth got his strength back, and she told someone about the enemies hidden in their midst.

CHAPTER NINETEEN

The village inn was much nicer than Kayla had expected. Most of the inns in Darthmoor had wooden tables and dirt floors and stank of ale and rotten food that had fallen between the rushes. This inn had stone floors, sticky here and there, but mostly clean, and instead of square wooden tables made of old weathered wood, they were made of stone. Slate, she guessed, though she didn't know for sure. It reminded her of the flooring at Dragonmeer. She'd asked about it once and Brant had told her it was slate from his family's quarry. She'd never forgotten the look or feel.

The whole group, minus Jayden, who seemed to have disappeared, sat at a large table together, wooden chairs pulled up to the round stone. Kayla wasn't sure how they managed it, but somehow Niefusu ended up on one side of her and Brant on the other. T'Kato sat across the table, shaking his head and grinning, and everyone else was oblivious to the competition still going on between the boys. Brant hadn't let go of her hand since they'd sat down, and it was really getting annoying. Actually, she'd been annoyed with the two of them pretty much all day. Niefusu would occasionally bump her leg or foot with his—she knew what he was doing. It turned out that her mother was right. All men were the same.

A cute red-headed waitress came to the table. "What can I get you?" She looked at Kayla first. She opened her mouth to answer, but Brant beat her to it.

"She'll have a glass of milk, some bread, and soup if you've got it. Same for me, while you're at it," he said, not even glancing at Kayla. Her jaw dropped open in disbelief. Since when did he order for her? It's not like they'd frequented inns very often, but he had never ordered for her. He should have known better. And when did a bowl of soup ever satisfy her hunger? She was starving. She wanted red meat and potatoes and a huge mug of cider, and that was just for starters, but she was too shocked by Brant's behavior to say a word.

The rest of the table ordered their food, and Kayla sat there and fumed. She tried to pull her hand out of Brant's, but he wouldn't let go, which made her even angrier. What was wrong with him? Why was he being so possessive? Didn't he trust her?

The longer she sat, the more livid she became. She couldn't look at anyone because she knew if she did, she would explode. The evening had been so beautiful—why did he have to ruin it?

When the food came, Kayla tried to pull her hand from Brant's so she could eat, but he squeezed even harder, eating with his left hand so he could cling to her with his right.

That was it. The final straw. Kayla yanked her hand out of his and stood in one motion, then picked up the bowl of warm soup and a cup of milk and dumped them both over Brant's head.

The entire table went silent, the room following shortly thereafter. Brant gasped and sputtered, his eyes more shocked than angry. Kayla leaned down close to him so she could speak softly. If she didn't, she would scream. "I am not your possession, Brant. You don't own me." She pulled all the bracelets off one by one. "I thought you trusted me. I thought you got it through your thick skull last night that I am not going anywhere, but no. The two of you have to continue this ridiculous competition for my attention." She glared at Niefusu too, who was grinning from ear to ear. He didn't care how upset she was. All the more reason to reject him.

Kayla leaned down until she was inches from Brant's face. "I belong to no man. Do you understand me? No man!" With that, she picked up the charm bracelet he had given her and threw it in his lap, then spun away from the table and marched up the stairs before she burst into tears. She did not know where she was going, only that her room was up there somewhere and that's where she wanted to be at the moment.

The wood creaked beneath her feet as she found the upper floors and walked down the long stretch, with doors on her left and railing overlooking the large dining room on her right. She could see Brant cleaning himself up. The men were all laughing at his predicament, and he seemed more embarrassed than anything. That stoked the fire of her fury. Stupid man. Stupid, stupid man! She mumbled it under her breath as a serving girl walked by, carrying an arm full of sheets. The girl looked at her funny as she went past.

Kayla kicked herself for her idiocy, then, despite her embarrassment, stopped the girl. "Can you tell me where my room is? I never found out which one was mine."

The girl cocked her head and smiled, looking over the railing. "Ah, you're that one, are you?" Kayla reddened. "He must have deserved it for that kind of act." The girl chuckled, and Kayla gave her a half smile. "I can show you the way, miss, but I know you've been on the road for a bit, and wondered if you'd like to use the bathing pools before you sleep."

Kayla nearly melted into the floor at just the thought of a bath. "Oh, yes, please!"

The girl nodded. "Let me just set these down and I'll show you your room and the baths both." She disappeared for a moment, then returned with one set of sheets, a towel, and a night robe for Kayla. Squeezing past, she beckoned with her head, not a word spoken. At the third from the last door, she stopped and fiddled with the knob and swung the door open. "This one is yours, miss," she said, setting the sheets on the bed.

"Here's your key." She handed Kayla a tarnished key and immediately exited the room. "The baths are this way."

Kayla left her bag in the room, pulled the door shut and made sure it was locked, then followed the girl. They continued down the hallway and descended three flights of stairs until they were actually beneath the inn. There the girl led her down another hallway, where the walkway ended and one had to turn either left or right. They turned right. "The other way is the men's baths," the girl explained as they entered the cave-like structure. "Laundry washing is in the small pool, bathing in the large. Soap for each is near the pool." She seemed in a hurry, but she paused for a moment and said, almost shyly, "I was there when you played tonight, Miss Kalandra. It was the most beautiful thing I've ever heard." And then she was all business again. "Enjoy your bath." The girl turned and disappeared.

Kayla intended to do just that.

After washing her clothes, her hair, and enjoying a long soak in the hot water, Kayla exited the pool and dried off. She wrapped herself in the robe, bundled her wet clothes in the towel, and, boots in hand, walked back up the hallway and stairs, and found her room with no trouble.

She shut the door behind her and tried to figure out a way to dry her clothes—there wasn't a clothesline strung across the window. She looked a little closer and smiled. There was a deck outside her overlooking the roof, and that deck had a railing. It would be the perfect place for the sun and wind to dry her clothes. She went outside and laid everything out, including her underthings. A week ago, she would have been embarrassed to have them hanging from a railing, but she was far beyond the point of being embarrassed over it now.

As she finished, her stomach grumbled once again. She'd hardly eaten all day, and what little food had been placed before her, she'd dumped on Brant's head. She shook her head, then wondered if the kitchens were still open and if anyone would care if she ate in her sleeping robe.

Well, there was only one way to find out.

Kayla picked up her bag with the flutes in it and exited the room. She made her way barefoot down the walkway, then down the stone stairs and into the dining room, and sat at a table.

The same girl who had taken her order earlier approached, a slight smirk on her face. Kayla ignored it. "Can I help you, miss? The kitchen is about to close, but there are plenty of leftover bits from before. I'm sure you're starving."

Kayla reddened. Evidently, her little run in with Brant hadn't gone unnoticed. She was honest with the girl. "What is your name?"

The girl's smirk blossomed into a full smile. "Wendalyn," she answered with a curtsy.

"Wendalyn," Kayla said, "I have an appetite like a horse. Maybe a pig." The girl giggled. "I eat more than three men put together, and I am famished. If you put it in front of me, I will eat it. I don't want your chef to go to any trouble, but if he has leftovers of a bunch of different things, if you could just bring them all out, I'd be ecstatic."

The girl's eyes widened. "All of it?"

Kayla nodded. "All of it. I am not lying when I say I am famished. I need a lot of food and I need it now. Oh! And cider or grape juice would be fantastic. Just not milk." She shivered. "I hate milk."

Wendalyn giggled again. "And now I know why you dumped it on that young man's head. I'll get some bread, cheese, and cider to get you started, then see what the cook has left."

"Thank you," Kayla said. The girl curtsied once again and almost ran to the kitchen. Kayla tapped her foot while she waited, but it wasn't for long. True to her word, the waitress was back with cold food almost as quickly as she left, and she didn't bring just a glass of cider—she brought an entire pitcher. Kayla could have kissed her for that alone.

An entire loaf of light bread and rich cheese were gone in a matter of minutes, but as she finished, Wendalyn appeared with three plates of food. One had several types of meat arranged on it, another had vegetables, and the last had more bread and cheese. Kayla kept eating. The meat was nearly as good as T'Kato's, though without the spice.

The girl refilled the pitcher of cider, and every time Kayla cleared a plate, Wendalyn brought another. Kayla hadn't eaten so much since the night Brant's father had thrown the ball in her honor. She had just about stuffed herself when the girl returned to collect plates and brought one last dish full of dessert. "That's all there is," Wendalyn said, almost apologetically.

Kayla leaned back and rubbed her stomach. "That's all right. I don't think I could fit much more, anyway. I am about as full as I can get."

The girl set the plate down and gathered up the dishes. "I hadn't believed you when you said you could eat as much as three men. Where do you put it? You're so small!" She glanced at Kayla, then quickly away.

Chuckling, Kayla answered, "My father is Evahn. I guess it's part of his heritage." She took a bite of cheesecake with fresh berries on top. It was heavenly. "Your cook is excellent. Tell him I said thank you."

Wendalyn nodded. "Certainly, though it's not a him. It's my mother. My father runs the lodging and my mother the kitchens." She wiped the table with a rag for a moment, then asked, "Your father truly is Evahn?"

Kayla nodded. "He is. I haven't seen him since I was but a girl, but yes, he married my human mother. Most of me is very human, but my appetite and my ears seem to come from him." Kayla couldn't believe she was telling the girl this.

Wendalyn looked like she wanted to sit down and just talk with Kayla, but she didn't. "I've never met an Evahn before," she said, her arms now loaded with all the dishes.

"I'm only half-Evahn, but it's better than nothing, right?" Kayla laughed. She was surprised at herself. Again, laughing at her heritage had never been her nature. She'd hated being different her entire life. What was it about this girl that made her open up so?

An older woman came out of the kitchen, her red hair pulled back in a bun. She had a cup of some kind of steaming drink in her hand as she approached Kayla's table. When she got close enough, she called out to the girl, who was obviously her daughter. "Wendalyn, are you talking this girl's ear off?"

The serving girl blushed, then left with all the dishes piled in her arms. The cook set the cup down in front of Kayla. "A little thank you for taking all the leavings off my hands. I would have had to feed them to the pigs in the morning, and I hate wasting food like that."

"I think you just did," Kayla answered, rubbing her waist. The woman tried not to laugh, but finally let it out. Kayla picked up the cup of steaming brown liquid and sniffed. "What's this?" she asked. "It's not coffee or tea."

Wendalyn's mother grinned. "We brew it from a soft bean that grows in these parts. Similar to coffee, but it tastes nothing like it. And it will help you sleep." She tapped the side of her nose. "Always a good thing after upsetting evenings."

Great. Even the cook knew about her fight with Brant. She took a sip of the drink and her taste buds erupted. Forget about dessert—the drink was divine. Better than anything she'd ever had. Sweet, but not overly so, and lightened with cream. She downed the cup in only a few swallows before asking, "What is this?"

Wendalyn's mother chuckled. "We call it hot chocolate. Isn't it amazing?"

Kayla couldn't help but agree. Just then, she felt the effect of all the food, and probably the hot chocolate, hitting her. She was exhausted. She scooted back her chair and stood, but before she left, she turned to the woman and said, "You are a fantastic cook, and believe me, I've tasted some of the best. Thank you for your hospitality and for feeding me tonight. It fed more than my body, let me assure you. You and your daughter have fed my soul. Thank you," she said, and stretched out her hand.

The woman smiled, took Kayla's hand and stood herself, then, impulsively, she threw her arms around Kayla. She stiffened at first, then slowly, she returned the hug. When the woman released her, Kayla looked at the cook and her daughter, who had returned by then. "I don't know what it is about the two of you, but you have a gift, one I've needed for too long. Thank you for easing my pain tonight." Mother and daughter looked at one another, both reddening as if they'd been caught doing something wrong. Kayla reassured them as she turned to go. "Don't worry. I won't tell anyone. But thank you again." She put her hands together in front of her, touched her forehead, and bowed. It was the Evahn gesture of gratitude and there was no higher form of praise. Somehow, these two women knew that and held hands, their heads bowing in response.

Kayla turned to go and made her way up to her room, though she became more tired with each step. She got her door open, locked it behind her, and dropped the flute bag in the corner behind the door. Someone had come in and made the bed up for her, and rather than resentment, all she felt was gratitude that she wouldn't have to do one more thing before sleeping. She almost felt drugged. Too much food is apt to do that to a person.

Without another thought or care, she crawled between the sheets and was asleep almost as soon as her head hit the pillow.

Kayla wasn't sure how long she was in her dreamless state before the noise woke her. Before her eyes opened, she knew someone was in the room. She went immediately from sleep to alert, with none of the confusion that usually accompanies a sudden awakening.

She stayed completely still, trying to feel with her newfound power where this intruder was, who he was, before she moved. She debated whether to call out for Brant or T'Kato, but she knew somehow that by the time they arrived in her room with its locked door, she would be dead. No, she would have to handle this on her own.

Somehow.

She was really wishing she had taken T'Kato up on his offer to teach her how to fight with a knife, though it would do her no good. The knife was with the flutes, and she remembered dropping the bag behind the door when she came in.

When her eyes adjusted to the darkness, she saw him—the figure of a man squatting down in the corner behind her door, rummaging through her things. Her heart beat faster as he pulled out the case of the Sapphire Flute. She knew what he was looking for now, but she couldn't let him have it any more than she could let C'Tan have it. She prepared herself by tapping into the flute's power. Kayla had done it before, though she didn't know how or why it was possible. Her plan was in place. She would tackle the man from behind and scream her lungs out to draw attention. She hoped she'd be able to turn the bolt to unlock the door as she approached.

She sat up slowly, drawing the covers back, and tensed her body, ready to leap, when the thief flipped the latch on the flute and opened the case. His back was to Kayla, but she could see the blue glow shining upon him, and she saw he wore a mask.

The deep blue glow touched his face, almost probing and caressing him. Kayla could see the moment the flute realized it lay in a stranger's hands. The blue glow turned an angry white and pulled back like a snake about to strike. The thief seemed oblivious, basking in the instrument's glow. It gathered energy that made Kayla's hair stand with the static charge, and then it struck, pushing against the thief with strength Kayla knew was inhumanly impossible. He dropped the flute when it picked up the man and threw him out the open window, where he sailed over her drying clothes and onto the roof and then the ground below. That was the first Kayla knew the window was open, and she realized he must have come into her room that way.

She heard him tumble from one surface to another and was too shocked to even chuckle as he groaned from far below. Instead, she ran and leaned over the balcony to try to glimpse the intruder, but he was gone. She looked at the distance he had fallen and the cracked tiles where he hit the roof on the level below. He shouldn't have survived the fall. There was something strange and wrong in that the man fell so far and left alive. She only hoped he would limp the following day so she could discover him that way.

She turned from the balcony and clambered back through the window, and went directly to the flute. The case was still open, the bluish-white energy still surrounding the instrument as if it were angry and grumbling. At least, that's what she would have thought, had it been human. She picked up the case and carried it to her bed, then lay back down with the instrument, her fingers gently trailing over the smooth crystal. Slowly, its color changed from near-white back to its original deep sapphire blue, and once it felt calm, she closed the case and latched it, then wrapped her arms around it and quickly went back to sleep with the song of the flute in her ears.

The next morning, Kayla awoke with the birds singing and the sunlight streaming through her open window. She stretched and yawned, her elbow bumping the case of the Sapphire Flute. She wondered what it was doing in her bed, and then she remembered. The intruder. That woke her up quicker than anything else could and in moments, she had collected her dry clothing from the bannister and changed from her night robe. Putting on her Ketahean-style clothing made her miss Sarali suddenly. The girl had become such an integral part of her life, and it just didn't seem right to be running off on a quest without her.

Still, it could not be helped. The world was falling apart, and Kayla held one of the keystones that would help to heal it. She needed to be on her way and find the Wolfchild so the healing could begin and she could go on with her life, though after the fight she'd had with Brant, she was no longer sure what that would be.

Setting aside the heavy thoughts, she pulled on her boots, collected her satchel, and went downstairs. The dining room was nearly empty but for a small group of soldiers talking near the fire. Wendalyn was up and about already, carrying mead or ale to the soldiers in the corner. Kayla shook her head. She had never been one for drinking and the effect it had on others, but to start so early in the morning seemed like it should be illegal.

The red-head stopped at Kayla's table. "You're back, I see. More of the same?" she asked.

Kayla grinned. "Not quite so much, but yes, I'll take whatever you've got, though I would love a half a dozen eggs, some kind of meat, and more of that lovely bread and cheese ought to do it. Oh, and the cider. It was fantastic." She laughed. "I tell you to bring me whatever, and then

I give you my order." She shook her head. "Sorry about that." The girl walked away, chuckling to herself. Kayla put her hands in her lap and watched the soldiers in the corner. The girl returned with the bread, cheese, and cider, just as she had the night before.

The soldiers got louder in their conversation as the alcohol took effect, and Kayla couldn't help but listen. "I can't believe you haven't seen the Shadow Weavers yet," the oldest said to the others. "They leave us alone mostly, unless they want something, but then all a man can do is get out of their way and let them have it. They will rip your heart out without a thought and steal any magic you may have."

"That's impossible," the youngest scoffed, slamming his drink down on the table. "No one can steal your magic."

The other soldiers looked at one another quietly, and one answered. "I used to have a charm I wore about my neck. Belonged to my gran and was passed down to me, since It had been touched by the Guardians. A Weaver found me one night, and with a single reach of his hand, he ate my magic charm and left me with nothing but a silver clasp on a leather leash. I swear it on my mother's grave. The Shadow Weavers can steal magic."

Most of the soldiers laughed. Kayla heard things like, "Superstitious old man," and "Been hitting the spirits, that one has." She almost felt sorry for him. The youngest looked thoughtful and not a little scared. The soldiers were mostly quiet after that, and Kayla inhaled her breakfast as quickly as she could. She wanted to find T'Kato and the others and warn Hadril and Graylin about the Shadow Weavers, if they hadn't heard of them already. She would hate for anything to happen to her new friends.

Wiping her mouth, she got up from the table, took up her bag, and walked out the front door of the inn, where she hoped they had parked the boxcar.

CHAPTER
TWENTY

C'Tan tapped her fingers against the sides of the scrying bowl, the water rippling back and forth with her disturbance. She was barely aware of it but for the patterns it caused to float beneath her eyes. It had been several hours since she'd sent out the call to her minions at the mage academy, and they had yet to respond. Could it really be that difficult to get some place private and contact her?

There would be serious consequences for the delay. She smiled, though it never reached her eyes, she knew. It never did. She dropped the call stones into the rippling water, each plunk a slightly different tone as the bowl filled with the added mass. Once all the stones were in the water, C'Tan tried something different, something Kardon had taught her when he had been the master. She put the tips of her long, manicured fingers into the water and sent out a jolt of power that was supposed to travel through the stones and into her servants—a jolt of pain that should send them scurrying to their hiding places and put them in contact with her shortly.

She was not disappointed.

Within minutes, the first of her minions had connected to her council and his illusionary face floated, glaring, on the surface of the water. One by one they locked in, and within twenty minutes, all were there.

"What is the meaning of this?" Dragon snarled when everyone was present in the council call. "I had to leave my students, claiming sickness to be here. Could this not have waited until evening?"

"Yes," Seer hissed. "I had to leave my station, also claiming sickness. It will not look well on my record, and then what will you do when I am released from my position?"

C'Tan silenced them with her fingers back in the bowl, the waves of pain she sent clear in their faces and in Shadow's flickering cover. C'Tan caught glimpses of her daughter beneath the fog that hid her and stopped when she felt she had their attention.

"I have no desire to hear your complaints," the mistress said quietly, but with no doubt she meant what she said. "When I call, you will answer, no matter what excuses or lies you must tell. You will answer me shortly and attentively. With silence," she said, staring pointedly at Dragon, then Seer.

"Now," she continued, placing both hands on the side of the bowl and leaning in toward it, knowing the effect it would have on their vision, making her seem to be a huge floating head. It was an intimidation tactic Kardon had taught her, one that worked well.

When she knew it ballooned her face large enough to fill a doorway, she stopped, her nose bare inches from the water's surface, and glared. "With Ember having been attacked so recently, you need to speed up your conversion and keep her safe in the meantime. S'Kotos wants her in one piece." This wasn't entirely true. He would *prefer* her in one piece, but if he could claim the keystones for himself, he would no longer need her, and would not care if she lived. For some reason, C'Tan did.

Master Dragon was, of course, the first to object. "She barely got here. How are we supposed to convert her when we haven't even had time to build her trust in us yet, especially when they keep her from classes?"

C'Tan snarled. "I don't care how you do it, Dragon. Get her on our side before it's too late. I doubt Lord S'Kotos will be nearly as patient as I have been. Make it happen."

"But—"

C'Tan put her fingertips in the water, giving just a taste of the pain she could inflict. A grunt sounded from behind the mask, and she stopped. "I said no arguing. Protect the girl. Convert her to our side. I don't care how you do it, but do it. Am I understood?"

The four faces floating in the water all nodded emphatically.

"Good. Now go. Protect her from the shadow weavers. Shadow, stay for a moment," she said as the other faces faded away. The figure that was her daughter re-solidified, but said nothing.

"Drop your cover for a moment. There are no others here, and I wish to see your face while we discuss something." C'Tan said, running her nails along the rim of the bowl and watching the ripples across the water from the movement.

Shadow hesitated for a moment, but then her cover dropped, and C'Tan saw her daughter. A pang of regret ran through her as she saw so much of what Shadow could have been if she hadn't destroyed her soul. There was still hope for this girl and C'Tan hated to use her this way, but she would do what she must. Ember was the key in freeing C'Tan from S'Kotos' chains, and she *would* be free of his chains somehow.

"The Shadow Weavers," C'Tan said, meeting her daughter's eyes. They were blank. Evidently she hadn't heard of them either. "Have you seen this before?" C'Tan held up the necklace Shadow had sent her earlier.

"Only when you had me steal it from him. Before that, no," Shadow answered.

C'Tan nodded. It was what she expected, and she was pleased to know her daughter was not betraying her. But the lack of knowledge about these people, these Shadow Weavers frustrated her. "Have you heard of them?"

Shadow shook her head.

C'Tan growled. "Let me show you what I have seen of them." She stepped back and replayed the scenes from her scrying bowl, specifically the scenes of the leader of the Shadow Weavers and their practice, so

Shadow could see their movement. When C'Tan was done, she leaned forward again, unconsciously this time. "Does anything look familiar?"

Shadow had excitement and fear in her eyes, but shook her head. C'Tan believed her. "I had hoped that since you share a similar gift, something might resonate with you." C'Tan switched topics. "How goes it in befriending the girl?"

Shadow shrugged.

C'Tan glared at her and motioned for her to continue.

Shadow sighed. "She does not trust me. She barely knows me. I will try, but she has not given me many opportunities to speak with her."

"Then make opportunities," C'Tan snarled. "You know more than anyone at that school, including most of the masters. Use your talents and get her to trust you. You, of all of them, have the best opportunity to get to her and pull her to our side. If we can convert her, we won't have to kill her."

Shadow's eyes widened, and C'Tan smiled to herself. Shadow had gotten to know the girl enough to like her. That was good. Perhaps it would push her to redouble her efforts.

"Yes, we will kill her if we must. S'Kotos commands it, Shadow. If you wish to save her life, pull her to our side. Those are my orders. Do you understand?"

Shadow hesitated for a moment, then nodded. "Yes, Moth—Mistress," she said, and faded from the scrying bowl.

C'Tan leaned back and smiled, for the first time feeling as if she might just have a chance at success. Ember was the key to so many things and she would have her, no matter the cost.

At *any* cost, the girl would be hers. She clasped her fingers together and began to laugh.

CHAPTER
TWENTY-ONE

Ember tried to walk normally, casually, so as not to seem bothered or afraid of the two corrupt guards following her and the daughter of C'Tan at her side, but in truth, she was terrified. Her hands wouldn't stop their constant shaking, so she put them inside her sleeves and gripped her forearms like she was a monk. She couldn't do anything about her knees or her heart, but both were hidden from sight—all except the pulse point on her neck that felt as if it were about to rupture and spew her life's blood all over the walls and do the traitors' jobs for them.

The sound of Rahdnee's voice made her jump, but she tried to cover it up with a cough. She couldn't afford to let him know she knew his secret. "Are you afraid of me, Ember? Is that why you are avoiding us?" When Ember didn't answer, he continued. "Because I can assure you, I'm not such a bad guy. Just ask Lily here. She'll tell you I'm okay. I may be a bit strict as a father, but nothing to fear." Ember glanced at Lily, who had gone rigid at her name. She looked back at Ember, and her eyes betrayed her. Lily, too, was afraid of the man. The silence stretched on, and Rahdnee let out a breath. "Seriously, child, why would you fear me?"

Ember took a chance. "I don't fear you—I resent the fact that you are here instead of DeMunth. Every time I see either of you, I think of him lying in the healer halls with no answers. Thank goodness he's finally getting well. I know it's not your fault he's there, and I appreciate your help. I miss him, but no—I don't fear you."

Ember heard a voice sound through her mind—a female voice. *"You should."* When she glanced over her shoulder at Brendae, she knew it had come from her. Mountainous chills coursed through Ember's body, not only because of Brendae's message, but also in the realization that twice in a single day, she had heard thoughts not directed at her. What was happening to her now? It scared her almost as much as the three of them did. She glanced at Lily. Well, the two of them did, anyway. She was feeling more and more as if Lily were caught in a trap, just like she was. She would talk to her today. No matter what, she would find a way to confront Lily about her parentage.

When they arrived at the shielded practice room, Rahdnee and Brendae stepped inside and glanced around the room as if they were checking it for her safety, then they stood inside the room, one on each side of the doorway. Ember turned around in horror, staring at them. She could tell they intended to stay in the room during her practice time. Had it come to this, then? Were they going to kill her now, or drug her and take her to C'Tan? They wouldn't have a better opportunity. There was no one else around.

Ember had walked right into their snare. In trying to save DeMunth, she had given up her own freedom. Perhaps her own life. She looked over at Lily, pleading with her eyes to make the guards go away. Ember wasn't sure whether Lily picked up on Ember's desperation, or had an agenda of her own, but she stood in front of the two guards and put her hands on her hips. "What do you two think you are doing? You will wait *outside* the practice room, not in it."

"If we are to protect the girl, we must be within sight of her," Brendae said in her gravelly voice. "We are not magi, to see through walls. We'll be staying."

"No. You'll be leaving," Lily demanded. She did nothing so dramatic as to point at the door, but her energy and desire pushed at them like a wave. They both swayed on their feet. "You said it yourself. You are not Magi. This room is protected, shielded. None may enter or leave without our consent, but my power does not extend to protecting the two of you when I must protect the two of us. What if Ember destroys the room, like she did the other day? Those breastplates won't protect you from flying boulders, will they?"

Rahdnee looked angry, but resigned. He leaned close to her, and though he spoke quietly, Ember heard him say, "We cannot delay this much longer."

Now Lily did what she hadn't before and pointed at the doorway. The two guards glared at her, but turned and went through the opening single file, the door snapping into place so quickly, Ember heard Brendae gasp and swear even through the stone. She wasn't sure whether it had bumped or nicked her, but either way, Ember was so filled with relief at their departure that she smiled at Lily, and Lily smiled back.

She got to business quickly. "Now, to work. Magic is all about control. You've shown that you have power, but the greatest challenge I think you're going to face, that *any* of us face, is controlling what you have. For some, it's a matter of ramping up the power to make it big enough to create change. For you, it's going to be about funneling it into a stream that will give you control over how quickly it is released. A magical valve, if you will, that you can make larger or smaller, depending on how big of a change you need to make. One thing you need to be aware of, though, is that magic takes power. It can either come from inside of you, which will eventually exhaust you and you will die—" Ember's eyes widened at that "—or you can pull it from people or things around you and funnel it outward. Most people use the latter as much as they can. It will delay the exhaustion, but channeling energy from your surroundings still requires a bit of your personal stock of energy, and it will eventually be depleted if you go too long. Still, it will give you longer use of power. Is that making sense?"

Ember nodded, trying to focus on what Lily was saying and *not* on the fact that she was C'Tan's daughter. "I did some practicing last night. I understand what you're talking about. I felt the valve effect—I thought of it like a nozzle."

Lily looked taken aback. "Really? I'm surprised, though I shouldn't be. You have impressed and surprised me more than once already. Tell me what happened."

Ember told her about her experiment with the floor the night before, and why she experimented on the stone rather than anything else. She told her about the difference in feeling the granite floor versus the crystalline wall, and how she couldn't get it to do anything until she thought of making it firm and made a fist. She also told, and then showed her, how she fixed it again.

"I am thoroughly impressed, Ember. What you did was dangerous to do alone. Your thoughts of being found dead a week later are not unfounded. It's happened before." Lily looked haunted at that. "But it seems as if instinct guided you where I could not. Excellent work."

"Thank you." Ember tried not to beam, but she couldn't help but be pleased with the way things were going. She still hoped Tyese could find a manual or a journal for her, but she was managing in the meantime.

Lily suddenly doubled over and groaned, clutching her stomach. When she glanced up at Ember, her face was white as a sheet. Ember went to her and took her by the shoulders. "Lily? What's wrong? Are you okay?"

C'Tan's daughter groaned again. "I think I must have eaten something that didn't agree with me. I ... I ... I think I need to run to the restroom. Will you be okay here until I get back?"

"Sure, sure, you go. I'll be okay. Just don't let those two in here when you leave, all right?" Ember said, using her chin to nod toward the door and the guards stationed outside.

Lily didn't answer, just nodded and dashed toward the door, opening and closing it so fast, Ember didn't even see Lily in its travel up and down. It was like she had turned to shadow or mist. Strange.

Ember lay down on the floor and started thinking. She knew she should practice, but she was worried about Lily, even knowing her genetics. Suddenly, her head exploded with an understanding. If Lily was C'Tan's daughter, and C'Tan was her father's sister, then didn't that make Lily her—cousin? For some odd reason, realizing that gave her a sense of comfort rather than fear. Lily was of her blood. Thinking of her now, she could see certain similarities between herself, father, and C'Tan.

She had a cousin. The thought made her all glowy inside, even with the complications it presented. She had family on her father's side, someone with whom she actually shared blood. She loved her step-brothers. They were like true brothers to her, but other than her mother and Uncle Shad, she'd not met anyone with whom she shared blood, and for that to once again come from her father's side, where she knew so little of his family, meant so very much.

Ember suddenly wondered if she had cousins on her mother's side. Did her mother have any brothers or sisters? If so, she'd never spoken of them. She made a mental note to ask the next time she saw her. It seemed odd that she was getting to know her dead father's family faster than her living mother's.

Lily came back sooner than Ember expected. She was only gone about ten or fifteen minutes before the door surged up and back down with normal speed. Ember quirked an eyebrow and glanced at the doorway. "Are you feeling any better?" Then, realizing she hadn't seen Rahdnee and Brendae outside, she asked, "Where are the guards?"

Lily shrugged. "Gone. I don't know where. Now, where were we?" She tried to jump right back into work, but the realizations Ember had while she was gone just couldn't be kept inside.

The words seemed to jump out of Ember. She didn't think she could have stopped them if she'd wanted. "I know who you are," she said, repeating the words Markis had thought at Lily earlier. They had the same effect coming from Ember as they had from him. Lily went white as Ember's robes and she backed away slowly. Ember took a step forward for every one Lily took back.

"I know your father is a traitor, a spy, sent from C'Tan." Lily's cheeks went red as the rest of her face went even whiter, if possible. At that point, she was against the wall and trembling. Ember took two more steps so that her mouth was by Lily's ear and she whispered, "I know who your mother is."

At those words, Lily disappeared, and in her place was a slightly human-shaped puff of smoke that seemed to blend in with the rock. Ember jerked back in surprise, and the smoke or shadow or whatever it was edged toward the doorway. Ember stepped over to block it and willed the door to stay closed. As the shadowy girl approached the door and it didn't open, she circled the room, seemingly in a panic, and eventually stopped, cowering near the vein of red gemstone.

"I'm not here to hurt you or turn you in," Ember said, still in front of the doorway. She had to get Lily to see reason. Once she left this room, she was afraid she'd disappear entirely, never to be seen again. "You're family, Lily. I wouldn't hurt you for anything, even if I've just met you." The shadow stopped shivering and seemed to focus its attention on Ember. Encouraged, she continued.

"I know it's hopeless for your father. I saw him talking to C'Tan and I know he is planning to hurt or kill me or something, and I can't let him do that. I'm here for a reason. I was *born* for a reason and given this gift of white magic, even if I don't know how to use it yet. And I think you were sent here for a reason, too. How many magi are there who can do all the colors of magic?"

There was a long pause, then Lily's cautious voice came from the corner. "Only one. You."

Frustrated, Ember stomped her foot. "No, Lily. I mean, yes, I'm the only white mage, but how many sixers are there? People like you?"

Again, a long pause before Lily answered. "Not many."

Ember took a step toward her. "Exactly! Why let C'Tan use you for her purposes when you can do so much good here? So much good with *me*. I need you, Lily. I need your help, your training, your understanding, and I'd very much like your friendship. We're family," she repeated. "I want us to act like one. Like a real one. Not the kind of unhealthy relationship your father gives you."

Lily's shadow got taller and Ember assumed she stood. Her shadow cover began flickering on and off, and it reminded Ember of the shadow weavers who had attacked her a few days before. How did she do that?

"We're family? How?" Lily asked, her voice suddenly taking on strength and genuine curiosity.

"Your mother was my father's sister. We're cousins," Ember said, leaning against the wall."

At that, Lily's shadow cover dropped completely, and she stood on the other side of the room with her mouth agape. Ember stole one of Aldarin's favorite lines. "Close your mouth, Lily. You look like a fish."

Lily's jaw closed with a snap. "We're cousins? But . . . my mother killed your father. They were siblings?"

Ember sobered at the reminder. "Yes, on both counts."

The color returned to Lily's face, and her mouth tightened. "I knew she was depraved, but I had no idea how much. How did you find out about me and my father?"

Ember debated whether to tell her, but she'd just exposed Lily—it was only fair to give her something in return. "The past few days, ever since the attack from the Shadow Weavers, sometimes I pop out of my body."

Lily looked alarmed at that, so Ember rushed to reassure her. "It's not like I'm dead. My body still works. It breathes, but it's in a dream-like state. Part of me separates from my body, and I can see strands of light that connect me to people." That reminded her of the chains binding her to DeMunth and she shivered, though whether it was from the memory of his kiss or his hands rubbing her back, or something else, she wasn't sure. "Last night after practice, I was so exhausted, I lay back on the ground and popped out of my body. I saw a strand I didn't recognize and followed it." She met Lily's eyes. "It led to C'Tan."

Lily's eyes narrowed at that, but Ember continued. "Her face was in a bowl and she was talking to Rahdnee, telling him she needed him to hurry and either convert me or bring me to her. When I realized they were talking about me, I left and went to DeMunth. That's why I slept in the healer hall. When I realized that not only was he a spy, but most likely Brendae and you as well, I didn't feel safe, so I went to the one person I felt safe with. And now even that is taken from me."

Lily ignored the last part and stepped toward Ember, stopping near the middle of the room. "If you know all this, why haven't you reported it to Ezeker? Why take the chance of telling me?"

For a long moment, Ember didn't answer. She hung her head, thinking, then lifted it to meet Lily's eyes, surprisingly much like her own. "Because you are family. And because I've seen the same fear of Rahdnee in you that I've felt in myself. He may be your father, but he terrifies you, too."

Lily's brows rose. Her mouth quirked, then she nodded once, sharply.

Encouraged by that admission, Ember continued. "I trust you, Lily. I don't know why, but there is something inside me that tells me I don't need to fear you."

At that, all the tension left Lily's shoulders, and she slumped to the ground, not in a faint, but as if the strength had left her. It was the most vulnerable Ember had seen her. Tears sprang up in the girl's eyes. "You have no reason to trust me, and every reason to spurn me, and yet you embrace me as one of your own. I don't understand it, but I am grateful for it. Surely, some part of me must be okay if we share the same family. I can't be all bad, can I?"

Ember came to her and sat cross-legged, just as Lily was. "I don't think any of you is bad, Lily. I think you've just been taught that you had no choice."

It was obvious Ember had hit the mark with the expression on Lily's face.

"You *do* have a choice. And from what I hear, our Grandma Asana is quite a woman. I have yet to meet her, but Uncle Shad says she would be a wonderful grandma to me. I can imagine how much happier it would make her to gain not one granddaughter, but two."

Lily's lip quivered. "I have a grandmother?" she whispered.

Ember nodded.

A single tear trailed down Lily's face before she got her emotions under control and seemed to come to a decision. "I'll help you, Ember. And if the day comes when you get to meet our grandmother—I'd love to come with you."

Ember put her hand on Lily's shoulder. "You've got it. I promise."

Lily smiled. "Okay then, we need to come up with a plan. I hear you're able to shift your shape, that it's not just an illusion, or an alternate form, but you can look like a different person. Is that true?"

Ember was surprised. That little bit of knowledge had been kept very quiet. She nodded her head slowly. "Yes, it's true. I was disguised as a boy most of the time I was in Javak, though I never changed the parts that make me a girl." Ember reddened. "I just couldn't do it."

Lily chuckled. "I don't blame you. I'd have a hard time with that as well." She looked Ember over for a moment. "Do you think you could shift your appearance as a girl just enough to keep Rahdnee and Brendae from recognizing you?"

Ember had already done exactly that to take her bath in Javak, so she knew she could. "Oh, yes. Absolutely."

The gleam in Lily's eye was wonderful to see. "Then let's sneak off to the baths, have you 'change,' and head to the dining room to test it out, shall we?"

"But how do we get past the guards?" Ember asked, glancing at the doorway.

Lily chuckled again. "There is a back exit. It's hidden, so the guards don't know about it. We'll go that way. It's closer to the baths, anyway."

Lily stepped to the other side of the room, pressed a knobby protrusion in the wall, and a hole opened into another tunnel. Ember could smell the water from there. Grinning, the two girls ducked through the doorway and moved down the hall, the stone door grating closed behind them.

CHAPTER
TWENTY-TWO

The box car was in the same place it had been the night before, and Hadril and Graylin were already doing a steady business. Everyone from the group was there, including the boy, Jayden, who seemed to have gotten over his anger. He helped the brothers by taking orders for Hadril and depositing items to be repaired around the back of the wagon for Graylin. They must have been up before daylight to beat her. That, or they hadn't eaten breakfast. At the moment, she didn't care. She tried to ignore Brant and Niefusu, who both stared at her, and instead she climbed into the back of the wagon and went to speak to the two peddlers.

"Do you have a minute?" she asked when there was a break in the crowd.

Graylin turned around, his hip against the counter, and said, "Sure. Go ahead." Hadril unconsciously took the same stance as his brother.

"Have you ever heard of the Shadow Weavers?" she asked, leaning against the shelves opposite them, her bag digging into her side.

The brothers looked at one another, then nodded. "We've heard rumors, but we thought that's all they were. Every community has some boogeyman or another," Hadril answered for the both of them. Graylin nodded.

Kayla gnawed at the inside of her cheek. "I was just in the dining room and I overheard some soldiers talking about the Shadow Weavers. One of them claims that a magicked charm that had been his grandmother's was turned to dust, leaving only the setting and leather behind. That doesn't sound made up to me," she said, adjusting her bag to swing around front.

Hadril shrugged and turned to a new customer, asking for something for her joint pain. Graylin answered instead. "True or not, there's not much we can do about them, but we appreciate the warning. We'll take it more seriously, now that you've said something." He looked her over and cocked his head. "Something else is wrong. What is it?"

She told him about the intruder who had come into her room during the night. Graylin laughed when he heard about the flute defending itself and throwing the thief out the window, but when she finished, he was serious.

"Are you all right?" he asked, putting a hand on her shoulder and staring into her eyes. She nodded, unable to look away for a moment. "I'm fine," she said, breaking the connection between them. "He didn't even know I was awake."

"And you're sure it was a man?" he asked. "I know plenty of women who would steal that instrument just for the beauty of its tones, never mind what it is."

She shook her head. "It was a man. He was thick in the shoulders. Athletic. I'm not sure how tall he was, but he definitely didn't have a womanly figure." Kayla blushed when she said that, but how else was she supposed to tell him it was not a woman? It didn't seem to bother Graylin.

"Hmmmm," he said, crossing back to the counter and stroking his short beard. "We'll have to look into that as well. You cannot afford to lose that instrument. Even on the road, we have heard stories of the bearer of The Sapphire Flute, and how she battled C'Tan and won."

Kayla reddened, not knowing what to say. She was saved by the entrance of T'Kato. He leaped into the wagon without using his hands, the whole thing shaking at his entrance. Most of the time, she forgot how big he was.

The tattooed man pointed out the back of the wagon, seeming angry. "We have got to do something about those two before they kill each other." He didn't need to explain who he meant. It had been obvious from the moment the two met that Brant and Niefusu would be enemies. That's just what happened when two men loved the same woman.

She sighed and buried her face in her hands, shaking her head. What was she to do?

Hadril, bless his soul, came up with the solution. "Separate them," he said while counting change to his customer.

Kayla and T'Kato looked at each other, then at Hadril as he finished doing business, then back at each other and smiled. She wasn't sure what T'Kato had in mind, but she could certainly think of several things that would keep Brant busy.

Now if only they hadn't just broken off their engagement. He would never forgive her impertinence and the embarrassment the soup and milk on his head would have caused. But forgiveness, both him toward her, and her toward him, was a key in separating Brant and Niefusu.

Hadril turned and addressed them fully. "I will ask Niefusu to help me here. Jihong has already taken the water horses to the lake to fill themselves. And he is searching for herbs. I need an assistant, and Niefusu will do nicely. He knows more about herbs than Brant does, anyway. Kayla, I know you are angry with Brant, but he truly loves you. Take him to the forest. Eat together. Spend time away from the village—perhaps even spend the night out there together."

Kayla blushed. "I don't . . . we haven't . . . I mean—" she started, but Hadril stopped her with an upraised hand.

"That is not what I meant. Just be together and heal. You haven't had time alone since you reunited, have you?"

She shook her head.

He continued. "Then now is the time. Go to him. Rent horses from the inn, collect a basket of food, and just leave. It is the best thing you can do." Hadril looked at T'Kato, a twinkle in his eye. "For all of us."

T'Kato looked like he wanted to object, and she knew exactly what he was thinking. He was worried about leaving them alone, unprotected, but the flute had proven it could protect her the night before. T'Kato was gracious enough not to say anything. Kayla pushed herself away from the counter, and as she passed T'Kato, she put a hand on his arm and said, "We'll be okay. I promise."

The tattooed man hesitated, then nodded stiffly and jumped down from the boxcar. Kayla's mind raced. She had to handle this just right if she was going to get Brant to cooperate. Rather than going in search of him, she ran back to the inn and told Wendalyn her plight, then went to the stable and asked the stable master if she could take two horses until the next day. He, being one of those who had kissed her cheek after her performance, did not hesitate to saddle two of his finest horses for her. She thanked him and promised to return the following day.

Back to the inn she went, tying the horses' reins to the ring post out front and running inside. Wendalyn approached her with a large satchel of food and two saddlebags full of cooking gear and bota water skins. Wendalyn grinned and helped Kayla put the saddlebags on the horses. Excited about the prospect of spending time with Brant, but still nervous, Kayla gave the serving girl a hug of thanks, put her foot in the stirrup, and mounted the black horse to return to the boxcar.

T'Kato had more supplies for her there, and somehow she found room for sleeping gear and something special from Hadril. It was a perfume he created from the combination of flowers Niefusu had braided into her hair. Probably not the best gift for Niefusu's competition, but there was no denying how wonderful it smelled, and Kayla hoped that wearing it without the visual reminder of the flowers would soften Brant toward her. She took it thankfully and dabbed a bit behind her ears.

Then came the hardest part. It was time to find Brant. Well, finding him wasn't hard. She knew exactly where he was—but facing him would be a challenge.

T'Kato pointed him out on the far side of the clearing, chopping wood with an axe in the blistering sun. He'd removed his shirt, and the sweat gleamed on his skin as she approached. She ached for him. So many times, she had watched him perform this exact task back home and admired the sheen of sweat that seemed to make his muscles so much larger. She knew it was an illusion, a silly thing, really, but she loved looking at him. She sat atop the horse for several minutes while he chopped and hacked, obviously trying to get his frustration to leave.

His hair was wet with sweat, but not sticky as it should have been from the soup and milk, so evidently she wasn't the only one who had bathed the night before. She was glad about that. She'd have felt even worse knowing he'd had to sleep in the mess she had created. She slid down from the horse and walked up behind him. When he straightened for a moment to wipe his brow and rest, she gently touched his shoulder.

Brant spun around quickly, the axe raised in front of him as if he expected an attack. Of course, with Niefusu around, he probably was. When he saw who was before him, he slowly lowered the axe, his eyes fastened on Kayla's as if she were a lifeline. She saw hurt there. Sadness and sorrow, but also love. Still, so much love shone in his eyes that she couldn't help herself. Despite his sweaty skin, she threw herself against him with a cry, the tears pouring from her eyes before she even knew they were there.

"Oh, Brant. I am so sorry. I should not have treated you the way I did. Please forgive me? Please, please, forgive me?" Her tears mingled with his sweat. It was only a fraction of a second before his arms were around her and he caressed her hair.

"Shhh. It's okay, Kayla. I forgive you. I was being unreasonable and deserved it. I wasn't thinking. I was so mad with jealousy. It should be me asking forgiveness, not you." He squeezed her tight, seeming almost afraid to let her go.

For several minutes, they stood that way, taking comfort from one another in touch before Brant pulled away and went to get his shirt. He pulled something out of his pocket, though Kayla could not see what it was. When he returned, he kissed her once, a gentle kiss that made the world spin, and then he dropped to one knee. "I know I have asked before, but I have been undeserving of your answer these past few days. Now I ask once more. Kayla Kalandra Felandian, would you be my wife?" He presented her with the charm bracelet he'd bought for her in Darthmoor.

Kayla held her breath. It was so beautiful, reflected in the sunlight. The tears started up again and Kayla could say nothing, but nodded her head and put out her left arm for him to fasten the bracelet. He did so with shaking hands, then stood and kissed her again. She kissed him with as much passion in return, and it wasn't until they broke apart that she appreciated the fact that they were alone.

Brant embedded the axe in the log with one swing, then put his shirt on and glanced at the horses, then looked again. "Are we going somewhere?"

Kayla laughed. "Oh, yes, Brant. We get a whole day and a night to ourselves. It's all planned. No Niefusu. No T'Kato. No villagers or family or friends to disturb us. Just you and me. Are you up for it?" she asked, waggling her eyebrows at him.

He puckered his lips as if he were fighting a smile and answered, "I've been dying to get you to myself for days. Let's go!"

Brant swung up onto the larger horse and Kayla mounted her mare, and together they rode into the woods, away from civilization and Brant's competition. She had twenty-four hours to convince him he was the love of her life, and she was determined to do everything she must to make it so.

CHAPTER
TWENTY-THREE

The pools were as wonderful as they had been after her disastrous classes, though not as impressive as the baths at Javak with their towering, heated waterfalls. Still, it was nice to clean up once again and get her hair washed, and even more fun doing it with Lily, now that the walls were down between them.

C'Tan's daughter seemed a different person, one Ember genuinely liked. It had been a long time since she'd had a female friend, someone other than Aldarin, and she found herself very grateful for it, and the fact that Lily was true family made it even better.

Once done, they got out of the pools, collected fresh robes and underclothes, and went into a private dressing room. Normally they would have each gotten their own, but Ember wanted Lily to check her work when she shifted and be sure that everything was in place. She would hate to go out in public with a droopy eye or something. So they dressed quickly, then Ember sat on the stool while Lily leaned against the wall, her hands behind her back, and Ember began to change. At least this time, it was just her face she was changing, and not her whole body. That would make it easier. And then she had second thoughts about that. Her body was part of who she was. If she was truly going to be in disguise, it would probably be best to make a few subtle shifts to her body as well. Ember sighed. It was going to hurt, but this time she wouldn't have an achy backside from sprouting a tail.

Ember started with her nose, pulling and lengthening it, then flaring the nostrils a bit. After that, she moved on to her eyes and cheekbones, her forehead and chin, then changed her hair from deep brown to a dark blonde and lengthened it, adding some natural wavy curls. She opened her eyes and looked at Lily then, checking her reaction. The girl's eyes were bugging out of her head. Ember grinned. Lily stepped forward and touched Ember's face, then shivered. "That's just eerie. I've never seen anything like it."

"Do you think I'm weird?" Ember asked, suddenly unsure of herself.

"No," Lily answered. "Just different. Are you going to make any other changes?"

"Yes," Ember said. "I think it would be a good idea to make a few body changes. A body can be as identifiable as a face, don't you think?"

"Oh, definitely," Lily answered, and leaned back against the wall. Ember prepared herself and went to the one thing she said she would never change. Her chest. She'd always been a modest size, and she considered going bigger, but was afraid that would draw a different kind of attention, one she didn't want, so she shrank her breast size down just a little. It would serve two purposes. One in making her more unidentifiable, and two, it would make her look younger. After that, she added about fifteen pounds to her body, broadened her shoulders, and shortened her neck.

She was drenched in sweat when she finished and wished she had waited to take her bath until after she had shifted, but it was too late now. She didn't want to bathe again. It took too long. One more change and she would be done. After having shrunk her chest to make herself look younger, she made her face look a few years younger as well. She rounded it a little more, made her eyes bigger, and called it good. She glanced at Lily, who was shaking her head.

"You don't look like you're even related to yourself," she said.

"That's kind of the point." Ember gathered up her towel and moved to open the door. "Is everything in place? Am I fit for public viewing?" she asked, her stomach suddenly aflutter.

Lily's smile was enough to reassure her. "Oh, yes. You look great. Hey," she said, grabbing Ember's elbow before she could leave. "Thank you. I don't know if I'll ever be able to tell you what you've done for me. I feel free for the first time in my life."

Ember put her hand on Lily's shoulder, then impulsively pulled her into a hug. Lily was stiff at first, then suddenly melted against her, as if all the walls had fallen down, and when they pulled away, there were tears in her eyes. The girl cleared her throat, then said, "I've been thinking. If we go anywhere together, people are eventually going to guess who you are. I'll go to the dining hall, but I'm going to sit apart from you, okay? We'll have to figure out sleeping arrangements later, but for now, let's pretend we don't know each other. It's safer."

Ember didn't like it, but she knew Lily was right. She nodded and finally opened the door and stepped through. After depositing her towel in the bin, she took a deep breath, stepped into the hall, and turned toward the eatery.

Ember walked casually down the hallway in her multi-colored robe, everyone oblivious to who they passed. Ember's first teacher, the one from the green room, strolled by, glancing her way, then moved by without pause. She sighed with relief and continued on, finding her way to the dining hall much more by smell than memory.

She scrambled a bit as she reached the doorway and came face-to-face with Tiva and Ren. "Excuse me," Ren said, smiling at her and stepping to the side.

"No, excuse me." Ember modulated her voice just a bit as she tried to squeeze past her twin half-brothers, and then Ezeker.

"Has anybody seen Ember today?" she heard Ren ask as they walked away from her.

"Nah," answered Tiva. "She probably found the bathing pools and is soaking her skin off." She hid her smile as she walked into the dining room. Yes, she had been to the baths, but she'd walked away with more than just clean skin.

Picking up her tray and getting her food, she watched the doorway and saw Lily enter. They both tried hard to ignore each other, but Ember was aware of everything Lily did.

After gathering her food, Ember decided to test her disguise on people she knew and headed toward her mother. It might not have been the best choice, but she'd fooled her once before, this woman who knew her better than anyone else. Marda was a good place to start. And Aldarin was sitting right beside her. Him, she had *never* fooled. This would be a major test as to whether or not she could fool Rahdnee.

Ember approached their table, set down her tray across from her mother, stuck out a hand and said, "Hi, I'm Bettina. What's your name?" She heightened the tone of her voice, just like she had for the twins, making herself sound slightly ditsy.

"Do I know you?" Marda asked, ignoring Ember's outstretched hand.

Ember wanted to laugh, but was partially worried that her mother had recognized her somehow. She shook her head and dropped her hand. "No, I'm new," she said, sitting down and digging into her food.

Ember could feel Aldarin's gaze dissecting her, but she said nothing as she ate. Finally Marda burst out with, "I'm rather new to the school myself, but I know you didn't come in with the last group, and I've never seen you before. Where are you from?" She sounded very suspicious and watched Ember's face as if trying to see beneath her skin.

Oh, boy. Ember thought, her brain scrambling for an answer. She took a guess and plastered on her most vapid smile. "Oh, I'm from one of the other schools. I just transferred in from a mage academy way east of here. They didn't know what to do with me," she said, leaning in toward her mother as if it were a big secret. "They said I didn't know the difference between granite and marble, but that's ridiculous. Of course, I know the difference."

"Really?" Marda didn't sound like she believed her. "What school? Maybe I know it."

Ember kept eating, snarfing down her food as if she were a bottomless pit. She felt like her stomach was going to eat its way right out of her belly with all the magic she'd done that morning. Shapeshifting was hard work.

Ember filled her mouth, then held a finger up in the universal sign of, "One minute," and wracked her brain for an answer while she chewed. She didn't even know if there was more than one mage academy. "It's a school for orange magic near the mountains of Kafutu." Were there mountains called Kafutu? She didn't know, but if there were, she hoped they were nowhere near here.

Marda scrunched her brow, obviously thinking, then shook her head. "No, I don't know that one. I have never heard of the Kafutu mountains. Where are they? Do you know?" she turned toward Aldarin, but he seemed to be trying to keep from laughing. He caught Ember's eye and winked. Ember wanted to shake her head. He'd seen through her disguise again. How did he do that?

"I told you, you wouldn't know it," Ember said, and laughed. "They're far, far away. Way east of here on another continent. I think my parents were trying to get rid of me, sending me out here where I don't know anyone." She should have thought of a better story before. She hadn't realized her own mother would interrogate her, though she should have. Marda always questioned everything. She was beginning to regret her choice in testing her disguise on her own mother.

She glanced across the room as Lily sat down with a group of kids Ember didn't know. She caught her eye across the room and Lily nodded her head quickly, a new version of a thumbs-up.

They ate in silence for several long moments, Ember feeling like a bug under a magnifying glass, when she felt a heavy hand on her shoulder. She glanced up, startled to see DeMunth staring down at her, a puzzled look on his face. He looked at Marda, then Aldarin, who was trying desperately not to laugh, then back at Ember. He opened his mouth to speak, then glanced at Marda again, who was openly staring at him, curiosity written all over her face, and closed his mouth with a snap.

"What is going on here? It's obviously something, as your mother doesn't seem to know you, and yet you look exactly as you should," he mindspoke, his eyes boring into hers like a worm into the earth.

"I was testing my disguise," she answered, glancing at her mother to gauge her reaction. *"And you are about to give it away. Will you just sit down already and pretend you don't know me? Please? And how did you see through it when no one else can?"*

DeMunth took his hand off her shoulder, his lips tight and eyes flaring. "I'm sorry," he said with his new tongue. "I thought you were someone else. Is this seat taken?" He moved next to her and sat down without an answer or invitation.

Ember shook her head and went back to her food. If she felt like a bug before, now she felt like she stood naked in a crowd. DeMunth continued to speak to her in his mind, though he didn't glance her way. *"I've always been able to see through your changes to the person beneath."*

Ember didn't know how DeMunth could see through her changes, no matter what they were, but knowing that he could explained a lot of things. It was no wonder he could be attracted to her, even as a boy. He didn't see the boy. He saw *her.* There was no escaping him. How could she manage this if she couldn't hide in plain sight? She filed his revelation in the back of her mind.

He continued. *"Why did you leave so quickly? We need to speak of things, Ember. How am I to guard you if you won't help yourself by staying nearby?"*

Ember stiffened at that question. She was so tired of being watched all the time. Couldn't people trust her to care for herself? She wasn't one of the littles who needed constant supervision. She was nearly a grown woman and had a power none had seen in millennia. Ember wanted him to treat her like a woman, not a little girl. *"I don't need a guard,"* she sent back to him. *"I can take care of myself."*

DeMunth choked at that, her response having made him inhale his food. He coughed and coughed, Aldarin coming around the table to slap him on the back.

Just then, Rahdnee and Brendae stepped through the doorway and looked around the room. They nodded to Lily, then glanced at Ember and past her as if she didn't exist at all. She sighed with relief, then looked back at DeMunth. They would figure it out soon because DeMunth was with her. He was still too weak to protect her. She couldn't let him get hurt, not because of her.

All eyes went to her as she stood. She wasn't sure why until she glanced down and realized her robes had gone from multicolored to their original white. She'd just given herself away. DeMunth stopped coughing and grabbed her arm. *"What's wrong?"* Ember didn't answer. Rahdnee and Brendae started toward her as a large group of kids came through the door. Ember took that moment of distraction to escape.

Ember shook off DeMunth's hand and jumped over the table, racing for the doorway. She knocked several of the kids aside as she ran, pounding feet sounding behind her. She didn't know if it was DeMunth, Lily, or the guards, but somebody was after her and she couldn't afford to be caught, not by any of them. Either she would be hurt or they would, and she couldn't let either happen.

The anger filled her like a bellows and stole away all other thought. She just wanted to be invisible, to blend in. Why couldn't things be easier?

The anger built to a breaking point and Ember's two legs couldn't carry her fast enough. Without thought, she pulled at the power within her, and in an instant she changed from girl to wolf and raced down the paths on all fours. Students and instructors alike scattered before her, some squealing, others trying to hurt or catch her, but she eluded them all and raced for the portals. She leaped through the first one, the trip long and breathless, but the trek got shorter with each jump. She went through portal number three, then back into familiar territory, and knowing there were no more portals if she continued, she turned and raced through the abandoned tunnels, looking for the scent of magic to pull her to more portals.

She had to find a place to be alone, a place that could be just hers, away from all the others so they wouldn't get hurt. Somehow, she would get word to Ezeker and DeMunth, but for now, she had to hide. No one was safe with her around. Not even the other students.

Ember found another portal just past the waterfall cavern. She jumped through it, this one a longer leap that left her on the other side without breath, but she kept running and searching for more until she was thoroughly lost.

She found one last portal and dove through. It was probably the eighth or ninth one she had entered, but this one was different. When she came out the other side, there was no open runway like the others had. This one came out mere feet from a quartz wall. She was racing so fast as she leaped through that she couldn't stop, despite her desperate attempt to skid to a halt. Ember slammed into the wall, but didn't stop there. She melted into the quartz like butter into toast and sat just inside the wall without moving, hoping against hope that the mountain hadn't just eaten her like it had the poor skeletal man Ezeker had shown her group on their way in.

When the stone didn't harden around her, Ember took a chance and moved forward, one paw at a time, her tail standing straight out as she walked through solid stone. She knew she could do this with her hands, but it had never occurred to her she could move her entire body through rock.

Moving through the quartz felt much as she imagined walking through honey would feel. Definite resistance, but she could still progress. Far away, a light shone. It looked like a white magelight bobbing in the distance, though what a magelight would be doing in solid stone, she did not know.

But Ember was curious and definitely did not want to go back at the moment. She couldn't take any chances of bringing attention to herself or the people she loved—not the kind of attention Rahdnee and Brendae had in mind for her. Here she was, the first white mage in three thousand years, and people wanted her dead.

Ember followed the light, hoping only that the consequence of doing so wouldn't kill her. She'd take just about any chance she could right now if it would free her from the failure of her magic, the treachery of the spies, and keep DeMunth safe.

Now, if only the white light would lead her to her father, she could finally have some peace. Not knowing where she was going, Ember put her focus on the light and slid through the stone.

CHAPTER
TWENTY-FOUR

As soon as Kayla and Brant entered the forest, the temperature dropped. The shade was very welcome after the heat of the morning rays. The sound changed as well. Rather than the noise of busy people, everything was muffled—even the steps of their mounts—and they were instead surrounded by birdsong and insect trills. It was a comforting sound. Kayla felt the forest calling to her, but she ignored it for the moment, instead just reveling in the feel of these ancient woods surrounding her. She didn't need to speak to them to know how old the trees were or how untouched these woods were by human hands.

They rode in silence for a while, not really caring where they went. It was just the quiet comradery of friendship grown to love that required no speech. Brant moved his mount close to Kayla's and reached out. She met his fingers, and they rode for several minutes that way, their fingers intertwined, healing the breach between them, until the uneven ground forced them apart. But it was all right. Just being together in this sacred place was healing for both of them. Kayla could feel it was indeed a sacred place, ancient as it was.

Brant finally spoke, asking she had dreaded most. "Why did you let him kiss you?" The hurt was still there, lacing his voice like acid.

She was quiet for a moment, trying to frame her thoughts into words. "I didn't let him, exactly," she said, then rushed on. "You have to understand something. In the sea world, no human can survive without gills or air bubbles surrounding their heads. Sarali created an air bubble for me and replenished it whenever I needed more. But they pop when you enter an oxygen-filled area, and beneath the bottom of the sea is a lattice of air tunnels connecting place to place."

"Really?" he asked, fascinated, and temporarily distracted from his question, though she knew that wouldn't last long.

"Truly," she answered. She took a deep breath and continued, knowing this was the part he would hate. "When Niefusu and Jihong came to the passage where T'Kato, Sarali, and I were staying, they demanded that Sarali go with them to see the king and queen. T'Kato would not let them take her without him, of course, and if I had stayed in the tunnel, I would have been all alone with no idea which direction to go, so I demanded that Niefusu take me with them." She looked down and fiddled with the reins, wrapping them loosely around the pommel of the saddle, then unwrapping them. "I thought Niefusu would do the same as Sarali and create a bubble for me and then place it over my head, but instead he pulled me to the edge, where water met air, and at that junction he kissed me, then pulled my head into the water, exhaling so that the bubble would cover me. I did not like it, Brant. Not at all," she said, looking at him.

Brant wouldn't meet her eye, but he seemed to listen, so she continued. "During the trip, my bubble almost disappeared, so he replenished my air the same way. I didn't understand at the time that he was taking advantage of me. He tried it a third time that evening, and I was about to fight him when he bit me and gave me the gills. I didn't know what it meant. I hadn't thought to tell him about you—not because I was hiding you, but because I didn't trust him. He didn't need to know. Does that make sense?"

She looked at Brant and he tried to flick away a tear as if it were nothing more than a bug, but she knew how deeply this hurt him. He remained silent, so she continued.

"I never encouraged him, Brant. I give you my word that I never once told him I was interested in him. Sarali said he was stubborn and would not give up easily, but I did not know how difficult it would be. I don't want anyone else. I don't trust anyone but you. How could I even think of wedding another?" Kayla tried to touch out to him, but he rode just out of reach.

Frustrated, she entered a clearing and stopped. Brant was nearly across the meadow and into the trees again before he realized she was not with him. He turned his horse, looking at her with questioning eyes. She stared at him, waiting for an answer. Finally, he sighed, his shoulders slumped, and he returned to her. When his horse was nearly beside hers, he pulled it to a halt and looked at her, tears brimming in his eyes. He didn't hide them this time, and Kayla's immediately filled in response.

"All I thought of was you," she said, her voice hoarse. "All I wanted was to get back to you and find out if you had survived the fall from the grasp of C'Tan's dragon. Your words as you fell those last few feet haunted me night after night. I wondered if I had killed you with my stupidity. I wondered if I had destroyed Dragonmeer. It nearly broke me to think of losing you. Why would I then turn to another?" She was sobbing by the time she ended, and now Brant brought his mount even closer so that at last he could reach out and take her fingers with his own.

He stared at the ground as he spoke; the light coming through the trees dappling them both. "I had the healer mend the worst of my injuries, and despite my parents' wishes, I left to find you. I took every hound we had, every tracker and hunter. We followed your path through the woods and saw the trees made into javelins. We found the place where one of you became the MerCat. Sarali, I'm assuming." Kayla nodded. "We followed you to the burned spots that still smoldered with dragon fire and followed your path as you separated from them. The hounds . . ." he choked up and struggled to continue. "The hounds led me to the

211

cliff where they found your blood. *Your blood!*" he cried, squeezing her fingers tight and at last lifted his head to meet her eyes. Both of them cried openly. "I couldn't find you, Kayla. You saved me by playing the flute, and I couldn't find you to save you in return." His voice choked on a sob. "I just wanted to save you. I couldn't live without you, Kayla. You're my everything. You always have been. Don't you know that?"

She reached across and pulled him into her arms, awkward though it was. The horses shuffled a little to compensate for the change of weight, but beyond that, they didn't move. Now it was Kayla's turn to soothe Brant as he sobbed into her shoulder. He wasn't one to show his feelings, unless it was anger or happiness. She had seen him cry on so few occasions she could remember them all, but she had never seen him cry like this.

"Hush, love. Hush, now. It's all right. I haven't gone anywhere, and I am *not going* anywhere. I am yours, remember? Yours. I will be Duchess Brant Domanta. I want no other. Not even the son of a king," she said, smoothing his hair and rubbing his back.

At her last words, he pulled back and searched her eyes. "Truly? You mean that?"

Exasperated, she answered, "Well, of course! Why would I be interested in the son of a king when the king of my heart is right here?"

It was a bit melodramatic, perhaps, but it was true. Brant ruled her heart and would forever. That made him smile.

With that settled, they pulled apart, and Brant circled his horse so they could continue on their way. They rode close beside one another now, their knees occasionally brushing, or one would reach out and touch the other as if to make sure they were still there. It was sweet, really, and exactly what Kayla needed to heal the ache in her soul. No matter what had happened, no matter the mistakes she had made or the pain it had caused Brant or his family, they were together and he loved her, and that was all that mattered.

They found the perfect camping spot just before lunch. It was a small meadow surrounded by mossy rocks that led to a beautiful waterfall pouring into a bend in the river. It created a small pond where they could see fish swimming in the stony depths.

"Gah! If only I'd thought to bring a pole!" Brant had always had loved fishing. Kayla didn't understand why, but she accepted it. It was just part of who he was.

"It's a good thing Wendalyn packed us such a lovely lunch then, isn't it?" Kayla said, pulling the food satchel down from her horse. "Much as you love to fish, I'm not much in the mood for it today." She glanced up at him from beneath her lashes. "I'm just in the mood for you."

Brant took her in his arms and gave her a kiss that shook her to the core. "It's a good thing. I'm in the mood for you, too." He gave her one last kiss, then took the lunch basket and set it on the ground. They quickly tended to the horses before they ate, removing saddles and hobbling the mounts near grass and water, then washed up in the clear pond before sitting down to eat.

They spent the afternoon talking and eating and talking some more. The perfect day, in Kayla's eyes, and all the hurts were healed long before they reached dessert. After a while, Brant packed up the basket and put it back with the saddles.

Kayla glanced up at the canopy of trees. The temperature had dropped so that it was almost chilly. It was going to be a cool autumn night. Kayla went to the horses and pulled out the hatchet and the sleeping rolls, then brought them back to the clearing and went off in search of some wood.

"What are you doing?" Brant called out.

"Looking for wood before it gets dark. We'll need a fire," she answered, then felt the fear and anguish of the ancient woods. She tried to send out a message to the forest, that she would be careful with the flame, but she wasn't sure if the woods had heard. The peace she had felt here before was now replaced with uneasy anger.

Brant caught up with her. "Give me that," he said, taking the axe from her hands. "Let me do something, too. I'll take care of the wood. Why don't you set up our bedrolls?" Kayla almost argued with him about it. She was no weakling and could have collected the wood herself, but then decided he was right. He was the stronger of the two, and she could create a fire ring to keep the flames away from the trees and hopefully calm their anxiety.

"Okay," she said. "Just don't cut any live wood. This forest is ancient and sacred and right now frightened at the mention of fire. Deadwood only, okay?"

His eyes got big, but he nodded and headed a little deeper into the woods to find dry deadwood. After a few moments, she could hear him chopping away, and she scurried back to their campsite. Kayla decided to create the fire ring first and set their sleeping rolls up around it. She looked around the clearing. She couldn't put the fire too close to the water. The moist soil would extinguish any flame they started. She also couldn't put it too close to the tree line. She walked around and found the perfect place in nearly the exact middle of the clearing. There was a large slab of granite with a slight indentation in the center, almost like a bowl of rock, free of weeds, and she quickly cleaned out the debris of leaves and grass, then collected rocks to encircle it, creating height to keep the fire within the pit. Brant returned with an armload of wood and stacked it neatly against one side, then went back to the woods for more.

By the time she finished, the fire ring was three feet across and three feet high and the trees were calming. Once that was done, she brought the horses and the remaining supplies near the fire pit and rehobbled them so the animals could feed.

Brant returned with another load of wood and stacked it neatly with the other, then went into the woods a third time. She took the bedrolls and put one on each side of the fire. She may be engaged to her best friend, and they may have slept together in innocence over the years, but things were different now. Even in the woods, they had to keep things proper.

About the time she got their bedrolls spread and the cooking equipment out, Kayla heard a splashing from the stream behind her. She turned, and her stomach sank. There in the pond were the two water horses, and standing on the shore, smirking at her, was Jihong.

CHAPTER TWENTY-FIVE

C'Tan inhaled the sweet smell of orange roasted chicken as it wafted beneath her nose. And did she detect a hint of rosemary? She leaned over her plate and shut her eyes to enjoy the scent. She rarely took the time to sit down and eat a meal, but this one was worth it. Fork and knife in hand, she sliced through the chicken and balanced it perfectly on the back of her fork.

She had just lifted a bite of baked sweet potato to her lips when a familiar sensation crackled up her spine. She stilled, stopping mid chew, every muscle in her body freezing as she felt *him* step from behind her and make his way around her side to sit in the chair opposite her. A duplicate of her meal suddenly appeared before him, and he began to eat. Within seconds, Kardon had joined them at the table. *Her* table. And S'Kotos accompanied him. She completely lost her appetite in the presence of the men who had once been her master and The Guardian who enslaved her. She set her fork and knife down across her plate and waited for the men to finish.

C'Tan's stomach boiled at having to share her space with either man, though she could not take her eyes off her master as he ate. He didn't need to eat, not really, nevertheless, she watched the muscles in his jaw with fascination as he chewed. She watched his larynx bulge as he swallowed. She hated that she couldn't help the admiration she felt for this man, this pit of darkness who ate at her soul. But she did. She both loved and hated him, but then, how could she not? He was divine, and she, a mere mortal.

The man and The Guardian finished their meal about the same time and shoved their plates away. C'Tan watched in silence, waiting for the words of S'Kotos. He would not be here without reason, especially after their last meeting on the bottom of the sea. She had nearly lost her place as his favored servant when Kayla left her locked behind a wall of ice and Kardon had been pulled into the scene by the master. She was not sure she cared to hear what S'Kotos had to say.

Beginning the conversation in his own way, as usual, S'Kotos didn't bother to clear his throat or look at her. He just spoke as he toyed with his knife. "I have a task for you. For both of you, and you must set aside your hatred of each other to accomplish it."

C'Tan glanced at Kardon. He turned slowly toward her and gave her a slight nod. She didn't deign to respond. Not until she knew what S'Kotos was asking of her.

"Another of the keystones has manifested itself," S'Kotos said, his voice showing no emotion but bored interest. "And strangest of coincidences, it is at The Academy of Magi. With Ember Shandae. Who should be in *our* power by now." S'Kotos stabbed the knife entirely through the table with that word. C'Tan didn't dare move.

S'Kotos continued. "The Armor of Light has come to life, and the fact that it is anywhere near Ember says the collecting has begun. This is why I wanted her sealed as a babe. The keystones are going to be naturally drawn to her until she has them all." S'Kotos slowly pulled the knife from the wood and laid it across his plate.

Neither Kardon nor C'Tan responded. They sat awaiting their Master's plan.

Still, he did not tell them what he wanted. "The Sapphire Flute will soon arrive at The Academy," he said. C'Tan's stomach churned. That, she had assumed. The master was right. The keystones were collecting around Ember. She finally dared to speak.

"What do you wish us to do, Master?" she asked, her head bowed. She wouldn't look at him directly, though she could still see him out of the corner of her eye. He smiled.

"I wish for you to destroy the mage academy and bring the keystones and Ember into the open so we can claim them." S'Kotos balanced his fork on the tip of his index finger.

Kardon finally spoke. "And how do you propose we do that, Master? We can't access the academy directly, and have so few agents in place, they would be destroyed before any major damage could be done."

S'Kotos stabbed his fork down into Kardon's hand, pinning him to the table, then released it and let the fork vibrate with the force of his thrust. The master steepled his fingers beneath his chin and ignored C'Tan's servant. Kardon paled, but didn't cry out. He reached and pulled the fork out with a jerk. Four dots of blood immediately appeared and spread from the injury, pooling between the tendons on the back of his hand. The old man put his left hand over the wound, hovering just inches from it, his hand glowing a pale green as he healed the punctures. He looked at his master as if nothing had happened while wiping the blood away with his napkin.

"I assume you know about the explosion of Devil's Mount, near Karsholm?" S'Kotos asked, using the dinner knife to trim his fingernails.

C'Tan and Kardon nodded. Of course they knew. C'Tan had fed the mount to create the explosion.

"And you know that the caves which house the mage academy are full of fissures that lead directly to that mount?" he said, glancing at C'Tan.

She saw where he was going. "You want us to direct the flow of magma into the academy?"

S'Kotos beamed at her. "Ah, you catch on quickly, my child." He stood. "Open the fissures slowly. We want to chase them out, not blow them up." He came around the table and placed a hand in benediction on each of their heads. "And do it *now,* my children, before The Sapphire Flute and Armor of Light have time to settle in with The Chosen One."

S'Kotos disappeared in a flash of red. C'Tan and Kardon looked at each other, Kardon's face a mask. C'Tan was filled with revulsion for what she had to do. What a waste. She knew what lay in those mountains. Forcing magma into the area would destroy so much magestone, specifically the birthplace of the keystones.

But she could not say no to the master. She pushed back her chair and stood. "Come, Kardon. The master has made his desires known. It's time to chase the rabbits from their hole."

CHAPTER
TWENTY-SIX

The light still bobbed in the distance, definitely leading Ember onward through the stone. She followed it like a lifeline. Every time she stopped to think about what she was doing, she found it hard to breathe. Not that the stone was choking her airway, but she felt like she shouldn't be able to breathe, and it was that which strangled her.

The light got brighter and Ember sped up her pace, curious now as to where it might take her. The panic and fear that had made her race from the dining hall left as she focused entirely on the white light.

She came out of the rock suddenly, passing through a thick vein of quartz and coming into a perfectly spherical room that took her breath away with its beauty. The white magelight glowed from the exact center, showering light on the ribbons of magestone that lined the entire room. Every surface, every single inch, was covered with some form of brilliant color. Emerald and blue sapphire, yellow and orange and purple sapphire, ruby and clear sapphire. Magestone. Sapphire wasn't just blue. Ezeker had taught her that when she was a little, and now, she remembered. Sapphire was all colors, and somehow, its construction made it ideal to store magic.

But she had never in her lifetime imagined a room like this. The floor curved, being spherical, and made Ember actually glad she was still in wolf form. Four feet let her pad around, examining the walls. The room was free of rubble, except for small bits that did not seem so much like random debris from the walls as remnants from carvings left purposely behind. The blue sapphire vein was as wide as a doorway and had a long, cylindrical shape cut from it, and below that was a long, blue rod and several round plugs, almost as if someone had pulled an instrument from the stone. She sniffed, sneezed at the power vibrating from the remains, then stepped forward to the next color. To her left was a green sapphire, almost emerald in color, with a reverse image of a wolf's head missing, but it was small enough to hold in her hand—or it would be if she were currently human. There were bits on the ground below it as well, as if the detail carving had taken place once they pulled it from the magestone.

Next to the green was yellow, and Ember's heart sped up as she recognized what this was. The image of a breastplate had been taken from the yellow sapphire, and Ember was absolutely sure it was the same breastplate DeMunth wore now. There was a larger amount of debris below the yellow than there had been any of the others, but then, there would be, if it had to be hollowed out. She pawed at the remnants and felt power buzzing at her fingertips.

Orange held only a small, round, flat void, almost as if a coin had been taken. The red was an odd shape, and Ember could not for the life of her figure out what it might be. The purple looked like several shards and one sphre had been taken from the stone. And that led her back to the blue.

After seeing the breastplate, and coming back to the blue, Ember was wondering if the long, cylindrical shape hadn't been that of a blue flute. A sapphire flute, just like in her dreams.

Her mind went back to something Ezeker had said earlier. He told her that the Guardians themselves had birthed the keystones in these very mountains. Was this that place? Could she really be standing in the birthplace of the keystones? And if so, where was the white keystone? Was there one?

She stood in the center of the room, directly under the magelight, and glanced upward. She saw the ceiling high above her, and there it was. The void looked much like a large mallet pulled from a pure white sapphire. The white keystone. Ember's heart suddenly yearned for it. Where were all these keystones? Was she responsible for bringing them together? Was that part of her job in helping heal the world?

She looked at the magelight, suddenly feeling there was more to it than just a magicked item. She looked beyond the orb to see what was guiding it and asked a question. *"Why did you bring me here? What am I supposed to do? None of the keystones are here,"* she asked in mindspeech, pleading, and a little angry at feeling so helpless.

The magelight suddenly pulsed and grew so bright, Ember had to look away. She covered her eyes and crouched down on her belly to cover her eyes with her paws. The light caught all the magestone and sent colors reflecting back and forth across the room to the point she felt bathed in light, washed clean by light alone.

When the brightness dimmed through her covered eyes, Ember took her paws away and looked up. A man in white stood in the air and looked down at her, a soft smile on his face. "Hello, Ember," he said aloud, his voice resonating in the crystal as if it recognized him and vibrated with his tones. "I've been waiting for you for a very long time."

Ember forgot she was a wolf for a second and tried to speak to him. As usual, all she got out was a series of yips and growls. It always frustrated and embarrassed her when she forgot her species, but she felt odd shifting in front of this man, this Guardian. His presence awed her, and she had so many questions to ask, but in order to ask them, she had to change.

She did it quickly to get it over with, and within moments she was back in her human form, quivering with pain and on her knees before the Guardian, for she knew him to be so.

"Sir, it is an honor to meet you," she said from the ground, her eyes lowered. "But why did you call me here?"

The Guardian chuckled. "You've prayed for a teacher, haven't you?"

Ember nodded.

The Guardian settled to the earth. "Well, here I am. This is the only place on Rasann I can stand and not have her rebel against me. My brother and I battled long ago and nearly destroyed her. Oddly, she will tolerate his presence, but not mine, though he was the one who did the most damage. Perhaps it is because I hold the remainder of the white magic and he holds only the red. Regardless, that does not matter. You prayed for a teacher, and I have come."

Ember looked up, stunned and thrilled all at once. "You will teach me how to be a white mage?"

He nodded. "Yes, my child. I am Mahal, leader of The Guardians, and the only one left who holds the wholeness of magic." Her mind reeled. She was speaking with one of the creators of Rasann, and he knew her by name. It seemed a dream. This was the man her father served. She was about to ask about her father when Mahal distracted her with his words. "Magic works differently when used together in the white than when separated, as I'm sure you've discovered."

Ember remembered the seedling suddenly becoming a six-foot bush, and the stone carving that ended with her hand embedded in soapstone. "Oh, yes, sir. I've discovered it all too well. I seem to do things that are near impossible, yet not manage the most simple of tasks."

Mahal nodded and sat back on thin air as if there were a stool beneath him. "That is because you are a binder. You cannot use just one color of magic. You must bring them together and bind them through you in order for them to work. Tell me about your experiences. Let us begin there, and then we shall practice."

It thrilled Ember to share. She started at the beginning, when magic first manifested for her, and ended with the day the Shadow people attacked—when she'd nearly torn the man's throat out, then healed and bound him at the same time. "He was on the verge of death," she said. "But I couldn't let him die, and yet he can no longer do his magic. He's a prisoner here, somewhere."

Mahal looked troubled by the last. "Shadow people? The shadow weavers are here, you say?"

Ember nodded.

Mahal was silent for a long moment. "That magic was banned long ago. It does not come of the light nor of The Guardians. It comes from the darkness of the universe. The Destroyer, S'Kotos, taps into that power to some extent, though this does not feel like it comes from him. I need to learn more. Could you bring the prisoner here to me? Would that be at all possible, so that I may study him?"

Ember wasn't sure, but she would promise this Guardian anything. Not only was he the equivalent of a god, but he was willing to teach her. She'd do anything for him. She nodded her head. "When do you want him?"

He tapped his lip in thought. "As soon as possible. Perhaps tonight or tomorrow?"

Ember's stomach jumped. She'd have to get permission or map out a way to steal the man from his cell. It wouldn't be easy either way, but she had agreed. She'd figure it out.

"Now," Mahal said, rubbing his hands together. "Time to work. Let's see what you can do with this." From the air, the Guardian pulled an animal Ember had never seen before. It looked to be a cross between a ram and a lion with taloned wings. The beast screeched at her and lunged. Ember's heart raced in her chest and she switched to wolf form. Mahal froze the creature in place and got up from the invisible stool.

"No, child, you must battle with your magic, not your genetics. Come back to human form and try again." He scratched her behind the ears to take away the sting and sat back down.

Ember transitioned back to human, getting tired from all the changing, and thought for a moment about how to defend herself. She had no weapons. Nothing but the bits of rubble strewn around the room, all things that had once been pieces of the keystones. That gave her an idea, and she raced around the room, gathering them up before Mahal released the creature.

It seemed strange for Mahal to start her off on such a dangerous level, but thus far, all the magic she'd been able to do had been when she'd had strong emotions and felt threatened, so maybe this was where she needed to learn—instinctively and through action. Hopefully, the easier stuff would come somewhere along the way.

Mahal nodded, and immediately the beast snarled and screeched at her again. Ember's heart raced, the adrenaline flooding through her like a tsunami. Not sure what to do, she reached out, one plug from the blue keystone in her hand, and touched the beast on the head just before it snapped at her. The animal stilled, air rushing around it like a windstorm that only surrounded the beast. Ember wanted to pick up an orange keystone and try something with change, but there was no orange rubble.

Instead, she reached out with the color of white and felt the other colors streaming into her as she calmed the beast. She had no desire to injure it. It did not understand what Mahal wished to use it for, and it attacked in fear. Ember touched its beak, then followed the neck and the wings and then to the tail, and as she did so, the animal divided. It became its three individual parts, rather than the mishmash of animals it had been before.

A lion, a ram, and a great eagle all stared at her, gratitude and understanding in their eyes. The beasts all turned back to Mahal, who was chuckling at her success.

"Ember, I'd like you to meet three of the original hundred guardians who fell to this earth to heal her when she nearly exploded on us. An evil mage merged them together centuries ago, and you just freed them." The lion bowed to her, one leg extended. The ram bowed his head. The eagle spread his wings and meowed. The last surprised Ember. An eagle meowing? But that was the best word she could use for the sound that came from the beast. They turned back to Mahal, who waved his hand, and the three animals disappeared. Ember was surprised. She hadn't meant to do anything—she was just trying to protect herself, and the magic led her in what to do.

Mahal must have heard her thoughts, for he answered as if she had spoken aloud. "Therein lies the greatest secret to white magic. It will lead you if you listen. Your emotions are a catalyst. Touch is the trigger, but what you do beyond that is led by the magic. You can't tear it apart and analyze it. There are no specific spells. White magic is about trust more than anything. Do you understand what I'm saying?"

Ember nodded. "I think so, sir." It was slowly sinking in that there was no guidebook to being a white mage, which made her feel bad that Tyese was still looking for a solution for her. When she left this place, she'd have to be sure to tell the girl to give up the search. Ember's kind of magic appeared to be all trial and error. That overwhelmed her more than anything—she wouldn't know what she could do until she did it—but it was also very freeing. She didn't have to take classes. Didn't even need to be at the mage school, really, except that she would still like to look through the library and see if she couldn't find some white mage's journal. His experiences might teach her something. Maybe Tyese would still be helpful after all, since they banned Ember from the library.

"Now, another task for you. See if you can do it. Get the prisoner you nearly killed and bring him to me. Get past the guards. Don't ask permission. Just do it and bring him here without getting caught. Are you ready for the challenge?"

Ember wanted to say "No." Actually, she wanted to ask him if he was crazy, but that would be a stupid question, so she nodded reluctantly.

"Great! Then go now. You needn't walk through the stone. Just picture yourself where you want to be and you shall arrive there. Have you seen the prisons?"

Ember shook her head, not trusting herself to speak. "Hmmm, that is unfortunate. But you know what this man looks like, yes?"

Ember nodded.

Mahal smiled, satisfied. "Then focus on that man in as much detail as you can and take yourself there. You can do this. It is part of your power."

Ember was doubtful. So much of what she had tried over the past few days had resulted in failure or disaster. What if she focused on this man and made him explode instead? What if she got stuck somewhere along the way and ended up trapped, like one of the mountain's victims? But if she couldn't trust a guardian, who could she trust?

In the end, she had to try.

Ember thought perhaps the man might be more cowed and cooperative if she were wolfen, so she changed back to her other form. Her stomach growled from all the extra energy expenditures. Once transformed, she sat on her haunches and concentrated on the man, specifically on the green and yellow band she'd somehow placed around his throat. When she had the picture of him firmly in her mind, she wished herself there, reaching toward him as best she could.

The connection between them snapped tight, like a fishing line caught in the mouth of a bass. The analogy worked for Ember. For once she felt the line catch, she "Reeled him in," pulling on the line and feeling as if she were moving through a very slow portal. She held her breath, her heart pounding in her ears, until she felt the line go slack and she opened her eyes.

She was there. In the room, alone with him. He stared at her with wide eyes, but couldn't yell. Her spell or the ripping of his throat had taken his voice and he could do nothing but scramble into the corner of the room and cower away from her. He darted toward the door, but Ember headed that off quickly. The last thing she needed was for him to pound on it and alert the guards. Instead, she moved to the doorway and snarled at him, then backed him into a corner. He was so terrified, he wet himself. Ember could smell it on him and it disgusted her, then, in a moment of clarity, she realized he was beyond terrified. She had nearly killed him, then brought him back to this miserable existence. He had to be wondering if she'd come to finish the job. Maybe coming in wolf form was a bad idea. Ember sighed, sat back on her haunches, and changed back to her human form. First, her body stretched upward, her clothing falling back into place as the fur disappeared. Then her face changed back to normal, and her tail receded, which always hurt, no matter how many times she did it. And finally, her limbs and paws became normal hands, legs, and arms.

Once the transformation was complete, she stood, her spine popping back into place as she rolled her shoulders. The man relaxed a little, but not much, his eyes burning with hate as he saw her as her true self once again.

"I'm not going to hurt you," she said. "But you need to take a little trip with me. Somebody wants to see you." She strolled toward him. When she got within reaching distance, he swiped out with a leg and knocked her down, then jumped on her and put an arm against her throat. She could see in his eyes that he meant to kill her.

Ember's initial reaction was to panic. She bucked against the man, trying to get some leverage, but he only pushed harder. Spots speckled her vision, and she knew if she didn't do something soon, she would be dead. She wasn't strong enough to throw him off or beat him physically. She could transform into a wolf again, but that would make her smaller than him still, and despite her teeth, she didn't feel that was the answer. There was one weapon left to her, and it was one she had no choice whether to use or not.

Her vision growing dim, Ember found the centered storm inside her and did as Mahal said—she called on her magic.

She closed her eyes so as not to be distracted by the spots and darkness. The pressure on her neck and in her chest was already distraction enough. Instead, she dove into the maelstrom of magic swirling inside of her and instinctively pulled on colors she knew she would need. Combining them, she gathered, just as she had with Lily in the practice room, then reached up and put a hand against his chest. To her surprise, he did not go flying across the room. Instead, her hand sank wrist-deep into his chest. She could feel his heart fluttering against her fingertips.

The man stilled, horror in his eyes as he looked down at her arm sticking out of his chest. The pressure on her neck let up a bit. Ember coughed, then sucked in a deep breath, never taking her eyes from his. When she had enough air to speak, she said, "I am not going to hurt you. You've got to believe me."

The man glanced down at her arm, then met her eyes with one eyebrow cocked. It was obvious he had no faith in her word.

She dragged her hand out of his chest, not sure how she did it, just grateful that she could. There was no blood on her hand, just a clear fluid. He backed away from her once again.

At that moment, there came a banging on the door. "Ember! Ember, I know you're in there! We need to talk. Quit running away from me," DeMunth's voice yelled as somebody came toward the door with jangling keys.

Ember swore. "How does he keep finding me?" she said aloud.

With no time to spare, she grabbed the prisoner by his collar and concentrated on going back to Mahal. The keys turned in the door, distracting her focus, and the door flew open. DeMunth, Aldarin, and two guards raced into the room. Ember felt the hook of magic sink into the spherical room. She felt the line go taut, and she pulled with all her strength.

Ember felt bad that not only had she failed Mahal's instructions to not get caught, but she'd just left DeMunth without an explanation—again. The hurt look on his face as she faded away was heartbreaking. She cared so much for him. How could she tell him she was doing this at the behest of a Guardian? When all this was done, she really owed him an explanation, and only hoped he would believe her.

CHAPTER
TWENTY-SEVEN

Jihong. Kayla stared at the prince, irritated that he chose now of all times to appear. This was her time with Brant, without interference, and here was one of her greatest enemies who'd been forced to pose as her defender. She said nothing. No words of welcome, no greeting, no telling him to leave. She just stared.

There was something different about him, a subtle antagonism that had been missing since he'd challenged her in his father's throne room. It made her nervous and her only thought, silly though it may have sounded, was to protect Brant. She finally broke the silence.

"What do you want?" she snarled, glancing behind her. Brant was gone, probably headed back into the woods to retrieve more wood. The man was nothing if not efficient.

She turned her back on Jihong for only a second, but before she could face him again, something stabbed her in the back of the neck—something that froze her in place, standing, unable to lift a hand or do anything more than blink her eyes. Panic set in, and if she'd been able to move, she would have run screaming. As it was, all she could do was scream inside at the excruciating pain in the back of her neck and feel the sweat form in her hair and slide down her body.

Jihong came up close behind her and whispered in her ear. "I be wanting the same thing I've always wanted—the flute. 'Tis unfortunate that last night's retrieval didn't work. Ye must *give* me the flute, for I cannot take it for meself. The instrument will not have me." He took her shoulders and twisted her around. Now, what would it be taking to have ye give over the flute? A threat to yer own self does not do it. Ye proved that in the battle under the sea. Ye gave it to me for a wee moment when T'Kato asked ye to heal the horse, and I should have taken it then. Foolish me." He walked around to face her, his footsteps light in the grass. "So it occurred to me that maybe if I threatened the one ye love most in this world, that might get ye to give up the flute." His grin was evil as he pulled a long blow gun from his side and loaded it with long spines.

Kayla stared at them, terrified, but she could do nothing. Was that what he had stuck in her neck? Jihong caught her staring. "I'd guess ye'd be wondering about these, wouldn't ye?"

She would have nodded if she could. He must have seen that in her eyes. "These be from the stonefish. Nasty beasts they be, though peaceful if ye leave them alone. But step on the spines at their tail, and yer in for a surprise. Many a man—and woman and child—have died from these spines." He continued to load the blow gun. "Paralysis. Seizures. Pain like ye've never felt afore. Death. Oh yes, they're mighty powerful weapons." He loaded the last spine, then lifted the blowgun to his shoulder. It looked like a long, hollow stick. "The spine I gave ye be the least of them. It will hold ye in place long enough for ye to watch me kill yer man."

He walked away, and inside, Kayla's mind raced. Jihong planned to kill Brant, and there was nothing she could do. She was frozen, stuck in place by his quill, and all she could do was watch. She couldn't even whistle to awaken the flute.

Jihong marched across the field and to the trees lining the edge of the meadow. He put plugs in each end of his dart gun, tucked the stick in the strap of his bag, and climbed. Not far up, he found the perfect limb on which to lie and wait for Brant.

He didn't have long. Kayla heard Brant's whistling before she saw him, and the panic within her grew until she thought she would pass out, her heart beat so hard. She had to warn him. She had to save him, but how? What could she do?

She remembered being under the ocean and using the flute's power without the flute itself, and she wondered if she could do the same again.

Kayla closed her eyes and reached out to the flute. She could feel its sapphire glow across the meadow near her sleeping place and felt it perk up at her request, but it didn't respond.

Brant was in sight now, just passing the edge of the trees and entering the field, his arms full of wood. He walked through the tall grass to the fire pit and set the pile down next to the others, then stood and brushed off his hands. He turned toward Kayla. "Well, it looks like that's it. We're ready to get supper started. What do you say?"

Kayla didn't answer. She couldn't. She nearly trembled with the effort.

Brant looked confused and then alarmed as he walked toward her. "Kayla? What's wrong, my love?"

Just then, a scream rang across the clearing and Brant spun, his hand immediately going to his sword hilt. Kayla wanted to close her eyes, for she knew what was coming next, but she couldn't. In quick succession, faster than she could see, Jihong blew the darts one after another into Brant's torso. The first one hit Brant's chest and he gasped, falling to one knee. The second and third hit him in the stomach, and he grunted, but didn't move. Kayla hated to watch the rest, but had no choice. She heard them sink into his flesh.

Jihong left the tree and ran across the clearing, pushing Brant to his back with one foot, then stood over him, chuckling. Kayla was furious at Jihong and terrified for Brant. If only she could get the flute to work for her again.

Jihong looked at her then, his eyes cold. "What say ye now, Miss Kayla? Would ye give me the flute to save his life?" She wouldn't answer even if she could. The prince laughed and walked to their fire pit, building it up like an expert, though she was too far away to feel the warmth.

Brant lay on the ground, gasping and groaning. Kayla knew how badly her neck burned and could only imagine what it must feel like for him to have so many venomous spines in his torso. She had to save him. She had to. Jihong would only save him if she gave him the flute—what choice did she have? And yet, she had given her word to guard the flute with her life, if need be. Did that mean Brant had to give his life to protect it, too? Oh, she was so confused.

Jihong stood near the fire and faced her. He pulled a vial from his waistband. "Do ye know what this be?" His smug smile said much more than his mouth. "Here be the antidote for yer man. But choose quickly, lass. He must use soon it or he'll seize. Once that begins, ye'll lose him. He be a dead man." He walked around the fire, his eyes never leaving hers, then stopped with his back to the flame. "What do ye say? Will ye give me the flute, or lose yer man? The choice be yourn."

She inwardly screamed at the flute to wake up and hear her.

Groggily, as if it were a child who slept too hard, the flute responded to her pleas. It awoke and attuned to her. *Pull the spine out of my neck!* She begged. For a moment it seemed baffled, and then with a will much like her own, she felt its power grasp the stonefish spine. The first movement sent waves of torment through her, but she was still frozen and could say nothing. She was grateful for that. If she could stay quiet, Jihong might not notice what was happening.

With agonizing slowness, the spine in her neck eased out and pulled free. Kayla heard it fall to the ground behind her and almost sagged with relief and pain. She kept herself still to avoid Jihong's notice, but it was horrible watching Brant suffer. She would do him no good if she were frozen again. She had to be careful and proceed with a plan—if she could only keep her emotions out of it.

Jihong had continued to speak all this time, but she had ignored him, focused solely on getting the flute to remove the spine. As Jihong paused, awaiting an answer he knew she could not provide, she came to a realization.

Jihong didn't intend to leave either of them alive.

And here was her chance. He didn't know she was free. She had to surprise and disable him, then force the antidote away from him to save

232

Brant. If that didn't work, she would use the flute to save her love, but Brant would not die this day.

Using all her strength, she called the flute to her. One second it was in her satchel, and the next, it was out of the case and glowing in her hands, a cyclone of energy surrounding her. Her hair crackled and stood out with static electricity, her entire body glowing blue as she trembled and pulled the flute to her lips, a single note echoing across the glade.

Lowering the flute slightly, she answered him. "Choose the flute or my love? I say neither! I will keep them both!" Jihong's face fell, his brows drawn down in fury.

He raced toward her across the field, his dart gun at his mouth as he ran. He blew, and a spine shot toward Kayla. The cyclone around her cast it aside. He blew again, and the spine stopped inches before her. She spun it around and shot it back, hoping to strike Jihong as he had Brant, but he deflected it with his blowgun, still running.

Remembering the electric bolts he shot at her under the sea, she put up a shield of ice, somehow knowing that was his next step, and sure enough, he dropped the blow gun and threw bolt after bolt of electricity. Kayla played the flute and strengthened the shield, then, using the power of air, she reached around it with the power of the flute, pulled the antidote from Jihong's hand, and threw it across the glade to Brant. It landed directly on his chest. Barely able to move, he picked it up with trembling hands, uncorked the top. And drank it in one swallow.

Jihong stopped, glancing down at his empty hand, then at her. Then he did the very last thing she expected him to do.

He laughed.

Hands on his hips, he leaned back and sent his laughter to the sky, then bent forward and laughed toward the ground, looking as if his knees were about to collapse beneath him, he laughed so hard.

Kayla hated this man. Hated him more than she'd hated anyone in her life. More than those aristocrats who had mocked her. More than the Evahn people who would not let her father come when she needed him so much. She hated Jihong more than she hated her grandfather. The fury built and built until it was a huge, tornado-like whirlwind of emotion, filled with jagged shards of ice.

233

She sent that whirlwind toward him and let the cold and wind sweep him from his feet and twist him into the sky. All she wanted to do was hurt this man who had hurt her so much. She wanted to stab him for every wound she had ever received. It was as if he became every pain, every taunt, every snub, every hurt, all rolled into one man, and she wanted to batter him with it.

The power. Oh, the power. No longer helpless, Kayla held Jihong immersed in the whirlwind, about to crush this being who had caused her so much pain.

And then he screamed. That single sound was so full of fear and pain that it brought her to her senses, and she at last heard Brant beg her to let him go. "It isn't worth it! Don't destroy your soul for him," he pled, his voice a mere whisper.

Brant was right—but she couldn't let Jihong just walk away.

She gathered up the power of the cold and the wind and pinned him against a tree, then wound ice around him in vast sheets that bound him in place, leaving only his head free. She knew he would be all right—she'd bound him in ice before.

For an instant, she wanted to throw the flute away, sickened by what she had done, but she didn't. She clung to it. She would make this right somehow. Jihong had to pay for what he'd done, but it was not her job to kill him for justice.

And what she had wanted to do was nothing like justice.

Kayla quickly ran to Brant's side. She reached for the spines to pull them out, but Jihong yelled at her from the tree. "I wouldn't touch those if I were ye. Unless ye want the poison yerself."

Kayla stopped, then turned and glared at him. "Then how do I get them out?"

"Give me the flute and I be telling you," he answered, still not giving up.

"I can't. I made a promise, and I won't break it for you or for anyone."

"Not even to save the life of yer love?" he asked.

She reached for the spines again when he spoke. "If ye pull the spines out, it will draw the venom into his skin. Pull them out, and ye'll kill him faster."

"What? That's impossible. There's got to be a way!" she yelled.

"There is. Give me the flute," he said, chattering from the ice, but calm as a summer day.

Kayla couldn't help herself. She screamed. She stomped around the fire for a moment, then came upon an idea. Heat drew things out. It had worked when she'd been sick as a child, and then there was that trick of drawing the egg into a bottle that Brant always loved to show the children. It was worth a try.

Kayla took a stick and burned the end, then ripped off a corner of the ground cloth and went to work. She moved to Brant and knelt down at his side. He was sweating, his face green, and he was foaming at the mouth. Whatever venom these spines held was nasty stuff. She knew it was killing him, and she had to work fast.

She took the smoldering stick and touched it to the end of the spine. Immediately, liquid boiled up and spilled out the top. She used the cloth scrap to mop it up, then grabbed hold of the spine and pulled it out. Brant gasped and turned a little more green, but she continued the process until all twelve were removed.

Jihong spoke again. "Ye've killed him for sure now, lass. What a shame. If ye'd just given me the flute, we could have avoided this." He tsked just as Brant groaned, turned on his side, and vomited. That was enough. Kayla faced Jihong, and screaming at him, pushed all the flute's power at the prince. She wanted to tear off his head and throw it across the world. Wanted to rip his arms from his sockets and pull out his still-beating heart. She wanted to destroy Jihong for what he had done to Brant. All her anger focused on him, the ice pressed, crushing him against the tree. He breathed shallowly then, still alive, but hopefully he would be silent for a while.

As if he could read her mind, Jihong laughed once more. "Yer too late, lass. The choice has been made for ye. It's not as if he would be surviving anyway. There be no cure for stonefish venom. He just dumped a vial of water into his mouth. That be all."

The anger returned like a storm. Kayla pulled the flute to her lips once again and directed it at Jihong. She couldn't take one more word from him. She only meant to seal his mouth, but her anger and the power of the flute made it so much more.

The ice crept up Jihong's neck and he thrashed back and forth, panicking now that he realized the price he would pay. The cold crept up his jaw, into his hair, and then just as he let out a scream of his own, the ice covered his head, his face forever frozen in fear. For a moment his eyes glared at her, still alive, and then they glazed over in death.

Horrified at what she had done, she ran to the tree where he was frozen and pounded on his bindings, but it was as hard as stone. She picked up a sharp rock and hammered at the ice, but it wouldn't even chip. The flute had done its job all too well.

Kayla sank to the ground and wept. She hadn't meant to kill Jihong. She'd wanted to for a brief moment, but it was in anger. She didn't mean it—and now it was done.

What was she going to tell Niefusu? And Sarali? She'd just killed their brother.

Brant groaned. Kayla wiped her face. She would deal with this later. Right now, Brant needed her. She turned back to him, rushing to his side as he hadn't moved since vomiting.

Perhaps the flute could heal him like it had her.

Desperate now, Kayla put the flute to her lips once more and played. It was beautiful music, but the magic was absent. The blue glow that usually surrounded her was missing, the feeling of power just—gone.

"No, no, no, no, no!" she said, speaking to the flute. "Why won't you work? You healed me before. Why not him? Come on!" She tried again, playing for Brant with all her heart and soul, pouring all the love she had into the song. For a moment, she thought it had worked. She felt the pull of life around her, saw the blue surround him, but then it drifted away, like water through cloth.

Brant looked up at her, sadness in his eyes, though he did not cry. "I'm dying, Kayla," he said. Then he went into a spasm, his entire body contorting in a seizure the likes of which Kayla had never seen. She didn't know what to do but hold his hand and be there. The poison worked within her, but the flute seemed to take care of it. So if it would help her, why not him?

236

And now she was angry at the flute as well. Why wouldn't it work? She picked it up and threw it against a rock, expecting it to shatter into a million pieces, but it didn't. It bounced off the stone as if it were made of rubber. Furious, Kayla picked up the instrument and smashed it against the stone over and over again, screaming her fury. But it would not break.

Exhausted, she sank to the ground next to Brant and cried. The tears flowed out of her like they never had, as if a dam had broken behind her eyes and just wouldn't stop. Brant reached over with a shaking hand and touched her fingers, as if that was all he had the strength to do. Kayla gripped his hands and kissed them, her tears washing the fingers that blood and venom had stained. She looked into his face and saw that he, too, had tears making tracks into his hair.

He looked at Kayla, exhausted from fighting the venom. "It's about time, love. Will you tell my parents that I love them and it wasn't your fault? Tell my brothers to lead well in my absence and do me and Father both proud." His breathing grew more shallow. "I love you, Kayla. I've always loved you. I would have married you even without a title," he said, his words more laborious with each breath.

Kayla began to sob. "Don't leave me, love! Please don't leave me!"

"I love you," he repeated, then expelled a breath and never took another. His eyes glazed and the foam at his mouth bubbled. Kayla threw back her head and screamed her anger and despair. Brant was gone. It seemed impossible, but he was gone. All because of greed.

She took the flute and laid it on his torso, begging it to heal him, to bring him back. But nothing happened. It hadn't worked when she played, and it didn't work with his touch. Why? What had gone so wrong? Was it her fault? Had she misused the power of the flute?

She knew the answer to that without even asking. She knelt at Brant's side and rocked back and forth, sobbing. What would she do without him? Who would she be? T'Kato couldn't be her protector forever, and if she continued to play the flute, eventually someone would find her, someone stronger, and they would take it from her.

The one thing she knew was she needed help.

She glanced at the flute still sitting on Brant's torso. It began to glow blue-white, then turned deep blue and made Brant's body glow. Something of himself was pulled upward and looked around.

Kayla gasped. It was Brant's spirit. The flute gathered it up out of his body and then sucked it into itself like a strawberry through a straw. And looking at Brant's body then, Kayla knew it was truly empty. What did it mean?

With shaking hands, Kayla took the flute from Brant's body and brought it to her chest. The instrument was warm and seemed to pulse with a rhythm that sounded strangely like a heartbeat.

Almost as if her hands were guided, she brought the flute to her lips and played a song she had written for Brant. She'd been saving it for their wedding day, but that was no longer to be. It was the song of their memories together, of the time they spent in the hay barn and watching grand balls through the slats on the stairs. It was of their hours together, staring at the stars and talking—always talking. And the newer memories of Brant's becoming the duke's heir and Kayla receiving her own duchy—and, of course, Brant's proposal. That had been the happiest day of her life. She trailed off with a single low note, now full of sadness, before a voice spoke out of the darkness, echoing and full of light.

"That was beautiful, Kayla. Play it again?" Brant's glowing blue spirit asked from in front of her. Kayla wasn't sure whether to scream or faint, so she did neither. She put the instrument to her lips and played again, tears streaming down her face as she stared into Brant's spirit eyes throughout the entire song.

CHAPTER
TWENTY-EIGHT

The travel through stone was much quicker this time around. Ember and the prisoner burst through the wall into the spherical room and rolled across the floor to collapse at Mahal's feet. The shadow weaver slammed into the crystal wall, crashing into it hard enough to make the breath explode from his lungs with an "Oooof," and he lay still.

Ember lay sprawled facedown across the floor in the middle of the room, her head aching from exertion, not enough food, despite having stuffed herself silly twice that day, and the crack her head had taken when she landed on the floor. She was sure she would have a goose egg the size of a fist in the middle of her forehead. It was amazing there wasn't blood pouring from her nose. It wasn't easy working for one of the Guardians, she decided.

She groaned and got to her knees, then her feet, her eyes closed as she swayed for a moment. In that state, she was completely unprepared for the explosion that planted in her stomach and threw her across the room.

Ember collided with the wall, then flowed through it like syrup. She was grateful for the softer landing this time around. She turned around, thrilled she could see through the stone, and was about to dive back through and attack the prisoner when Mahal stepped forward more quickly than she imagined a man his apparent age could and gripped the prisoner's head with his large hand. The man who had attacked her knelt completely still, frozen by some power Mahal held over him. Curious, Ember watched as the Guardian closed his eyes and seemed to concentrate on the man kneeling at his feet.

Mahal's brows knitted together and his eyes snapped open. He stared at the man before him in clear horror before letting go and stepping back, then beckoned to Ember. She slid forward through the stone and stepped into the room. "He . . . that man . . . it's unbelievable," Mahal stammered. "I know it to be the truth, but I had never thought to see the like again." He seemed to ramble. Ember watched him with growing concern.

He shook himself and put a hand on Ember's shoulder. "Return the man to the prisons. I must report to my brothers. They need to know the danger he represents." Ember nodded. She was full of questions, wanted desperately to ask what he had found in the man's head, but she didn't dare. Mahal squeezed her shoulder, and suddenly he was gone. Disappeared. Poof. Just like a soap bubble popped against a finger. She looked around the room and scratched her head. She was tired. So very, very tired, and the thought of dragging the man back to the prisons was nearly overwhelming. She turned her back on him and tried to steel herself for the effort ahead. A sharp blow hit the small of her back, throwing her forward against the floor. She hit her head once more, and this time she saw stars. The darkness glazed the edges of her vision and she couldn't think. She felt herself lifted and tossed through the wall as if she weighed no more than a child. She skipped through the rock and finally came to rest just outside the ring of light that passed through the crystal. For several long moments she floated in the empty space, disoriented, stunned from the pain and in shock. She watched through the wall as the shadow weaver stood in the middle of the room, his arms outstretched. The crystal lining the walls evaporated, turning to dust that flowed to his hands and ate at the tattoo on his neck. She wasn't sure what he was doing exactly, but it was obvious it wasn't good. Stone of any kind shouldn't turn to dust without a hammer, but for the most powerful magestone in the world to be etched away with this shadow weaver's power, was beyond bad. It was an atrocity. Sacrilege.

Evidently, she had brought him to the wrong place. His power was eating the magestone like it was bread, turning it to dust that flowed into him in a rainbow of colors. Ember was afraid to move. Her first impulse was to run away, but she couldn't. She'd brought him here, and even though it was at Mahal's request, she was responsible for him and couldn't stand the idea of the man doing something so awful to such a sacred place.

The anger in her built as she saw the pitted magestone continue to erode and flow into the man. The shadow she'd seen when he'd first attacked her outside of Javak began to flicker, and she knew if she had any chance at all, she had to attack him now. She knew what Mahal had said about using her white magic and not her genetics, but her greatest success against the shadow weavers had been when she'd been in wolf form, so she changed, still embedded in stone, and charged the shadow weaver.

The man had made her same mistake in closing his eyes, so she caught him by surprise as she barreled into him, lunging for his throat. This time, he was more prepared and threw up an arm just in time to protect his throat. Ember tore into his flesh before he flung her away. She got her feet under her and bounced off the wall, using her momentum to strike at him like an arrow. She couldn't get her teeth in him, but she was at least able to knock him into and through the wall. They tumbled through the stone and, much to her surprise, he flickered away from her, moving through the mountain like a fish through water.

She shifted back to her human form to better pursue him. The crystal gave way to gray granite that was harder for her to move through, and she got caught up on one particularly dark vein of stone. And in a flash, he was gone. Ember looked all around, twisting this way and that, but the shadow weaver had disappeared and she did not know where to find him.

She stood still, trying to sense what she couldn't see with her eyes, but the man was just as elusive to her magic as he was to her eyes and ears.

"Oh," she mumbled, "This is so very, very wrong. They are going to kill me." Visions of Mahal, Ezeker, Aldarin, her mother, and DeMunth flashed through her head. She was going to be in so much trouble, and what was she supposed to say? Mahal made me do it?

Like they would believe that.

With nothing else to do and definitely not willing to go back to the mage academy yet, Ember swam through the stone and back toward the crystal sphere, the birthplace of the keystones. It wasn't hard to find. It was the only thing glowing in this dark place. A strange thought passed through her head. Most people talked about feeling the weight of the mountain on them when they were in caves or underground, but she had felt nothing but safe since she had entered the caverns. Why was it she felt so safe underground?

She had no answers, and the point was moot, anyway. What did it matter? It was just one more quirky thing about her, but one that made no difference.

She passed through the magestone and into the crystal sphere to find that Mahal had brought in a table and set it with supper for the both of them. It seemed a strange thing to do, considering she had just battled with a shadow weaver and lost him, and Mahal was supposed to be speaking with his brothers. She had done nothing right, and here Mahal was *feeding* her?

She stood there, unable to find any words as she stared at the Guardian. He stared right back at her, unsmiling, unmoving, then suddenly he grinned, reminding her of Tiva. He waved an arm expansively, gesturing toward the chair he pulled out for her. "Come, come. Sit and eat. You need your strength."

Ember's stomach rumbled long and deep at the sight and smell of the food, her mouth salivating. But how could she accept his generosity when she had just failed? Didn't he realize what had happened?

"Sir," she began, but he waved her to silence.

"Mahal is fine. Or Master, if you so desire, though I prefer the familiar form." He sat in the chair opposite the seat he had pulled out for her.

"Master Mahal," Ember started, then stopped, her mouth suddenly unable to form the words that echoed through her heart. Tears sprang to her eyes as she took a step forward. "Mahal, I have failed you. I am so sorry, Master. The Shadow Weaver was strong—too strong. He pulled the magestone right from the walls, powdered into pure energy. He got away. I lost him. I am so, so sorry," she said, biting off the last with a sob.

Mahal was instantly at her side, his arms around her. "Shhh, child, it is not your fault. I had not realized how powerful the dark ones had become, had not even known they were upon Rasann until they attacked you. I was wrong to have left you alone with him. I should be the one to apologize, not you." He held her tight and rubbed her back in a soothing motion. Normally she would have felt smothered, but Mahal's arms were strangely comforting.

"But it's not just that," she said, pulling back a bit. "Aldarin and DeMunth saw me leaving with him. They know I took the prisoner, and now he's loose. They'll have to tell Ezeker, and I am going to get into trouble. This is big, Master. They are going to be really, furious with me." Ember was near tears again, thinking about the reaction she would get when she saw them again. They would probably throw her in prison now, too.

Mahal chuckled. "And who was it who asked you to take the prisoner?"

"You," Ember said, slightly reluctant.

"And who was it who left you alone to battle him when you needed help the most?"

She was even more reluctant to answer this time. Her voice came out as a croak. "You, Master."

"Then whose fault is it he escaped?" Mahal asked.

"Mine," Ember answered, her chin jutting stubbornly.

Mahal took her chin and lifted it so she would meet his eyes. "No, my child. It was my error, not yours. I will accept responsibility. No harm will come to you. Now, leave this for the moment. Magic takes energy, and you need to restock. Come and eat. We will talk." He took her by the forearm and led her to the table that was laden with all kinds of delicacies. Even with the delay, the food was still hot, steam rising from the chicken and mashed potatoes and greens—and there were scones with butter and honey, melt-in-your mouth warm as if straight from the oven. Ember loved scones. Moisture collected on the chilled fruit and beaded on the outside of their glasses of cider.

Ember didn't resist any longer. She sat down, scooted her chair forward, and set to eating. The taste was exquisite, better than anything she'd ever had before, and she ate until she could eat no more, and when she sat back in her chair, the table disappeared.

Ember would have jumped at the table vanishing before her if she had more energy, but she was exhausted and stuffed to the point of stupor. Mahal stood and his chair disappeared, so Ember did the same, trying not to groan. Now that she was fed and her strength was returning, her thoughts returned to the shadow weaver. What was he, exactly? And how had he pulled power from the magestone? It bothered her so much, she eventually voiced her questions.

Mahal was quiet for a moment, then he waved his hand. Floating balls appeared in the air and grew until they were so large, Ember could see clouds moving across an ocean of the deepest blue. "This is your home, Ember. Rasann as we intended her, the way we created her in the beginning. Pure and pristine, full of abundant life and a place of peace and rest." Mahal gestured, and Ember felt as if she were zooming across the landscape, seeing the vast fields of grass, the lakes and rivers, and diving beneath the ocean depths.

"Let me give you a bit of the history of this world. I know your uncle has taught you about white magic and how it was divided into colors to hold Rasann together until she could be healed, but what he did not tell you, and could not have known, is that white magic is not the only magic the universe holds. There is a much darker magic out there, a destructive magic, and it is that which the shadow weavers use."

Ember shivered as a wave of darkness covered the illusion of Rasann.

"This battle between light and dark has been found on all the worlds the Ones created. I'd thought we had avoided it here, but I see now it is most likely that which corrupted my brother in the beginning, and not the lust for power I'd thought had changed him." Mahal's face was drawn, his mouth drooping in obvious sorrow. He waved his hand again and brought up the image of a man—tall, with dark eyes, and hair the color of the silvery moon and dimples when he smiled. He looked much like Mahal, but Mahal was sunshine and light to this man's darkness and night.

"This is my twin as I once knew him," Mahal said, confirming Ember's suspicions. "Before the dark changed him and he lost his way. Once, he was known as Sthadal. You might know him better as S'Kotos." As Mahal spoke, the man changed. Not in appearance, but in demeanor, as if all the light were sucked from him. His expressive eyes became flat and his ready smile transformed into a cruel smirk. "I wish I knew how he found the darkness. I wish I'd known then and had removed it from him, rather than let it nearly destroy this jewel of Rasann we created together."

As Ember watched, the world shook and trembled, the oceans rising and the land exploding upward into mountains and volcanoes. At last, the shaking stopped, and bands of color encircled the globe, alternating streaks north and south, then east and west that squeezed the world back into shape like a hand molding a ball. This was the net of magic that encircled Rasann, the net that was unraveling. As she watched, Ember saw bits of it deteriorate and be woven together again with magic, then other spots deteriorate, until it unraveled faster than it could be patched. She understood her mission.

What she didn't understand was how to do it. Mahal was teaching her to trust her instincts and let the magic flow through her, but she was only one person, and a young one at that. How was she supposed to heal a world?

The illusion disappeared with a wave of The Guardian's hand, and in its place was a bed centered neatly in the middle of the room. Mahal lowered his arm, and the glowing crystal dimmed.

"But that is enough for today. You, my child, need to sleep."

"But—"

Mahal shook his head. "No, Ember Shandae. Tomorrow is another day. Your head is full and your heart aches, and tomorrow I must ask you to do some things that will be difficult for you. Sleep now, my child. We shall visit more in the morning."

Ember didn't want to argue with him, couldn't, with the yawns that now cracked her jaw and sent her tumbling into bed and almost instantly into dreams. Only one thought crossed her mind before she gave in to the soft mattress and warm blankets. What task could Mahal have for her that could be harder than today?

CHAPTER TWENTY-NINE

The fourth time Kayla played her wedding song for Brant, the flute began to fade, and Brant along with it. The sun had set by this time, so it was dark but for the glow of the flute and the embers of the fire that still burned. When she finished the song, Brant's spirit spoke in that echoing voice that sounded as if it came from one of the domed cathedrals in Darthmoor.

"Kayla, I can't stay much longer. The flute powers me, and you have used much of its reserves tonight in your battle with Jihong. So listen now, while I have the time, my sweet." Kayla hadn't noticed until now that he hovered a few inches above the ground. "I never expected the chance to tell you anything beyond death, my love, but the flute has claimed me as its own. I am now its tool, its weapon. I wish more than anything that we could have stayed together in life, but the Guardians must have other plans for us. We'll be together as long as you have possession of the flute." He walked across the fire without harm, and that's when she knew this was real. He was a ghost, there but not there, and the tears started anew.

"Why couldn't I save you?" She buried her face in her hands and wept. "Why would the flute save me and not you?"

"Kayla, it's not your fault," his spirit said. A breath of touch whispered along her arms, making her shiver. "You protected me. You battled for me, and if you had not, Jihong would have killed us both. You know that. The flute used so much of its power, there was none left to heal me. That, and—" he paused. Kayla looked up and met his ghostly eyes.

"And what?" she asked. She was desperate to know.

"I hesitate to tell you," he said.

She was walking the line of sanity after this night. "Why, Brant? Is it so hard to tell me I killed you? That it's my fault you are dead?" She stormed away from the fire and walked to the pool beneath the waterfall, trying to hide the tears that would not stop.

But hiding from Brant was like hiding from a hound. He came to her shortly after she calmed and spoke, though she kept her back to him.

"You did not kill me," he said. "Jihong did. But—" and here he paused again before continuing, sounding reluctant. "Your emotion. I know what the flute felt, love. I am now a part of it. You rejoiced in Jihong's pain and destruction. You used dark magic to subdue him, and that conflict between your true nature and the dark battled the magic within the flute. It is but a tool, feeding off the emotion of its user, but you were . . ." He searched for the right word. "Conflicted," he said. "It used much more of its power, and that is why it took me into itself rather than let me die. I am basically an interpreter now, so that it understands you and knows how to properly work for you, its player. I am also to be your protector and guardian, and believe me, I take that very seriously."

Kayla listened and grew more horrified the longer he spoke. She kept her back to him, tortured by knowing he spoke the truth.

And her feelings had drained the flute more quickly than it would have otherwise. If she had not given in to her darker emotions, Brant may still be alive. The flute could have saved him.

Without turning to face him, she spoke. "So it is my fault. I killed you, whether or not I meant to."

Brant didn't answer, which was unlike him. She chuckled bitterly. He was changing already. He was now a creature of truth, and not compassion. The realization sat like a stone in her heart.

The silence stretched between them for much too long. It was Brant who finally broke it.

"I know this is a topic you do not wish to discuss, love, but it is necessary. Will you hear me?" he asked.

She nodded without turning.

"It's about my body," he said, clearing his throat.

Kayla tensed.

Brant rushed on. "You cannot take my body back to Dragonmeer, though that is where it should rightfully be. Too many in Dragonmeer blame you for C'Tan's attack and, unsurprisingly, my mother is one of them. If you took me home, she would do everything in her power to have you destroyed."

Kayla hung her head. She blamed herself for the destruction of Dragonmeer. Her carelessness had brought C'Tan down upon them and, as a result, the attack upon its people. She turned and faced Brant, tears still running down her face.

"Then what am I to do? I cannot leave you there to . . . to . . ." she couldn't even say the word, but visions of animals left by the side of the roadways filled her mind.

"To rot," he finished for her. "I know I told you to get word to my family, and I would still like you to do so—but not in person. It may seem impersonal, but send word of my death by messenger or letter and tell them how to find me. Do you understand?" She nodded and he grinned his usual grin, which was just one more knife in her heart. "I have an idea. This meadow," he gestured around him, "Is secluded and beautiful. It's also the last place where I have wonderful, happy memories with the person I love most in this world. You. I want my body to stay here, but not in this ground. I do not want to be hidden away."

Puzzled, she asked, "Then what?"

"Ice," he said, a full-fledged smile spreading across his face. "I want you to create an ice casket for me here. One that will not melt, like the wall you created in the waterways." He saw her question before she asked it. "Yes, I know about that. The flute has shown me many things. Create an icy bier and casket for me and lay me upon it, then freeze me inside so I will always look the same. It will be a place my mother can come to mourn and see me, alive or not. Please, Kayla. Do this for me?"

Kayla thought. An ice casket. Like glass, but one that would freeze him forever. She didn't know how.

But the flute did, and she knew it would guide her in this creation, especially if it was for Brant. She nodded slowly. "I'm assuming the flute needs to recharge?"

He nodded.

"Then I shall do so at first light. There are preparations to be made before I can seal you, anyway. I can't have your mother looking upon you forever with blood and sweat and grime coating you. I need to prepare your . . ." She gulped. "Your body," she almost whispered.

Brant looked as if that had not even occurred to him. It probably hadn't, being the type of man he was. "I am sorry," was all he said. He was nearly transparent now. He blew her a kiss and disappeared into the flute.

Kayla burst into sobs that felt as if she were being ripped inside out. It hurt so much, she didn't know how she would ever bear the pain. But crying accomplished nothing. She couldn't stop the tears, but she could get to work.

Moving back to the fireside, she stoked it and added more wood to the embers that barely burned until the flames leaped high enough to illuminate Brant's body. Rolling him back and forth, she got his shirt up over the top of his head until he was bare-chested, then rummaged through his leather bag. Thankfully, she had thought to pack an extra set of clothes for him, and though they were nothing fancy, at least they were clean.

Trying not to blush, she pulled off his boots and then his pants, extremely grateful he had underclothing. She had been told that not all men wore them.

With her fiancé's body laid out in his underwear, she tore the blankets into large pieces. Several of them she ripped into smaller squares and took them to the pond, then returned with them dripping with clean water. Very gently, she wiped the blood and venom from Brant's torso, then used a dry rag to wipe away the water. She took another wet rag and cleaned his face and neck, and another for his hands and legs and feet. She cleaned every bare inch of him, even turning him over to clean his back.

The entire time, she cried. She knew it was silly to clean the parts of him that would be covered with clothing, but she could not bear to encase him otherwise.

Once he was as clean as she could get him, she pulled out the leather pants she'd brought and somehow pulled them up his legs and over his hips, though she was drenched with sweat by the time she finished.

The shirt was much easier. She tucked it down inside his breaches, then buttoned it up. She wished she had a cape for him. He would look so much more handsome with a cape.

She pulled his boots on, then polished them as best she could. She combed his hair back, styling it just the way he always had. His lips were turning blue already. Her heart ached to be reminded once again that he was truly dead. Gone. She couldn't take the blue of his lips. It hurt too much. At least she could create the illusion of life. She found the berries they had planned to eat with dinner and crushed one, dabbing it gently on his lips. She didn't want him too red, but she couldn't let him be blue. Between the berries and a wet rag to wipe off the excess, she got the color just right.

And then it was her turn. Stripping, she walked naked to the pool and stepped into its depths. It was cold, but she relished it. She needed the cold. It was part punishment and part wake-up, but whatever it was, it was the first thing to bring her any sense of comfort since she'd first seen Jihong.

She wondered what happened to the water horses, but couldn't summon the energy to care. Instead, she dipped herself beneath the water and scrubbed away the blood from the back of her neck, then rinsed the sweat from her hair and her body.

Once finished and shivering from the cold, she climbed from the water and walked to the fire. She couldn't bear to put her dirty clothes back on, and wanted to save her clean dress for the actual act of creating the casket and returning to the village. She put on her nightclothes instead and sat staring into the fire that had once again died down to embers.

The flute lay next to Brant and pulsed with a soft glow. She wondered what that meant. Was it stealing memories from what remained of his mind? Was it charging? Was it Brant's spirit that made it pulse?

She didn't know. Perhaps now that Brant was part of the flute, he could explain it to her at some point.

It was strange how her mind could wander over such meaningless things when she felt so empty and cold. It was as if some giant scoop had come along and hollowed her out. She was a husk. A shell. Empty.

"What be happening here, lass?" a familiar voice called from the darkness.

Kayla froze. Niefusu. When he saw Jihong, there was no predicting what he would do. She stood slowly and turned toward him, then began to walk without saying a word.

"Kayla?" He didn't sound angry. Evidently, he hadn't found his brother yet.

Kayla was still lost in shock, but she knew enough she had to reach him before he saw Jihong. She had to explain, or she could very well find herself joining Brant in death.

Niefusu must have seen something about her that wasn't right, for he stepped out of the trees and into the light, not realizing that his brother was frozen to a tree directly to his right.

"Kaya, lass, tell me what be wrong!" he begged.

"Brant," she somehow choked out and watched Niefusu's eyes darken. She knew she had to continue. She had to explain. "Brant is dead." At the words, she broke into sobs, and Niefusu was instantly there, trying to take her into his arms, but she backed away. "No! I have to tell you everything. I doubt very much you'll want anything to do with me after you hear what I have to say." She stoked up the flame a third time and chose her seat carefully, knowing Niefusu would want to face her, and she wanted his back toward Jihong.

It worked perfectly. He sat, pointing away from his frozen brother. Kayla heard a soft neigh and looked to the pool where she had bathed. The water horses were back. Somehow, it brought her some small measure of comfort and relief, knowing they were okay.

"Tell me what happened," Niefusu said. There was no arguing with his tone, and Kayla didn't want to, anyway. She had to tell him what she had done, though the realization sickened her. She had taken a human life, deserved or not.

"Brant is dead," she repeated, then told him about the entire experience. She was honest about it all.

"I'm sorry, Niefusu. I never wanted this. I lost control, and now Brant is dead, and I killed Jihong. I'm sorry. I'm so, so sorry!" she sobbed, burying her face in her hands once again.

Niefusu was quiet for quite some time before he asked, "Where is he?"

Without raising her head, she pointed behind him to the tree where Jihong was imprisoned. She heard Niefusu get up and walk over to his brother. Again, there was silence for much too long. She expected him to turn and kill her at any moment, but there was nothing. Instead, he whistled. Not the appreciative whistle a man gives a beautiful woman, but a calling whistle.

The water horses came, and Kayla lifted her head. She watched as they trotted over to Niefusu and stood awaiting his direction. Without facing her, the MerCat spoke. "Can you release him?"

She understood what he was asking, but she didn't know. She wasn't sure if the flute was charged enough to melt the ice from the tree. "I can try." She stood and retrieved the flute from near Brant's body. Her hand brushed against his and she shivered. His skin was chilled.

Kayla tried to put it out of her mind and raised the flute to her lips, trying to focus her thoughts on releasing Jihong from the tree without thawing the ice that surrounded him.

A crack sounded across the glade, and Jihong fell into his brother's arms, still completely encased. The flute's light dimmed, and Kayla set it back down next to Brant, where the pulsing light continued to build again.

"That's all the flute can do," she said. "I used too much of its power fighting Jihong. That's why it couldn't save Brant." Niefusu still hadn't turned, so she addressed his back. "What are you going to do?"

"I'm going to take him home," he said, pain filling his voice. "I don't know if he be dead or alive frozen in this ice, but either way, he needs to go home. If dead, he be buried. If alive, to face trial and justice for his actions." He was quiet a moment before continuing. "You be right, Kayla. Yer actions were just and defensive. But Jihong still be me brother, and I cannot easily forgive this harm to him, justified or not." Niefusu clucked his tongue to the two horses, then said something to them she didn't hear. The water horses sidestepped into one another, their watery forms merging until where two horses had stood, one giant steed took their place.

Niefusu took Jihong and pressed his frozen body into the animal so that he floated inside its belly. It was strange to see, but it made sense that it would be the easiest way to carry him.

Niefusu climbed the nearest tree and lowered himself to the huge water steed's back, then turned to Kayla. "Farewell, lass. If I see ye again, I shall reconsider me feelings, but if not, know that I do not hate ye. I am angered, yes, but just as much at me brother as at ye. Ye were in the right. I pray we meet again." And with those words, he clicked his tongue again and the water steed rode off into the darkness, leaving Kayla alone with the body of her dead fiancé and a depleted flute.

Knowing she could never sleep that night, Kayla was determined to greet the sun. She sat back by the fire, put her head in her hands, and planned the music to create Brant's casket. And in the back of her mind, she wondered how she would ever tell his mother.

CHAPTER THIRTY

C'Tan paced her room, waiting for Kardon to arrive so they could go do their master's will. The hour she had set for their departure had long since passed, and her anger grew with every minute. She wished the man would just hurry and looked forward to punishing him for his tardiness—but that didn't help the fact that she was itching to leave now.

Impatient and desperate for something to do, she went to the scrying bowl and contacted her servant Magnet. She watched him laughing in bed with his partner, Seer, for a moment before she sent streaks of pain to them both to get their attention. They immediately stiffened and turned toward the bowl over which she knew the projection of her head floated. Magnet scrambled off the bed and knelt before her. Seer did the same, though much more slowly, and with a sneer C'Tan was determined to wipe from her face one of these days. She ignored the woman, knowing Kardon could come at any moment. She wanted to take care of this quickly.

"Report, Magnet. What is your progress with Ember Shandae?"

Magnet glanced up at her, then let his head hang, the silence between them terse for a long moment before he muttered, "She is gone, Mistress. We have lost the girl, and know not where she is."

"What?" C'Tan snarled. "How can that be? You are in a closed system in those caves. There is nowhere for her to go. She can't be far. Have you tried tracking her?" She paced again.

"Yes, Mistress. The tracking leads us to blank walls. We cannot find her." Magnet shifted uneasily.

C'Tan turned and sent pain through the scrying stones once more. When he and the woman stopped writhing, she asked, "Have you spoken to Shadow? Does she know where Ember has gone?"

"No, Mistress, not yet," he said sullenly.

She was tempted to kill them both right then, but decided on a better course of action. "Give me your body," she demanded.

He looked at her as if she were dense.

C'Tan growled. "Loan me your body. I wish to speak to my daughter, and this requires more than a scrying stone. I must do it in person. I'll use yours."

He looked fearful now. Good. That was much more acceptable than the resentful answers he'd been giving her lately. This woman he had partnered with was not good for him. C'Tan determined to be rid of her soon—she was corrupting C'Tan's servants. The irony of that thought was not lost on her and she chuckled as she entered Magnet's body and shrugged her shoulders back.

"Ah, that's better," she said through his mouth, then, dressing him in only a robe, she strode out of his rooms and headed toward Lily's room.

The halls were mostly empty at this hour, so she ran across no one, unfortunately. She would have liked to further humiliate her servant for his failure, but having to share his body with her was humiliation enough for the moment. The woman, Seer, followed behind, confused and angry at Magnet's behavior and C'Tan's touch upon him.

When they reached Lily's room, she strode through the curtain as if it weren't even there and looked around the darkened space. Her daughter was asleep on her bed. C'Tan forced Magnet's body to stride over to the bed and shake her roughly.

Lily sat up with a start, her eyes fearful at the sight of Magnet there. She glanced behind his body to Seer, then back to Magnet. "What do you need?" At least her fear did not show in her voice. C'Tan was proud of that in her daughter. She said nothing to let the girl think she was anything other than what she saw.

"Where is Ember? You were supposed to keep a close eye on her," Magnet's voice asked.

Lily shrugged. "I don't know. She ran out of the dining room when you two came in and I haven't seen her since. I thought you caught her."

C'Tan felt Magnet's anger burn and let it fuel her. "So you've wasted all this time in bed, waiting for her to come back, instead of going out to search for her? Haven't I taught you better than that, Lily? Hasn't your mother?"

Lily turned red and glanced at Seer again, and C'Tan realized her mistake. They had mostly been anonymous to one another until now. She had just given away her daughter's identity. She cursed her stupidity, but what was done was done.

Lily threw herself off her bed and stood up to them, just inches below her father. "Yes, that's exactly what I did, *Rahdnee* and *Brendae*. You saw her last, and you never came to me. What else was I supposed to do? At least I've kept you notified when things happen. Nobody has bothered to return that favor, though I thought C'Tan told us to work together. And where has Ian been in all this? I haven't seen him trying very hard. Have you?"

C'Tan couldn't help herself. She pulled back and slapped the girl hard across the mouth, drawing blood. Lily used her fist to wipe it away and fought the tears that sprang into her eyes. "At least I've done my part," she said as if nothing had happened, despite the blood still trailing down her chin where her lip had split open.

Magnet leaned in until he was almost nose to nose with Lily, with C'Tan pushing him closer still, though he fought her. "Find her, Lily. Get her back here and do your job," he said. Then C'Tan forced his body to turn and storm out of Lily's room and back toward his own.

Kardon chose that moment to knock on her door, so C'Tan abandoned Magnet's body, knowing it would force him to collapse in the hallway, but she didn't care. Her use for these two had just about been spent, and she had another job to do.

Once back in her own body, she strode across the room and opened the door to Kardon, who waited in his riding leathers, unrepentant at his tardiness. C'Tan thought of punishing him then, but she'd just spent most of her anger on Rahdnee and Lily. She thought she'd let it pass this once.

She pulled the door to her room shut behind her, and together they headed up the long spiral of stairs to the dragon aerie. They had a purpose, a task to do S'Kotos' bidding and destroy the mage academy at last.

CHAPTER THIRTY-ONE

Ember stretched and yawned, awakening slowly. C'Tan had plagued her dreams all night long. First she had been scarred and with no hair, but then she was beautiful, in a terrifying way, with long golden locks and eyes as cold as a midwinter freeze.

For once, C'Tan had done nothing in her dreams. She'd just watched, as if she could see Ember from wherever she was. It was haunting, the way she'd looked at her and examined her, as if the woman were actually two people battling for control. The scarred and terrifying woman was angry and hated Ember. It radiated off her in waves that were nearly palpable. The blonde woman was softer, even with the cold eyes, and seemed to want something from Ember she could never provide. It had not been a restful night, despite the comfortable bed and warm blankets.

Ember sat up and swung her legs over the side, her feet barely brushing the cool, crystalline floor. She looked around her, the colored bands of magestone shining with their own inner light. It was a wonder no one had found this place sooner. It wasn't far off the paths that were already beaten through the mountain. A few feet in this direction would have made the transparent room visible to the pathway.

Obviously, someone had been protecting it for all these years. People knew it was here—they just didn't know where. Even Ezeker had spoken of it. It was like a whispered secret, something everybody knew but nobody believed, and yet here she was, waking up surrounded by the very crystal that formed the keystones to the net of magic.

Ember yawned again, smacking her lips together, and realized just how badly she needed to brush her teeth—and bathe. She had definitely surpassed the "Overly ripe" category and now ran toward just plain stinky, despite her bath the day before. The frequent shape shifting and battling with the Shadow Weaver had made another bath not just appealing, but absolutely necessary.

Once again, Mahal was nowhere to be found. Ember didn't dare try the public baths. There were too many people who would recognize her, and she was sure there were many people looking for her with questions she couldn't answer. She ran her hand through her tangled hair and sighed. She couldn't hide forever. Eventually, she would face the fact that she had stolen a prisoner, and he had escaped. She would deal with DeMunth and Ezeker and Aldarin and everyone else, including the students who kept staring at her.

A small glow of relief started in her stomach. At least now she knew she wasn't useless. She had a teacher, even if his teaching consisted of putting her in dangerous situations more often than not. She still had no idea how she was supposed to heal a world, but now she knew it wasn't hopeless.

With that thought, Ember made up her mind. She would hide long enough to bathe and make herself look decent, but she would face whatever consequences were necessary today. There was no point in putting it off, and with DeMunth as upset as she'd seen him at the prison, she could only imagine how upset her mother must be with her disappearance.

Ember put her hands on her face and molded it to look like someone different. Lily's face came to mind, and she was suddenly curious about the girl. What had made her so untrusting of others? Of course, it had something to do with being raised by Rahdnee and having C'Tan for a mother, but what had they done to her exactly? What kind of pain had they put her through?

Without consciously realizing what she was doing, Ember made herself look like her roommate, the girl she now knew was family. When she realized what she had done, she almost changed her face to that she'd worn the night before and lost in the constant switching between human and wolf, but then thought better of it. Lily was one of those people others avoided, which is just what Ember wanted. Why not leave it the way it was?

That settled, Ember kept Lily's face and moved through the stone again. She found the pathway that led to the portals and eventually the baths. There were a few people swimming in the large pool, but not enough for Ember to be worried, though she did pause for a moment when she realized she had no soap or toothbrush. She talked to the bath girl and finagled a toothbrush, tooth powder, and some soap, along with a change of clothes.

Once free of the nameless bath girl, Ember undressed, tossing her ruined clothing into the chute that evidently led to the wash and repair room, then she slid into the warm water and sank below the surface. The water was invigorating. She swam a couple of lengths, going from cool edges to overly hot near the falls, but she didn't care. She needed a moment to not think, not feel anything emotionally, and moving her body had always been therapeutic that way. After a while, she stopped swimming long enough to climb the stone steps to the falls and wash her hair. It took two rounds of washing and rinsing before she felt clean again and leaped from the ledge into the water.

When she surfaced, there was a woman next to her. Startled, Ember turned and swam away, but the woman grabbed her ankle and pulled her back. Ember's head went under the water, and she came up spluttering. She was about to yell at the woman when she realized who it was.

Brendae. Ember froze as she recognized the guard who'd been following her. The woman grabbed her arm, leaned in close, and whispered in Ember's ear. The same words she'd heard earlier the day Markis sent his thoughts to Lily. "I know who you are," Brendae whispered. Ember's heart banged against her chest. Could the woman see through the shifting features, like Aldarin and DeMunth could? That thought was quickly dispelled by her next words. "I knew you were his daughter, and after last night, it became rather obvious, don't you think?"

The guard's smile was scary—the bared teeth of a predator. "Your father wants to marry me, see. All these years of working and being together, and he finally wants to wed. You won't be able to get away with these games of yours once I'm in charge." She squeezed Ember's arm hard. "Why do you keep the girl from us? You know what the Mistress wants. We're supposed to be a team, and yet you shut us out of your practice rooms and now hide her away. Where is the girl, Lily?" She shook Ember with that question and it took a moment for Ember to get past the fear and find the words to answer.

"I don't know, Brendae. I haven't seen her since she ran away from you at the dining hall yesterday. She disappeared, just like you two did from guarding the door." Brendae looked slightly guilty at that, then stood taller.

"You know as well as I do the Mistress called us away. Our discussions with her always leave me in a somewhat pained state, especially when she is angry, and she was furious—all because of you. How can we convert the girl to our side if we don't have time to be with her? Are you trying to keep her to yourself and get all the glory?"

Ember went with it as best she could. "Why would I do that? Do you really think I want C'Tan's attention on me?" She snorted. "Far from it. If I can find the girl, you'll get your chance. She seems to have hidden somewhere. Are you sure you haven't given something away? You know she's terrified of you."

Brendae snarled. "And well she should be."

"Not if you're trying to gain her trust," Ember said. "Try being a little nicer. And smile a bit. I promise, your face won't split." She patted

Brendae on the cheek and pulled free of her grasp. "Now, if you'll excuse me, I've got a wolfchild to find." Ember moved away from Brendae and hoped she wouldn't grab her again. It was terrifying turning her back on a woman she very well knew to be her enemy, but to keep up the appearance of being Lily, she had no choice. It was the kind of thing Lily would do.

Ember swam to the edge of the pool, gathered up her towel and clothes, and headed to the dressing room. She dried off as best she could, braiding her hair and tying the end off with a leather cord someone had left in the room before her, hoping the whole time that Brendae wouldn't follow her.

She pulled on her underthings, slipped on the dull gray robe, and stepped out of the room. She headed for the door, passing several girls on their way to the bathing pools who stopped, their eyes following her as she walked by. It wasn't until most of the room had stopped and looked at her oddly that Ember realized her gray robe had turned pristine white. She sighed.

One girl ran over to the doorway and beckoned to someone, probably a guard, and pointed in Ember's direction, just as a voice shouted from the pools. "Hey!" Ember didn't have to turn and look. She knew it was Brendae.

She would let nothing come of that. She ran straight at the granite wall of the bathing room and hit it like a diver doing a belly flop in the water. The granite was much more solid than the crystal structure. She'd forgotten in her race to get away. There was a moment of pain, much like that of hitting the water stomach first, but she quickly recovered and moved on, though much more slowly than through the more refined crystal. Silence gathered around her. Here there was no one to watch her, no guards to run from. She didn't know of anyone else who could walk through stone—certainly none of the guards. They didn't have magic.

Ember waded through the rock like it was mud and eventually reached out with a magical hook and grasped the crystalline sphere once again. She popped through the wall and threw herself on the bed, grateful she'd gotten her bath, and she still had her toothbrush and powder with her. She took a moment to change her face back to her own and sighed with relief. It always felt strange to be someone else, like squeezing into clothes two sizes too small.

Ember looked around for some water, but found none. She growled in frustration, then tucked the toothbrush and toothpaste in the pockets of her robe and determined to use them later.

Mahal was still gone, and Ember's stomach was growling. Had he decided to leave her to her own devices? To let her face consequences alone? She certainly hoped not. She lay back on the bed and rested her eyes, trying to plan how she would handle this if Mahal did not return.

She hadn't even gotten past the image of showing up in Ezeker's office to explain what happened when an abrasive, bell-like tone resonated throughout the chamber. Ember sat up, cringing at the discordance it created clear to her bones. She was just starting to relax and wonder what in the world the sound was when it struck again. And again. And again. Faster and faster, the strikes came until she could stand it no longer. She slapped her hands over her ears, but still felt the vibrations like a ripple from foot to head.

Curiosity got the best of her and she stepped through the nearest wall, making her way in the direction of the noise. Not directly toward it, but in the general direction. When she knew she was close, she circled around the stone and came out of the wall about thirty feet down the pathway from where a shining man struck chunks of rock from the wall with his sword.

Even buried in stone, DeMunth had found her again.

CHAPTER THIRTY-TWO

The dark hours swept by much faster than she wanted with such a dreaded act in front of her. She would have had the night last forever if it were in her power.

As soon as the sky began to brighten and Kayla no longer needed the fire to see, she began her preparations. She couldn't put Brant's funeral bier just anywhere. It needed to be somewhere special, and so she spent time in the earliest hours of morning finding just the perfect spot.

She found it almost immediately. Just inside the tree line on the eastern side of the meadow was a small glade full of wildflowers of all kinds. The smell was heady, and though she knew Brant could not smell the flowers, their fragrance would comfort and uplift any who came to visit. She would place the bier here, directly in the center.

The decision made, she went back to Brant's body and picked up the flute. This time, she felt the iciness of his body without even touching it. She reached out to his arm to find it frozen solid, though his color remained perfectly normal. Surprised, she looked at the flute and wondered. Was this its way of apologizing for being unable to save him? Was that why it pulsed so strangely the night before, creating a slow freeze that left his color normal so he looked almost alive?

She didn't know, and it didn't matter, really, but one thing it did accomplish—she no longer wanted to destroy the flute. It restored a small measure of love toward the instrument. She brought her mouth close to the instrument, but instead of playing, she whispered two simple words. "I'm sorry." The flute glowed as if it heard her and Kayla felt warmth settle in her heart, even if just for a moment.

Setting aside her questions for the moment, she went back to the glade, stood at the edge of the trees, and played. She closed her eyes and visualized what she wanted—a long rectangle about two and a half feet high, made of clear ice. She poured her heart into the music, but kept the image in her mind, frozen as solid as that which she tried to create.

Somehow, she knew when it was done. She finished her song and opened her eyes. The bier was exactly how she had envisioned it. Once again, she wished for a cloak, or some kind of padding to put beneath Brant, so he wouldn't look quite so stark against the ice.

As if the flute had read her mind, Kayla felt its power come to life. A blue mist covered the bier, then solidified into what looked like sapphire-colored velvet. A blanket, padding for her love to lie upon.

Tears sprang to her eyes at the gift the flute gave her and Brant, but she blinked them away. She couldn't afford to fall apart yet. There was still too much to do. Kayla made her way back to Brant. There was no way through this next part besides sheer physical effort. She heard a sound to her left and looked up in surprise. The horses! She had completely forgotten about their horses. They could do the work for which she didn't have the strength. She probably could have used the flute, but she didn't want to waste the power on something so unimportant. She needed to save it to create Brant's casket.

Nearly sobbing with relief, Kayla saddled up both horses and brought them near Brant's body. During the dark of night, she had taken rope and scraps of blanket and made a framed sling, tying it all directly to the blanket on which Brant already rested. Now she took those long poles and tied them to the stirrups. When she was sure Brant was secure, she took the reins and led the horses to the bier. The most challenging part was yet to come in getting him from the sling to the bier.

Thankfully, the horses held still as she untied Brant's upper half and tipped the device upward. He slid headfirst toward the bier. She untied everything but his feet, leaving the ropes around his ankles trailing off the end so she could hold on to him, then she clucked her tongue. The horses moved forward slowly until Brant's head was just where she wanted it. She halted the horses, then tipped the frame again and ordered the horses backwards. She backed up with them, letting go of the rope around his ankles, and at last he was free of the sling and resting on his bier. The blue cloth wasn't even out of place. It seemed a miracle.

Kayla removed the sling from the horses' saddles and took the animals back out to the meadow, hobbling them near some clover they were likely to enjoy.

Once again, Kayla entered the glade, and her breath stopped for a moment upon seeing the ghost of Brant looking at his body resting on the blue cloth. He glanced up at her entrance. "Is that how I looked? Really?"

She nodded slowly. "Mostly. Usually you've got more color, but the cold—" her voice wouldn't continue beyond that. Seeing the two of them, both the same man, one physical, the other spirit, and knowing the one she could speak to could never touch her again was almost more than she could bear. Her vision swam, and she blinked away the tears, putting a lid on her emotions, much like she would a top on a kettle. It may boil over later, but not now. She couldn't afford it now.

Instead, she got back to work. She took Brant's sword belt from the ground and pulled the blade from the scabbard. She moved to Brant's side and lifted his hands, clasped at his chest, as best she could to put the hilt beneath them.

"Wait," he said, looking at her across his body.

"What? Why?" Staring at his face with his body laying at her waist was just so odd.

"You keep the sword. A gift. I'll never use it again." Brant put his spirit hand over his physical ones. "I'll leave this instead."

Mist swirled in ropes down his frozen body, blue sparkles permeating its length. Then it solidified into an icy sword, pommel beneath his hands as if he had died with it there.

Kayla stopped breathing for a moment. It was exquisite. Much more beautiful than his own sword would have been, and now she had something of his to keep, something he had held every day as he practiced. Now she couldn't hold back the tears that had been threatening all morning, and they streamed down her face like rain on a window.

"It's . . . stunning," she choked out.

"I know," he said, grinning his usual cocky grin. "A lot better than my actual sword, since people are going to be seeing me for eternity. One has to think about appearances." He posed, his nose in the air for a moment before he winked at her.

Kayla laughed. A genuine laugh, carefree for just a moment as the old Brant was reflected in his ghostly image. She wiped the tears from her face and, setting the scabbard back in the grass and flowers, retrieved the flute.

"Well, shall we finish this?" she asked.

Both somber now, he nodded. "Yes. It's time." He backed away from the bier, clasped his hands before him, and waited.

Kayla took a deep breath to steady herself, then played. It was similar to the song she had played the night before. Soft and slow, her shared memories with Brant spun out with her breath, and with it came the icy cold that built the dome. She kept her eyes open this time, watching as layer upon layer of frozen water grew over his body, cloudy and creating mist in the early autumn air. It curled away like smoke from a giant pipe, covering the grass and wildflowers and even the trees. It covered Brant's spirit and she would have lost his position entirely if not for the faint blue glow that gave him away.

After a while, the mist blew away and the icy dome cover grew clear. When Kayla could see Brant's body through the lid, she concentrated on making it harder and so cold that neither heat nor sunlight could melt it. She truly meant for his casket to last forever, like the legends she'd heard of the ends of Rasann, where significant chunks of land were made entirely of ice that never melted.

This would be her final farewell gift to Brant and the best apology she could give to his family. He may not be home, but he was in a beautifully tranquil spot where his parents, his brothers, their children, and grandchildren, and great-grandchildren could come to see him for generations to come. And she would be sure to spread the tales of Brant Domanta far and wide. He would forever be her hero, if nothing else.

Kayla finished her song on a soft and low note, letting it trail into frail echoes that sounded off the rocky walls in the distance. The flute still clung to her lip. She couldn't let it come down, for to do so would mean Brant was truly gone.

"Kayla," she heard his voice whisper. "It is done. Let me go," he said from just beside her.

She could say nothing, could only bow her head and let the tears fall silently.

"Kayla," he whispered again, and she felt his icy breath of touch trail down her arm. "Let the flute down. It is done. You did a beautiful job—everything I could have asked for. Now, take care of yourself. I'm a part of the flute now, remember? I'm not going anywhere."

Even that reminder didn't ease the ache in her heart, in her very soul. Brant was gone, and it was again her fault. When would she ever learn? If she had just insisted that Jihong stay behind in the water kingdom, Brant would never have been harmed. She knew Jihong was—evil, and yet she said nothing. When would she be strong enough to stand for what she knew to be right?

Lowering the flute, she slowly straightened. Now. The time was now. She nodded to Brant, then turned to retrieve the horses and her things. T'Kato was sure to be wondering about her and Brant by now. It was time to return to the village and be on her way. She still needed to find the Wolfchild.

A flickering figure appeared at the edge of the trees and zipped toward her. The figure was dark, like a shadow come to life, but it made her sick to look at it—nauseated from the movement and from the sense of emptiness that emanated from it. It felt like a void, a black hole, hungry for anything magical. Sensitive because of her recent commitment to fight wrong, she felt the depravity, the lightlessness within this being. Whether man or woman, she could not tell, only that it was full of a corruption so sinister she could not name it, and that it was after the flute.

She put the flute back to her lips and played a single long and shrieking note. Brant immediately appeared once more, but this time he glowed a brilliant blue and had muscles as big as T'Kato's. For a moment he looked pretty normal, but then he raised his hands, and the entire bottom half of him turned into a whirlwind that raced toward the shadowy figure. They collided, and Brant's color faded as it flowed into the darkness. She remembered the conversation she'd overheard the day before, and suddenly she knew what this was.

A shadow weaver.

Panicked, Kayla played, hoping to aid Brant in his battle with the ominous being. The blue power that sparked to life around her streaked toward the darkness, but it grew in size and seemed to become stronger.

She stopped playing. This creature ate magic like it was supper. She could not afford to feed it more power under any circumstances, but especially when it fought Brant.

She watched in helpless silence as the two tore through the trees and out into the meadow. She wondered if the shadow weaver would as easily absorb a stone or a spear as it did magic.

And then she had an idea.

Racing out into the meadow, she watched as the shadow weaver zipped this way and that, trying to get around Brant and to her and the flute, but Brant met it at every turn. Knowing the being was distracted for the moment, she stood at the edge of the meadow, put the flute to her lips, and played.

The power streaked toward the being again, but at the last second, she turned it—she didn't know how—and she took up the stonefish spines that had paralyzed her and Brant the night before, thrusting them into the shadow weaver's back.

A piercing scream echoed across the meadow and the creature fell face down into the grass, unable to stop the momentum that threw him forward, for she could see a bearded face and muscular torso. It was indeed a he and not an it.

As soon as he was on the ground, she raced to Brant, who now looked more inhuman than human. His features had sharpened and his muscles bulged beyond human ability, but as she approached, he softened. The whirlwind that swirled beneath him stopped, and he met her halfway. He looked like himself once more, though he was slightly transparent.

"That thing nearly drained me of everything. I can stay but a moment. Get your things, take the horses, and ride like the wind. Get back to T'Kato and tell him what you saw here. Tell him the flute recognized these beings. Tell him the Ne'Goi have returned." He faded with each word, and by the time he finished, his voice floated on the wind and he was gone.

She followed his instructions, running to the horses, grateful she had packed the early that morning so everything was ready to go. She stopped to pick up Brant's sword at the edge of his glade. With one last look at his icy tomb, she tied the reins of Brant's horse to a hook at the back of her saddle, mounted the horse, and kicked it with a loud, "Hyah!"

Startled, the mare lurched forward, pulling Brant's horse with her. The saddle moved for just a second until the stallion caught up with the mare. In all likelihood, he could probably have passed her, but he followed well, and in a very short time Kayla barreled out of the tree line and straight toward Hadril's wagon.

The men saw her coming, and before she arrived, all three of them stood outside. The boy, Jayden, perched on the roof, his usual scowl in place.

She pulled back on the reins so hard, the horses almost skidded on their backsides to obey her command. Under most circumstances, she would never treat an animal that way, but she was too distraught to care. As soon as she saw T'Kato, her eyes teared up. She wanted to throw herself into his arms for comfort, but she knew she wouldn't receive it from him. T'Kato was all business where the flute and magic were concerned.

271

She blinked furiously for a moment as the men approached and at least pushed the tears back, though she couldn't ease the emptiness of her heart and soul.

"What happened?" T'Kato demanded. "Where is Brant?"

"Dead," she answered, not sure if she could expound.

The ride back had given her time to think, and she knew why the shadow weavers, or the Ne'Goi, as Brant had called them, had come.

They heard the flute. Just like C'Tan, they had heard the flute and come to claim it.

The shock on T'Kato's face forced her to explain, though there wasn't time for details. "Brant died at the hand of Jihong. I killed Jihong without meaning to and Niefusu took his body home. They are gone, but there is something more you need to know," she said, interrupting him before he could ask questions. "Brant's spirit was taken into the flute and he is turning into some kind of elemental. After I sealed his body in an ice casket, a shadowy figure attacked us. Brant appeared to fight him. I paralyzed the man with the stonefish spines Jihong used to kill my love." She choked on that for a minute, then continued. "Brant said to tell you that the flute recognized our attacker. His last words were 'the Ne'Goi have returned.'"

T'Kato paled. Kayla was pretty sure she'd never seen him do that before. Even Hadril and Graylin went white as cotton at those words. They looked at one another, then turned in unison and sprinted for the wagon. They took down the awning that acted as a side cover, stowed the poles, sent Jayden to the inn with a load of items Graylin had repaired, then hitched up the other two horses to the wagon.

Kayla objected. "Wait, don't those horses belong to the stable at the inn?"

Graylin came around and opened the door in back for her. "They did. We are taking them as payment for the work done. Jayden will tell the innkeeper, telling him to collect from those who still owe us money. It will work out, and to tell you the truth, the inn will make out better. We are losing money on this. Now get in the wagon. We need to go."

Kayla understood their fear. She still shook from her encounter with the shadow weaver. "But why so fast? Surely we have a few hours before the Ne'Goi come to investigate the absence of the one. He is frozen, paralyzed. How can he send word to others?"

Graylin seemed exasperated. "We don't know how it works, and it has been a long time since the Ne'Goi have been here. I only know the tales, but from what I understand, their minds are like a hive. What one knows, all know. They will be here shortly. There is no time to waste. Get in." He gestured to the boxcar.

This time, Kayla listened. She hitched up her skirt and stepped into the wagon. the door shutting tightly behind her.

CHAPTER THIRTY-THREE

DeMunth continued to strike at the stone wall as if he were cutting down a tree, sparks and rubble flying with each hit. Her first thought was, *He's going to destroy his sword if he doesn't stop.*

Rather than say anything, she watched for a bit as fist-and-head-sized pieces of stone leaped from the wall with each strike. What he was doing shouldn't be possible. The walls were granite. They should have shattered his sword with the first blow, but then, he didn't have just any sword. His weapon was a piece of the Armor of Light, and that was a keystone. When she thought of it that way, it was completely reasonable that he could cut through the rock.

DeMunth stopped his swinging and stretched his back, arching for just a moment, then stiffened and held still. Ember knew he sensed her presence, and now his attack on the wall made sense. He knew she was in there somehow, and he was desperate to find her. How she knew that, she couldn't say, but she knew.

The instant he spun and charged her, she stepped back into the stone, suddenly afraid of him and what that sword could do. He pounded on the wall with his fists, clearly able to see and feel her. Ember slid to the right, and he followed. She stepped back a few steps, and he took up his sword again, obviously determined to pull her out of the stone if he didn't kill her first.

At first, Ember was scared. Her heart raced as she watched this man she cared for so much swing at the wall in fury. But after a moment, she found herself suddenly furious. Why couldn't people just leave her alone? Couldn't they trust that maybe she knew what she was doing? First her mother, and now DeMunth, thought she needed constant protecting. The anger built until she shoved a hand forward through the stone and pushed. Not physically, but with something inside her, perhaps even that chain that seemed to bind them. She shoved DeMunth away from her with more strength than she thought she had.

The man sailed across the pathway and collided with the wall on the other side. The air escaped him in a rush, his eyes widening with evident surprise, then narrowed in anger. He rushed toward her again, leaping off the wall as if from a cliff. Ember's hand caught him in the middle of the pathway once more and shoved him back against the opposing wall, but this time, she held him there. His muscles bulged, the tendons in his neck straining against her hold, but he wasn't going anywhere, Armor of Light or not.

Ember stepped from the rock, her hand still outstretched, and walked toward DeMunth, who still struggled. "What are you doing here?" she asked, but he didn't answer.

"What are you doing here?" she asked within her mind, and still, she got no response. Frustrated, she touched him, taking his sword arm in her hand, and sent the question a third time, both in her head and with her mouth. ***"What are you doing here?"*** she almost shouted.

At her touch, he relaxed, and his eyes came into focus. *"Ember?"* he asked in his mind.

Ember nodded. "Ezeker is going to have your hide for destroying the halls."

DeMunth looked at her. His mouth quirked and head tilted, before he started to laugh. "Ezeker's going to have *my* hide? He's been nearly panicked since you disappeared. Only my reassurance that I could feel you somewhere near has kept him from destroying the academy looking for you. Your mother has been constantly harping at him, alternating between fits of fury and tears, and your step-brothers are interrogating everyone, terrorizing the students in their search. And to top that off, I caught you stealing away our prisoner. Do you have any idea how much trouble *you* are in?"

Ember refused to hang her head, though the shame she felt would normally have had her doing so. Instead, she nodded, solemn and accepting. DeMunth stopped laughing. Some of the anger was still there, but she could feel through whatever bound them it was because he feared for her safety, not because he was truly upset.

She wanted so much to tell him everything that had happened, starting with the spies within their midst, how she'd found the birthplace of the keystones, and that Mahal himself was training her, but she couldn't find the words. She stood there looking at him, helpless. If she told him a Guardian made her do it, he would think she was absolutely insane.

"Explain yourself, Ember Shandae," DeMunth said, crossing his arms over his chest.

Ember squeezed the back of her neck with frustration. "I can't." A realization dawned on her, and she only hoped her idea would work. "But I can show you. Come on," she said, taking him by the hand and stepping into the wall. He pulled against her, objecting, but she didn't listen. She threw out her magical hook into the crystal sphere and pulled, taking him with her just as she had the shadow weaver, though much more gently. They flew through the stone at a normal rate, DeMunth choking behind her, probably in fear, though she wasn't sure.

Soon they were through the wall and into the birthplace of the keystones. DeMunth quit trying to speak, though his mouth was agape.

"This is why I've been gone. I'll explain more later, but while we're here where it's safe, I need you to know why I left without telling anyone."

They sat on the edge of the bed that was still in the middle of the room, and Ember told him almost everything—about popping out of her body, the strands she followed, Rahdnee and Brendae and how they worked for C'Tan. For some reason, she didn't tell him about Lily. It didn't feel necessary.

When Ember was done, DeMunth was pacing the floor, oblivious to his surroundings. He stopped and faced her. "And all this happened while I was asleep?"

Ember nodded. "Most of it, yes."

"How could Ezeker not realize he had traitors in his midst? And why would he assign them to you? When I met them, even I could feel the darkness oozing from those two, and Ezeker is supposed to feel things like that. Lily has a little of that too, as does one of the other students in your class."

That surprised Ember. She hadn't felt that from any of her other classmates.

"How could others have not seen this? Those two have been here for nearly twenty years. Surely someone noticed!" DeMunth was nearly out of his mind with fury. Ember stood and went to him, taking his hands in her own.

"Calm down, would you? We'll get it figured out. I wanted to tell you earlier, but I was afraid they would hurt you and you wouldn't be strong enough to handle them, having just awakened from a coma. I kept quiet for you."

DeMunth stilled at that. He froze, as if he had instantly turned to stone. Then he raised his arm, cupped her face in his hand, and spoke her name aloud. "Ember, you did that for me?" When she looked at the floor and nodded, he raised her chin so she would meet his eyes and asked one simple question. "Why?"

She didn't have an answer. Or, she had one, but she wasn't ready to express it yet. She tried to tear her eyes away from his, but his magnetic gaze locked her in and she couldn't look away.

"Why?" he asked again, his voice nearly a whisper.

"I . . ." she couldn't say it. She barely knew him—how could she feel the emotions that rocked her to the soul? How could her heart be chained to a man she'd met only a week ago? That thought made her pause, and she realized he hadn't chained them together. She had done it—her heart had done it.

His thumb stroked her eyebrow, and he asked one last time. "Why, Ember? Why?"

She crumbled under his gaze. "Because I love you." Her knees gave out, and she collapsed to the stone floor, her back propped against the bed. Ember hung her head and tears dripped from her chin to her knees as she waited for him to step away from her in disgust. Instead, he sat at her side, put an arm around her, and pulled her to him. Her head safely on his shoulder, she let out the emotion that had been bottled inside her for much too long. The fear, the sorrow, the frustration all poured out with her tears, and DeMunth held her until the storm passed and she could lean quietly against him. This is what love was. Real love, whether from mother to child, friend to friend, or soul mates. Love was about being there for one another, and Ember felt her heart finally acknowledge the fact that she was in love with DeMunth.

They sat quietly a little longer before curiosity got the best of her, and she asked, "How old are you?"

DeMunth chuckled and answered in his musical voice, "Twenty-two."

Ember sat up and looked at him. "Really? I would have thought you were older."

The chuckle answered her again. "Well, thanks a lot. Do I really look that old?"

Ember rolled her eyes. "No, it's not about looks. It's your wisdom. Your strength. The small lines by your eyes."

"That's just bad eyesight," he said.

Ember laughed now. "No, it's not. They're laugh lines. But you have a position of such power. Most members of the mage council are at least forty. Why are you on the council so young?"

DeMunth was quiet for a long moment before answering. "The council keeps itself as varied as possible so as to have a broad range of experience to draw from. That is how they try to maintain balance. They seek members who are diverse in experience, religion, gender, and age, though the age thing has been overlooked for a long time. The only reason they chose me was because of my experience being a priest of Sha'iim. I am okay with that. They needed my knowledge, and I needed to be accepted and belong to a group. Once the priests threw me out, I was lost. It was only in joining the mage council that I found myself once more."

"Well, however it came about, I'm glad you found yourself." Ember looked down at her lap and shyly asked, "Now that you have your tongue back, could you sing for me? Sing the words to your prayer song for me at last?"

DeMunth leaned over and kissed the top of her head. She could feel his smile through her hair before he stood and walked a short distance from her, kneeling and opening himself up to the heavens. He began his song, wordless, as usual, the magestone picking up the magic of it and beginning a soft glow that pulsed with his song.

Ember didn't close her eyes, though she probably should have. He was praying, after all, but she couldn't take her eyes from him and the effect he was having on the magestone. She didn't know if it was because of the Armor of Light, that it recognized a piece of itself, or if it was responding to the song, but it liked it one way or the other. That much was obvious.

After several minutes of wordlessness, DeMunth sang the words—words that Ember had felt in her heart when he sang all this time, but hadn't recognized them as being what they were. Interestingly enough, the words didn't matter. The song was the same. The meaning was the same with or without them. She just listened to the song, to the divine gift given to DeMunth—his voice.

When he was done, Ember sighed. She had missed hearing him sing. "I think I prefer it wordless, don't you?" he asked.

Ember was reluctant to admit it, but she nodded. He looked ponderous for a moment. "When I don't use the words, I put the meaning into the song itself. It feels more sincere, more genuine when I sing the melody alone. It astounds me." He came back to her and sat at her side. "I don't know why, but I am genuinely surprised."

A white light grew above their heads and DeMunth jumped, then scrambled to the wall and stood, his sword at the ready and his armor immediately springing into place. Ember went after him and put her hand on his arm. "Easy, DeMunth. Believe me, there's nothing to fear."

He growled at the light descending to the ground. "Then what do you call that?"

The light disappeared and a man stepped forward. "She calls that her Guardian," Mahal said. "Welcome, DeMunth. Welcome to my home."

CHAPTER THIRTY-FOUR

With nothing to do and little light in the apothecary's boxcar, Kayla lay on one of the sleeping mats stuffed beneath the counter and stared at the roof she could barely see. She replayed the events of the last twenty-four hours in her mind over and over again, wondering what she could have done differently, and was still pondering the question when the rocking motion of the boxcar sent her to sleep. It was no wonder, really. She had been up the entire night before and had been running on adrenaline for most of those hours.

Thankfully, she didn't have to be alone, even in her dreams.

The familiar cave greeted her almost as soon as she shut her eyes, and for once, she didn't have to wait for him. Her father sat on a boulder—or he did, until she entered the room. As soon as she walked out of the water and into the cave, he stood and came to her. Without a single word, he took her gently in his arms and held her as if he knew all that had transpired.

The barrier between them broke. The lid she had put on her emotions shattered into a million pieces and everything came boiling up. Her anger at Jihong. Her fear for Brant. Her terror at being unable to do anything while he held her captive. Grief over losing Brant and not knowing what was to become of him now that he was a tool of the flute. Fear, anger, loss, and grief. They boiled from her and she sobbed into her father's shoulder like she'd never had the chance before.

After the initial burst of tears, she pounded on his chest, and still he held her. "Why?" she screamed. "Why did this have to happen? Why? Why? Why?" Pounding on his chest wasn't enough, nor was screaming, so she pushed herself away from him, picked up a handful of rocks and threw it at the cave wall, then a larger stone, and a larger, until they were too big for her to lift.

Then she pulled on her magic while her father stood by and watched, letting her release her anger. She picked up a large boulder, drawing on the power of the flute, and guided it with her hand, smashing it against the wall again and again and again, until even that wasn't enough, and with a heart-wrenching scream, she made the boulder explode into a billion pieces.

None of the pieces touched either of them—she made sure of that. She may have been out of her mind with grief, but she wasn't crazy.

With stones pinging around her, she collapsed to the ground, exhausted from the emotional release. The sobs had turned to whimpers, though the tears fell just as hard. She lay there but a moment before she felt strong arms curl under her shoulders and knees and pick her up, holding her tight. Unable to move after her tantrum, she tucked her face into her father's chest as he walked up the hill and exited the cave.

There was mist everywhere, and she could see nothing. It was the thickest fog she had ever seen. For now, she only knew her heart was broken and her father held her. She still hurt, but being so near and feeling his love and touch was a balm to her wounded soul.

Upon reaching the grass, he turned to his right and settled to the ground. The grass was wet from the fog. It soaked through her dress as she sat between her father's legs and leaned back against him. He kept his arms around her the whole time and never said a word.

When she stopped whimpering, she became aware of sounds coming from the cave. The explosions continued, just like her boulder fragmenting into little shards. She also heard swords coming together, and a battle scream. It sounded like T'Kato. She didn't even have the energy to sit up, but the tears slowed to a stop with her curiosity piqued and turning quickly to alarm. She was the first to speak.

"What is that? There was no one there when we left the cave. Is that a battle?" she asked, still leaning against her father's chest and completely uncaring that her backside was as wet as if she had sat in a river.

"Yes," he answered in his deep voice. It made her smile as she felt it rumble through his chest. She'd forgotten how his voice felt. She basked in it a moment before what he said registered. Kayla sat up and turned around.

"Yes, it's a battle?" she asked.

He nodded.

"But—how is that possible? The cave was empty."

He pulled himself up and brought a knee to his chest, meeting her eyes. "What you hear are the sounds of battle around your sleeping body. There is no one in the cave, but T'Kato, Hadril, Graylin—they all fight to protect you and the flute."

"What?" Kayla surged to her feet. "I have to go help them. I can't be here now." In a panic, she turned toward the cave. Her father's hand around her arm stopped her.

"Wait," he said. "You need rest more than they need you. You will be useless to them if you go back now. Besides, there may be another way." He looked at the cave, seeming to decide, his chin firmed and he walked ahead of her. "Come. Let's help how we can."

Kayla was confused, but she followed. In barely a moment, they were back in the cave and looking at the water. She could see the battle in the reflection of the silvery liquid.

"This place," her father said, "Is the borderland between asleep and awake. It is the one place where we can make a difference and still let your body rest. You've already seen that you can use the power of the flute here, and though its use may require you to sleep a bit longer, you would need much, much more rest if you awaken yourself right now. Using the flute there would drain you."

She started to object.

"Trust me," he said, his eyes the deepest blue she had ever seen, and so sincere. How could she not trust him? She nodded. "Now look," he said, pointing to the water. The boxcar raced down the path, the shadow weavers zipping in and out, keeping up with the boxcar no matter how fast it went. An arrow shot out of the distance and embedded in the cart's side that carried her sleeping body, and that was when she realized it wasn't the first. Arrows covered the wagon, making it look like a square porcupine with wheels. T'Kato was on his horse, engaging the Ne'Goi whenever he could catch them. That was the sound of clashing swords she'd heard, and also his battle scream, she realized as he shouted again, which startled a Ne'Goi and stopped its shadowy zipping long enough for T'Kato to engage it.

T'Kato killed him in moments. And that made her realize something else.

As strong as their magic was, these people were not immortal.

They could be killed.

Graylin had a bow and was rather adept with it, she discovered as he released an arrow toward empty space, only to strike home as one of the female Ne'Goi appeared there at the exact moment as his arrow. The woman flew backwards and hit the dirt with a thud. Kayla could hear through the dream water. For a moment, the Ne'Goi struggled to breathe, blood gurgling in her throat and leaking out the corner of her mouth, and then her arms relaxed, her eyes staring into the empty sky.

She was dead. How Graylin had done that, Kayla did not know, but the man was brilliant with a bow.

Hadril threw out small bottles that broke upon hitting the rocky ground. Some of them sent up gasses that stopped the shadow weavers, leaving them confused and wandering. Other potions created small pools of acid that ate anyone who stepped into them. Those were rather gruesome, and Kayla shivered. Another potion transformed the people who were caught in its cloud, making them into harmless creatures like deer, squirrels, and rabbits. It must have frustrated them terribly, and if the situation wasn't so dire, Kayla would have laughed. Instead, she turned to her father.

"What can I do?" she asked, determined to help.

"Do you remember how you picked up those stonefish spines and killed the Ne'Goi you confronted in the glade?" he asked, his eyes peering intently into her face.

"How did you . . ." she started, but then she knew. Of course, he had been watching her. What father wouldn't, if he had the chance? She shook her head, then changed her words. "Okay. I remember. What do I do?"

"The Ne'Goi are immune to magical attacks. You saw that. They eat magic. That is their purpose. They are a vacuum that powers itself in the magic of others. The more magic you toss at them, the stronger they become."

"Then how do I fight them?" She threw her arms out with irritation. "The flute is magic, and it's the only weapon I have."

"You're not understanding," he said, a little of his own frustration showing. "Think of the spines, Kayla. The Ne'Goi tried to eat the flute's magic, but you turned it and sent the spines into his body. They cannot defend themselves against physical attacks. Look at what your friends are doing. They do not use magic to fight them. They use physical things. Potions. Arrows. Swords. Use your magic to create weapons. Do you understand?"

"I think so," she said, though she didn't. What was there to use in that rocky wasteland?

And then she understood. It was a *rocky* wasteland. Grinning, Kayla stepped to the water's edge, not quite in it, but as close as she could get. She didn't have the flute with her, but she could feel its power pulling, and she reached out a hand and pulled back. The flute answered her call in an instant and her hair flared around her, the blue glow that always accompanied the power surrounding her.

Kayla now understood why her father wanted her to work from this side. The power of the flute in this dreamland was so much stronger than in the real world. She may have to reach between worlds to make it work, but the flute had power enough to do so. And this time, Brant came along with it.

He spun to life, the sharp elemental force of his whirlwind as strong as a tornado. She didn't have to tell him what to do. As soon as he saw the Ne'Goi, he began annihilating their numbers, tearing them apart with his power. She couldn't watch. These people may be her enemies, but they were still people, and seeing the man she'd loved for most of her life destroy them as if they were nothing more than a piece of paper was hard to take.

Instead, she focused on picking up rocks. At first she tried throwing them at the shadow weavers, but the Ne'Goi were so fast they were gone before the rock was anywhere near them. Instead, her earlier tantrum inspired her, and as soon as a shadow weaver was anywhere near a floating rock, she made it explode, sending the shards toward them. That proved much more successful, as it's a lot harder to escape an exploding cloud of stone than it is a single rock.

The only problem—there were a lot of shadow weavers. It seemed that for every one they killed, two more took their place. Graylin, Hadril, and T'Kato did their best, but they were going to lose. It was becoming obvious.

Kayla turned to her father. "What more can I do? They're winning!"

He looked at her with sad eyes. "I don't know, Kayla. I wish I had an answer for you."

Kayla stomped her foot in frustration and the ground near the boxcar surged, throwing a shadow weaver who'd been about to climb in the back off his feet. Surprised by this effect, she stomped both her feet and saw several of the Ne'Goi stumble.

The boxcar approached a steep valley, the vertical stone leading to more rock above. This gave Kayla to an idea, but she'd have to be careful to time it right. If not, she'd kill the people she considered her friends.

As soon as the boxcar entered the valley, Kayla focused on the stone just behind them and jumped up and down as hard as she could. The stone shook, but did nothing more than that for several seconds. Then, just as the shadow weavers followed and began running along the vertical walls, sheets of rock fell. Whooping at her success, Kayla focused her energy wherever the Ne'Goi happened to be and created a huge avalanche of stone that followed close behind the boxcar. She could see Hadril and Graylin's eyes as big as eggs as they raced ahead of the stone. Of course, they would not understand what was happening, since her body still lay asleep in their boxcar, but she was doing what she could to save their lives.

And then Brant got involved in the game. An ear-splitting grin seemed to permanently slash across his face. By now, Brant was taller than the highest building she had ever seen. His head was even with the top of the ravine. He pulled the Ne'Goi off the walls and threw them into the path of the falling rocks so they were sure to be buried. It didn't seem fair, but Kayla couldn't afford to care at the moment. She was protecting people that were like family.

The boxcar raced out the other side of the ravine and drew to a skidding stop. The wheels locked into place as Jayden grabbed a bag, leaped from the driver's seat, and ran to the Ne'Goi. Kayla noticed a jeweled sheath at his side. *Her* sheath. The sheath her father had given her with the knife. The one T'Kato had asked to take for a while, and had yet to return.

"Jayden Hancock, you get back here!" Hadril yelled. The boy ignored him and ran to the shadow weavers—what few remained after the disaster in the ravine—and spoke to one of them, who stopped long enough to talk. The man grinned and clapped a hand on Jayden's shoulders, then yelled, "It looks like we have a new recruit!" The shadow weavers surrounded the boy, all welcoming him as if he had just joined a club.

In the meantime, Hadril, Graylin, and T'Kato were doing all in their power to unlock the brakes that had been pulled so hard, it nearly glued them to the boxcar. Seeing their plight, Kayla sent an icy breath of air, shrinking the metal so the brakes popped back into place.

Surprised, but taking it in stride, the men got back on the wagon and took off, the Ne'Goi letting them go for now. They'd gained a recruit and lost hundreds of men in this battle. They could have easily pursued, but instead, they looked to the sky, took Jayden by the arms, and, leaping upwards, they disappeared.

CHAPTER
THIRTY-FIVE

The flight to Devil's Mount took most of the night and a portion of the day. C'Tan and Kardon slept strapped to their dragons and awoke with the sun's light just above Karsholm. They veered south toward Javak and the mountains, and dove into the first of a series of caverns that were the mouths of fissures running through the entire mountain chain.

The wind streaked past as they rode, C'Tan's hair streaming behind her, free, as she wished so much to be—and then they swung beneath the lip of the cavern and descended into the bowels of the mountain. When the path became too narrow to fly safely, the great black beasts landed. Once C'Tan and Kardon got their legs steady beneath them, they took a deep breath and began.

"I'll take this wall. You take the one behind me," C'Tan demanded. Kardon, even less talkative than usual, nodded and moved to the opposite wall like a man much younger than his years. C'Tan went to the wall in front of her, placed her hands on its surface, then sank them elbow-deep and began to work her magic. She called fire to her and the heat rose toward her hands, making the room warmer than its normal cooled state. In a few minutes, she was sweating, but the magma listened to her commands. *Go to the academy. Fill the empty places and send the intruders into the light.*

The magma sent its response with pleasure and moved onward in the school's direction.

Assured that it began the job, C'Tan spun and went back to her dragon. Kardon was already there, waiting for her. "Finished?" she asked. He nodded. "Then on to the next," she said, turning the dragon back in the direction they had come and taking flight. It was going to be a long day, but if all went according to plan, the school should be vacant and destroyed by the next morning, and she would finally have a chance to retrieve two of the keystones—and capture Ember at long last.

That thought kept her happy for quite some time.

CHAPTER THIRTY-SIX

Ember wasn't sure why Mahal had been missing all morning and now was suddenly back, but there he was in all his god-like glory. Ember's bed disappeared to be replaced by a table groaning with food, three chairs set around its edges. Mahal walked around the table and stood with a hand on the back of one chair.

"Come in, come in!" he said, sweeping his arm with a grand gesture toward the other two chairs. "Come, enjoy the food of the gods. Or the food of The Guardians. However, you want to say it. Goodness, you even get to enjoy it *with* one of the Guardians." Mahal chuckled at his own joke, though Ember didn't think it was really all that funny, especially considering how pale DeMunth had suddenly gone at Mahal's words.

"You . . . you're . . ." DeMunth stammered, his knees collapsing beneath him as he knelt on the stone floor before the Guardian.

"The great Mahal, yes," the white Guardian said before sitting. He served himself, then gestured with his fork toward DeMunth. "You got our gift, I see." When DeMunth stared at him, he pointed at DeMunth's face with his other hand, which held a knife. "The tongue. The armor healed your tongue?"

DeMunth nodded slowly, still kneeling in place, then, seeming to come to himself, he leaned forward and placed his forehead on the ground, his arms stretched out before him.

Mahal stopped eating when he saw DeMunth's actions and stood, suddenly the regal Guardian Ember had expected him to be and rarely saw. His voice echoed through the cavern as if it sang along with his words. "DeMunth, arise. I do not require the veneration my brother does. I was once a man, just as you, until my father raised me up to something more. There is no need to bow before me. Now come. Join me at this feast before I send you on your errands."

DeMunth's head slowly rose. Then he sat up, but stayed on his knees, examining the Guardian for a long moment before he pulled himself to his feet. Ember sighed with relief when he stepped forward, pulled a chair out from the table, and sat across from Mahal. Ember threw herself into the other chair and grabbed whatever was in front of her before passing it on to DeMunth. Her stomach growled loudly. She did not know how long it had been since she'd eaten. The night before, she remembered well, but with no way to tell time, she didn't know if it had been mere hours or near a day. Her body rebelled at the lapse.

When she'd taken from every plate and passed it on, she dug in, then stopped chewing almost immediately as the most amazing flavors danced across her tongue. Food of the Guardians, for sure. She'd never tasted anything like it and didn't want to swallow for fear she'd never taste it again, but unless she wanted to gag or start drooling over her plate, she had no choice. She swallowed slowly and took another bite of something different. Sweet and tart and cool, she devoured a kind of fruit she had never encountered.

For the next little while, Ember thought about nothing but food, as she sampled all the flavors Mahal had set before her. It was a feast that surpassed even that of the night before, and all the energy she had spent in walking through stone and battling with Brendae and DeMunth was replenished. She felt like a new woman—changed somehow.

When she was so full she thought she would explode if she ate one more bite, the table disappeared as if it were mist. Ember and DeMunth looked at each other, and it suddenly dawned on her how amazing this meal must have been for him. He said he was twenty-two, and had told her once he'd lost his tongue when he was seventeen, just a year older than she was now. That meant he'd been without a tongue for five years. He had tasted nothing he ate in all that time. She could hardly imagine what it must have been like.

They all stood, and the chairs and utensils in their hands turned to mist that settled into the ground and disappeared. Ember found herself oddly quiet as Mahal put his arm around DeMunth and took him around the room, teaching him about the keystones and how they had been formed from this place. Then Mahal reached down to pick up the pieces that had fallen after the Armor of Light was taken from the vein of yellow sapphire that arched across the room. He glanced at DeMunth, his mouth twisted in concentration as he looked him up and down. "There was one thing we neglected to create when we made the Armor of Light. Something my brother Sha'iim has bemoaned since the creation of the net that encircles Rasann. We gave you a breastplate to guard your most vulnerable parts. A helm, that you might never lose your head. Gauntlets, shin guards, leg and arm guards, and even gave you a sword. But never did it occur to us you might need a shield."

Mahal tossed all but the largest piece of rubble back to the ground, then took that piece in his hands and pulled. Ember felt that pull deep in her bones as he tugged not just at the physical stone, but somehow dipped into life itself to create. She watched, entranced, as the fist-sized piece of golden stone was stretched and molded and thinned until Mahal held in his hands a large, round shield, the crest of Sha'iim emblazoned on its surface in white light. When it was done, Mahal turned it around to look at the crest, and Ember could see two loops inside that looked a perfect fit for DeMunth's arm and hand.

Mahal nodded once, then thrust it at the wide-eyed DeMunth, the shield seeming to bond to his arm without him ever sliding his hand through the loops. The silver-tongued man lifted the shield as if it were weightless, the sword appearing suddenly in his other hand. He glowed brightly, so brightly that Ember blinked away the tears that sprang to her eyes, but she refused to shut them. DeMunth was beautiful. He'd always been beautiful, but since the Armor of Light had grown, he had become beautiful the way a dragon was beautiful, in an untouchable, majestic sort of way. It made Ember's heart ache, though she still felt the chain that bound them. Instead of waning with his growing power, their bond waxed stronger.

She was afraid to let him get close, but couldn't stand to have him gone. What was wrong with her? She had expressed her love for him, but he had said nothing in return. Did he feel the same?

Slowly, the armor's brilliant glare faded and the sword retracted into DeMunth's arm. The shield shrank until it was a small button on his sleeve. The helmet faded into his skull, and the breastplate and gauntlets and all the rest just seemed to melt away. They were still there—Ember could feel the buzz of life emanating from him, something different from his own energy—but they were no longer visible.

Ember released a breath she hadn't known she'd been holding and went to DeMunth, who was examining his hands and arms with amazement. She reached out and touched his hand, just to be sure it truly was flesh. It was warm and soft and strong—just as his hand ought to be. She took both of them in her own and squeezed, meeting his eyes, then turned and faced Mahal, still not sure what to say. Mahal took the chance for speech away from her.

"DeMunth, my boy, have you not noticed the draw you feel toward young Ember here?" Mahal put his hands behind his back and walked in a slow circle around them. "Can you not feel the tie, the chain that binds you?"

Ember startled at his use of the word "Chain" after what she had seen earlier.

Her friend glanced at her and nodded slowly. "I have, sir. Yes, I've felt it."

Mahal chuckled softly. "Good. The greatest purpose the Armor of Light serves is that of protecting the Chosen One. Ember is the servant of white magic. My servant, just as her father is my servant, though in a different capacity," the Guardian said, stopping in front of them. "Know this, my son. Your greatest call is to keep her safe. Guard her with your life, your light, your breath, for only she can bring the colors of magic together once more and heal our world."

DeMunth dropped Ember's hand as he fell to one knee before Mahal. Under other circumstances, she would have rolled her eyes, but this moment felt sacred somehow. She stood at his side and watched as Mahal placed his hands on top of DeMunth's head. A light bell-tone rang out through the room at the touch, and DeMunth seemed visibly shaken and strengthened by the act. He came to his feet once more, and Mahal took both their hands in his own.

"My children, there is a mighty task before you. One that will involve much sacrifice and pain, but in the end, you will find joy like none other has seen, not since the hundred Guardians were spawned from the tree of life." A flash of memory crossed Mahal's face and then disappeared. "Now listen closely, for my time here is almost gone."

Ember startled at that. "What? No! How else am I supposed to learn? I need—" she started, but he cut her off with the shake of his head. "You have enough, my child. All you need to know is inside you. Just trust it." He turned to DeMunth. "Guard her with every bit of you, my son. She will save us all in the end, if she can only live long enough to take the chances given her." He then turned to Ember and took both of her hands in his own. "Go with my blessing, Ember Shandae." With his words came a blanket of warmth that settled over her soul. "You have found one of the keystones of Rasann, but there are six more. One holder will soon be on her way. The others will find you as the time is right. When all the keystones are together, you must bind them and use their light to heal the net of magic."

Ember was sure her eyes were as large as saucers. "But how—"

Mahal cut her off once more. "You will know when the time is right. I shall never be far away, and my servants shall be even closer still. And yes, my child, that includes your father. You shall see him again." The wave of relief Ember felt over that was almost more than she could bear, but she tried to set it aside and listen.

"Now, the first thing you must do is speak to Ezeker. He must know what is happening. Tell him the time of the Chosen One is here, and he must send you out in search of the stones." Mahal stared off into the distance behind them. "He also needs to know that S'Kotos is bent on destroying the mage academy and will nearly succeed. He needs to prepare now, for if he waits even another day, the cause will be lost and S'Kotos will have won."

Mahal's gaze came back to the two of them. "Now go! Find Ezeker and deliver my words. You have enough, my daughter. Have no fear." He caressed Ember's face, then disappeared in the same mist with which he had taken his table and food.

Ember and DeMunth looked at each other, overwhelmed by what they'd just heard, then with resolve in his eyes, DeMunth pulled Ember toward the wall and waited for her to take him through.

CHAPTER THIRTY-SEVEN

Kayla shouted for joy when the shadow weavers disappeared, though it did not thrill her that Jayden had taken off with her jeweled sheath. She only had two things that had belonged to her father, and that was one of them.

She turned away from the water that had shown her the battle and looked at Felandian. He was so handsome with his long, curly hair and regal nose. "Did we really just do that?" she asked.

He smiled and put an arm around her. "We really just did. Pretty amazing, wouldn't you say?"

"Oh, yes," she answered, unable to fight the giddy joy that resulted from a battle well fought and won. She was actually thankful for it. It was a much better feeling than the numb emptiness she'd arrived with and the explosion of emotion after.

"And now it is time for you to go," her father said, taking her hands and gently squeezing.

Her face fell. "Really? Already? But we hardly got to talk." She knew she was whining, but she couldn't help herself.

"No, we did much better than just talk, wouldn't you say? We saved your friends, and you received the comfort you needed. Do you think you can go on now?" he asked, reminding her of the loss she still had to face. She swallowed hard.

"I think so. I will always miss Brant. He was my best friend. And strange as it sounds, having him as part of the flute makes things even harder."

Felandian nodded. "I believe I can understand that. Seeing him is a constant reminder of that which you lost, and his changes make it impossible to pick up where you left off."

She nodded. "Exactly! I don't know who he is anymore, or how to treat him. I guess all I can do is what I've always done—take it one step at a time." Those words said, she reached out and embraced her father. "Thank you for being here for me," she whispered in his ear. "It meant more than I can ever tell you." She pulled back to arm's length, then kissed him on the cheek.

Releasing her, Felandian brought his hands together in front of him and bowed his head. It was his way of saying, "I love you." Kayla appreciated it, but it wasn't enough for her. Laughing, she threw herself back into her father's arms and squeezed him tight. "I love you, Daddy," she said, calling him by the name he had always been in her heart.

Tears actually sprang to his eyes. She saw before he could blink them away. "I love you too, Kay," he answered with the nickname he'd given her as a babe. It felt so good, so normal to stand here with him. She couldn't help but wish they could meet in person, and she could tell he felt the same way. He squeezed her hand as if he didn't want to let go.

Finally, he released her. "It's time to go," he said. "If you wait much longer, they will worry as to why you won't awaken." He put his hand on the small of her back and gently pushed her toward the water. "Go. I'll be here the next time you need me."

Kayla believed that. He had nearly made up for all the missing years with his help today. She finally knew that he loved her, not just in her mind, but in her heart and soul as well. "Goodbye, Daddy. I'll see you again soon."

He winked at her. "You can count on it."

Kayla smiled and stepped into the water. In an instant, she was awake. She stretched and yawned, and though she was still exhausted, she felt better in ways she never would have if she'd stayed here with T'Kato and the others. Sitting up, she saw she was not alone.

"I was worried," the tattooed hulk of a man said. "You wouldn't wake, but I know you helped with the battle." He didn't question her directly, but it was implied in his tone.

"I dreamed," she said. "I was with my father and he taught me how to fight from the dream world. The power of the flute was stronger there and my body needed the rest here. I've not had much sleep."

She knew those words went without saying, but she said them anyway. T'Kato, in his usual silent way, digested this for a moment before answering. "Your help was vital to winning this battle, and since you did not play the flute, the Ne'Goi did not know you were with us. I believe that is why they left in the end. Thank you," he said, and left it at that.

From T'Kato, those words were raving praise, but she offered him the same dignified, wordless response he would have given. She slowly nodded her head, acknowledging his words, then stood up. The boxcar was hot and sweat ran down her entire body in streams. She wished she could bathe.

The boxcar hit a rut and bounced, throwing her off balance. She caught herself on the counter to her left and regained her footing, then, taking up her bag, she moved toward T'Kato and the back of the wagon. "It's too hot in here and I need air. Would you mind?" she asked, pointing at the door. T'Kato strolled to the back of the wagon and threw open the top half of the door and latched it against the wall, then opened the bottom half and did the same. They sat down beside one another, their legs dangling out the back.

They sat in silence for long moments before T'Kato gestured at Hadril and Graylin with his head. "They will have questions for you. Many questions."

She nodded. "I'll answer as I can. When the time is right."

Knowing the brothers sat in the driver's seat reminded her of Jayden and his theft. "Did you know Jayden stole my sheath before he left with the Ne'Goi?"

T'Kato grinned. "I hadn't, but I'm not surprised. He's been eyeballing it since we met the travelers and fingering it since I first took it from you. That's why I asked for it," he said.

Kayla turned and leaned against the side of the doorway to better face T'Kato. "What do you mean?"

He untied a small bag that hung at his side and handed it to her.

Kayla pulled on the drawstring and opened it up, then dumped the contents in her hand. Jewels. Precious stones of all sizes, color, and cuts sparkled in her hand. She looked up questioningly at T'Kato, whose grin had turned mischievous. It was a look she had not seen on him before.

He put his back against the frame as she did and faced her. "Do you remember when I told you at Dragonmeer that your sheath was candy for a thief, and you were a walking target?"

Kayla nodded.

"I had Graylin replace the gems with fakes." He pointed at the stones in her hand. "Those are the true stones from your sheath. I am sorry you lost the leather, but at least you have the valuable stones."

Kayla could have kissed the man. Jayden had stolen fakes—he was going to be so disappointed when he realized it. Somehow, she had a hard time feeling bad for him. Instead, she threw back her head and laughed. When she stopped, she pointed a long finger at T'Kato and said, "You, my friend, are a genius. Thank you."

He nodded. "It was my pleasure, Lady Kayla."

Just before reaching the next village, Hadril pulled off the road and came around back.

"I don't know how you did it while sound asleep, Lady Kayla, but thank you for your help. I believe things would have turned out much differently if you had not interfered and brought your elemental friend to do battle with the Ne'Goi. Thank you." He bowed and offered his arm to help her down. "I hate to ask anything more of you, but we need to get these arrows out of the boxcar before we go into town. It is better for business if people don't ask questions."

Kayla agreed and nodded her affirmation.

"Would you mind helping us and perhaps smoothing out the holes the arrows leave behind?" he asked, sounding hopeful.

Kayla wasn't sure what she could and couldn't do, but she would certainly try, and she told him as much.

"That's good enough for me," he answered, and then the lot of them set to work. T'Kato and Kayla worked on the right side and Hadril and Graylin on the left. She ended up being the one to climb onto the roof and pull the arrows out there, as she was the lightest and most spry. The men tried to object, but they knew she was right, so their objections were half-hearted at best.

Once the boxcar was free of arrows, Graylin gathered them up into bundles and tied string around them. When he saw Kayla watching, he explained. "There's no point in wasting perfectly good arrows. I can use them or sell them, but either way, they are of value."

And now came the challenge. Kayla had the flute in her satchel, but she didn't want to play it, not with people near. The last thing she wanted to do was draw the shadow weavers here, so she reached with her own energy and just touched the flute's case, feeling the power buzz within. It whispered to her, and rather than try to guess what she needed to do, she asked the flute, just as she had in Sarli's kingdom before healing the fissures in the hotpot. Images sprang immediately to mind. She hadn't expected that, but thankful for the instruction, she turned around, and running her hand along the surface, she walked entirely around the boxcar, smoothing the dents and holes in the wood until it looked as if it were freshly painted. She hadn't been sure she could do it, but it appeared she could.

Pleased she could do something more to help, and happy for the distraction it provided her, she admired her handiwork. Hadril and Graylin were full of praise and gratitude, and she accepted it graciously.

Hadril pulled her aside and spoke to her after that. "We had thought a stop in this village would be good for all of us and keep us invisible to the Ne'Goi. But—can we perform without the Sapphire Flute? I don't know about you, but I have no wish to call them here, with so many people around."

Kayla stopped him there. "Neither do I. We're minus four, though. Can we do without them?"

Hadril nodded. "We've been doing this by ourselves for so many years, a show with only a few of us is no problem at all. It may not be as entertaining as the last, but the village will not know that." He was quiet for a moment, then met her eyes. "Are you sure you'll be okay with this? I know you have suffered a tremendous loss—"

"I'll be fine," she interrupted. She couldn't afford to think of Brant at the moment.

But then again . . . "What about using Brant's elemental spirit as part of the show? He would be unique enough to replace Niefusu and Jihong and their horses, don't you think?"

Hadril scratched at his beard, thinking. "Perhaps. Can you control him without playing the flute?"

As unladylike as it sounded, she snorted. "He's sentient. All I need do is ask. He is still new to this elemental business, so he cannot stay for long, but he could give a show while he was here. Shall I ask him?"

Hadril hesitated only a moment. "Certainly. Tell me what he's willing to do."

"I'll do better than that," she said, smiling, and touched the flute. "Brant. Will you come out?" she asked, and even before she finished, he was there, looking nearly normal, though he was still tinged blue and slightly transparent.

"Yes?" he asked.

"Would you be willing to help us with our show today? Get the people's minds off things and bring something unique to their lives?"

"You mean something like this?" he asked, turning instantly into his elemental form with its sharp features, bulging muscles, and whirlwind bottom. Hadril gasped and took a step back before Brant dropped the form and became his spirit self again.

Kayla glanced at Hadril, who seemed speechless. "Yes, something like that. Just don't hurt anyone, okay?"

He looked offended. "I only hurt those who wish to harm you," he answered before disappearing.

Hadril looked partially relieved he was gone, but his eyes glowed with excitement. "He would be a fantastic addition to the show. Let me work out the schedule, and I'll get back to you shortly. Why don't you get something to eat while we wait? I've got apples and cheese in the boxcar."

Kayla shook her head. She was still too sick over her experience with Jihong and losing Brant—the thought of food turned her stomach. "No, I'll be okay. I'll get something after the show. It's still early in the day."

"As you wish," he said before jogging to the boxcar and talking to T'Kato and Graylin.

Kayla took a moment to look around her. This village was nothing like the one they had left. It was wealthier, and it was larger. The fields were full and ripe, the roads better kept, and she suspected Graylin would have less work and Hadril more. It would be an interesting evening.

The arrows removed, the dents fixed, and a schedule in place, they drove into town. This time, instead of parking in a fallow field, they drive directly to the center of the town near its well and set up shop. Graylin went to the inn to inform the innkeeper that they had arrived. He would spread the word more quickly than a town crier.

Or maybe he would use the town crier, Kayla thought as a man left the inn and walked the roads, yelling out the news that a show would begin at noon, which came much faster than Kayla had imagined. The battle with the Ne'Goi had seemed to go on for so long, and she had begun her day so early, that it felt as if it should be nearing sundown, but it was far from it.

Still exhausted, she followed their schedule. Graylin did an archery exhibition and created wire animals for the children. Hadril used one of his potions to transform the blacksmith into a rabbit, and then back into a man. The people loved that one. Kayla played her silver flute, then drew Brant from the Sapphire Flute and let him show off for the crowd.

At first, people were terrified. Several women screamed when he first appeared, but then he took up a curious child into his whirlwind. Kayla almost stopped pulling power from the flute, but Brant had slowed and softened his miniature tornado so that it only lifted the boy from the ground and spun him around a few times before Brant caught him in his arms and returned him to his mother. The giggling boy immediately tried to scramble down and go back to the funny blue man, but seeing the adventure the young boy had, the other children had lined up for a ride.

Brant stole the show. It made Kayla proud to see. Her heart panged for a moment—he would have been such a wonderful father. But there was no point thinking of it now. What was done was done.

The show continued, ending with the duet of Graylin and Kayla in song and with the flute, though this time she used her silver flute alone. Finally, the travelers announced they would be in town for the remainder of that day and the next for any repairs or potions needed, and that was the end. It seemed much faster than the last time and probably was because of the missing people. Fewer people meant less chaos—easier to keep things simple, and definitely less to do.

Finally hungry, Kayla headed to the inn and found a table near the fireplace, though the hearth was not burning at the moment. A young girl of probably twelve came to take her order, and Kayla did as she had the last time, asking them to bring whatever leftovers remained in the kitchen from the lunch rush, as well as a pitcher of cider.

As before, a plate of bread and butter arrived with the cider, though this time there were three different types of bread—a white, a medium brown, and a very dark. She guessed white flour, whole wheat, and rye, and found herself delightfully pleased to be right. She ate the bread and drank the cider, and looked around the room. Being several hours past lunch, there were few people in the dining area, which suited Kayla just fine.

A tall, thin woman walked through the doorway and paused, scanning the room, her eyes stopping on Kayla. She walked gracefully across the room, pulled up a chair, and seated herself.

Kayla was so surprised, she didn't know what to say to the woman who was so bold as to seat herself at a table uninvited.

"You have been very hard to find, young lady."

For a moment, Kayla was afraid this woman was one of the shadow weavers, but her next words both eased that fear and created a new one. "I am Mistress Shiona of the Council of the Magi. We have heard rumors regarding the Sapphire Flute and C'Tan's attack on the court of Dragonmeer. I have also heard that Duke Brant travels with you, and I have many questions. May we speak?"

Kayla didn't know how to answer, but she realized things had just caught up with her. If the Council of Magi was involved, there would be no escaping this. She was going to have to tell the truth of C'Tan's attack to someone outside her circle of friends. She would have to explain Brant's death and the change the flute made in him when even his parents didn't know.

Oh, boy.

CHAPTER THIRTY-EIGHT

Ember swam through the stone, dragging DeMunth behind her until she broke through the wall and onto a main pathway, startling several girls into squeals. The girls scrambled and ran the opposite direction back toward the bathing rooms. Ember couldn't help the smile that spread across her face. If she had known that was all it would take to get people to leave her alone, she'd have walked through the walls ages ago. Then it dawned on her that she hadn't known she *could* walk through walls until just before she met Mahal. She had many things for which to thank him the next time she saw the Guardian. She was about to tell DeMunth about her new ability to travel almost instantly from one place to the next when he grabbed her by the hand and took off at a run.

"Come on," DeMunth said, seeming to get his bearings and dragging Ember down the paths that led to the central areas. He ran through the eatery, past several classrooms, and then turned down a corridor Ember hadn't noticed before. It took them to another portal. Ember really didn't like portal travel. It made her slightly nauseated to be zipped along like that, but she had no choice as DeMunth ran straight forward and then into the buzzing space between the pillars. Ember felt herself pulled along at extreme speeds, then she stumbled out of the next portal and into an empty cavern. She and DeMunth raced again as soon as she got her equilibrium, and before she knew it, they had entered another portal. This one lasted longer, and when they stumbled out of it, DeMunth let her sit and rest for a few moments before he pulled her along again.

The last portal was the longest yet, and when they exited, Ember tripped and nearly fell flat on her face. DeMunth caught her just before she hit and turned her so that she fell on her side with him. They lay almost nose to nose for a long second, gasping for breath, when she became very aware of just how close they were. Without even thinking about it, she reached a hand out and caressed his soft brown hair, pushing it back from his face so she could see his beautiful green eyes. His arm brushed up until it lay along the side of her head, his thumb flicking along her jawline as he brushed her curls back. And then, with their hands on the backs of each other's heads, they slowly drew close until their breath intermingled, and with a sigh, their lips met.

Ember had thought their first kiss a fluke—some things could only be that beautiful once. Never twice. But here she was with her lips pressed against DeMunth's, and the world faded away. She completely lost herself in him with a single kiss, but this time when she saw the chain that joined them, she remembered what Mahal said and was not afraid. Instead, she loved that they were bound. She didn't feel as if her freedom had been taken away—she felt DeMunth was almost an extension of herself and it thrilled her in a way nothing else could. She wanted to spend forever with this man.

He pulled away, as if suddenly realizing they were on the floor in the middle of a crisis and had a job to do—which they did. She just hadn't wanted to stop kissing him to do it. Ember sat up with a sigh and pulled her knees to her chest for a moment, trying to gather herself together, and she'd have been lying if she didn't admit her knees were a little wobbly when she stood. DeMunth was that good.

She followed him as he raced down the stairs and into the room where Ember had received her birthing day gifts from her father. She heard the voices before she came around the last bend and tried to slow DeMunth to warn him, but he wouldn't stop. As they rounded the last corner, Ember came into full view of her family and half the staff of the mage academy.

DeMunth stopped suddenly, Ember slamming into his back, as Ezeker turned. She rubbed her nose, then stepped out from behind him. Ezeker's eyes grew wide, then narrowed in what looked to be anger, though if so, it was a look Ember had never seen on his face before.

"Where in the world have you been, young lady?" Ezeker's voice rose above the rest of the room, which momentarily quieted as they turned in the direction he was facing. A gasp came from Ember's right. Then her mother swept her up in her arms, alternately crying and yelling at her.

"Where have you been? I've been looking all over for you, and was so worried something had happened. Don't you *ever* do that to me again, Ember Shandae! Do you hear me? Never again! Oh, I'm so glad you're safe!" Her mother went on and on until Ember could untangle herself and start talking.

"I'm okay! Really, I'm okay. There were some things I had to work out and I think I finally did, but we need to give you a message. We'll tell you everything, but you need to let me talk." Ember looked across the room at Ezeker, who still looked angry and ready to burst any moment, so she hurried on as quickly as she could.

"After I left, I was drawn toward a light that led me into a spherical room. You wouldn't *believe* this place. Ezeker, you know how you always said the birthplace of the keystones was somewhere inside these mountains?" She waited for Ezeker's cautious nod before she continued. "Well, you were right. I was there! There was a light in the stone, and I walked right through the rock and came to this room that looked like a giant ball had been cut out of rainbow crystal. It was the most beautiful thing I'd ever seen."

"You saw the birthplace of the keystones?" Ezeker asked, the anger fading with his awe.

Ember nodded. "I did. And more than that. I found a teacher. The only person still alive who could show me how to use white magic."

Stunned silence followed.

"Ember, there *is* no one left alive who could have taught you. We'd have known—" Ezeker started, then realization made his eyes wide and his mouth form into a silent "O."

Ember nodded. "The Guardian Mahal brought me there and taught me. He was the one who told me to bring the shadow weaver to him. I would never have done so otherwise. We were just going to question him and then take him back, but the shadow weaver ate the magic from the walls somehow and disappeared. Mahal told me to come here and give you a message. He said that S'Kotos is trying to destroy the mage academy and has nearly succeeded. He said that within a day, the time would be upon you."

The entire room burst into an uproar at that, completely ignoring the fact she had just told them her teacher was one of the Guardians. Ezeker raced to her side while the others talked amongst themselves. Ember noticed one of the professors and a couple of the guards in the corner talking, though they weren't Rahdnee or Brendae, thankfully. They kept glancing at Ember. Lily was there too, and she just stared at Ember as if unsure of what to do.

"Ember, did he tell you anything more? How is S'Kotos to destroy the mage academy? What is coming? What can we do?" Ezeker asked, his hand on her arm shaking and squeezing more with each question until Ember winced in pain.

"I don't know, Uncle Ezzie. He just told me to warn you, then he disappeared. I'd tell you more if I knew." She wanted to tell him about the traitors in their midst, but with so many people in the room, she wasn't sure who she could trust. That would have to wait until they were in private.

Ezeker was quiet for a moment, his lips pursed in thought, then he took Ember by the arm and dragged her back toward the portal. "Take me to him," he said, slightly breathless from the race up the stairs.

"He's gone, Uncle. I told you that," Ember said, trying to pull out of his surprisingly strong grip.

"I don't care. Take me there. Take me to the sphere of the keystones. Perhaps it will give me answers if he truly is gone."

"I'm coming too," Marda said, and the look on her face made it obvious she was not to be argued with. Ezeker gave a sharp nod before racing up the stairs, then, without even bothering to pull aside the tapestry, he pulled Ember into the portal, right through the cloth. It was a strange sensation, almost a tearing, as they moved through and went back the way they had come. Ember wasn't sure how much time had passed since she had left the crystal sphere. She knew Mahal would not be there and was frustrated with Ezeker's stubbornness. They needed to be working on a solution, not going on tour.

After pulling Ezeker, her mother, and DeMunth through the rock and into the sphere, Ember was exhausted. What energy she'd built up from the delicious meal was nearly depleted, but it was almost worth it to see Ezeker's face as he walked around the room, his fingers trailing along the different colors of stone and feeling the indentations where the keystones had once been.

Ember wiped the sweat from her brow. It sure was hot in here. The stone had always seemed so cool before, but now it was as if she were sleeping too close to the fire. It was odd. *It must be from all the exertion,* she thought. *I've never had to pull three people through stone. Helar, before yesterday, I'd never pulled anyone through stone, including myself.*

Marda stood in the middle of the room and turned in a circle, taking everything in, then ambled to the blue vein and touched the rod-like void. "The Sapphire Flute," she whispered, then moved on to the green. "The Emerald Wolf," she continued. "The Armor of Light," she said at the yellow, glancing at DeMunth and moving on to the orange. "The Hidden Coin." At the red, she named the one Ember could not figure out. "The Ruby Heart." At the purple, she fingered the four rough-looking shard holes. "The Amethyst Eye." Then looking around and up, just as Ember had, she pointed to the ceiling. "The Crystal Mallet. They are all here. This truly is the birthplace of the keystones."

Ember had never heard her mother sound so reverent, but she understood the feeling. This was a holy place. A sacred room. She was glad it had been protected from sightseers all these years. Obviously, someone had found it at some point or the rumor it was here wouldn't have been so prevalent, but if so, it had been long enough ago that no one remembered the story or who it was.

DeMunth knelt and hummed softly, bringing the magestone to life around them once again. The pitted etchings where the Shadow Weaver had stolen the magestone and turned it into dust smoothed when DeMunth sang, as if he had the power to not only heal the stone, but almost to replicate it.

Ezeker came to her, Marda still lost in the room's ambiance. "Ember, thank you for bringing me here. This room is magnificent, all I ever dreamed it would be and more." His eyes were misty, though he tried to blink it away. "But you need to know that freeing the Shadow Weaver as you did has put the academy and yourself in grave danger."

Ember hung her head. "I know, Uncle Ezzie." She met his eye then. "But whether or not you believe it, Master Mahal truly asked me to bring him here. He hadn't known the dark magic was in our world and believes it is that which corrupted S'Kotos. I'm sorry the prisoner got away from me. I didn't know what he could do, and the master left me alone to handle it."

Ezeker put his hand on her shoulder and squeezed. "I'm not placing blame here, child, but you need to be aware. Now," he said, changing the subject. "You look exhausted. How much magic have you used today?"

Ember tried to quantify, but her brain was so tired, she couldn't process the numbers. She finally gave up and admitted, "A lot."

Ezeker harrumphed, then wrapped an arm around her and guided her back to the wall. "I'm going to ask you to perform one more feat of amazing magic, this walking through walls thing, and then I'm sending you to your room for an extended night's sleep. DeMunth will bring you supper and guard you through the night. That's not a request," he said when he saw she was about to object. "It's late enough in the evening that you can go to bed with no one thinking the worse of you for it, and rest and food are the two most important parts of regaining your magic. While you sleep, the council and I will come up with a plan to thwart S'Kotos."

"Uncle Ezzie—" Ember started, wanting to tell him about the traitors in their midst, but he cut her off.

"I don't want to hear anything about it. You rest and come talk to me tomorrow, okay?"

Ember supposed it could wait another day. She really was exhausted. Taking each other by the hand, she gathered what energy she had left and pulled them back through the wall and into the hallway before she nearly collapsed. DeMunth picked her up and carried her to her room. She was asleep in his arms long before he reached her room.

CHAPTER THIRTY-NINE

Kayla spent an uncomfortable hour explaining to Mistress Shiona of the mage council what happened at Dragonmeer, the part she had played in drawing C'Tan to the Domanta family home by breathing on the flute, and how she'd tried to lure the evil woman away and save Brant at the same time.

After that, she told her all about Brant's death at the hand of Jihong, and Niefusu taking his brother back to his homeland for justice, if he still lived. And then she told Shiona about the flute taking Brant into itself and changing him, using him as a tool, and how he helped to fight the Ne'Goi.

"Ne'Goi?" Shiona asked. She sounded startled and slightly terrified. "The Ne'Goi have returned?" At Kayla's nod, she continued, "Oh, this does not bode well." And then realization crossed her face. She let her head fall forward to bang against her fist repeatedly. Muttering under her breath, Kayla overheard her say, "Why did I not see this? How could we not connect the two? The shadow weavers are the Ne'Goi! It's obvious." She pounded her forehead a few more times, then stopped, resting her head on her fist.

Kayla was concerned. She didn't know if the woman was crazy or distraught. One thing was certain—something was terribly wrong, and it had much to do with what Kayla had just told the councilwoman. She remained quiet, eating her food when it came, but barely tasting it. She ate until her stomach stopped rumbling, then pushed the plate away, keeping only the pitcher of cider. Finally, the councilwoman sat up and met Kayla's eyes. "You must come with me to the mage academy and address the council," she said.

Kayla pulled back. "Why?"

"Because no one else knows what you know. None other has seen what you've seen. So many things you've seen," she added more softly, placing her hand over Kayla's. "So young to see so much." She pulled back away and straightened herself. "The council needs to know about C'Tan's attack on Dragonmeer. They need to know about the Ne'Goi. They need to know how the keystones are adapting and using your Brant to do their bidding. And the most important reason—the Wolfchild is there, and the keystones are collecting around her. One is there already, and finding you seems like a manipulation by the Guardians to gather you together. We knew this day would come, and I believe it is here."

Kayla felt the truth of the councilwoman's words like a hammer in her heart with each revelation, but when she told her that the Wolfchild was at the mage academy, Kayla knew she had to go. It wasn't a matter of choice or desire. She'd been seeking the Wolfchild since King Rojan had given her the flute. And now she not only knew how to find her, she had a guide.

"I will go," she said.

Shiona didn't smile, but she did smack the table enthusiastically. "Good! The sooner the better. We must find swift horses to get us to the portal before nightfall. We shan't be able to enter tonight, but we can camp outside and enter at first light. I wish there was an inn closer to that portal." Shiona wasn't complaining, but Kayla could understand her feelings. The thought of sleeping on the grass didn't particularly excite her, either.

"Where is the portal?" Kayla poured the last of the cider into her cup and took a large swallow.

"Just outside of Driane," Shiona answered.

Kayla choked on her cider, then laughed. "Driane?" she asked when she could breathe again.

"Yes." Shiona seemed confused by Kayla's reaction, which made her laugh all the more.

"Well, if your Guardians are arranging things to get the keystones together, they are doing a fine job of it." She tried to smother her laughter. "It so happens that King Rojan has just made me the duchess of Driane. I own the manor there. If you don't want to sleep on the grass, it looks as if your wish has been granted."

Councilwoman Shiona's jaw dropped at Kayla's revelation, then slowly picked itself up and broke into a wholehearted smile. At that point, she, too, began to laugh.

There was a lot to do before they could leave, but they did it quickly. Graylin and Hadril chose not to continue on with them, so instead, Kayla begged a favor.

They stood beside the boxcar, absent of customers for the moment, while she spoke with them. "Which direction are you heading next?"

"We usually take a circuitous route that will lead us back to Dragonmeer, then on to some of the coastal kingdoms. Why do you ask?" Hadril said.

"I wondered if perhaps you could do something for me when you reach Dragonmeer."

"Anything," he answered, and Graylin nodded his head in agreement.

"I want to implant a memory, a route memory, into the mind of the horse that belonged to Brant, so he can find his way back to Brant's casket and lead his family there. Would you be willing to give the horse to his family and deliver this letter to Duke Domanta for me? I have no idea how long it will be until I return." She hated having to ask, but Brant's family needed to know what had become of their son, and Kayla knew she would not be welcome there. She'd spent a good hour composing the message and telling the duke all that had happened, knowing he would want the truth of it, hard as it would be to hear. The duke could choose what he would tell others.

The brothers looked at one another, and this time Graylin answered. "Lady Kayla, you have done more to help us than anyone ever has. We will honor your wishes with pleasure, despite the heaviness of the news."

Kayla's eyes brimmed with tears and overflowed. "Thank you," she choked out, handing him the sealed letter addressed to Duke Domanta.

With nothing else to say, she hugged each man and said her goodbyes, then moved to the white stallion that was Brant's engagement gift from his father. She wasn't sure how to implant the trail into the horse's mind, but she knew it was possible. She put her hands on its head and tried to stare into its eyes, but nothing happened. Kayla could feel the power of the flute, but it seemed just out of reach. Exasperated, she called Brant's name. He was immediately at her side, standing actually inside the horse, his head and arms poking up from its body. It was a bit unsettling, but she tried to ignore it.

"Yes?" he asked.

"Brant, I'm trying to tell the horse how to take your parents to your ice casket, but I don't know how. Can you tell me what to do?"

He grinned his usual Brant smile. "I can do better than that." He took three steps forward until his head overlapped with that of the white stallion. It startled up at first, then settled down and into Brant's head. It looked very odd. Kayla shivered, but after a minute or two, Brant stepped to the side. "There. Done. The horse can take them there now."

Relief flooded Kayla. "Really? That simple?"

"That simple," he responded. Then, showing a bit of his human warmth, he said, "Thank you for thinking of them and making this right. It will mean much to them, I am sure."

Brant disappeared before she could answer.

Finally, all the preparations were made and Shiona, Kayla, and T'Kato saddled up and rode to the south toward Driane. It was a few hours' travel, but the company was nice, and the roads were in good condition. The sun was just beginning to set when they arrived at what would someday be Kayla's home.

Driane was a large, blocky castle made of reddish sandstone. It wasn't the prettiest castle she had ever seen, but she could envision the changes that would make it a home. A beautiful home, with her mother's touch.

Thoughts of her mother made her homesick, but her heart was already so full of ache and loss that homesickness was just a raindrop in a hurricane. Such a small thing to deal with when she felt so lost. It was good to have a purpose and something to do. She needed the distraction more than ever before.

The sun was falling behind the western mountains when the group rode up to Driane Keep. She led the group into the courtyard as if she knew what she was doing, when in reality she knew nothing of her new home, and only hoped the king had sent a stable master or at the very least a groomsman to ready things for her after he gave her the duchy.

She was in luck, for before her feet touched the cobbled ground, a young boy ran up from the west end of the building. "Are you Lady Kayla?" he asked her. She smiled and nodded as he took the reins of her mount. "It's good to meet you, Duchess. My name is Tobyn and I'm your stableboy." He bowed at the end of his little speech. "Would the rest of you like to follow me, or have me come for your mounts as soon as I get this one settled?"

T'Kato looked at Shiona, then answered the boy. "We'll just leave them here, if you don't mind. We've been on the road for quite a while, and I know the ladies would like to clean up before dinner."

Tobyn bobbed his head. "No problem at all, sir. I'll be right back and take good care of them for you. Will you be needing them again tomorrow?"

Kayla was about to say yes when Shiona spoke up. "No, Tobyn. We'll be departing for a while, but the mounts will stay here. They won't like where we're going."

Tobyn grew serious at that, but bobbed his head once more and turned to lead the horses down toward what Kayla assumed were the stables.

Kayla wanted to ask Shiona about that, but the woman turned and entered the building, where a lovely young maid curtsied. "So nice to meet you, Duchess Kayla," she said to Shiona. The tall woman chuckled and gestured toward Kayla with her chin. "I'm not the duchess, just an old mage on her way home. The duchess is the pretty, young blonde in the back."

The girl blushed, then turned to Kayla. "Pardons, Mistress, I just assumed. Welcome home. It's good to have you here," she said, leading the group upstairs. "We've done a lot of cleaning in the past few days, and we have just enough rooms for you. We would have better prepared if we'd known you were coming."

"It's all right," Kayla said. "We didn't know we were coming until this afternoon. I'm sure it will be just fine."

They climbed the stairs, rounding up to the top floor. The maid turned and smiled. "Let me show you to your rooms, and then I'll take you to the baths and the kitchens, if that is all right. If you'd like a tour, duchess," she said, now directing her words to Kayla, "I'd be happy to escort you."

Kayla thought about it. "Yes, actually, I think that would be nice. Perhaps after dinner?"

The girl nodded. "Excellent. We'll have things ready for you."

"What's your name, maid?" Kayla asked the girl as they approached the first door.

"I'm sorry, duchess, I didn't even think—"

"No need to apologize. And no need to call me duchess all the time. Lady Kayla or Mistress are fine for now. I'm not quite used to the duchess title as of yet," Kayla said, thinking of Brant's mother. She would forever be the duchess in Kayla's eyes.

"I can imagine," the maid said. She opened the door on the right and beckoned T'Kato forward. "This one is for you, and this one," she said, opening a door across the hall, "Is yours, Magemaster," she said to Shiona. "It's got the longest bed. I thought you might appreciate that, considering your height."

This girl reminded Kayla of Sarali. She immediately liked her. Shiona answered, "How delightful! If there's one thing I hate, it's a short bed," she said, then entered her room and examined it, Kayla saw, before she moved on. The girl still hadn't told them her name.

She went to the end of the hall, where the double doors stood. "This is the master suite. It's got two rooms, though I know you're the only one. That is all right, isn't it, duchess—I mean, Lady Kayla?"

Kayla smiled at her correction. "Yes, that should be just fine . . ." she paused expectantly.

The girl reddened. "Ah, I apologize, Mistress. My name is Elayna." She curtsied. "It's grand to meet you."

"As it is you, Elayna," Kayla answered. The girl opened the double doors and took Kayla on a tour of the suite. The entryway held a sitting room and a fireplace, with doors to each side leading into large bedrooms. There was even a mage-spelled water closet, so she wouldn't have to go outside in the night.

After a bath, they were seated around a large butcher-block table just inside the kitchen and served a delicious stew and fresh bread light enough to float away. Kayla slathered it with butter and dropped a dollop of sour cream in her soup.

After sopping up the last of her broth with some of the bread, she sat back and looked at the group surrounding her. T'Kato was so protective of her and the flute, and he had treated Sarali with so much tenderness and respect, it was easy to overlook the tattoos and fierce appearance to see the man underneath. And Mistress Shiona, a mage councilwoman who had already impressed Kayla—now she would take them to the Wolfchild. When Kayla's father had told her to find the birthplace of the flute and the Wolfchild, she had thought it an impossible task, and now this woman had come to her, opening the door where she could not see one before. The Guardians must truly be guiding their people. There was no other explanation for what was happening.

Suddenly exhausted from the week's events, Kayla scooted back her chair. Elayna was immediately at her side. "Would you like to see the books tonight, Mistress?"

Kayla shook her head. "No, not tonight. To be honest, I'm exhausted, and we're leaving in the morning, and I'm not sure when I'll be back. When I return, I'd love a more thorough tour, and hopefully, at that time, I'll be staying. In the meantime, do you think someone could pack up some rations for us to travel with? Perhaps a week's supply? And any coin we can spare."

Elayna's smile left her face at the mention of Kayla's departure, but she nodded her head. "I'll get on that right away, Mistress. Is there anything else you would have me do?"

"No, I imagine that would be it. If you'll just have the stable boy watch our mounts until we return."

"Absolutely, Miss Kayla. You can count on me." The girl curtseyed, then spun and walked across the room to speak with the cook.

Kayla turned back to her companions. "I'm exhausted. I'm assuming we'll be leaving with the sun?" she asked Shiona, who nodded once. "Then I'm off to bed." She pushed her chair in and leaned on it. "I'll see you in the morning."

They all said good night, and Kayla made her way up the stairs and to the end of the hall to her room. She took the door on the right, leaving the left side empty, and undressed. She left her clothes in a pile on the floor and pulled on the nightdress that had been laid on the end of the bed for her.

After using the water closet and washing her face, Kayla went back to her room and put her satchel on the chest at the end of her bed, pulling the Sapphire Flute from its depths. She went around the side of the enormous bed, climbed up on it, and sat down in the middle, the glowing blue instrument pulsing in her lap. She tried something different for a change, and placing her hand on the instrument, she hummed rather than playing the flute, like she had in Sarali's kingdom.

Brant spiraled out from the flute as if she had placed it to her lips. This time when he spun out, it was quite literally. He looked like a dust devil or a small tornado, and rather fierce at that, reminding her once again of what he could become. Once he was settled before her, he resumed his normal human shape, but the blue sparkles still spun around him as if in a current of air.

He continued to change, and so quickly. Kayla brushed away a tear that escaped down her cheek and smiled at her love. He didn't smile back this time.

"What did you need, Kayla?" he asked, his voice echoing. Even the sound of it was changing. She couldn't bear it. Having him so close was almost worse than knowing he was gone.

She choked on a sob. "You. I just needed—you," she said, then buried her face in her hands.She felt a light breeze brush by her, then a slight weight settle beside her as Brant's almost solid hand brushed back her hair and rested on her head. It was cold, but still so familiar.

"I know, love," he said, sounding more himself. "But you can't have me anymore. I'm here, but I'm changing. The flute needs to use me, and I'll be here for you, always, but I won't be the same me you've always known."

"But why? Why can't you just be you?" she asked, the pain pouring out of her like steam from a kettle.

"Because I'm dead."

The bluntness of it shocked Kayla. She raised her face from her hands and turned her head to look at him. The blue sparkles still spun around him, though they didn't stir her hair. He repeated, "I'm dead, Kayla. Much as you hate it and we would both change it if we could, that's the truth of it. You have to let me go." He said the last tenderly, but she knew he meant it, and she understood what he was saying.

"There is so much more out there for you, Kayla," he continued. "It's not the end. You *will* love again."

"I feel so lost without you. Why did you have to die?" she asked, the bitterness leaching away the tears.

He put his hand over her fist, so cold. "Because it was my time, love. The flute has let me see things I'd never imagined, including little bits of the future, and believe me, you have so much more in store for you than to rule a small duchy at my side. You, my dear, are one of the chosen ones, created to play this flute you love so much."

Kayla was confused. "But what about the player? I'm supposed to give it to the Wolfchild, aren't I?"

Brant shook his head and grinned his usual mischievous smile. "No. *You* are the player. *You* are the chosen one."

Kayla's head was swimming. "But how can that be? The Wolfchild is the chosen one. I'm just an outcast half-Evahn, nothing. I've never been chosen for anything." She tried to run her hands through her hair and found it still in a bun. She yanked out the sticks and pins, needing to do something, anything, with her hands.

"They gave you the Sapphire Flute," he said. "There can be more than one chosen one," He slid off her bed and faced her. "You are part of a group of chosen ones, Kayla, and it is your destiny and purpose to play the flute, standing beside the Wolfchild, not subservient to her. She is the point of the arrow, but you and the others are the shaft and the fletching. You are all part of one whole." Brant was fading, but it seemed intentional this time, that he was truly leaving her, at least in the capacity she had always known him.

"Wait!" she said before he could disappear altogether. "How do you know this? How can it be true? Don't leave me, love! I need you!"

The sparkles spun more quickly around him now. He smiled and placed a hand on the side of her face. "You can and will live without me. I'm here, just changed. The flute needs me to be your guardian, and I can't do that while we are still so emotionally attached. Everything I said is true, Kayla. Trust it. Trust me. Now let me go," he whispered.

The tears streamed down Kayla's face. She knew he was right. She couldn't keep loving a dead man, not like this. Nothing would come of it. Though it tore her apart to say it, she knew she had to speak the words. She had to let him go for either of them to progress. "I release you, love. Just stay my friend?"

"Forever and ever," he said, the wind spinning around him now as he prepared to rejoin the flute. "I am here whenever you need me, but as time goes on, I shall be more elemental and less human. Be prepared, Kayla. Friend, I can be. Warrior, protector, and guardian, I am. Goodbye, Kayla. Find the one who is meant for you. Just remember me fondly," he said, then with a blast of wind that stirred her clothes and hair, he surged upward and dove into the flute.

CHAPTER FORTY

C'Tan pulled her hands out of the cavern's floor with a sigh. Exhaustion was settling in and she was happy this was the last fissure they needed to widen and direct to destroy the mage academy. She stumbled backward and leaned against her dragon, waiting for Kardon to finish. He fell out of the wall, rather than stepping out of it, and C'Tan was afraid he had used all his strength and was going to die right there. It wouldn't have been a terrible death, really, but he got up and staggered to his dragon just as she had, then met her eyes across the cavern. They still burned fiery red from the magic he had worked.

"You were hoping, weren't you?" he asked, almost casually. If C'Tan had a soul, she would have felt guilty for thinking exactly that. She gave him a tight-lipped smile and leaned against her dragon.

"It might have crossed my mind, I must admit," she said.

He snorted. "You wouldn't have been my star pupil if it hadn't."

C'Tan hated the reminder. S'Kotos may have drawn her in like a fly to a trap, but it was Kardon who had chiseled her into the person she was. She chose not to answer, and instead mounted her dragon, strapped herself in, and waited for him to do the same. It took him longer than it once did, but at last they were ready and flew back out of the mountain's belly. C'Tan glanced to the east and saw that Devil's Mount was pumping out more ash and smoke than it had when they'd started this process. From here, it looked as if S'Kotos' plan was working. Now it was just a matter of finding a place to rest while they waited for the action to start. They flew back to Karsholm and found a spot high in the mountains. It was cold up there, but there was no chance someone would spot them from the ground.

They settled their dragons, undid all the straps and chains that held them to the beasts, and dismounted. C'Tan's Drake rolled over on his side, one wing on the ground, and created a curved place for her to rest against his warmth. She thanked him quietly with a scratch to his belly and lay down gently on his wing. He covered her with the other and within moments she was asleep, not caring what Kardon did to keep warm in the hours it would take for the school to explode. She needed to regain what strength she could. She would rest now and eat when she awoke.

She fell asleep and dreamed of fire and smoke and running children. It was perfect.

CHAPTER FORTY-ONE

For the second time, Ember was lost in dreams of C'Tan when she awoke with Lily's hand on her shoulder. Thankfully, they didn't repeat the painful head-butting they'd endured last time, but she was still startled at the abrupt awakening. Ember rubbed the sleep out of her eyes and sat up, only a low-powered magelight illuminating the girl.

C'Tan's daughter, she remembered then, and almost squirmed away. Ember let out a sigh and ran her hand over her face from forehead to chin. "What do you need, Lily? I'm exhausted," she said, trying to be civil and not entirely sure she succeeded.

Lily rubbed at the side of her face as if it were tender, and Ember could tell she had been crying. "My father, who it turns out is not really my father, is in on C'Tan's entire plan and he just laid it all out for me, fully expecting my cooperation. They are going to flood the school with lava, Ember. They plan to either flush us out or kill us all, but we can't let it

329

happen. I can't be a part of killing any of the littles." Lily choked on a sob, then sucked her emotion back down and ducked her chin, her voice shaking as she spoke. "We have to tell Ezeker." Her glance at Ember held a lot more meaning than her voice expressed. "Everything," she finished, her voice determined, but scared.

Ember called up a magelight and saw the hand-shaped bruise on Lily's face. "Your father did this to you?"

Lily's eyes darkened. "He's not my father. Evidently C'Tan just threw me on him as a babe."

Ember tried to shake herself awake. Surely this was a dream, but no, Lily was still there, bruised and crying. "I'd say I'm sorry, but I admit I'm glad he's not your father. You know I've never liked him." The rest of what Lily had said sank in. "Wait, C'Tan is doing *what?* And you want to tell Ezeker about *you?*" She was fully awake now.

Lily nodded.

Ember's brows shot up toward her hairline. "Aren't you taking a big chance?"

"I don't care!" Lily's voice rose. "I won't let them hurt the littles. They've got no one else to protect them." Lily looked down and twisted Ember's covers into little mountains of cloth. "Will you come with me?" she asked, almost shyly.

Ember didn't even have to think about it. "Of course I will, Cousin." She grinned.

Lily looked up, surprise registering on her face as once again she was reminded of their relationship. "Cousin." She paused, then smiled. "I like the sound of that."

Ember was grateful Lily didn't ask about Ember's absence. "Me too," she said. She touched Lily's hand briefly, then threw back the covers and got dressed in record time. When they stepped through the curtain, they found DeMunth sitting on a stool and leaning back against the wall, wide awake, as if he were expecting them. Lily didn't say a word, just gave him a nod, turned right, and headed back toward Ezeker's tower. Ember smiled as she passed him and let her fingers trail across his. DeMunth immediately stood and followed them, letting his own fingers brush hers every now and again.

Ember had almost figured out the path, though it was still a little vague. If she'd been more awake, she would have hooked into Ezeker's tower and pulled them all there, but she was too caught up in what lay ahead of them, too nervous to think. DeMunth trailed behind them rather like a puppy, but Ember knew he was anything but. He was more a lion than a dog.

C'Tan was going to flood the school with lava. Ember shivered. Now that she knew what C'Tan was planning, she realized why things seemed warmer. The halls were getting beyond warm to straight-out hot, and Ember hated the sweat that broke out, and not just on her brow. It was pouring off her like on the hottest summer days. She picked up the pace. If it was that hot already, C'Tan's plan was much closer to fulfillment than any of them had realized.

Evidently Lily had the same thought, because she broke into a run as they neared the first portal. Ember and DeMunth both chased after her like there was a demon on their tail. Again, Ember thought of how much faster it would be to just throw out that magical hook and immediately be in Ezeker's tower, but before she could say anything, she had doubts. She'd taken the shadow weaver through, yes—had even pulled three of them to and from the magestone sphere, so she knew she could, but what if she hit a patch of lava entering the mountain? Would she pass through it like she had the stone? Or would she burn to a crisp? She didn't know and didn't want to take the chance, so she followed Lily as they raced to Ezeker's quarters.

When they stepped through the final portal and into the top floor of Ezeker's tower, they could see that sunrise was fast approaching. The light coming through the windows was faint, but it was there. They raced, spiraling down the tower to find Aldarin standing at the bottom, his hand on his hilt, prepared to battle whoever clattered down the stairs. Lily pulled to a swift halt and put her hands up. Ember and DeMunth did the same, then DeMunth stepped past the girls and Aldarin recognized him, and now that he saw Ember in the dim light, he relaxed further, though he still put his hands on his hips and asked, "Now, what is so pressing it can't wait a few more hours?"

Lily told him in the briefest of terms about C'Tan's spies in their midst and that there was a plan about to be realized that would cost many lives. "I need to see Ezeker right now. This can't wait any longer. Please, Aldarin," Lily said, stepping forward and putting a hand on his arm. "Please wake him. There is much he needs to know."

Aldarin looked over Lily's head to Ember, who nodded slowly. He looked back at Lily, then seemed to decide. "Sit. All of you. I'll get Ezeker here as quickly as possible." He had barely finished speaking when he stormed to the cellar and raced down the stairs, his armor and boots making quite a racket as he made his way down. Ember couldn't help but wonder if there was another portal in the cellar. Aldarin seemed to retrieve Ezeker from there an awful lot and there just wasn't much to do down there.

The three of them looked at each other and found seats around the giant stone table. Ember sat at the same place she had when Ezeker had given her the gifts from her father. She looked at them in the early morning light, the emerald eyes twinkling at her now and again.

"How did you do that?" Lily asked, touching Ember's wrists.

Ember looked up at her. "What? The bracelets?" Lily nodded. "I didn't. They did it all on their own. They were a gift, and when I first got them, they looked like normal bracelets and rings. When I put them on, they sank into my skin. I don't know why, nor do I know why they keep winking at me, but I don't mind." She was quiet for a moment, then said softly, "I know I already told you, but they were a gift from my father—the only things of his I've ever seen, let alone owned, aside from this matching pendant he put on my neck when I was a babe. It sank into my skin at the same time as the bracelets. How strange is that?"

Lily looked as if she was trying not to be bitter. She glanced down at her hands gripping the table. "Well, at least you have a father. It turns out mine was just a babysitter and shares nothing but an occasional meal with me."

Ember had already heard some of it, but the girl's pain was so fresh and raw, Ember couldn't help but hurt for her. She wasn't even sure what to say, but she managed to muster a sincere, "I'm sorry," before Ezeker raced into the room, his hair in disarray, and still in his bedclothes.

"What? What's going on?" He glanced from Ember to Lily and threw himself into a chair, completely ignoring DeMunth. Lily started to stand, but he waved her down. "No need for that, child. Sit, sit, sit."

Lily sat. She glanced once at Ember, took a deep breath, then began her story. "My mother is C'Tan." Her first words shocked Ezeker white and sent him leaning back in his chair as if his bones had suddenly departed.

After, she told him of C'Tan's secret meeting with her spies in the hills above Javak. She told him of the spy they planted with Ember's class, and how they would either convert Ember to their side or destroy her. If Ember had heard that before, it hadn't registered, and she went a bit green at the thought.

father," she nearly spat, "Came to me looking for Ember, not once, but twice, and told me about the new plan. They are going to flood the caverns with lava. The process has already begun and the school is getting really hot. I don't know what we can do to stop it, but we can at least evacuate everyone and seal off the most important rooms, like the library." Lily chewed her lip, then leaned forward, her gaze boring into Ezeker's. "If you want to be rid of the spies from inside your ranks, I will admit, I have been one, though unwilling. The man who called himself my father is another, and his partner Brendae. One of your teachers is also a spy, and one of the new students. I can give you their names, if you wish. In the meantime, I'm giving myself up into your custody." Lily fought back tears, and Ember could tell she was trying to remain stoic.

Ezeker shook his head, completely serious. "No, Lily, I won't arrest you."

"But why? C'Tan is my *mother*." The word seemed as appealing as vomit, and now the tears fell. "How can you not want to put my head on a pole for that alone?"

Ezeker reached across the table and took her hand. "I will not punish you for your blood. That you came here speaks much of your character, and it is that of a person I would like to have on my side." He shook his head. "No, I will not take you into custody. I intend to use you in this battle. For our side. The side of right."

Lily's face softened like Ember had never seen it. Then her chin quivered and she burst into tears. Ezeker pulled her in with his long arms and let her sob on his shoulder. Ember could see his smile over the top of Lily's head.

When she was finished, gained her composure, and turned a curious shade of red, Ezeker said, "Now, about those names . . . I most definitely need them." Ember started chewing on her nails and bouncing her knee up and down, waiting to hear the names of the teacher and student who were involved. Lily spoke quietly, and it was hard to hear, though she leaned forward.

DeMunth must have seen her distress and distracted Ember by taking her hand and speaking to her in his mind. *"So, what are we going to do about this thing between you and me?"*

The question surprised Ember. She didn't even know what if they had a relationship yet, though it felt like they did. He had yet to tell her he loved her, though she felt he did. She didn't know how to define it, let alone how to answer. She knew he wasn't proposing to her, but she couldn't help that marriage was already on her mind. Ember was too young to get married yet, but she already knew that if she was ever to marry, DeMunth was the man for her. *"For right now, we save the school,"* she said. *"Once we do that, we save the world. Who knows what can happen after?"*

He chuckled in his mind. What *would* happen after? It was something worth considering.

Ezeker turned toward Ember and DeMunth. "Would you two go back to the school and let the elders and guards know to get everyone out? Then go to the library and tell Master Earl to seal it up against fire and heat. Get anything you need from your rooms, then come back. I need Lily here. I'm sure you understand why." Ember most certainly did. Lily had all the information they needed. Ezeker continued. "Ember, I'm assuming you know who the traitors are?" She nodded, not bothering to tell him she only knew half of the traitors. She was too worried about the children to care about her own safety. Ember would do whatever she could to help them, even if it meant putting her life in danger. She felt an urgency like she never had before. "Stay away from them," he said, referring back to the traitors. "I'll send Aldarin and his guard to find them. You just get those children out of the school."

Ember stood and nodded, DeMunth at her side. She didn't bother to speak. What more was there to say? Together, they raced up the stairs toward the portal.

CHAPTER FORTY-TWO

The magelight woke Kayla before the door to her room even opened. She turned over and watched as the door swung open and the servant Elayna crept in with the magelight floating overhead and her arms full of clothing. She set the clothes on the end of the bed and put her hand out to wake Kayla, but before she could touch her, Kayla said, "I'm awake."

The girl jumped and squeaked, then put her hand on her chest. "Oh, Miss Kayla, you scared the Helar out of me. If I'd known you'd roused already, I would have knocked."

Kayla sat up. "It's all right, Elayna. I appreciate you coming to get me up. It's the light that does it. I've always been that way."

"I'll remember that," the serving girl said, then changed the subject. "Mistress Shiona asked me to fetch you. She says you need to be ready to leave within half an hour. I've got rations packed and breakfast set aside so you can eat on your way." The girl paused, then pursed her mouth before saying, "Do you mind my asking—where are you going without your horses? There's nothing around here, Miss. Nothing worth walking to, anyway."

Kayla chuckled. "Mistress Shiona is a master of the mage council. She is going to open a portal for us and it would scare the horses. We'll be several weeks' distance within a day or two. It should be interesting."

Elayna's eyes got big. "I would imagine so. I've heard of portal travel. I'm not sure I'd have the courage to do that. I'll just say I'm glad it's you, if you'll pardon the expression, Mistress."

Kayla threw back the covers and got out of bed. "Yes, well, one does what one must. Thank you for your help, Elayna. You may tell Mistress Shiona I'll be down momentarily."

The girl nodded and backed her way out of the room as if Kayla were royalty. It was odd, but Kayla ignored her to get dressed. She pulled off the nightgown and put on the blue Ketahean outfit, braiding up the sleeves and pants to fit her before tying on the sash, then pulled on her freshly cleaned boots. That done, she went downstairs and met T'Kato and Shiona by the front door. T'Kato had thrown a large bag over his shoulder, and there were smaller packs for each of them set along the wall. "Does it matter which one I take?" she asked. T'Kato shook his head, so Kayla grabbed the nearest one and put it on, Shiona quickly following suit. Once the packs were donned, Elayna brought them each a paper-wrapped bundle that smelled delicious. Kayla was thankful to note that her parcel was as big as T'Kato's. Evidently, her enormous appetite had been noticed.

She opened the package and took a bite. Two sandwiches made with the bread from the night before, and an omelet with vegetables, bacon, and cheese in the middle. Kayla had one completely gone before they even opened the door to leave. She wiped her mouth with the paper wrapping and thanked Elayna, then walked out the door behind Shiona.

They didn't go far, just outside and around the southern side of the castle. The sun was peeking over the eastern mountains as Shiona started to chant, holding her arms out to her sides. Her voice rose in intensity, then with a sharp clap, a large oval opened before them.

Shiona spoke over the hum of the portal. "I'm not sure how many of you have traveled the portals before, but the best suggestion I have is to hold your breath and calm your heart. You *will* eventually come out on the other side. Are you ready?"

T'Kato nodded. Kayla followed his example, though her heart raced, and her hands shook with anticipation and nervousness.

Shiona stepped into the darkness and disappeared, and T'Kato went next. Kayla took a deep breath, settled her bag more steadily over her shoulder, and stepped into the portal.

She couldn't help the hammering of her heart as she streaked like light through the portal. She tried to breathe, but found she could not. Her gills did not work, either. It was as if she were stuck in perpetual sunlight with all the air sucked from the room. She panicked and would have thrashed about, but her body was either frozen or missing. She could feel nothing but the pounding of her heart and the pressure in her chest as it begged for air.

When she stumbled out the other side, she was screaming. She stopped quickly when she realized the air was entering her lungs again. She felt weak, as if someone had pierced her with a straw and sucked out all the energy. Her knees wobbled as she stepped forward, though whether it was from the energy drain or the adrenaline rushing through her body, she wasn't sure.

Once she stumbled through the portal, it closed with a whoosh behind her. They stood in pitch black for several seconds before a magelight burst into life above Shiona. Kayla had never been so glad to see light in her life. She wished she could create a magelight, then wondered if she could. She dug in her satchel and pulled out the Sapphire Flute, just touching it, not playing, then creating the thought of what she wanted in her head, she hummed softly.

The flute pulsed and grew in light, then threw a blue magelight upward to float above her. It had worked! Kayla was thrilled. Now both the lights lit the way before them and showed Kayla their environment. She almost wished the magelight away then.

They were buried deep within a mountain, a tunnel stretching before them endlessly, and a blank wall behind. Now Kayla had a hard time breathing again as she felt the weight of the mountain press down on her. She stumbled to her knees. The weight was so heavy.

The flute lit again, and Brant spun from the instrument. He looked like he'd gained forty pounds of muscle overnight, and his eyes and hair were a little wild. Brant was truly becoming a creature of the flute. He came to Kayla's side, and the instant he touched her, the weight lifted, and she could breathe again and finally stand.

T'Kato and Shiona stood apart from them, talking, and Kayla and Brant joined them. He didn't look like he was going to leave anytime soon, so she tried to ignore the ache that still gnawed at her chest at the sight of him and listened to Shiona.

"The mountain doesn't recognize you. I should have thought of this. Neither of you have been to the academy before, and the mountain has been trained to destroy all intruders. We'll have to get it to allow us access to the academy, or this mountain will swallow us whole," the mage said, glancing around her, for the first time seeming fearful.

"What do you mean, swallow us whole?" T'Kato asked, his gravelly voice even more threatening than usual.

A wall to their right lit up, showing a man frozen in its crystalline depths. He looked as if he were caught trying to claw his way out, terror clear in his eyes and face.

"Like that," Shiona said, her voice resigned. "If the mountain is showing them to us already, we have little time. We need a plan."

"Well, can't you take us back out the way we came in?" Kayla asked, her voice squeaky with fright.

Shiona shook her head. "I'm afraid not. I don't have the energy to call up the portal again. It would kill me. Other suggestions?"

Brant spoke, his voice still sounding as if it came from that deep well, and made even more hollow with the cavern surrounding them. "If this truly is the mountain that birthed the keystones, then it should recognize the Sapphire Flute. Do you think that will give us a pass?"

Shiona's eyes lit up. "It might. Kayla, play for us, would you? Play for our lives."

Kayla was fine until Shiona said the last. Then her heart raced and her hands shook as she brought the flute to her lips and played the song she wrote for Brant. It was the only one that came to mind at the moment, so she played, pouring her heart into the music like never before. Brant glowed brighter, the blue sparkles swirling around him so quickly they almost hid him from view. He rose off the ground, his arms outstretched as she played, as if he gained strength from her music.

Well, that would make sense, since he was now an extension of the instrument.

A deep groan sounded around them, as if the walls themselves were speaking. A sharp crack sounded from above and the group scrambled back as a stone the size of a horse fell from the roof and landed near where they had stood. Now desperation set in like never before and Kayla picked up the pace, throwing every bit of passion she had into the song. Brant was glowing so brightly, it almost hurt to look at him, but Kayla looked anyway. She couldn't take her eyes off him as he rose higher and higher until he reached the roof, then he stretched his arms up and touched the stone.

A bell-like tone sounded throughout the cavern and the walls flickered around them, showing light, then darkness, a man buried in the midst, then another ahead of them in armor that looked hundreds of years old. Brant kept his hands on the ceiling, almost as if he were communing with the stone itself, and shortly after, the flickering and groaning stopped and the weight lifted from them.

Brant dropped slowly toward the ground, his light fading gradually until he looked almost normal by the time his feet touched the floor. "It is done. We may pass," he said, then disappeared in a poof that shot back into the flute. Evidently, saving them had used up every bit of energy he had.

It had used most of Kayla's as well. She found herself on her knees as she lowered the flute, put it in its case, and back in the satchel. She set a shaky hand on the ground to press herself up, then suddenly found T'Kato on one side and Shiona on the other, helping her to her feet. T'Kato let go as soon as she stood, but Shiona stayed at her side.

"Lean on me, if you will. Let me be your support," she said, wrapping her arm around Kayla.

It was the most comforting sound and feeling in the world. She put her arm around the woman's waist, and together they moved forward into the darkness.

CHAPTER
FORTY-THREE

Ember and DeMunth reached the top of the stairs and were about to go through the portal when Ember stopped. This was a waste of time. She had to take a chance, whether or not there was lava in the school. "There is a faster way," she said, and without telling him, she threw out a hook to the library, and sent the two of them hurtling through the stone until they stopped in front of the library. DeMunth wobbled on his feet for a second, then stepped forward and pushed against the double doors. The heat was almost unbearable. DeMunth spoke to Master Earl, their mumblings coming to Ember, but completely unintelligible. Tyese was still there, her books sailing through the air as she scribbled in her notebook. Ember wanted to talk to her, to ask her about anything she may have found, but there just wasn't time. Tyese looked up just as DeMunth took Ember by the arm and said, "Take me to your room."

"Wait!" the girl called out, but it was too late. Ember was already locked on and plunging through the stone to stand in her room. There wasn't much here to take. She grabbed her satchel with her birthing day gifts from the week before, picked up the script stones her step-brothers had given her, a few robes and slippers, and that was it. There was nothing here to make it seem like home, and nothing on Lily's side of the room that seemed personal at all.

At the doorway, DeMunth turned her to face him. "You can make your way back to Ezeker's tower using that hook and pull trick of yours, right?"

Ember nodded. DeMunth squeezed her shoulders. "Good. I want you to go back there. I'm going to go on and warn the guard and the elders so they can get this place evacuated. With traitors running about, I don't want you anywhere near here. You need to be safe with your mother and Ezeker. I'll send her to you as soon as I find her, all right?

"But—" Ember started, but DeMunth cut her off. "I can't work knowing you are in danger, love." Ember's heart twittered. He'd never called her that before. He pulled her to him and gave her a sound kiss on the lips, and even the brusqueness of it had her head in a whirl. "Now, go! I'll see you soon." He smiled, turned on his heel, and ran down the hall in the opposite direction, leaving Ember alone and a little discombobulated from his kiss.

She was readying her power and about to send out her magical hook to Ezeker's tower when she heard a child sobbing. She considered letting DeMunth handle it, but he was far away by now, and she was here. What harm would it do to get one child to safety?

She followed the sound and found the boy just down the hall around the corner, crouched in a doorway, hugging his knees. When he looked up with his tear-stained face, it surprised Ember to see that it was Markis, the little one she had helped through the caverns on the trip here, the one Lily hated so much. She debated. If Lily hated him, maybe there was a reason for it. Maybe he was the traitor. But then he looked at her with those pleading eyes, and when he saw her, he stood and raced to her side, wrapping his arms around her waist as he sobbed.

"Oh, Miss Ember! I'm so lost! It's getting so hot in here, and I can't find my way out. Can you help me? Please?"

Powerless at his plea, she nodded. "Certainly. We'll get you out of here, Markis."

"Thank you, Miss Ember! I just need to get something from my room. It's very special to me. I can't leave it behind."

Ember was worried, but she couldn't refuse. She had come back to collect her own things, after all. "All right, but we have to hurry. Some bad things are going to happen here soon, and we need to get to Ezeker's tower where it will be safe, okay?"

Markis nodded and ran the direction DeMunth had, full tilt. He was fast. Ember could barely keep up with him. He kept gesturing for her to hurry and come, and she was doing her best. Finally, he ran straight through a wall. Ember almost stopped at that, and she most certainly slowed down, but then she realized, if she could go through a wall, there was no reason he couldn't do it as well, and so without further thought, she stepped through what turned out to be sheer illusion and into a dimly lit room, much like Rahdnee's. There was a large stone basin filled with water, the walls red and glowing with the heat.

This was no bedroom.

Ember turned to step out when a puff of dust was thrown in her face. She gasped, breathing it in before she could help herself, then immediately stiffened and fell to the ground as if she were a board. She could move nothing. Not her arms or legs, nor fingers or toes. Only her eyes still moved as she watched Markis, now with that same evil look on his face as he had with Lily. He circled her, laughing in tones that were familiar, but that she could not place.

"Not so easy to get away this time, is it, Ember?" The boy knelt at her side, a slim rope in his fingers, and tied her hands together in a complex knot. In her mind she exerted every effort she could to pulling away, but she couldn't move. Evidently, her muscles were only wooden to herself, as he seemed able to move her limbs easily. Furious and terrified, she tried calling to DeMunth, praying he would hear her and come to her rescue, but she remained alone. She couldn't help the despair that filled her. There truly was a limit to mindspeech.

Markis dragged her to the wall, propped her against it, and tied her ankles together, then tied ankles and hands together so she was hunched over uncomfortably, draped over her knees and unable to sit up. It was uncomfortable and humiliating. Markis shoved her head back hard, slamming it against the stone. The kit was stronger than he looked. "You thought you were so smart, shifting into a wolf to get away from me before. Well, not this time."

Ember tried to throw out a magical hook to pull herself away, but evidently her power had been frozen along with her body. Her heart sank with the realization. She hadn't felt this helpless since she'd been chained to the floor in a cave after Ian Covainis had kidnapped her. Her eyes widened—the one thing she could still control.

Suddenly, Ember knew who Markis was. It was obvious he was the spy who had come in with her class, and done such a good job of gaining her trust that she had gone with him without thinking. But beyond that, he'd done this to her once before. Only then he had bound her with chains and pounded them into stone. Somehow, Markis the boy was also Ian Covainis, the man who had kidnapped her and traveled with her family to Javak.

If Ember's heart hadn't been pounding with fear before, now it did a triple beat. Her stomach was in turmoil, and adrenaline raced through her system.

He must have seen the fear in her eyes, for her face wouldn't move. "You know me now, don't you? I'm glad you know who brought down the mighty Ember Shandae. I'm glad you know who destroyed the first and last white mage." He laughed again. "I've got someone here who wants to speak with you." At that, he turned to the stone basin and dropped something in the water. A fuzzy shape appeared in the air above it, one Ember knew better than she ever wanted to.

C'Tan.

When the image was fully in place, it looked over Ember with a quirked eyebrow and a smirk on her face. "So, the mighty one who would save the world has been to her knees at last. I must say, I'm rather disappointed we didn't get to continue our game any longer." C'Tan was quiet for a moment and looked almost sad as she said, "You have much of your father in you." Then she wiped the emotion from her face and the snarl was back.

"I have a proposition for you, and I don't see where you have much choice at the moment. You will join my ranks, become one of my servants and a servant of the Guardian S'Kotos in our venture to heal the world in our own way. You will accept my master—or we will leave here you to die, to burn in the lava that is even now racing toward you, and believe me, I have no problem letting you die. If I can kill my own brother, it will be easy to kill his child. You were the reason I had to kill him to begin with. Now I can be forever rid of you both. So, what will it be? Will you join with me? Or will you choose to die?"

What a choice. Ember couldn't speak. Her mouth and tongue were frozen, but she had no questions for this woman—not really. She was choosing death either way. A living death with the guardian of fire and evil, or a permanent death that would take her back to Mahal and her father. She didn't want to die, but it was the better choice. She knew it.

Still unable to vocalize, she sent her thoughts out as strong as she could and hoped the woman could hear them. *No! I will never serve you, nor your master. I would rather die than serve a living death with you two.*

C'Tan's smile was wintry and never reached her eyes. "I had a feeling you would make that choice. Too much like your father, you are."

Well, I'm happy my apple doesn't fall far from his tree, unlike your own daughter.

The red-headed woman stopped at that. "What do you mean?"

Ember was happy to deliver a little bad news to this woman who had destroyed so much. *Your daughter? Lily? She's telling Ezeker all about your plans to flood the school with lava, and she told him the identity of your spies. I'm afraid your time here at the mage academy is over. They are a step ahead of you now.*

C'Tan looked aghast, then furious. "Die, then," was all she said before she disappeared.

Ian came to her and, still grinning like a maniacal kid, kicked her in the side as hard as he could. Ember felt something give, and pain started up her side. Tears streamed from her eyes and she could do nothing to wipe them. She slowly fell over until she was curled up on her side against the hot stone. "Not smart to get the Mistress angry. I'd say it's been nice knowing you, but that would be a lie," he said. Then, laughing, he stepped through the illusory wall, and Ember was left in the room by herself.

CHAPTER FORTY-FOUR

The caverns seemed to go on forever, much like the waterway under the sea, but at least there Kayla had something interesting to look at in the fish and the turtles and the manta ray that swam just outside of the air passage. Here there was nothing but rock, rock, and more rock. It wasn't even pretty, except for the clear quartz that held the prisoners of the mountain—the prisoners the mountain showed them every time they neared. It may have given them permission to pass, but it was obviously not happy about it.

Kayla ate her other breakfast sandwich shortly after their showdown with the mountain and found herself still hungry. She had used a lot of energy between passing through the portal and playing the flute. Though Brant battled for her, he had pulled from her energy and the magic of the flute, and she was weak with hunger.

Finally, after what seemed hours of walking, they came upon another portal. Shiona glanced around at them. "Are you ready?" T'Kato nodded. Kayla did not. She wasn't ready, but she didn't really have much choice at this point. T'Kato pulled her forward, and they went through the portal side-by-side.

This time, it wasn't as difficult. It was a much shorter journey, and having T'Kato with her made the transition easier. When they exited this portal, they were in an enormous cavern, the sound of rushing water overshadowing all else.

"Where are we?" she asked.

Shiona came over, evidently so she wouldn't have to shout to be heard. "We call this place Deirdre's tears. Just look," she said, sending her magelight high above them, brightening as it rose. At its apex, Kayla could see what she meant. Water streamed from two holes in the rock to cascade down the face of the cavern, making it look as if the holes were weeping eyes. It was a beautifully sorrowful sight.

Kayla sat down on a boulder, nearly collapsing from exhaustion. Shiona looked at her more carefully, then dug in Kayla's pack and brought out some dried fruit and jerky. "Here, eat this. You need to restore your strength. I'll get you some water, and you might want to cool your feet in the pool."

Kayla nodded and absently chewed on the tough meat. She had never really liked jerky. At least this had some flavor to it, much better than the soggy rations she'd eaten after being dropped into and then dragged through the sea.

Shiona dug through her pack and pulled out a cup, then filled it with water and gave it to Kayla. Kayla downed that with the rest of the meat while sipping at the cool liquid. She ate the dried apples slowly, enjoying the treat, then went to the pool, took off her boots and socks, and put her feet in the water. Between the food and water, Kayla began to feel better and regain a bit of energy. Shiona sat beside her.

"You are obviously new to magic," she said quietly.

Kayla nodded. "Yes, it's only been a week since I got the flute."

Shiona pursed her lips, obviously thinking, then spoke. "Normally I would wait for you to get to the school to give any kind of instruction, but you need a few basics right now, things someone should have told you when you received the flute."

"Yeah, they should have told me a lot of things," Kayla said, knowing the bitterness of her heart crept into her voice. She scooped up a handful of pebbles and tossed them into the water one by one.

"Yes, well, nothing to be done about it now, except give you what I can," the mage said. "First, magic uses energy, and the only ways to recoup that energy are to rest and to eat." Shiona joined Kayla in tossing pebbles into the water. It surprised Kayla that she would take part in what seemed a childish activity, but it was mindless and gave their hands something to do. Kayla watched ripples grow from the plunks of the stones.

"That makes sense, and I certainly have no trouble eating or sleeping," Kayla said.

"Yes, I've noticed, and it actually has me concerned. I realize it is the fact that you are part Evahn, but you metabolize your food quickly, so to keep you energized, you truly need to be eating all the time, or you are going to run out of magic fast."

"And what happens then?" she asked.

"Then you die," the mage answered, throwing the rest of her stones all at once.

Kayla froze at her words. "Seriously? I'll die if I run out of energy?"

Shiona nodded, brushed her hands off on her knees, and stood. "Yes. You will die. Always remember that food is your most important ally. Keep something with you at all times, and eat every spare moment you've got. I doubt you'll ever have to worry about your weight, with that super metabolism the Evahn all seem to have. Protein will give you more lasting energy. Nuts, jerky, eggs, and such. For a quick boost, grab something sweet, like fruit. The more natural it is, the better your body will utilize the energy."

Kayla dropped her rocks and stood when Shiona reached out to pull her up. "Always remember," the woman repeated.

"I will," Kayla answered, knowing that was something she would never forget. And really, she didn't mind. It might be a little inconvenient, but she could do magic now, thanks to the flute. What a blessing that was.

Kayla pulled her socks and boots back on after drying her feet with a rag. T'Kato lay down on the moss and chewed something. Evidently, she wasn't the only one who needed to refuel.

Kayla wiped her brow. The room seemed to have suddenly grown warm. Was that another effect of using too much energy?

She was about to ask Shiona when the mage turned in apparent alarm and looked at the wall of Deirdre's tears. Kayla followed her eye and was stunned to see that the wall glowed. The heat continued to increase, and Kayla felt like she was stuck in a metal bin on the hottest of summer days.

Shiona yelled. "Come on! We've got to go now! Get up! Get up!" she screamed at T'Kato and Kayla.

Kayla's heart stilled. Deirdre's eyes were leaking magma. Lava flowed into the lake, the steam rising and rolling toward them.

"Run!" Shiona screamed and raced for the other side of the cavern, where another portal stood shimmering in the distance. Kayla glanced over her shoulder. The steam came faster than they could run. They weren't going to make it. She'd already lost Brant—she couldn't lose anyone else. She didn't even think of herself.

Kayla stopped and turned, the flute having made its way into her hands somehow as she ran. She raised the instrument to her lips and did as she had once before on the bottom of the sea—she pulled the power of cold and ice to her, but instead of creating a wall, like she had then, she blew the cold back toward the steam and the magma.

T'Kato tugged at her arm, but Kayla was like iron. She pulled every bit of cold to her she could, and it was a lot. The stone, forever buried from the sunlight, held the chill she needed.

And suddenly Brant was there, blowing her icy wind faster than she could send it herself. His light spun around him, and then he gathered the frost up in his arms and herded it forward like a shepherd with his sheep. It was amazing to watch. He sent the icy breath out to collide with the lava, and with a hiss and crack, the two met. Kayla's ears ached from the meeting as the lava turned instantly from melting, flowing rock into exploding stone. The pebbles from the blast reached the group and they covered their heads, though by the time the rubble arrived, it had lost its momentum.

Kayla stopped playing and turned to face Brant. "Thank you," she said.

He grinned and bobbed his head toward her. "Just doing my job, love. Just doing my job." And instantly he was gone. Kayla put the flute back in her bag and turned to the group.

T'Kato looked as if he didn't know whether to be angry, terrified, or proud of her. Mistress Shiona looked astonished. She pursed her lips, like she was so prone to doing, and quirked her head at Kayla.

"Had it for a week, you say?"

Kayla nodded.

"Hmph," the magi said. "You are one quick learner. Ezeker's going to love you." And with that, they continued on their way to the portal, no longer chased by lava, but feeling an urgency that hadn't been there before.

An urgency that felt as if it came from the mountain.

CHAPTER
FORTY-FIVE

C'Tan awoke with a start, her dreams trailing off into unremembered nonsense. Only one thing remained, and that was an idea that should have come in her waking hours. It was a sign of how exhausted she truly was that she hadn't thought to put it in place sooner.

She gently scrambled out from between Drake's wings so as not to damage the fragile membranes and glanced over at Kardon. He was asleep sitting up, leaning against his dragon, which was barely tolerating his presence. It let as little of itself touch him as possible. C'Tan chuckled under her breath. It served the old man right. He had never treated the dragons with the respect they deserved.

Unable to use her scrying bowl here, C'Tan pulled out a small scriptstone from her pocket and a small pad of homemade paper. She had no ink, but she found a small stick and used her power to blacken its end and scratched a note to her servant, Dragon. The last she had heard, the teacher's identity was still unknown, and she needed to save at least one of her spies for future use. They were hard enough to find, let alone train, and Dragon was one of the best.

She laid the paper in the snow and set the scriptstone on it, then told it to send. In an instant, the words had spiraled into the stone and were sent to her hidden servant inside the school. She hoped Dragon had done as she asked and left the stone sitting on paper.

Within a few minutes, she received her answer to both questions. The teacher had received her message and agreed immediately.

Ian's attempts at converting the girl disappointed her. He had been too rough with her, and revealing himself as her kidnapper had only terrified her more. Converting her to their side was a useless idea. She hoped S'Kotos would accept the girl's death if it came to it. Ember had become a threat to all of them, and if she were allowed to collect the keystones, C'Tan knew her own life would be over. That had to be prevented at all costs.

The scriptstone lit up once more and C'Tan read Dragon's last note. "I am just outside of Javak. Shall I walk home, or have I done well enough to deserve a ride on one of your mighty dragons?" she read, the tone whimsical.

Oh, C'Tan liked that. She liked that idea very much. Grinning, she composed a return message. *A dragon will be sent. Await.* She then went to wake Kardon. She needed him to take her spy to safety. At least one of her converts must live through this adventure, and she was already tired of the old man. It was time for him to go home.

Grumbling, Kardon awoke and scrambled atop his dragon, then launched into the air. C'Tan felt better with each minute he was gone. She turned and watched Ezeker's tower and the small village of Karsholm, and waited for the fireworks to begin.

CHAPTER FORTY-SIX

Ember glanced around the room where Ian had taken her. There was nothing but the rock, the stone water basin, walls, ceiling, and a red-hot floor. Ember still couldn't move from whatever Ian had thrown in her face, and even if she could move, there was nothing sharp enough to cut the ropes.

The wall across from her began to glow and give off tremendous heat. Ember felt as if she were going to be baked alive, but she didn't regret her decision. She would serve Mahal, never his twin, S'Kotos, and she could never work for the woman who had killed her father, family or not. Ember closed her eyes and resigned herself to her fate when she felt a slight tug on her soul, almost like when she left her body. Hopeful, she tried to leave like she had in the past, but it didn't work. She wasn't sure if it was the freezing potion or her own issues, but she was stuck here.

Then the pull came again, stronger this time, as if someone was settling a hook into her soul, and then suddenly she was flying, yanked through the stone and rooms, and all sorts of things. Who would have ever thought she could travel through furniture and people—as if she were a ghost flying from one side of the school to another, and she did not know who was on the other end. She didn't know of anyone else who could walk through walls, and very few people knew she could do it, so who could pull her?

She got her answer quickly when she landed on the library floor at Tyese's feet. The girl looked at her red, sweating face and bound hands and feet with surprising calm, and said in tones much too old for her, "Well, you certainly got yourself into a mess, didn't you?" She scribbled in her notebook again and the ropes turned to dust and drifted to the ground, but still Ember couldn't move. She looked at the girl, pleading, hoping she could read her mind.

Puzzled, Tyese leaned over and sniffed at Ember's shoulder, then sneezed and backed away quickly. "Who did this, Ember? That kind of magic is not allowed."

Ember still couldn't answer. Tyese scowled, then scribbled furiously in her notebook, her hand practically flying across the page. Ember felt a strange sensation, as if moths were fluttering up from her lungs and out her nose. She sneezed and coughed and finally groaned as she turned over. The girl closed her book with a snap. "Who did this to you?"

"Ian," Ember croaked. "Ian Covainis entered the school as a boy named Markis."

Tyese turned white and sat down on the bench. "It was Ian who stormed our village and took my father. He's here, you say?"

Ember nodded, grateful she could move.

Tyese's jaw clenched, and she stood as if she were going after the man on her own. Ember sat up weakly. "Tyese! Stop. You can't pursue him alone. I'll help you, if you'll help me."

Tyese stopped and turned, looking at Ember as if she were weighing it out. She was not like any other child Ember had known. She was more like a grown-up stuck in a kid's body. After a moment, the redhead nodded, came back to Ember, and helped her to her feet. Ember was wobbly, but she could stand. Tyese steadied her, then reached into the pocket of her robe and handed Ember a book. "I found this for you. I don't know if it will help, but it's a journal belonging to the last white mage. Want me to put it in your bag?"

Ember had completely forgotten she had her satchel slung over her shoulders. She nodded. "Thank you, yes." Ember waited until she was finished, then turned. "Tyese, you need to get out of here. The school is going to be full of lava, and soon. You need to get to safety. Where's your home?" That's when Ember remembered the girl was an orphan.

Tyese shook her head. "Home is too far away and I think I'm needed here. I'll stick around." When Ember objected, the shy girl put her hand on Ember's arm and said, "Don't worry. I'll be okay."

Ember believed her. She nodded, gave the girl a hug and said goodbye, then sent a hook to her mother and pulled herself outside of the school and to Paeder's house. The sun was still just rising. Funny, it seemed like more time had gone by than that, but no, it was still sunrise, and Marda and Paeder were only now stirring. She landed in their bedroom, went to her mother's side of the bed, and shook her awake.

Marda sat up with a start, almost repeating Ember's collision with Lily the day before, but thankfully Ember moved out of the way quickly enough to avoid it. "What? What?" Marda demanded when she was awake enough to realize who was there.

Ember quickly outlined the problem and what she needed her mother to do in calling the council to meet. Half in Javak, half at Ezeker's, to fight the battle C'Tan was bringing to them. If they were going to save Karsholm and Javak, they needed magi there to fight the destructive power of the lava. Marda got out of bed quickly. "I'll call the rest of the council. We have a way of doing that without my having to leave the village. You stay with me. I'm not letting you out of my sight again."

Ember groaned inwardly. "Mum, I can't stay here. Ezeker needs me back at the tower." A brilliant flash of idea came to her. "Look," she said, "Take half of the scriptstone the boys made for me. We can keep in touch that way, okay? It's small enough that you can fit it in your robes or a pocket or a satchel. No problem. You can know where I am, I can keep you posted, and I can still do my duty to the mage academy." Ember wanted to stress that last bit, as it wasn't personal. She was old enough to be on her own, but more importantly, she had made a commitment and she needed to follow through on it, whether or not her mother liked it.

Marda stopped getting dressed and looked at her daughter, her eyes welling with tears, but Ember was surprised to discover they weren't tears of fear or sadness. Marda put her hand on the side of Ember's face and said, "I'm so proud of you. Despite my interference, you've grown up to be a much better woman than I could have ever imagined." She took her daughter in her arms for a quick hug, then pulled away. "Now give me that scriptstone so I can stop worrying, and you be on your way. I'll see you later, okay?"

Ember dug half of the stone from her satchel and handed it to her mother, gave her another hug, then sent out the hook of magic to Ezeker's tower and returned to his dining room. Several of the council members had already arrived, along with many of the students. The room seemed to be stuffed to the top, with more coming every moment. It was a wonder Ember hadn't hit one of them landing in the room.

DeMunth spotted her and waved, then came through the crowd to stand at her side. Ezeker was still talking to Lily, who seemed much more at ease now that the truth was out. She seemed to be the kind of girl Ember could really like, proving her first impression of the girl correct.

Everyone was winding things up, getting ready to send the kids away and abandon the tower and school, when a tremendous blast shook the tower to its foundation. Several people screamed, children and adults alike, then everything went silent as they all waited. Ember did not know how the tower still stood with that kind of pressure pounding against it.

Whatever it was slammed into the tower again, several stones coming loose and showering down on the crowd. Ezeker took control at that point, yelling over the noise, "Everybody out! The fight is on. You know what to do!"

And then the doorway was flooded with people racing out as fast as they could, several groups heading off toward the mountains, and others, mostly the elders and council members, heading toward Karsholm. Ember, Lily, and DeMunth were some of the last to leave, and when they stepped out the door, they stopped in surprise and terror.

The lava flow had started.

Ember looked farther down the road. Rahdnee and Brendae stood on the hillside, directing the magma into two streams—one up the hill toward Ezeker's tower, and another fountaining out toward the village of Karsholm.

Ember's home.

At first she wanted to race to the farm and warn Paeder, but then she realized her mother had probably already done that. He would take care of the animals, including her precious horses, Brownie and Diamond Girl.

The more immediate problem was much closer, for it wasn't C'Tan's people who had started the attack on Ezeker's tower.

The shadow weavers were back and en masse. Uncle Shad had already turned wolf and several of the weavers littered the surrounding ground.

DeMunth's Armor of Light had come on in blazing force the instant he had spotted them, his brilliant new shield gleaming on his arm. His other had become the sword that seemed to grow from his fist. His left hand held a hooked knife beneath the shield.

To her left, Lily had taken on her own kind of armor. It wasn't made of light, but appeared to be made of ice. Her weapons were long knives, barbed and hooked, but transparent. The three charged forward as one, directly into the midst of the shadow weavers. Ember stood stock-still in fear. They didn't know what she knew about these weavers. Weapons and armor wouldn't last long against them—they ate magic like candy.

Sure enough, Lily's knife shattered into a cloud of ice-crystal dust, but instantly she had another weapon, a flaming sword she swung at the shadow weavers when she could see them. Within moments, the flame had gone out and the dull metal crumbled like charcoal. How could they fight a war when the enemy kept eating their weapons and only gained in strength?

Ember did not know. She watched as her friends battled for her in a losing war.

CHAPTER FORTY-SEVEN

After a series of several portals, Kayla found herself in a building rather than a cave. The floor tiles were smooth and even, probably marble, though after so many hops through the portals, Kayla was too exhausted and dizzy to care. The sound of rushing water pounded at her ears, and with the dizziness, she thought it was just her head making the sound until the others focused in on the waterfall that fell from high above into a pool nearby.

In that moment, her head cleared, and excitement fluttered to life in her chest like a butterfly taking flight from a sunflower. "Are we in Javak?" she asked, turning to Shiona.

The tall mage nodded without looking at her. "Yes. We should be at the mage academy shortly. We are nearly there."

Kayla could hardly believe how far they had traveled. These portals were amazing—it was a shame more people couldn't use them.

"Come on," Shiona said, leading them out of the building and across a wooden bridge that floated directly on the water. The group walked through a field toward a small city that was nearly deserted, then past some stone buildings and toward the mountains on the other side. They followed what looked like a goat trail up to the side of the mountain, then Shiona touched one of the knobby protuberances with her hand and a hole grew slowly in the mountain's side, gravel and dirt falling as it opened like a yawning mouth. When it was barely big enough for them to step through, they all entered and continued their trek into the mountain.

They were not even twelve steps into this part of the journey when the ground beneath them shook. At first, Kayla thought it was the mountain fighting with them again, but when the temperature in the room shot up like it had in the cavern, they ran without Shiona having to say a word.

A crack appeared in the trail ahead of them, glowing red from the heat beneath, steam shooting upward as they lunged away. Thankfully, no one was injured, but it spurred them on faster until they were sprinting at a breakneck pace.

They made it to the next portal, steam geysers shooting up behind them as they dove through the oval and into the icy stillness of the transfer. Kayla couldn't catch her breath before the long jump, and when she sprinted out of the portal, she bent over, gasping, her knees shaking with the effort to hold her up.

"Sit," Shiona wheezed, and even T'Kato listened, collapsing on the spot. "Catch your breath for a moment, then we need to go. Something is wrong."

Kayla chuckled. "That is rather obvious."

Shiona glanced at her without humor. "It's not just about the lava. Can't you feel the mountain calling for help?" she said, throwing her arm out toward the wall as if she barely had the strength to hold her limb up. She probably didn't.

Kayla tipped her head to the side and listened, then felt stupid for doing so. The mountain did not have a voice she could hear with her ears, only one that spoke to her heart. She closed her eyes and tried to open herself to it, and there, in the deepest, most quiet part of her soul, she found its voice.

Pain. Confusion. Fear for its charges. Helplessness. All these emotions came through. Shiona was right. The mountain really was calling for help.

Kayla came back to herself and looked at Shiona. "I heard it. You're right."

Shiona stood. "Let's go." They groaned, but got to their feet and followed her, more slowly this time. But the last few hops through the portals were the shortest ones yet, and Kayla saw evidence of habitation. Stock rooms here. Bathing pools there. When they made their last jump and exited into the midst of a group of youngsters, they all stopped.

One small, red-headed girl was yelling at the group, but no one was listening. The children were in a panic, like a spooked herd of cattle.

"You've got to leave," the girl cried. "Ezeker commands it. You are in danger here." No one listened. Instead, they tried to push past Kayla's group to reach the portal.

Mistress Shiona put a stop to that. She achieved the volume the young, desperate girl could not. "And what do you think you are doing?" she yelled at the crowd. Everyone stilled and turned toward her. No one dared answer. The red-headed girl swam through the group and nearly pleaded with Mistress Shiona.

"Please, councilwoman, make them listen! The lava is coming and they are not safe here. They won't listen to me, but they have to leave. Help me, please!" she cried.

Shiona bent over so she was eye-to-eye with the girl. "It's okay, Tyese. I'll take it from here. Why don't you run on, find Ezeker, and tell him we're here with the Sapphire Flute?"

Tyese's eyes got huge, but she nodded to the councilwoman, turned, and ran from the group. Shiona went back to crowd control. "I am ashamed of all of you. All of you!" she said in almost normal tones. Several of the kids hung their heads. "You know the codes. Why won't you listen? Are you trying to get yourselves killed?"

A few mumbles came from the group now.

"We just barely escaped the lava and steam geysers ourselves. Do you want to be roasted alive? Why won't you listen?"

"We didn't know," one kid said. Whether stupid or brave, Kayla wasn't sure.

"Well, you should have. When Tyese told you that Ezeker sent her, you should have listened. Now go. Get! All of you go out. *That* way," she said, pointing in the direction Tyese had just taken. "Do what you can to help, but get out of harm's way." When nobody moved, she shouted. "Now!"

That got them moving, and they truly sounded like a cattle stampede as they ran away from the tall woman.

She turned back to the two of them. "I'm not sure what's going on here, but if Ezeker is evacuating the school, it's bad. We need to go fast too. Can you do it?"

They nodded, and in an instant they were racing after the children, who, after having to be prodded so hard, were traveling at a tremendous pace, going so fast, the long-legged adults could not catch them.

The group jumped through one last portal and stumbled out behind a tapestry that was half pulled down. Kayla tripped over it and went to her knees, crying out in pain. Immediately, T'Kato was there, lifting her up, and when he was sure she was stable, they all raced down the spiral staircase and out the door.

Once out in the open, they stopped in shock.

To her right were two wolves, a girl, and a man in glowing armor battling what seemed an endless army of people who zipped here and there like shadows caught on a kite string. She froze—the Ne'Goi had beat them here. The group seemed to handle themselves well, so Kayla turned her attention elsewhere.

It looked as if Helar had surfaced outside the mage academy. Lava flowed freely, not down toward the village, but *up* toward the tower where they stood. It was impossible, and yet there it was, against all the laws of nature. Kayla looked around. There was no way the lava could flow uphill without magic. That was the only answer. Setting aside the shock and terror of running into the middle of a battle, she looked around to find the source.

Down the lane, there was a magic battle taking place with two people at its center, surrounded by a barrier. Kayla guessed they were the ones pushing the lava toward her. Kayla squelched the horror she felt. She had faced down C'Tan, swam to the deepest parts of the sea, ridden behind a water horse, and been given gills by a prince of the MerCats. She had defeated a legion of Ne'Goi and survived the death of the man she loved. If she could do all of that, she could deal with this.

Kayla took a deep, steadying breath, pulled the Sapphire Flute from her bag, and raised it to her lips. She closed her eyes to block out the distraction, though she couldn't shut out the battle and death screams, nor the heat of the molten rock. She pulled in a breath, sucking in the hot air, then blew out a long stream of notes.

She felt it when Brant boiled out of the flute in a cyclone, the wind screaming and tearing at her clothes, and she couldn't help but open her eyes for a moment. This time he didn't resolve himself to his old appearance, but stayed the ferocious-looking air elemental that he had become, bigger than she had ever seen. He looked at her without speaking. Kayla waited for a moment, but when she realized he would not say anything, she nodded toward the mage battle and said, "Help them! Freeze the lava!" The elemental that was Brant nodded and leaped toward the group down the hill.

Kayla kept playing, but seeing Brant deal with the two magi controlling the lava, she realized there was someone else in need of her help. They had separated a woman of medium size with dark hair from the others who fought around her, and though she fought as hard as T'Kato, she stood alone against the Ne'Goi and several dragons. The woman seemed familiar somehow, but Kayla knew there was no way she could know her. She only knew she needed to help, so walking slowly toward the brown-haired woman, Kayla continued to play and turned the lava against the Ne'Goi. She spun fist-sized pieces of rock up from the river and threw them at the shadow weavers. It worked, and soon the numbers were gone, and the dragons had disappeared as well.

Kayla took her flute from her mouth for a moment to introduce herself to the woman. She reached out a hand and was greeted with a smile that again reminded her of someone. The woman spoke before Kayla could.

"Thank you for your help. I'm not sure I could have kept them away much longer. Would you help my daughter now?" she asked, pointing to one of the wolves in the group Kayla had initially seen. She fought the surprise she felt. If there were MerCat shapeshifters, why not wolves? They had been in legend for it seemed forever. This was just the first proof she had seen.

"Absolutely," Kayla answered. Her fingers grasped the woman's, and they shook hands. "I'm Kayla Kalandra Felandian," she said, not sure why she used her full name.

The woman froze. Even her breathing stopped for a moment, and then she laughed. "This is impossible. The Guardians must be manipulating things again," she said. Kayla was confused, and it must have shown on her face.

"My name is Marda, but your mother knows me as Brina. Brina Balania. I'm your mother's sister."

Brina or Marda or whatever-her-name-was reached out and took Kayla into her arms. "You look just like your mother. I should have known. Now, come help your cousin, the Wolfchild, would you?"

Kayla remained speechless, but she ran uphill alongside her aunt to aid her cousin.

The Wolfchild.

CHAPTER
FORTY-EIGHT

Music floated across the lava river, sending a wave of cool air wafting toward Ember. For a moment, she forgot the battle as she turned toward the sound. It was beautiful music, but it seemed to have a purpose. Ember saw an elemental form at the sound, nod to the girl, and head down the flow of melted rock toward Rahdnee and Brendae, leaving cold in its wake. Ember had never seen an elemental before, but she knew what he was the moment she saw him and stood in awe, despite the battle before her. The lava river darkened and slowed, then suddenly froze with cracks and pops and bits of shattering glass flying upward. The stream of magma went from a glowing orange to a glassy black.

The girl glanced at Ember before slowly walking down the hill toward Ember's mother. Even from here, Ember could tell that her eyes were blue as the deepest ocean—as blue as the flute she played.

It was the girl from her dreams. Ember was beginning to believe more and more that those dreams she'd been having her whole life were not just nighttime visions, but were actual prophetic dreams, and this girl was part of them. She hoped she lived through the battle to meet her.

And speaking of the battle, she came to herself, realizing it was nearly upon her now. Still wolf, she lunged at the weaver nearest her. It was the tactic that had worked best when they first ambushed her—but there were so many. She didn't know how the four of them would last long enough to eliminate the entire group. There had to be a way to destroy them as a whole. If only they had archers. The Weavers didn't seem to fare as well against non-magical weapons, DeMunth's sword being the exception.

Her fangs were non-magical, and so were Shad's. They had proven most effective against the enemy. They couldn't take down many at once, but she'd destroyed the weavers before. She could do it again. Ember dove into the action, biting left and right, dodging swords and knives as the shadow weavers focused on her and came in force. Ember fought her hardest, moved her fastest, but still it wasn't enough. Even she could see that they were fighting a losing battle, and felt it even more when a strike caught her across the leg, slashing clear across one of the bracelet tattoos visible even in her fur. She yelped, backed out of the fight, and went to higher ground.

Quickly shifting to human, Ember tore off the hem of her robe and bandaged her arm. Thankfully, it was her left and not her right so she could allow it time to rest and heal, but being wounded took her out of the fight. What could she do to help?

That brought her back to her previous thought. Archers. Ember glanced around. They didn't have arrows, but she had an entire river full of potentially lethal glass, if she could break it up and somehow throw it at the Shadow Weavers. But she still hadn't had enough training to know what she was doing. How was she supposed to take the still-hot glass and throw it at them? She couldn't do it by hand. There wasn't enough force behind it, and she would get horribly burned.

Perhaps if she used magic like a wave to shove it at them? It had worked in her training with Lily, so why not here? Mahal had told her repeatedly to trust her heart when it came to magic, that her heart would lead her in how to use it more often than not.

This felt like one of those times.

Ember tentatively reached out, both physically and magically, and sent thoughts of broken glass, about the size of her thumbnail, at the frozen lava. The ground shook, everyone standing nearly knocked to the ground, rocks tumbling down the hillside and taking out several of the shadow weavers. She hadn't thought of that, but was grateful the mountain was throwing its own rocks at their enemies, then wondered if it really was, or if it was an accident. She hoped for the former.

In the meantime, great cracks formed in the river of glass, then more spider-webbed out until there were millions of bits of broken glass lying there, just waiting to be made into something useful. Ember intended to use them, all right.

She didn't know how she did it, but she lifted up a large swathe of sharpened lava rock without using her hands. The black shards floated in midair as if held on strings, just awaiting her command. Ember could feel little strands of herself flung out to each one, and it gave her an idea. She mentally yelled, *"Lily, Shad, DeMunth! Get down! Now!"* The three of them dove on the ground, and Ember used those strings like a sling, the glass arcing overhead with power she'd never find in using her arm alone. The pieces of glass bit into the shadow weavers, breaking through armor and shields and helms. It took out at least thirty of the dark magic users all at once. Grinning, Ember picked up another swathe and flung it at the next wave of shadow weavers charging her over the bodies of those she had already killed.

"Good work, pup," she heard Uncle Shad's voice whisper in her head. *"Keep going!"* Again, she raised the shards and flung them forward as hard as she could. Ember was successful and took down several groups, but now, as she raised the glass up for the third time, she could feel the drain on her energy and knew she wouldn't be able to keep it up for long—she was already exhausted, and the shadow weavers seemed endless.

She flung the glass, then instantly went wolf again, forgetting the slice in her leg. She climbed, but she couldn't go much higher. Lily, Shad, and

DeMunth joined her, and they all put their backs together to fight off what they knew would only end in their death.

Better to die fighting for something that had meaning than to die tied up in a room because you said no to C'Tan.

The battle was never-ending. Ember's fangs were getting sore from all the biting. Lily had run out of weapons and resorted to using the fallen Shadow Weavers' own weapons against them. She had no shield, no helm, and Ember was scared for the girl. It would take one hit to disable or kill her. DeMunth, of course, looked none the worse for wear. He fought unwearyingly, but one man standing against the army was not enough. Shad looked tired, but charged endlessly. She knew he wouldn't give up until he took his last breath.

Ember wanted to pray for a miracle, but she knew it would never come. Life just didn't work that way. You did your best. Fought the good fight. And then you died and hoped you had lived well enough to deserve at least a small corner in heaven. Miracles were for the kind of believer she could never be.

In an instant, she was proven wrong.

Ember lunged at a Shadow Weaver and sailed beneath him. She looked up, leaping into the air at the man just out of her reach. He seemed as surprised as she was when he continued to rise into the air. When Ember looked around, she saw he was not the only one. The entire group of shadow weavers were hanging in the sky as if they were puppets on a string. They looked left and right and tried to get down, but nothing moved them until they began to spin.

As if their heads were caught on a string, they swung outward, faster and faster, until they spun in a giant circle above the three tired fighters. The Shadow Weavers thrashed about, and a few of them got sick as they swung and swung and swung. Then, suddenly, they disappeared with a distinct pop.

Ember looked around and didn't see any more Shadow Weavers. None near her, anyway. She glanced behind her, saw the miracle worker, and trotted up to stand beside her. Not knowing if the girl could hear her, she mind spoke. *What did you do? Where did they go?* Tyese must have heard, for she answered.

"I sent them away. Home." The girl turned red, but beamed at Ember, snapping her notebook closed and sliding her charcoal stick behind her ear. "You looked like you needed a little help."

I did. Thank you, Tyese. You saved us. You saved all of us.

The girl went more red and ducked her head. "It was just something I had to do. Thanks for your kindness, Ember." At that, the girl shifted into wolf shape and took off down the road to help the others who still fought against C'Tan and her agents.

Tyese was Bendanatu as well? Who would have thought? Shaking her head, Ember headed up the frozen lava field. It was time to meet this flute player from her dreams.

CHAPTER FORTY-NINE

Kayla had watched with admiration as the girl across the lava flow had taken the glassy river of cooled lava, broken it into bits with her magic, and used it like shrapnel to destroy the Ne'Goi who attacked her. This had to be the Wolfchild, she thought as she watched the girl slip casually from human to wolf in the blink of an eye. She had known the term meant she was the Chosen One, but she hadn't realized it would be so literal. She was part wolf. Only the Bendanatu could change shape the way she did. Kayla was fascinated by this Wolfchild cousin of hers.

"I guess she didn't need our help after all," Marda said. "Why am I not surprised?"

Kayla chuckled. "What should I call you? Marda? Brina? Auntie?"

Marda laughed. "I hadn't thought of that. Auntie is too odd after all these years, and I haven't been called Brina much at all for fifteen years.

How about Marda or Aunt Marda?" She followed the river of lava to meet her daughter, who was headed the same way.

Kayla ran to catch up. "Aunt Marda, it is then. I've only known Uncle Tomas and always wanted an aunt." She knew she was rambling, but couldn't help it. "Mother will be thrilled. She's been looking for you for so long."

Marda stopped and looked at her, surprise obvious on her face. "Really? Last I talked to Kalandra, she wanted nothing to do with me." There was a bitter note in her voice.

Kayla took a guess here, but somehow knew she was right. She put her hand on her aunt's shoulder and met her eyes. Blue, like her mother's. "She has regretted it ever since."

A wave of relief seemed to cross over Marda. She nodded, blinked hard for a moment, then smiled and headed back up the stream toward her daughter. Kayla didn't know if her words meant anything, but she hoped they did. Somehow, she would get these sisters together once again.

When the Wolfchild reached the top of the lava flow and bounded around it, her companions close behind, Kayla was almost nervous. She wondered once more if Brant was truly right and that she was the player, one of the chosen ones, and not Ember.

When the group reached them, Ember shifted to human once more and went to her mother. "Who's this?" she asked, using her chin to indicate Kayla.

"Kayla, meet my daughter, Ember Shandae." Kayla watched Ember for a response, but she didn't get one. The girl didn't seem impressed at all, and Kayla wondered if she was wrong about this Wolfchild. She took a chance.

"I recently became guardian to one of the keystones, the Sapphire Flute, and was told to guard the flute until I found the player, and I've always assumed that would be you," she said, holding the flute out to Ember. The girl searched Kayla's face, and looked at the flute, entranced—then slowly, she put her hands behind her back and stepped away. "I'm not the player," she said, meeting Kayla's eyes at last. "You are." She paused for a moment, as if considering what to say, then added quickly. "I've dreamed of you since I was young. You've always been the player. I won't take it from you, though I'd love if you would help me in collecting the other keystones."

Kayla nodded. "I assumed as much when I heard about you. I'd be honored to help Mistress Ember," she said.

Ember held up a dirty and torn hand. "Just Ember. Please."

Kayla grinned.

"Oh, and one other thing," Marda said. "Kayla is your cousin. My sister's daughter."

Ember turned to stare at Kayla. "Truly? I didn't know you had any family, Mother," she said.

"Oh, yes. A sister and a brother. I had two other sisters, but they were—killed." It was as if she were about to say something else, but changed her words at the last moment. Kayla would have to look into that later.

Several people ran up at that point. The golden man Kayla had seen before hugged Ember. "Are you all right?" She nodded and introduced Kayla, just as T'Kato and Shiona walked up.

"This is T'Kato. He isn't as scary as he looks." Ember's three step-brothers, one older and two younger twins, approached and were introduced as well. It seemed strange to have a family reunion amid a battle, but it didn't last long.

Kayla was about to ask Ember about her ability to shift shape when the river of lava stone melted and moved toward the mage tower once again.

Kayla looked around, trying to find the source, and there, down the river, stood the man and woman pulling the lava from the rock and directing it up the hill against gravity. The same couple Brant had attacked earlier. Where was Brant, anyway? Evidently, he had run out of power before finishing them. That was where the fight needed to be taken.

She pointed. "Look! There they are!" Ember's twin step-brothers, Tiva and Ren, she thought their names were, and the glowing DeMunth ran down the hill and leaped over the lava at a narrow channel, then went to battle with the man and woman. That left Ember's older brother, Aldarin, Aunt Marda, T'Kato, and the girl who fought with Ember, Lily, behind with Ember and Kayla. Most of them watched, but Kayla decided to do something to help. Once again, she froze the lava and sent her cold spell out toward the two who were fighting to push the molten rock up the hill.

She sent a wave of cold that caught them unprepared and they froze in place. Then the golden man swung his sword at them, and in an instant, they went from living beings to puffs of dust floating down to the village. Lily cried out and fell to her knees with their destruction. Kayla looked at her oddly until Ember leaned over and whispered, "The man raised her as his daughter, evil and hateful as he was. She didn't know until recently that he was not her father."

Kayla's heart panged for the girl then. She knew what it felt to lose a loved one.

Ember turned to Kayla. "Well, that was easier than I imagined it would be. The Shadow Weavers are gone, thanks to Tyese, and now the spies in the academy are gone," she glanced at Lily, then back to Kayla "thanks to you and my brothers. It looks like things are over." Ember grinned, greeting her brothers as they returned.

Kayla wasn't so easily convinced. She turned in a circle, but saw no one else to fight. A group of scraggly children were coming back to the school, and another group of battle-weary wizards marched directly toward Marda. Kayla prepared herself by keeping the knife her father had given her ready to be used, just in case.

Unfortunately, she wasn't watching the children.

As they neared, one of the boys broke off and came toward the group. Everyone had their backs to him or were occupied with other things. Only Kayla saw him approach, but never realized what a danger he was until he shoved one of Ember's twin step-brothers into the lava that still burned hot, his hands and face hitting the stream and sinking through the thin layer of frozen magma. The smell of charred skin reached her even there, and his scream was a sound she would never forget. Kayla wanted to rush to the boy, but his brothers beat her to it. He screamed again as they pulled him out, his blackened flesh dropping off like an overly cooked chicken.

Everything slowed down and Kayla was stuck on the outside, unable to help. She didn't understand why, except to wonder if someone had cast a spell on her. She wanted to help. She'd been useless to Brant and so many others, and here she was with a flute in her hands and she couldn't raise it to her lips to play.

Ember also stood frozen, her mouth open in obvious horror. She spun, saw the boy who had pushed her brother, and her eyes narrowed. They obviously had some history. She pulled the magic to herself and thrust it at him, but he deflected it back at her, then ran toward her with a knife. She dodged to the side, but there was nowhere to go. She was pinned between the lava and the people.

The Wolfchild tried pulling the fight away from the group, but the boy followed her, tossing small bags of dust. She turned her head and held her breath every time they came near. People all around them were dropping to the ground, frozen as they inhaled whatever was in the bags. Kayla wondered if she had inhaled it herself, then realized that could not be. She was still standing. All the others were flat on the ground.

That was when she realized what had held her frozen in place, and it surprised her to no end.

Fear. It was simply fear.

The understanding freed her. She raised the flute to her lips and played, pulling ice and air to her again, then realized she no longer had to battle alone. She sent out a request to the flute, and suddenly Brant was there. He went after the boy, and most likely to defend Kayla's newfound cousin, but before he could get there, T'Kato stepped into the fray.

The tattooed man disarmed the boy of his poison by slicing the child's belt off without breaking the skin. That left them in a more fair fight—except that one of them was a huge, trained warrior, and the other was just a little boy. Kayla called out to him. "T'Kato, no! He's just a boy!" But the tattooed man wouldn't listen. He and the boy circled one another, one dashing in for a strike, and then the other, and quickly Kayla came to realize this was not just an ordinary boy. Despite his age and size, he was a match for T'Kato.

A dome of fire spun up around them just before Brant reached the two. He howled in frustration, his fists beating the ground near Ember, but there was nothing any of them could do. The power of air that Brant lived with would just spur the flames higher. Only water could battle the shield, and none seemed to be in sight.

The girl who had fought with Ember, Lily, glowed with purple light. Dark clouds gathered above her and the battling man and boy. The clouds pulled moisture into them, and within seconds, it had rained.

Kayla watched, fascinated, and as soon as the fire shield was down, she played her flute. Brant was fading fast, and she needed to power him, even if she had to pull it from herself.

He glanced at her, then at the fight, and back at her, then shook his head. Even from that distance, she heard his voice. "I can't battle if it will hurt you, love. Another day, maybe, but today you aren't strong enough."

In a swirl of air he was gone, back into the flute, and it left her alone and unable to do anything as the fight between man and boy heated up. Although T'Kato fought with a sword and the boy with a knife in each hand, it was unclear who was winning. Kayla stepped to Ember's side and watched, feeling helpless.

And then the tide turned. Lily jumped into the battle, knife in hand, trying to put an end to the boy. T'Kato raised his hand to stop her, yelling, "No!" But it was too late. The moment T'Kato's guard was down and his arm raised, the boy threw his knife at T'Kato's armpit, the one place where he could get in a fatal shot. T'Kato cried out and instantly went to his knees, blood spurting from beneath his arm. Kayla cried out and ran toward him, her stomach sick with dread. She'd already killed Sarali's brother. Would her friend ever forgive her if she let T'Kato die?

Everyone ran to him, and the boy was forgotten in the race to save T'Kato. Only Kayla saw the child look up at her, his expression the most evil one she had ever seen, save only C'Tan. He disappeared in a flare of smoke.

Kayla reached him first and fell to her knees to press strips of cloth she tore from her tunic and pressed them to his wound. T'Kato's hand covered hers and pressed against the hole under his arm, but the blood came fast, and Kayla knew that he most likely would not recover from that wound. Perhaps the flute could save him like it had helped heal her? She pulled it out and tried to play, her fingers covered with T'Kato's blood, but no sound came forth. Shocked, she tried again. And again. And again.

The flute would not sound. Evidently Brant was serious when he told her she wouldn't fight today. It was Brant's death all over again—only this time, he had control of the flute. It wasn't fair! Kayla went to T'Kato's side. Ember's older brother, Aldarin, knelt at the big tattooed man's other side and held his hand. "What can I do for you? Is there any magic to fix this? I'm not sure how to help," he said, trying to get the breastplate off and fumbling with buckles he obviously didn't understand. The tattooed man put his hand over Aldarin's and got his attention.

"There is one thing you can do for me, boy. I sense you are a good man. Are you a good man, Aldarin?"

He nodded, though reluctantly. "I try to be, sir."

"Good," T'Kato nearly whispered. "I have a charge for you. Will you fulfill my last request?" He was getting weaker by the moment.

"Yes sir. If it's in my power to do it, I certainly shall," Aldarin said, holding both hands now.

"Take my magic, son. Take it and return it to my people in the Ketahean jungles. Do this for me. Please. A last request of a dying man and disciple of Klii'kunn."

Aldarin's eyes grew wide at that. "But—how, sir?"

"Don't you worry," T'Kato whispered. "Giving you the magic is my job. Getting it to Ketahe is yours." T'Kato squeezed Aldarin's hands. "Thank you, son, for son you are taking this magic. Are you ready?"

"For what?" Aldarin asked, obviously confused.

T'Kato grinned. "You'll see," he said, then lay back and gripped Aldarin's hands hard. The tattoos on his skin swirled, from head to hand and every bit that Kayla could see through her tears. Aldarin shook and cried out with pain as the tattoos crept from T'Kato's hands to his, then up his arms, under his sleeves, and disappeared for a moment, only to reappear crawling up his neck, face, and into his hairline. For a long moment he glowed blue, then, as T'Kato's grip on him relaxed, Aldarin sat back on his knees, his entire body stiffening as the blue glow shifted quickly to orange that flared as bright as the flowing magma, then settled into his skin.

When the glow was gone, every bit of showing skin was covered with T'Kato's tattoos in bright, vibrant orange, and the huge Ketahean lay dead at Aldarin's feet.

Kayla didn't even have tears to cry, though T'Kato deserved them. She had failed again. Another beloved man was dead and she could do nothing to save him. What good was the flute if she couldn't help the people she loved?

Numb with grief and having to handle too much for too long, Kayla sat down on the ground and stared at her protector, now minus his tattoos. Sarali was right—he wasn't much to look at, but he had a heart of gold. He was strong and kind and did the right thing, even when it was hard.

Inside, Kayla found parts of her were softening, and others strengthened by knowing this man. Here was a man worth emulating, a man who had given her an example with his life. He was the kind of person she wanted to be. Her grief for Brant, she now realized, had been selfish, focused inwardly, on *her* life and how it affected *her*.

In T'Kato's death, she realized, he had given her a gift—one that let Kayla see that the guardianship of the flute was difficult, no, but what made one worthy to hold it was the kind of\ life one lived, and until now, hers had been rather shallow.

But no more. Kayla stood, walked to T'Kato's body, and knelt beside it. Taking his blood-soaked hand in her own, she made a promise she knew she would keep. "I'll live like you, T'Kato. I'll devote myself to the flute. I'll fight for right and forget myself. You taught me that. Thank you, my friend." She bent her head over his hand and finally cried. When she was done, she left her tears with him. It was time to leave them behind.

CHAPTER FIFTY

C'Tan watched the fight from the side of the mountain, her power allowing her to zoom in on parts of the battle at will. She was angered when Magnet and Seer were destroyed, but had not been surprised. She hadn't expected them to survive this attack. When Ian killed the big Ketahean, she was rejoiced. He had been bothersome for many years and she was glad to have him gone, though she would have been happier if Ian had captured or killed the Chosen One.

Evidently, the hard jobs were left up to her, and she still had one agent in place. With Lily standing amid her enemies, perhaps they could get this job done properly.

C'Tan clambered up the side of her dragon and strapped herself in, then pulled her red leather hood up over her hair to keep it out of the way as she rode into battle. She pulled a handful of throwing daggers from that special place where she kept things, between reality, the void, and prepared herself. She nudged Drake, and without a word, he took to the air and dove directly toward Ember and Kayla. Finally, she had the two girls in the same place. She'd be happy to destroy one, but if she could get them both, her master would be extremely pleased with her, and she could really use his favor.

The girls didn't seem to be aware of who was coming. She kept quiet and bided her time until she was close enough for her daggers to do some good. She waited until the perfect moment, then drew back and threw two daggers at a time as fast as she could.

The first two daggers missed, but the third and fourth ricocheted off the shield of the priest who wore the Armor of Light, and a smaller man covered head to toe in orange tattoos. It was not a color she would have chosen for herself, if she had been one to be tattooed, but people were strange.

She continued to throw daggers until suddenly a shadow shield went up before the group and pushed C'Tan and her dragon away.

Stunned, C'Tan hovered above the lava river for a moment before she called out. "Lily? *dare you* challenge me now? I thought you were made of noodles, for the backbone you've had."

Lily's voice came from the cloud. "I've never wanted to be like you, *Mother*. I just never felt I had a choice with you and Rahdnee as parents, but finding out he was not my father made me realize I didn't have to be you. Ember is my friend. I won't let you hurt her."

C'Tan had mixed feelings. Part of her was proud of her daughter for standing up to her. Part of her was livid that the girl would dare oppose her. And another part was just sad that it had come to this. "You may not have a choice, child. Just let me have Ember, and I'll leave everyone unharmed."

"No, Mother. You can't have her." Lily said, standing firm. The shadow cloud didn't move.

"I'll only say it once more, child. Give me the girl and everyone will live." C'Tan was quickly losing patience.

"And I said no. I'll die first."

"That can be arranged," C'Tan said, then dove into the shadow. It was cold and wet and her dragon bellowed in pain at the moisture, but she pushed on until she was past the cloud and could see her daughter standing next to Ember, but her daughter was not the problem. The strange tattooed man was on the other side of the girl and the man in the Armor of Light was in front of her.

The only one who stood unprotected was Jarin's wife. She had aged, but C'Tan knew her. The wife of her half-brother. She could reach no one else, but taking the Wolfchild's mother might make things go her way.

Quickly diving, C'Tan's dragon took hold of Brina and pulled her into the sky. One of the girls screamed, probably Ember, and the magic started shooting toward her. C'Tan put up her own shield of fire, surrounding herself, the dragon, and Brina, who dangled below her mount like Kayla had the week before. She moved away from the scene of the fight as quickly as she had moved toward it, then went to the mountainside where she had waited all morning long, put Brina down, and tied her up while she still shook with fright.

She threw the woman over the back of the dragon and strapped her in for the long flight back to her castle, then took a moment to cast a spell she knew she'd pay for later, since it was so hard to do without her scrying bowl.

C'Tan sent her image to the group below her and spoke. The boys held Ember back as she tried to run after C'Tan. It would have done her no good anyway, as she could never go as fast as Drake, not even in her wolven form.

She created an immense head to float over the cooling river of Magma. "Chosen One. Wolfchild. Ember Shandae. Whatever name you choose to go by, I wish to make a trade. Are you open to hearing my terms?"

Ember growled at the head, her wolf nature coming out despite her human appearance at the moment, so C'Tan repeated herself. "I wish to make a trade. Will you hear my terms?"

Ember didn't growl this time and seemed to calm. She met the eye of C'Tan's projected image and nodded.

"Good. I have your mother, and if you are anything at all like your father, you will move heaven and Rasann to get her back." She didn't bother waiting for Ember's response. "I wish for you to do that which you had planned, anyway. Collect the keystones. Find them all and bring them to me. I'm sure someone will give you directions. I'm not asking you to give them to me—just bring them to my castle, and we will battle out who is the real master of the keystones. Will you accept?"

Ember seemed to ponder C'Tan's words, though her eyes were furious and tears continuously leaked from her eyes. "I do not see where I have any choice. I shall accept."

Lily sucked in a breath. "Ember, no! You don't know what you're saying!"

"I know exactly what I'm saying. I'm promising C'Tan a fight with the weapons I had planned to use anyway. This fight has been coming since the day I was born, and if it will save my mother, then even better," she said.

C'Tan nodded, serious for a change, relieved that the girl accepted her terms. She had a few tricks up her sleeve that might weigh things in her favor, but she had a feeling that either side could win.

The deal made, C'Tan let the projection fall, climbed astride her dragon, and, ignoring Brina's threats and screams, she took off into the air and flew in the direction of her castle. It was a long ride home, and though she knew her master would be angry with her failures, she hoped he would give her leniency just once more with the prizes she brought in exchange.

All was not lost after all. Smiling, C'Tan settled herself in for the journey, and headed west into the setting sun and home.

CHAPTER
FIFTY-ONE

Ezeker's voice brought Ember out of her fog. "What just happened here? Was that C'Tan I saw?"

Ember turned toward him. The mage council and many of the straggling students marched up the hill from Karsholm. "Yes. She has my mum," Ember said, trying not to cry, but the panic bounded inside of her like a jackrabbit in her chest, and it felt as if a rock were embedded in her stomach.

Ezeker froze. "What?" he roared. "How did this happen?"

At that, Ember burst into tears, and Ezeker hurried his step and wrapped her in his arms. His voice shook. "Oh, sweetheart, I'm sorry. Tell me what happened."

So Ember told him. She told him everything, from the moment they burst through the door until C'Tan had flown away with Marda in tow, and her offer of a trade. Ember was sure he was going to tear into her for agreeing to such a thing, but he stroked his beard thoughtfully. "This ties in to your dreams, doesn't it?"

Ember nodded. She had told him about the dreams many times, especially because her mother would neither listen to nor believe in them. "Yes, it does. The people of my dreams are becoming real, Uncle Ezzie. This girl here—Kayla," she said, pointing to the girl who played the Sapphire Flute. "She plays the blue flute in my dreams whenever we win. And DeMunth. He's also part of the group when we succeed. If either of them is ever missing in my dreams, we are defeated."

Ezeker continued to stroke his beard. "She charged you to find all the keystones, you say? And then come challenge her in her castle? Why didn't she just demand that you give them up?"

Ember shrugged. "I do not know. I'm just grateful for a way to get my mum back. I won't give them to her, but at least by having them, I'll stand a chance, and hopefully she'll leave us be now so we can search them out in peace. So long as we can find them, the only challenge I really see is learning to use them quickly enough to do any good." Ember scuffed her toe and glanced out at the destruction surrounding Karsholm.

"I may have a solution for you," Ezeker said. "But I'm not sure you will like it."

Ember drew her attention back to the headmaster. "Try me," she said. "I'm open to anything right now."

"Your grandmother Asana knows more about the keystones and magestone than anyone I know. She may not be a mage, but she knows how the stone works, and the only other stone I can direct you to lies with the Bendanatu. She can take you there and teach all of you at the same time. It looks like Aldarin is going to need some training as well. I hate to lose the best captain I've ever had, but it's obvious he needs to go with you."

"What?" Ember said, having not even noticed what happened to her step-brother until then. She turned around and her jaw dropped. Glowing orange tattoos completely covered him. Now Ember realized where the big Ketahean's tattoos had gone, but why had they changed from blue to orange? Ember had no answers. Aldarin wasn't all too happy with them either. In that instant, she remembered one of her dreams, where her step-brother was covered with orange tattoos and battled alongside her. It was one of the winning battle dreams. She smiled to herself.

Ezeker beckoned him over and he came without pause. "Aldarin, you realize you need to go with Ember now, don't you?"

He nodded, most definitely unhappy.

"Hopefully once you get to the Ketaheans, they'll be able to take the magic back and you can return, but I can't have a mage for a guard. If I had realized Rahdnee and Brendae were both mage and guard, they would have been released from duty. If I'd known they were traitors, I would have destroyed them long ago," he said, anger tingeing his voice.

Aldarin only nodded. He must be really upset, to not be speaking.

Ezeker pulled at his beard again. "I have not checked the school yet, but if it's anything like out here, we're going to have some major repairs to do before we are ready to teach again. I'm going to ask a favor of you, since you'll be traveling, anyway. Take the children home, as many as will be on your way."

Ember wanted to object. The kids were just going to slow them down, and she wanted to save her mother, blast it! But the kids needed to be safe. Ember thought of Tyese, so helpful, and all alone. But if she was Bendanatu, she had people to take care of her, and suddenly she felt like Uncle Ezzie did. She answered for all of them.

"We'll do it."

"That's my girl," he said, putting an arm around her. "We'll get your mother back, don't you worry."

The tears blurred her vision again, and she nodded before turning away and glancing toward the girl with the blue flute, who stood talking to DeMunth. For a moment, she was insanely jealous. DeMunth was hers! But when he turned to her and winked, she realized they belonged to one another, and he wasn't going anywhere. After all, Mahal had named him her guardian for life. He was stuck with her and she couldn't be happier for those chains.

"Now," Ezeker said, walking back to his tower. "Let's go see what we can do to help Tiva, shall we? That boy has a way of finding trouble, no matter where it is." Ezeker shook his head, but his levity did nothing for any of them.

Everyone followed the wizened mage as he led them to his home, which was still intact, if a little shaken up. He had people bring more chairs and magically increased the size of his stone table to seat Kayla's group around the table with them. Lily stood to the side, as if unsure what to do. Ember beckoned her over, and the girl came, slowly. She stopped at Ember's side and said so softly Ember could barely hear. "You still want me here?"

"Of course I do! You're family, remember?"

"Yes, but what a family. I knew my mother was capable of anything, but to take yours like that—" Lily choked up. "I'm sorry, Ember. I'm truly sorry. I tried to protect you, and didn't think to protect her."

Ember put her arm around her cousin and new friend, trying very hard not to think about her mother. She put the emotion in the back of her mind. She'd deal with it later, when she was alone. "It's not your fault. We'll get her back, I know it." Ember chewed her lip. Should she ask her now? "Actually, I have been thinking, and you were about to graduate anyway, so would you be willing to come with me in my search for the keystones? I could really use your help and experience, and you can continue to teach me."

Lily's eyes got huge as she turned toward Ember, then they filled with tears. "You would have me do that? After all I've done, and all my mother has done to you?"

Ember nodded. "I told you before, Lily. I trust you. You're not like your mother, and I think being a part of the search and even the battle that *will* defeat her would be the best medicine you could have, wouldn't you agree?"

Lily nodded, then suddenly, she reached out and hugged Ember as if she were the stone holding her to Rasann. Ember hugged her back, then took her by the hand and led her to the table.

Across from her was Kayla, and next to Ember sat Lily and then DeMunth, butting Aldarin out of the spot just before he sat next to her. Aldarin playfully backed away and sat on the other side next to Kayla, who looked at him with curiosity.

Ezeker was the first to speak. "T'Kato is dead. I'm sure all of you know that by now. We will bury him where he fell, as is the tradition of his people. I've already set some of our best on that task," he said. Kayla mouthed a thank you in his direction.

"We have a more serious challenge at the moment with Tiva. Paeder and Ren are with him now. Father and brother," he explained to the newcomers. "His hands and face can be healed and rebuilt, but I am afraid the fire took his sight, and about that, there is nothing we can do but teach him to use his other senses. For that, I have assigned Mistress Vanine to him. She knows better than any other how to cross that boundary, and hopefully he will recover and function close to normal."

Ember was shocked. She knew burns could be healed. She'd seen miracles done through Ezeker's power, but she hadn't realized that vision was an exception, though she should have known. Shed seen the orange teacher's blindness. But if Tiva could learn to accept his challenge as well as Mistress Vanine had, he would be okay. She breathed an internal sigh of relief, though her heart still ached for him.

"There is nothing any of you can do. His sight is even beyond the power of the flute." He nodded to Kayla. "Or your white magic, Ember. Instead, I need all of you to begin the task C'Tan set for you, whether or not you like it. You are now a unit, acting as one. Ember shall lead you, but she cannot do this task alone, and needs all of your help to make it happen. Let me rectify that. Aldarin. Kayla. DeMunth. Shad. Lily. You are needed for this venture. Any of the rest of you who choose to assist may go, but for the five of you, plus Ember, this journey is necessary. You will go places you've only dreamed about in the search for the keystones, but it will be worth it in the end, and I believe you will triumph if you work together."

Ezeker stood, walked around the table to the end, then put his hands flat on the stone top and leaned forward. "There is a legend rarely retold that the Chosen One is not just one person, but a group acting as a unit. A group of chosen ones, each selected by the keystones to be their bearers." He let the silence at the table speak for a moment before continuing. "I believe that legend to be truth more than any other. You are the chosen ones. You are the guardian," he said, turning to DeMunth.

"And you, my dear, are the player," he said to Kayla, who reddened and teared up, though she tried to hide it. "Ember, you are the Wolfchild, also known as the whitewalker, or the healer. You have yet to find the wolf, the eye, the heart, and the chameleon." At the blank look on their faces, he continued. "The chameleon is also known as the Hidden Coin. The keystones will come to you when the time is right, along with their companions. And even you have a keystone to hold, Ember. The Crystal Mallet is out there somewhere. I promise, it will find you, just as the armor and the flute have found these two."

What Ezeker said made sense to Ember. It felt right, more right than anything she had before seen or heard.

They were the chosen ones. Not just her. The group. She looked around, and from her dreams, remembered many of these people using the keystones. She felt like the bearers were right here—they just had yet to find their matching stones.

A group of chosen ones. Ember was thrilled to know she was not alone.

KUDOS

You'd think I'd have this acknowledgements thing down by now. After all, I've written a couple of books already, but I still sweat over forgetting somebody. Crazy me.

First, I want to thank Tristi Pinkston for the marvelous edits (as always), and Deirdre Eden Coppel for the fabulous artwork.

Second, I want to thank all the many people who have read my early drafts and told me to keep going. Shari Bird, Laura Taggart, Jannell Locke, Shanna Blythe, Rebecca Blevins, Nicole Burton, and many more. If you read it and I forgot to add your name, know that I am thanking you now. I couldn't have done this without you guys. Thank you for pointing me in the right directions when my characters were floundering, and for cheering me on when I was down. You guys rock!

Third, I want to thank the wonderful people who let me write them into The Armor of Light. Brenda Clarke (Brendae), Rodney G.(Rah dnee), Jayden Hancock, my husband Gary Lynn (Graylin), and Tyese Burton. It was a total blast making real people into characters and giving them powers. I hope I get the chance to do it for many years to come.

A very Special thanks to my husband, Gary, for filling in for his often absent wife. For cooking, cleaning, taking care of kids, and being patient with me when deadlines loomed. Also to my sons, Austin and Robert, for loving me even when I crankily tell them I have to finish this chapter and no I can't watch TV with them right now. I could never do this without your support, and I love you guys more than anything in the world.

Lastly, I'd like to thank my Heavenly Father, for the inspiration and gifts He has given me to use. Without Him I am nothing.

PRONUNCIATION GUIDE

EMBER'S GROUP:

- Brina—BREE-nuh
- Marda—MAR-duh
- Ember—EM-burr
- Shandae—shawn-DAY
- Paeder—PAY-dur
- Ezeker—EZZ-ick-cur
- Aldarin—AHL-duh-rin
- Tiva—TEE-vuh
- Ren—REHN
- Shad—Shad
- DeMunth—di-MOONTH
- Tyese—tye-EES
- Lily—LILL-ee

BAD GUYS:

- C'Tan—seh-TAHN
- Kardon—KAR-dawn
- Ian Covainis—EE-in co-VANE-us
- Rahdnee—ROD-nee
- Brendae—brin-DAY

GUARDIANS of RASANN:

- Mahal—muh-HALL
- S'Kotos—SKOE-toess

- Bendanatu—behn-duh-Nah-too
- Klii'kunn—klee-KOON
- Lahonra—luh-HONE-rah
- Hwalan—hwa-LAHN
- Sha'iim--shaw-EEM

KAYLA's GROUP:

- Kayla—KAY-luh
- Kalandra—kuh-LAN-druh
- Felandian—feh-LAN-dee-in
- Brant—(Like rant with a B)
- Sarali—suh-RAH-lee
- T'Kato—tuh-KAH-toe
- Niefusu—nee-FOO-soo
- Jihong—jee-HONG
- Graelin—GRAY-linn
- Hadril—HAD-rill
- Shiona—she-OH-nuh

PLACES:

- Rasann—Ruh-SAHN
- Karsholm—KAR-showlm
- Darthmoor—DARTH-more
- Dragonmeer—DRA-gun-meer
- Peldane—PEHL-dayne
- Javak—JAH-vuk
- Driane—dree-ANE

SHAPESHIFTERS/RACES

- MerCat—MUR-kat
- Bendanatu—BEN-duh-NAH-too
- Ne'Goi—neh-GOY
- Ketahe—keh-TAW-hee
- Ketahean—keh-TAW-hee-in

ALSO BY THE AUTHOR

The Wolfchild Saga:

The Sapphire Flute

The Armor of Light

The Emerald Wolf
The Amethyst Eye
The Ruby Heart
The Hidden Coin
The Crystal Mallet

Newtimber:

Fractured

The Misadventures of a Teenage Wizard:

Two Souls are Better Than One

Poetry:

And the Mountain Burns

ABOUT THE AUTHOR

Karen E. Hoover has loved the written word for as long as she can remember. Her favorite memory of her dad is the time he spent with Karen on his lap, telling her stories for hours on end, everything from Dr. Seuss' Green Eggs and Ham (which he thought was disgusting) to sharing his love of poetry in reciting Jabberwocky enough times she memorized it at a young age. Her dad promised he would have Karen reading on her own by the time she was four years old . . . and he very nearly did.

Karen took the gift of words her dad gave her and ran with it. Since then, she's written many novels and reams of poetry. Her head is fairly popping with ideas, so she plans to write until she's ninety-four or maybe even a hundred and four. Inspiration is found everywhere, but Karen's heart is fueled by her husband, two sons and her grandson, the Rocky Mountains, her chronic addiction to pens and paper, excessive office supplies, and the smell of her laser printer in the morning.

Thank you so much for reading The Armor of Light! If you enjoyed the experience, I would greatly appreciate your leaving a review on Amazon and Goodreads. It is one of the best and easiest ways to help your favorite authors. There are many more stories about Ember and Kayla and C'Tan to come, and I hope you will join me in continuing their journey in saving their world.

You can find me at the following:

Website: karenEhoover.com

Amazon Author page: amazon.com/author/karenEhoover

Instagram: author_karen_e_hoover

Facebook: @karenEhoover

Tik Tok: @

k

eghoover

Goodreads: Karen E. Hoover

Bookbub: Karen E. Hoover

MyBookCave.com: Karen E. Hoover

Sign up for my newsletter to receive behind the scenes content and much, much more! Character and location pictures. First glimpses at upcoming books. The chance to join my street team and spread the word. Games. Prizes. FUN! Come and join me! The link can be found at www.karenEhoover.com.

Made in the USA
Middletown, DE
25 May 2023

31470489R00229